## "Trust me, I would rather die than see the girl come to harm."

March searched his eyes, then nodded once, sharply, turning away. "All right. I will accept it. But I will be somewhere close, where she can find me if she needs me."

"Not too close," cautioned Feor. "Sif may not know her, but you are another matter. And where you are, he might well expect to find Anghara."

"I cannot abandon her!"

"You will not," Feor said softly. "None of us can. None of us will. But we can be more useful to her now if we let her go. She tried to fly tonight, and almost broke her wings beyond repair; we must let her go, to learn what she might of survival. She is strong, March; strong enough to doom herself if we let her."

Unexpectedly, March's warrior eyes prickled with tears. "She's a little girl," he whispered.

Feor shook his head rising. "She is a queen," he said, very softly.

**THE REMARKABLE EPIC JOURNEY OF ANGHARA KIR HAMA WILL BE CONCLUDED IN *CHANGER OF DAYS***

# THE
# HIDDEN QUEEN

## ALMA ALEXANDER

*An Imprint of HarperCollinsPublishers*

This is a work of fiction. Names, characters, places, and incidents are products of the author's imagination or are used fictitiously and are not to be construed as real. Any resemblance to actual events, locales, organizations, or persons, living or dead, is entirely coincidental.

EOS
*An Imprint of* HarperCollins*Publishers*
10 East 53rd Street
New York, New York 10022-5299

First Eos paperback printing: May 2005

First published in New Zealand under the title *Changer of Days*, Volume 1, by Voyager, an imprint of HarperCollins*Publishers*

HarperCollins® and Eos® are trademarks of HarperCollins Publishers Inc.

Printed in the U.S.A.

10  9  8  7  6  5  4  3  2  1

To David, who was there when the story set sail,
and to Deck , who was there to see it sail into harbor.

# THE
# HIDDEN QUEEN

Se' thara pan
(Staren pan)
Shaymir Desert
Kadun Khajir'i'id
Shaymir Dance
Ul Khari'ma
ai' Jihaar's hai'r
Coba
Al' haria
Aymer
Castle Bresse
Radas Han
KHELDRIN
Miranei
Halas Han
Sayar'dun
Kadun Shod
(Fihra) hai'r
Dodmer Forest
Kharg'in'dun'an
Gul Qara
Beit'el'Sihaya
Tanass
Han
Arad Shod
(Fira) Hai'r
Sa'alah
Arad Khajir'i'id
Calabra
Beku
ROISINAN
Collas Han
Algira
TATH
Vallen
Fen
N
Mabin Archipelago

# Prologue

There were still echoes of sporadic fighting, but night was drawing in fast. Fodrun, finding himself suddenly alone in the middle of what had until less than an hour ago been a fierce battlefield, paused and looked around, taking stock. There was blood on him, none of it his own, but fatigue ached like a wound and his wrists throbbed with the pain of simply holding his sword. He remembered very little after the incandescent moment when he had seen Red Dynan, the king, stagger and slide off his horse with a cursed Rashin arrow in his eye. Fodrun had succumbed to pure battle frenzy, leading his small knot of men directly into the Tath army's flank, exposing all to certain death for an instant of revenge. All were now dead. All except him. And he seemed only now to have woken from a nightmare.

Sticking his sword point first into the turf, he sank down on one knee beside it, pulling off his helm. Scattered around his feet were broken weapons, discarded shields, the corpses of men and horses. There was one whose staring eyes implacably met Fodrun's own as he looked in the dead man's direction. The man wore Roisinan colors; he might well have been one of the men in Fodrun's command, but then, he could have been almost anyone. He'd taken a slash across the face and his features were twisted beyond recognition in a frozen mess of mangled flesh and congealing blood. Even Fodrun, a battle-tempered soldier used to death, turned away at the sight.

Another memory surfaced, unbidden, vivid: a Rashin mace swinging inexorably . . . *'Ware!* he had shouted, and

Kalas had ducked, turned and met the mace with his shoulder. Fodrun remembered seeing his general stagger . . . did he fall? Are they dead? Are they both dead?

"My lord . . ."

The voice was hesitant, very young. One of the pages. Fodrun looked up.

"My lord," gasped the boy. He couldn't have been more than thirteen or fourteen, and his eyes were round with horror. He had probably been sent to find Fodrun, or his body; instead he had found this blood-bespattered gargoyle with wild eyes . . . Fodrun tried to smile, the expression more grimace than anything else.

"Do not mind, boy, can you not tell black Tath blood when you see it?"

The wince that followed his words was lost on the young messenger, but Fodrun knew the reason behind it would soon spread its insidious poison in the army ranks. Not many knew he was Tath-born, but enough did. Enough to make men balk at following him against the army on the other side of the river. His lineage tainted his loyalty. "What is it? Who sent you?"

"The healers, sir . . . they have the general in their tent . . ."
Fodrun straightened, fatigue forgotten. His eyes blazed. "He is alive? Kalas is alive?"

"Yes, lord, but wounded . . . badly wounded . . . the healers say he is in pain, and he has not been himself since they brought him in. The army, sir . . . they bid me find you . . . they need orders, sir, and the general . . ."

As quickly as they had kindled, Fodrun's eyes faded into dullness again. His shoulders slumped. "The king . . ."

The page hung his head. "Dead, sir."

Dynan dead. Kalas, by all accounts, racked with battle fever. The army . . . headless. Except for him. Second General Fodrun. Tath-born.

Fodrun allowed his eyes to range across the churned plain that had been the day's killing field. Somewhere in the distance he could see the blurred gleam of moonlight on the River Ronval; and beyond the river . . . what remained of

Duerin Rashin's army. They had withdrawn across the ford. Yes, he remembered that too. They would be back tomorrow. And the army . . .

Fodrun sheathed his sword with a weary gesture. There would likely be no sleep for him that night. "Where are the other lords?" he asked the page, who stood shivering in the moonlight, whether from cold or the horrors of warfare, it was hard to tell. Faced with a direct question, something to do, the lad looked up with what was almost anticipation.

"I'll take you to them, sir."

They went the long way round, first stopping by the healers' tent, where Kalas was not alone. Perhaps more than a hundred men were laid awkwardly about, filling the tent almost to overflowing; Kalas, his rank pulling privilege even when he was unconscious, had been given a screened-off corner of his own. That much they could do for him, and bind his shattered shoulder; but even if he came out of the delirium which whipped his head back and forth on his pillow, already soaked with his sweat, Kalas would never be a soldier again. The arm hanging from his broken shoulder would never again be able to lift a sword.

And then, the other tent. There were even more men here, with more arriving as Fodrun watched; but inside, on a bier made from bloodied shields, the body of Red Dynan, King of Roisinan, lay in state in an open space within a ring of flaming torches. They had plucked out the arrow that had claimed him; he looked almost whole, almost asleep, until one looked closer and noticed the waxy pallor of his skin and the ruined eye socket beneath one of the two heavy gold coins marking his state, payment for passage into Glas Coil. Fodrun stood for what seemed an inordinately long time, helmet in hand, and looked upon the king. Dynan had named him second general only a month ago, a deliberate act of faith against the background of rumbling discontent from those who knew the new general's lineage; but the king had chosen to trust him. Fodrun remembered the day, Dynan's laughing eyes, the strong brown hand that raised him from his knees. As chaotic thoughts tumbled through his brain, one suddenly coalesced out of the turmoil, presenting him with the narrow, thoughtful face of Dynan's lawful heir. Princess Anghara. She was back in Miranei, with the queen. The only child of Dynan's marriage, Anghara was heir to the chaos that had taken and slain her father—to this resurgent Rashin aggression, to war. She was only nine years old.

Fodrun shivered with what was almost a touch of pre-science. Anghara would ascend the throne at Miranei, a puppet for a Regent Council for at least five or six more years. And in that time, Roisinan . . . Roisinan and the cursed Tath . . .

He turned to the page, who still hovered by him, waiting patiently until he had concluded his business. "Where are the lords?" Fodrun demanded again, his voice harsher than he had intended. "Take me there. Now."

Behind Fodrun, a shadow that had waited for his departure slipped into the tent almost before the flaps fell from Fodrun's hand. It was shrouded in a dark cloak, but armor gleamed beneath. The hood of the cloak was up, the figure's face shadowed. It came to the king's body slowly, almost hesitantly, and stood rigidly motionless beside the makeshift bier, shoulders stiff with pain. A guard, who had thought the cloaked figure was with the general, woke up to its unsanctioned presence. "Hey! You there! Out!"

The cloaked man ignored the words, bending to plant a kiss on Dynan's pale, lifeless brow. The guard strode over, took hold of the other's shoulder, spinning him around. "You! What is your name? What are you doing here? You have no right to . . ."

The man threw back his cloak. His hair was a burnished red, almost the precise shade of the dead king's, and his pale eyes, faded blue, were implacable steel as he haughtily met the guard's angry stare. "My name," he said in a low, precise voice, "in this army is Horun; I took that name because otherwise my father would have discovered I had disobeyed him. But I have every right to be here, soldier. My true name is Sif. Sif Kir Hama. And that," he said looking down on the king, "is the father whom I disobeyed."

The guard was out of his depth. There *was* a son, a young man called Sif, but how to prove . . . "My lord," muttered the guard indecisively, "I must insist . . ."

Sif laughed, a harsh bark that had nothing of mirth in it. "I won't be far away," he said, and his words had the force of a vow, or a threat. He plucked the guard's fingers from his shoulder, flung his hood back up again and melted into the shadows outside.

His name remained, a whisper in the dark, spreading from the death-tent out into the night—*Sif is in camp, Sif Kir Hama, Dynan's son.*

Before long a messenger page stumbled into the tent where Fodrun sat with his war council, debating the morrow. Fodrun looked up sharply. "I thought I gave orders not to be disturbed," he snapped. Already there was doubt in some of the commanders' eyes; he could sense it, a cold, clammy touch on his skin like a dead man's hand. Everything depended on him being able to hold them, and they were already wavering. And now this boy, breaking into the meeting, unravelling what Fodrun had already spent almost two hours trying to weave . . .

The page raised frightened eyes. "Lord," he said, in a hoarse whisper, "forgive me . . . there is important news."

"Well," said Fodrun impatiently after a pause, "what is it?"

The page's voice dropped even further, Fodrun had to lean forward to hear him. "It is rumored that Sif is in the camp, lord, Sif Kir Hama, King Dynan's son."

"Rumored?" Fodrun said. "What use do I have for rumors?" He would have been a lot more forceful a few hours ago, but exhaustion and cold dread were beginning to take their toll; he was slow to kindle his swift and much-feared anger.

"Sir," said the page, "one of the king's own guards spoke to him . . ."

Fatigue or not, Fodrun got up so fast his chair overturned behind him. "What?"

The message was repeated. Fodrun stood rigid for a moment, his jaw clenched. Anghara's face swam into his consciousness again, the wide, guileless gray eyes of a child. He forgot, for the moment, the cool, precocious measuring those eyes had given him when he was presented to the queen and the princess at Miranei only a few short months ago. All he could think of was the Tath army across the river, the dead king, the Rashin pretenders raising their hands again to a kingdom they had claimed once before in rebellion, a kingdom won back from them in days not too long gone. Bitter, bloody tales from the Rashin interregnum survived in the minds of the people. Roisinan could not hold against a renewed threat from the hungry Rashin clan, not with a nine-year-old girl on the throne and a foreign-born general leading her armies . . .

And now, this gift—Dynan's first-born. Illegitimate, but a man of age who could fight, hold, rule. A soldier. A king.

Fodrun turned burning eyes to the frightened page. "This guard, take me to him at once. My lords . . . I will not be long."

He chose not to notice the eyes that would not meet his own as he swept out of the tent.

The guard could provide little further information, but he did volunteer a name. Horun. Feverish now, Fodrun sent messengers amongst the campfires. The soldier called Horun, or anyone who knows of him, was to come to Second General Fodrun at once. *At once.*

Even as he strode back to his own tent someone touched his arm. Fodrun whirled. A young soldier stepped back from the general's haunted face, but stood his ground. "You are looking for a man named Horun, my lord?"

Fodrun closed the distance between them. "Yes. *Yes!* Where is he?"

"He is in my cheta, lord. My commander ordered him to picket duty tonight. He should be with the horses."

Fodrun had not even waited to hear the end of the sentence, already turned and halfway to the picket lines before the soldier finished speaking.

In the dimness of the horse-lines, far from the campfires, a shadowy figure stood amongst the beasts, lightly stroking the arched neck of a hobbled stallion. Almost stumbling upon him in the dark, Fodrun had to reach out and steady himself against the other's shoulder. His breath came short. "Horun?"

It was too dark to see, but Fodrun felt rather than saw the other man smile. "It is one of my names."

Fodrun drew a deep breath. "I hear," he said, "that you claim another."

"I do."

The unconscious arrogance in those words convinced Fodrun of the truth. Still he asked, to hear it spoken. "What name?"

The soldier who called himself Horun stepped forward, flinging back his hood with high royal pride. "I am Sif Kir Hama."

Fodrun closed his eyes for a moment, the burden on his shoulders lifted by a blessed relief; the evanescent image of Anghara Kir Hama's gray eyes in the fastness of Miranei was gone almost before he was aware he had seen it. The only thing he could think of was Tath, and the honed blade he had just been handed to vanquish the Rashin clan. "Lord," he said, opening his eyes. "You are an answer to a prayer."

Sif offered no help, standing loose and relaxed, waiting for the general. Fodrun stumbled on, all soldier in this instant, a man whose friends were actions, not words. "An hour ago I sat with my commanders to plan tomorrow's battle, knowing full well we face disaster. Now . . . now I believe we have a chance. King Dynan is dead; but if we had you to lead us in his place . . . Will you take this army, Sif Kir Hama? Will you lead us against the Rashin in the morning?"

Sif's eyes were smoky, veiled. "And what of the aftermath, general?"

"The aftermath?" echoed Fodrun, caught off guard.

"When the battle is over, general. What then?"

And Fodrun met Sif's eyes steadily, read the ambition there, accepted it. "They tell me Kalas is dying," he said. "I command this army, set in my place by Red Dynan himself. You are no less his child than the girl at Miranei. Lead us tomorrow, lord, and I lay the army at your feet until you are crowned. We need a strong hand at the helm; Anghara cannot lead us, not now. You can. You must." There was no disloyalty, no sense of betrayal; Fodrun was giving Roisinan into the hands most fit to hold it. He sank to one knee before Sif, his eyes never leaving the younger man's for an instant. "Take us to victory tomorrow, Sif Kir Hama, and I will call you king in Roisinan; so will every man in this army. We will take Miranei for you. You are the only one who can hold your father's realm."

Sif reached out a hand and raised Fodrun, his own eyes burning intensely with a pale blue fire. There was something wolfish in his smile, something that, for the last time, called up Anghara's gentle image in Fodrun's mind, this time accompanied by what might have been regret. But the regret was swept away into a fierce joy as Sif spoke. Only two words, words that put a seal on the fate of a land and a small girl who did not yet know how easily she had been supplanted.

"I accept."

# PART 1

# Brynna

1

"**O**ne. Already—and he was Anghara's."

Rima, Red Dynan's widowed queen, paced her chambers, lacing restless fingers in and out of one another in palpable frustration.

"How, my lady?"

"Poison, they think. The healers who tended him say he died in great pain. And now there are six in council. And I can be sure of only two." She looked up, her eyes haunted. "How long, March? How long before some poisoned sweet is handed to Anghara? I cannot be with her constantly, I cannot protect her all the time, not while I am trying to save her throne!"

March, the queen's man from long before her marriage, stirred from where he stood staring into the leaping flames on the great stone hearth. "It might not be too much longer," he said carefully. "There has been other news."

"What? When? Why wasn't I told?"

March smiled, an indulgent smile from an old retainer for a mistress he had known from her cradle. "You are the first to know, my lady. The messenger arrived less than an hour ago."

Rima crossed the room and stood before him. She had to look up at his face; she had always been physically frail, small-boned, almost bird-like. In moments of tenderness, Dynan used to call her his little sparrow. But there was that in her face right now, which would make many a man twice her size tread lightly. "The message?"

"They are coming. They are coming here, for Miranei, for the throne. Sif will never be content with less, not with the army behind him. We knew this would happen."

"Damn Kalas!" murmured Rima, looking away into the fire. "Now, when I needed him most, he lies dying. He would never have given Sif the army."

"They won the second battle," March pointed out. "Perhaps Fodrun knew what he was doing."

Rima made an impatient gesture. "Tath!" she said. "They have always been a thorn in our side. Our men were not that wanting. If only Fodrun hadn't lost heart. If only . . ."

They both knew if only what. If Dynan had lived . . . But if Dynan had lived, Sif would have still been waiting for his chance. Now at least he had declared himself, as openly as he could; his first act of defiance was to claim his father for himself, and for Clera, his mother. It was to Clera's manor that the messenger bearing the news of Dynan's death had gone, not to Miranei. Rima had known of it, probably as it had happened; she was Sighted, and gifted that way. She had known, perhaps, that she would never see Dynan again when she had girded his sword on him for this battle. But Sif had sent her no official messenger. What she could not have foreseen was just how fast things would fall apart at Miranei, after one of the squires had galloped from the battlefield at Ronval to gasp out the news of Dynan's death and Sif's bid for the kingdom.

Rima had always been very good at hiding her feelings. Her court face was a carefully cultivated mask, pleasant, pretty, interested, a little abstracted—people said a lot in the presence of someone who seemed not to be listening half the time, and not fully comprehending what she heard even when she did pay attention. They had always thought her weak, the council lords and those who jostled for favors at Dynan's flanks. But here, in the presence of someone whom she trusted and who would not have been fooled for an instant with her court pretenses, Rima allowed her true feelings to percolate across her features. March, watching the play of emotion there, smiled, a little grimly. The court was about to learn how badly they had underestimated Dynan's "little sparrow."

"They have accepted Anghara as queen, in full council," Rima was saying softly.

"And when they see Dynan's own banners on the moors before Miranei?" said March.

Rima glanced up briefly, acknowledging the question as one she had pondered herself. "I must get them to seal their vows. In writing. Now, while I can still control the council. You say nobody knows of Sif's coming as yet?"

"Nobody, my lady."

"Good. Make sure the messenger is rewarded for his trouble—I am sure he is another whose interests do not lie with Sif—but don't let him speak to anyone until I have done with the council. Where is he now?"

"I told him to wait in my chambers, my lady."

They exchanged conspiratorial smiles. "Keep him there," Rima said, "for the time being. And tell the stewards to convene the council. Now, within the hour."

March made her a slight bow and turned to leave. Her voice stopped him even as he reached for the door. "March."

"My lady?"

"Which of Anghara's ladies do you think we can trust?"

March considered this. A little too long; Rima's mouth thinned. Had it really come to this? That she couldn't find one of her daughter's ladies who would be loyal to the future Queen of Roisinan? But March met her eyes steadily enough. "I would think Lady Catlin, or Lady Nessa. I would keep Lady Deira as far from any secret plan as I could."

Rima smiled despite herself. Deira was an elderly gossip, to whom one could entrust any rumor one wanted spread around Miranei and the surrounding countryside within the space of a single day. The warning was well-placed. There was an equal warning in March's words, though, in the two names he had omitted to mention. Those who might sell Anghara, if they had the chance. Rima considered the two ladies March had named for a brief moment, while he waited patiently by the door for further instructions. "Catlin," she decided finally. "Send Lady Catlin to me. And make sure Anghara is attended by Lady Nessa at all times, when Catlin or I are not with her."

"Yes, my lady." March took a moment to gaze at the queen with something like pity. There was desolation in Rima's eyes. She had already suffered a sundering, one beyond repair; she was contemplating another at that very minute, one which could well be instrumental in saving her daughter's life. For nine-year-old Anghara had never been as vulnerable as she was right now, with a stronger claimant than she on his way to tear her from the throne she held so precariously.

By the time the council was assembled, grumbling at the haste, Rima had set a great deal into motion. She swept into the room clad in royal robes of scarlet and ermine, glittering with gems. She knew very well that any direct order she gave this dangerously unbalanced council might all too easily be ignored—at worst, they could rise up against her, against Anghara, there and then. But she knew how to play them; the judicious show of a little royal splendor was never wasted. With a mixture of courtly deference and a delicate pulling of Dynan's rank, Rima did not find it hard to lull them into believing they had been sweet-talked into adding their signatures and seals to the document she had already prepared—the least of things, merely a declaration of succession. They woke up abruptly at Rima's rather grim chuckle as she picked up both the original document and the copy she had also given them to sign and proceeded to read to them what they had just agreed. They, the undersigned, council lords appointed by King Dynan of blessed memory of the Realm of Roisinan, lawful king in unbroken descent of the Kir Hama dynasty, undertook to preserve and protect the successor to King Dynan, his only heir and legitimate child of his marriage, against all comers. They agreed to accept her as their sovereign queen. It was more than a simple declaration, it was an oath of allegiance.

"Majesty, was this really necessary?" protested one of the lords, one Rima was far from sure of. She could see beads of sweat gathering on his forehead.

*Yes. Yes! You have already chosen a different master. Let's see where you go from here.* "I believed so, my lords. None of you forget for a moment, I am sure, that the princess is still very young." It was a sharp little gibe—of course they couldn't put from their minds that, technically, they were ruled by a nine-year-old. One or two councillors had the grace to look abashed. "There is one more thing I would ask of you. Would you please follow me?"

They did so, not without grumbling, but she was still queen and Miranei was still her court. They stopped abruptly as they entered the Great Hall. Openly displayed on a purple cushion was the crown of Roisinan—and next to it, sitting very still in a chair only one step down from the dais on which stood the throne of Miranei, the princess they had just sworn to uphold. Anghara Kir Hama sat straight, not touching the back of the chair, her dignity almost frightening in one barely turned nine. She watched them enter with calm gray eyes, meeting no lord's direct look but seeming to encompass them all with her still, royal gaze.

"What is this, majesty?" one of the lords asked. "The princess? The crown?"

"Yes," said Rima, and cold steel rang in her voice. The lords looked at her, surprised. This was not the gentle queen they had learned to know. This was a she-lynx from the mountains, and on the dais was her young. The time was past for preening and purring. The claws were out. "We must wait for her crowning, her formal crowning. But today you, the council of lords, have all set your names to a document naming Anghara as Queen of Roisinan. And today the council of lords will witness her first crowning. You, the council, will crown her. Once bestowed in this way, we all know the crown cannot be taken except by a usurper. And if it is so taken, you will all bear witness that it is worn by a false claimant. Lord Egan, Lord Garig, if you will."

One or two of the lords had glanced back at the door through which they had entered, but it had been quietly closed behind them. So were all the other doors. Rima noticed their furtive glances and smiled. "All doors are barred from the outside at my command," she said, "until this ceremony is over, and until I give the word. My lords, your queen waits."

There were those who still contemplated some sort of escape, but the two lords Rima had named glanced warily at one another and began walking toward the dais where Anghara sat. She had turned her head slightly to look at them, and their spirits quailed at the piercing power in her eyes. So unexpected in a child—eyes which seemed to see past the lords' council robes, expensive jin'aaz silk from Kheldrin, and into the sins festering beneath in their souls. Lord Egan was the first to look away. Lord Garig had declared openly for Anghara; that was partly why Rima had named him. He looked at the child with love and loyalty. But even he could not bear her direct gaze for long. Her eyes, the same gray as Rima's, were all Dynan's in that moment—the blood in her veins was royal, by the Gods, and it showed.

Rima shepherded the remaining four lords closer, so they might miss nothing. Lord Egan picked up the crown and could not prevent a scowl as he turned to hand the jewelled treasure into Lord Garig's waiting hands. He did so in silence; but Garig suddenly felt moved to say a few words, to legitimize what ought to have been a rite of royal pomp and panoply with a few phrases of ceremony. He lifted the crown he held high over Anghara's head.

"With this," he said formally, lapsing into the high tongue of all ritual, "we accept thee as our queen, Anghara Kir Hama, daughter of Dynan. We hold thy life and safety above our own, and we pledge our lives to thee in this place today. May the Gods bless and protect you."

The crown touched Anghara's bright hair and rested there for a few moments—then Garig lifted it away, with something like reluctance. It was not his place to crown her properly; but it was written in his face how much he wished Anghara could walk from this room his queen in more than just his dreams and wishes. Rima could see his expression, and also the daggers Egan's eyes cast at him over the crown as he received it back. She suddenly wondered if this little charade of hers would cost Garig his life.

None of this had been rehearsed; there had been no time, and Rima had to rely on Anghara's natural awareness of what was going on. The girl now startled them by suddenly rising from her chair. She might have been small-boned, like her mother, and still a child, but at that moment she had the presence Red Dynan had commanded.

"Thank you," she said to the two lords who had leaned their hand to her "crowning." She included them both in her thanks, but the smile hovering in her eyes was for Garig alone. Garig suddenly saw the means to cement the ceremony he had just performed in terms that would bind the lords irrevocably, far more so than Rima's document. He dropped to one knee before the child-queen, lifting up his hands to hers, palms together. He caught her eye, this time fearlessly, and she read there his intent and raised her own small hands to cover his.

"I, Lord Garig, do swear fealty and allegiance and do take thee as my liege lady and my queen . . ."

This Rima had not planned, and the blood rushed to her face as she realized what Garig had done. Now he had sworn, they would all have to, or be instantly proclaimed traitors. The ancient oath might not mean much if Sif knocked on the doors of Miranei, but it was honor-binding. Rima blessed Garig for thinking of it, wondering how she ought to reward this most loyal of lords, while it was still in her power to do so.

She focused once more on the dais, where Garig had completed his oath and been raised by Anghara. Egan's color was also high, but not from joy. His face was thunderous. Still, under the challenging gaze of Lord Garig and Anghara's serenely expectant smile, he stumbled onto his knees and forced out the words of the oath of allegiance as though through clenched teeth. All the same, he had done it. When he rose, the next lord was already stepping onto the dais to take his place. Rima sought Garig's eyes, and he met her look across the heads of the file of lords waiting for their turn at the oath taking. He gave her a barely perceptible nod, approval of what she had done, acknowledgment of her gratitude, which must have blazed from her eyes like a beacon. He looked away again, at Anghara, who stood less than half the height of the burly men who bowed before her but seemed to tower over them as they approached. Yes, thought Rima, she would do. She had it in her, the queenship; only why, in the name of all the Gods, did Dynan have to die before his daughter had turned fifteen? They would have accepted her then, even with Sif hovering in the background like a bad dream. But she was still a child, especially now, in the afterglow of Sif's martial exploits. They would look for confirmation of the right to rule Roisinan in Sif's abilities on the battlefield, not in the quiet qualities of a girl-child who had never lifted a sword . . .

"Majesty?"

Egan's voice beside her woke Rima from what had almost been a dream. She glanced up at the dais, where Anghara now stood alone, and then around the faces of the lords who had rejoined her in the hall. Egan looked as if he might well break every court protocol he had ever known, and go so far as to demand to be released from the room. But Garig forestalled him, stepping forward in the instant of silence following Egan's challenge, and bowed to her.

"Our duty is accomplished," he said smoothly, "and the young queen has given us leave to go. Have we yours?"

"Yes, and my blessing," she said impulsively. She held his eyes for one last instant and then turned to walk to the nearest door and knock on it. "Open," she called, "in the name of the queen!"

The doors swung open at this invocation, and the lords, with a sketchy obeisance in Rima's direction, filed out. When the last had left, Rima turned to her daughter. Anghara had descended the steps of the dais and stood, gray eyes wide and questioning, looking more delicate and fragile than ever. "Mama?"

Rima held out a hand, and Anghara ran to hug her mother around her slender waist. "Oh, my little queen, you did beautifully. They will not forget this. They might try, but this day will never leave their memory. You may not have been crowned yet, but they saw the crown upon your head, and it looked as if it belonged there. They will not forget."

March popped his head around the door he had been guarding. "My lady?"

Rima, her arm around her daughter's shoulders, looked up.

"I have released the messenger," he said, cryptically.

"Good," said Rima. The news would greet the lords as they came from Anghara's crowning. Only now would they realize what they had done. "Catlin?"

"She is ready, majesty," said March, a little more slowly. Rima's eyes were distant, looking inward, sifting through the memories. Then she roused herself, allowing a small moment of triumph to sweeten what had to follow, and hugged Anghara closer.

"Come," she said, "there are still a lot of things to be done, and we have little time. Come, Anghara."

Lady Catlin of Anghara's suite waited in Rima's private quarters with two small travelling trunks. One was already corded and scaled; the other still open. Catlin had finished with it, however; the final space above the layer of fine silk-paper covering the meticulously packed clothing was left for another's hand.

Anghara had been told nothing of travel plans. Yet the trunks were hers, and Catlin was a familar attendant, and Anghara's eyes widened as she saw them secreted away in her mother's rooms. March led Catlin out into the anteroom for the moment, giving mother and daughter a few moments alone together.

"My darling," said Rima, in a voice which was steady enough to an untutored ear, "you must go away for a while. Things could get a little dangerous for you here, and I'd have you well away from Miranei until you can come back to the court and be properly crowned."

"And you, Mama?" Anghara had no need to hide her feelings. The tremble in her own voice was all too apparent, and threatened to completely undo Rima's hard-won composure.

"I will stay here," she said. "Someone needs to hold the castle for you."

"But March could . . ."

"March is going with you. And Catlin. They will take care of you while we are parted."

Anghara was a child, but she was a child born to duty. She lifted her chin. "How long must I stay away?"

"I don't know, my darling. I will send for you when it is safe. Now listen to me. This I will give to you." She wrapped Anghara's small hands around the document the lords had signed. "Don't ever lose it. The other one, the copy, I shall hide in a safe place, if you should ever need it."

"Where, Mama?"

"March will know. Keep him close. And one more thing I will give you."

She rose and went to a casket by her bed, taking from it a massive gold ring, a man's ring, set with a great red stone carved with the crest of Roisinan. A fine gold chain had been looped through the ring. Rima stood looking at it for a few breathless seconds as the unhealed wounds in her heart began to bleed anew at the sight of Dynan's seal. And then she turned and placed the ring in Anghara's small palm, pouring the chain after it. "This was your father's," she said, and her voice was husky. "It is the seal of the kingdom. While it is yours, you are the Queen of Roisinan. Do not let it out of your sight."

Anghara bit her lip and then took the treasure, looping the chain over her head until the great seal hung dull red against the bodice of her dress. Rima smiled, and reached to tuck it inside. "Do not let it out of your sight, but do not reveal it to that of others. Not until you are ready to claim it again here in Miranei."

Anghara accepted this in silence. Her eyes strayed toward the half-packed trunk. Rima noticed. "I asked Catlin to pack for you," she said, "but that space is for you, if there is something you want to take, something she did not know about. She's waiting for you now, and there is nobody in your chambers. Go quickly and quietly, and bring whatever you might want. And then . . ."

"There is nothing," said Anghara. "What she chose to bring, I will take. I am content."

Rima gazed at her child for a long moment, with a mixture of pride and sheer incomprehension. "Are you sure?" she murmured. "It might be awhile. Is there some special treasure . . ."

"I will be back," said Anghara, with a certainty that dragged Rima's sleeping Sight into full wakefulness. Looking down at her daughter, she saw curiously double, the face of a young woman superimposed on the child's—a face that was no stranger to suffering. "Yes," Rima said slowly, recognizing the abyss of pain-filled years lying between the two images. "You will."

She bent to kiss Anghara on the brow, then turned away to open the door of her chambers. "Lady Catlin, the princess needs to change into her travelling costume, and then you will take her down to the north courtyard. There is a wagon waiting. March will be there presently, he will be your escort on your journey. Make sure . . . nobody sees where you go."

"Yes, majesty," murmured Catlin, her voice a pleasant smoky alto. "Come, princess."

Anghara, who had laid her copy of the council document carefully into the open trunk, obeyed. Her last farewell to her mother was a swift backward glance of those strange gray eyes, filled with a depth of understanding too great for her tender years. Rima blew her a kiss from the tips of her fingers, and Anghara smiled a little as she turned away. "March," said Rima, and March slipped into the room as Anghara left it, closing the door behind him.

"Lady?"

"The other scroll . . . if she should ever have need . . . in our secret place in Cascin."

March took the document, folding it into the breast of his travelling tunic. "I will keep it safe."

"March . . ."

"And her, my lady. I will keep her safe."

Rima turned away, unable to bear the compassion in his eyes. He waited for a moment, but she said no more. "I will send a man for the trunks," March said at length. "He can be trusted. The Gods watch over you, my lady."

Rima kept her back to him, hearing him quietly close the door behind him. She had no intention of being here when March's man arrived. The departure of her daughter had already left a great gaping hole in her soul, added to the wound of Dynan's passing. Somehow, seeing those two small trunks disappear would be worse than saying goodbye. It would be a haunting and permanent farewell.

Rima had no illusions; when Sif came to Miranei any siege would last a bare day or two—a week, if the defenses held at all. There were too many who were Miranei born and bred in the ranks of his army, too many who knew Miranei far too well. If there was a weakness, they would know it as well as the defenders. There would be someone in his army who knew rumors about secret passages; and they would know all the postern gates. There weren't enough men in Miranei to keep out Miranei's own army, even if all chose to fight, which was by no means certain. And when Sif gained the castle, Rima knew she was dead. As would Anghara be, if she were to wait within those walls, so secure against anyone but their own children. But Rima could buy precious time. She could stay behind, inviting speculation; she could send three different expeditions in three different directions, at least one, with a girl answering Anghara's description, into a sanctuary of Nual. The priests wouldn't lie, but they would be fed only half-truths—if anyone did come knocking, the priests could not swear they were not harboring the vanished princess. Perhaps Sif would be content to leave her there, knowing she could never leave the sanctuary alive.

And other, truer paths she had already swept clean of tracks. She had sent a letter with March. By the time Anghara Kir Hama arrived at the manor of Cascin, Rima's childhood home now belonging to her sister Chella and her husband, Lyme, the fosterling by the name of Brynna Kelen, whose identity Anghara would assume, would have been "living" there for two years. Rima trusted her sister—Chella had the ability to make the entire household swear to that, if Sif should choose to inquire. Even the children . . . Rima allowed herself a moment of bitterness. There, at Cascin, no more than a small manor in the hinterland of Roisinan, were three sons waiting to inherit—while here, at Miranei, there was but one small girl to take up the burden of a kingdom. It was not fair. It was not fair! If only she had been able to give Dynan a son to supplant his first-born child by another woman—a true-born son instead of Sif, who gloried in his right to bear Dynan's name. Because Dynan had taken him, accepted him, set his stamp on him that all might know the boy for the king's own. He had loved Anghara, but Red Dynan came of a line of warriors, and all his pride had been for Sif. And now the daughter of his love could easily fall beneath the onslaught of the son of his pride. And Rima was a frail enough barrier to raise between them. Yet—there was still one last thing she could do, one thing her Sight could do for her daughter.

She left her room, and climbed the battlements facing south. There were several carts on the road from Miranei, folk fleeing the inevitable attack. One of them might well be the one carrying Dynan's daughter away from his keep. In a last moment of full and free memory, Rima was deeply grateful for the numbers on that road; they would mask Anghara's departure even more thoroughly than Rima could have hoped. Then she ruthlessly erased all traces of Anghara from her mind after the last bright vision of her daughter's small face beneath Roisinan's crown, deliberately left to torment Sif if he ever came close enough to Rima to question her. There was one small trigger, inaccessible to anyone but herself, that would restore her memory of Anghara's sanctuary; but Sif could not get at it. Even if she survived his assault on Miranei long enough to become his prisoner, he would never be able to drag the secret from her. He could not force her to divulge what she no longer knew.

Both were gone from her now, Dynan whom she had loved and the daughter for whom she fought even as she chose to forget her. There was a great yawning hollowness inside her, a longing that could never be met, part of a puzzle that could only be resolved when Sif arrived in Miranei and she, Rima, went to whatever fate that hour held for her.

But now she was tired, empty. She crossed her arms upon the cold stone of Miranei's ancient stone battlements and rested her chin on them, staring unblinkingly across the moors into the flat horizon, as if she could already see in her mind's eye the dust raised by Dynan's army. Sif's army, coming to conquer. Roisinan's army, death behind them, death before, coming to bring a new king to the keep under the mountains.

2

It was not that Sif had counted on having Miranei handed to him without a blow struck in anger, given his manner of having claimed its mastery, although it would have gratified him to have been welcomed there with acclamations. But neither did he expect the keep to hold out against him for so long. Even Rima had not realized the depth of the feelings that ran in the keep's defenders. Faced with a horrifying choice, divided within itself, its people's loyalties shredded in the storm of Sif's coming like cobwebs in a high wind, Miranei was still the king's keep and he that waited beyond it, for all the claims of his blood, was not yet the king. And what was the king's was still within the walls, and would be defended. The garrison fought like men demented, even against those who rose up in Sif's favor in its own ranks. Miranei suffered agonies of both body and soul, but it held out for the heiress of Red Dynan for almost ten days.

Even then, Miranei's gates were opened to Sif from within. Once in, the army's superior numbers made short work of any remaining pockets of resistance. But the aftermath, the picture that met Sif's eyes when he rode in to claim his city, was a swathe of blood and destruction. There were bodies in the courtyards, bodies hanging awkwardly from battlements. Torn, bloodied cloaks lay trampled underfoot; bright blood pooled on stairwells, left long, dull smears on walls. Those men who were still alive wandered about in a daze. A few recognized and greeted Sif according to the manner of their most recent feelings about him—some with a weary kind of joy, others, less subtle, simply turning tail and running for cover. There was an odd smell in the air, partly that of death, partly something more intangible, a smell, perhaps, of treachery, or regret. Someone had torched a grain storehouse and the fire hadn't fully caught—the roof still smoldered dully, adding acrid, murky smoke to the already polluted atmosphere. Sif, unaccountably, felt cheated.

"I wanted to ride into my father's city in glory," he said to Fodrun, riding beside him. He lifted a hand from his black stallion's reins, waving a waft of smoke from before his face. "There is no glory in this."

Fodrun could only agree. It was easy to forget in the heat of battle, but what they had just vanquished was not simply a body of men opposed to their own, it was the spirit behind those men, the spirit of a nine-year-old girl. There was something bitter in the thought, something dismal about Miranei, something that jarred badly at Fodrun's bright memories of it. But he could not put his feelings into words. He merely nodded. "But there is time for that, my lord. You will make the glory."

Sif's mood was too bleak for prophecies of splendor. He merely signalled forward a pair of troopers who rode at his back. "Go," he said to them, "take a detail and secure the royal tower. If there is anyone there, detain them in comfortable confinement. Go."

One of the men bowed from the saddle in acquiescence, raised a hand, motioning to a company of mounted men. They peeled off from the main group and made for the royal gate; a few, obeying a sharp hand signal, wheeled and passed under an archway leading from the yard, rounding the tower and vanishing from sight. Going for the postern, Sif noticed fleetingly, with approval; he made a mental note to commend the men whom he had set in command of this cheta for their thoroughness. The men would not be surprised to find their new king knew them by name. That was part of Sif's power, part of the reason the army cohorts at his back, who had not all been entirely happy in the beginning at what they saw as Fodrun's treachery, were now behind Sif to a man, as once they had belonged to his father. This, if nothing else, had stamped Sif as Dynan's, and their own.

Sif made a thorough tour of the battlements, offering a few well-chosen words to men he met on his way. But there was nothing he could have usefully done or changed there, all orders having been given and confirmed before Sif had ridden into the keep. Fodrun, walking two steps behind, could not help but think the tour was little more than a delaying tactic; Sif was as reluctant to join his men in the royal tower as Fodrun himself. Suddenly, here, Princess Anghara had returned to haunt Sif's general with a persistence he had never expected; being a practical man, he saw no pleasant future for the little princess once Sif had time to think about her potential as a focus for those who might plot his downfall. If he wanted to hold on to what he had won, Sif could not afford to let Anghara live at liberty, if he could afford to allow her to live at all.

At last Sif turned toward the royal chambers where a hard decision awaited. Dynan's queen had never liked him, and Sif had accepted that—how could she? She resented him; he resented her. How much more he could have had than the crumbs from Dynan's table, had Clera been queen, had he been born prince instead of king's bastard?

But Anghara . . . After Dynan had acknowledged him and had him brought to court, Sif had seen his half-sister frequently. He vividly remembered the day of her birth, the day his hopes of Dynan's putting aside his queen, marrying Clera and announcing his only son as his heir had been finally dashed. If Rima had resented Sif, he had paid it back tenfold by resenting Anghara, with the implacable hostility of a twelve-year-old boy who saw in Dynan's new daughter the ruination of his dreams. But she had never hated him. She always had a way of keeping a friendly distance, a knack many an adult woman would have envied, if their paths happened to cross a little more closely than usual for a high-born girl-child and a bastard-born youth who spent most of his time in places she rarely frequented. She had never found occasion to pay him much attention, both from the point of view of being secure and unchallenged in her exalted position, and from the natural disinterest and incomprehension bound to follow from the discrepancy in their age and sex. Before that, she had been too young. And now Sif held her life in his hands. His face was clean of expression, but his hands were tightly clenched at his sides; Fodrun could tell his self-possession was hard-won.

It shattered without warning when they entered the queen's private chambers, and Sif saw the woman laid out on the bed. He slid from tight-leashed composure into a blistering rage within the time it took to blink.

"I wanted her alive!" Sif snarled, having paused aghast in the doorway. The guard who stood at the foot of the carved four-poster bed cringed.

"She is, lord!" he had time to squeak, wincing in anticipation of a stinging blow across his face.

The blow never landed. Sif had himself in hand. "Explain," he said brusquely, and the naked edge of his voice was no less dangerous for having been sheathed in a brittle control.

"Lord," the soldier began warily, "somebody was here before us. The room was a mess . . . whoever was here might have been looking for something, but it looked as though she had not fought her assailant—perhaps she knew them—but by the time we got here they had already gone."

"Did you search the tower?"

"Yes, lord, we did. But there were blood-spattered men everywhere. If some of that blood was the quee . . . was hers . . . we could not know."

Fodrun allowed himself a small grim smile at the man's frantic attempt to retrieve his slip of the tongue. Sif would not want reminding of who had been queen in Miranei. And the guard's clumsy reconstruction of events may not have been far from the mark. Rima may well have known who attacked her. What she may not have known when they entered her chambers was where their loyalties had been given.

"She was wounded," the guard was still babbling, "but she was not yet dead, and three of us came to see if we could help. But she had a knife, lord, one of those wretched small ones so damnably easy to hide, and if she had failed to fight the one who came to murder her, she certainly fought us, who came to help. She slashed at Radis' face—and then Talin grabbed at her arm—he didn't mean to break it, lord—and I . . . I pushed her away . . . and she fell . . . across that." The fender he indicated ringed the hearth, and was delicately spiked. Some of the spikes, ornamental but deadly, were anointed with blood. There was more pooling by the hearth.

They had lifted the half-swooning queen onto the bed, the guard explained, and tried to bind the worst of her hurts, but by the time Sif had arrived the bed was soaked with blood that seeped through their makeshift bandages. Rima lay still, her face a bloody mask; her eyes were closed, but she was still breathing, very shallowly. Fodrun, no stranger to death, saw it stamped on her brow; but it was no part of his soldier's brief to see women laid out thus. He found himself feeling queasy. Part of the reason for this supplied itself a moment later when Sif asked the question Fodrun's subconscious could not formulate.

"And the girl? The princess?"

"Some of the men are still searching, lord. She was not in her quarters, nor here. Perhaps she is hiding somewhere; or perhaps . . ."

Yes. Perhaps somebody had already solved Sif's dilemma for him. Perhaps whoever had tried to do away with the mother had succeeded where the child was concerned. Sif dismissed Anghara from his mind for a moment, crossing over to the bed and bending over Rima's prone form. As though aware of his presence, her eyes flickered open. They were already filmed, glazing.

Sif reached out and shook her, none too gently. "Who was it? Why attack you? Why now?" he demanded. "Where is Anghara?"

She murmured something, and both Sif and the guard instinctively leaned closer to hear. "What was that?" said Sif impatiently.

"She said . . . sign? Signed?" volunteered the guard. Rima made a faint movement of her hand toward her breast, but lacked the strength to carry it through; the hand fell back. Sif's eyes narrowed.

"Did you search her?"

"No, lord!" said the guard, sounding faintly shocked at the idea.

Sif had no such scruples. He'd followed the unfinished gesture to where it would have landed, and saw a subtle bulge there that belonged on no woman's body. Now he reached out and ran his hand over it, not able to suppress a quick grim smile as his fingers met parchment.

"It's my guess it was for this she was attacked. 'Sign,' she said. Or 'signed.' Something signed. What document is this?"

It was much crumpled and partly stained with Rima's blood, but it was still legible enough. As Sif tried to make sense of it, Fodrun watched his face change again, sliding into the cold fury only lately quelled. When he looked up, even Fodrun quailed at his icy eyes even though the anger was not for him. Sif spoke to the guard without even turning his head in that direction. "Find me one of those Sighted women; there used to be dozens in the keep. Find me one, now. I want her here within five minutes. Move!"

The guard, suddenly anxious to depart from Sif's volatile presence, scurried to obey.

"My lord?" Fodrun ventured.

"She wasn't attacked for this, but for that of which it tells," Sif spat, tossing the unsavoury parchment to Fodrun, who caught it awkwardly. "She had the council sign a declaration. That's just a statement of its existence; but that declaration, the original document, is a confirmation of Anghara's succession, signed by every lord on my father's own council. I can form a new council, but this, this will bind them, too— this is a legal document, signed by a legal government in its full powers. Anyone producing the original, or proof of its existence, can hold a sword at my throat. This can bury me. I want that document. If none know of it but she and the council, then I can still . . ."

"Lord, you wanted . . ."

Sif grabbed the dishevelled, elderly woman whom the

guard dispatched for Sighted prey had produced, his hand closing round her arm like a vice. Her eyes were round with horror, and she whimpered like a puppy at the new pain. Sif shook her, and she blinked, seeming to start out of deep shock, staring at him in fear.

"This woman is dying," Sif said, "and you will read her for me. I want answers, and I can no longer extract them myself. Come on."

"The queen . . ." moaned the Sighted woman, suddenly catching her first sight of the subject she was to probe. "I can't . . ."

"Oh yes, you can," said Sif grimly. "She *was* your queen. Right now, I am your king, and you will obey me. What is your name?"

"D . . . Deira . . ."

"Listen to me, Lady Deira, and listen very carefully. I want to know two things. I want to know where the original is of the document the general is holding. Do you need to see it to know what to ask?"

She seemed to have lost her voice completely; Sif made an impatient motion and Fodrun handed him the document. Sif thrust it at the woman, who received it almost mechanically. "Look at it!" he snapped, and she did, although it was doubtful she took any of it in. Sif didn't mind, he would have preferred her never to have seen it at all—if she couldn't understand what she was holding, all the better, as long as she had the vital link to get the truth out of Rima.

"The other thing . . . look at me, woman . . . the other thing I must know is the whereabouts of her daughter . . . what is it now?"

Large round tears rolled out of Deira's eyes at the mention of the princess. Sif shook her again. "I don't have much time. What is it? Do you know something?"

"She was my young lady . . . my lamb . . . she is gone . . ."

That could have meant a number of things. Sif jerked his captive forward, desperately afraid Rima might yet cheat him of the information he wanted. He could not let her die before he got it out of her. Deira stumbled against the bed, making no effort to wipe her tears; Rima's eyes opened again. Deira gasped at the sight, her hands, one still holding the document, flying to her mouth.

"Ask!" said Sif violently. "The original! The princess!"

Rima whispered something, very low. Deira's breath hissed out again as Sif tightened his fingers on her arm; she bent over her to listen, and then, sobbing, murmured the questions Sif had put. Rima was silent then, for so long that Sif already tasted defeat, but then her lips, almost bloodless now, opened again. Sif almost pushed Deira into Rima's face. The queen's voice rustled faintly, like the sound of wind in dying leaves, and then she was simply . . . gone. Fodrun could see the instant of her going, her breath stopping, her head lolling sideways, lifeless. Her eyes had stayed open, though, and if Fodrun had been called upon to interpret the expression that remained on her face he would have had to call it triumph. The thought gave him an odd shiver of apprehension. What was it she thought she'd won?

"She said," Deira said slowly, without being prompted, although Sif's fingers were possibly prompt enough, "the original is with Princess Anghara."

"And where," said Sif, who couldn't keep the sarcasm out of his voice, "is the princess?"

Deira looked up, her eyes clear and very candid. "She does not know, and she is speaking the truth. There is no memory of Princess Anghara in her mind, after the crowning."

Fodrun felt the temperature in the room drop. Sif took his fingers from the woman's arm as though she were unclean. "Crowning?" he echoed, and his voice was glacial.

"The council crowned her, and swore allegiance," said Deira, recounting the memory she had just read. Fodrun watched Sif's face change. Even if he had wanted to spare Anghara it was now too late. There was no room for two crowned sovereigns in Roisinan, and Sif had already staked everything on the gamble he had taken to win the crown for himself. Rima's plan had doomed her daughter; if Sif's searchers found the child-queen, she was dead.

"Who knew of this?" Sif asked, his voice flat.

"The council lords, who were there. And the queen's guard," said Deira.

"None else?"

"I did not know until this moment," said Deira, suddenly gathering the tattered rags of dignity befitting a lady of the royal chamber, "and I was Princess Anghara's own attendant."

"Go," Sif said abruptly. "Leave us. Guard!"

"Lord?"

"Get the woman out of here."

Deira went with alacrity, stealing a tender look at the woman whose last memories she had stolen for Miranei's new lord.

One of Sif's captains returned at this point to report no trace of Anghara Kir Hama could be found in the keep, living or dead.

"Could she have spirited her away under my very nose? Where would she have sent her?" Sif said, speaking only partly to Fodrun, demanding answers from himself.

"I could make enquiries, lord. Even in the chaos . . . someone might have noticed something," Fodrun volunteered. Sif gave him a swift glance from beneath lowered eyelids.

"Yes. Do so. But if . . . when . . . we run her to ground, it will be for me alone to know. As far as anyone else is concerned, she is dead, Fodrun. Anghara Kir Hama is dead, and will be buried with her mother. They cannot crown a dead queen; this way, even the damned document . . . where is that parchment, Fodrun?"

Fodrun's eyes widened. "The woman . . . the woman had it . . . you gave it into her hand . . ."

Sif was already at the door. "Domar!" he called, and the man who had reported not finding the princess stood to attention. "The woman who was just here. She has in her possession a document. I want it back. Find her."

"Yes, lord!"

Leaning against the doorway of Rima's room, Sif laughed joylessly, his head bent, seeming to study with rapt attention the dust on his riding boots, so inappropriate for a royal lady's bedchamber. Then he looked up, and his eyes glinted with a savage determination. "I've been careless," he said. "It won't happen again."

He turned around and contemplated the dead woman in what had also been his father's bed. He could let that specter drive him from this room, from this palace, but it would take more than the dead to keep him from the dreams he had clung to for so long. "Get someone to clear up this mess," he ordered abruptly. "I want this room habitable again before tonight. For now . . . I need a drink. Come, Fodrun, king-maker. Shall I show you a place where a would-be prince-in-waiting often used to go?"

It came as something of a surprise to Fodrun to realize the last thing he wanted to do was walk into some Miranei tavern with the man who would be crowned king within days. When he had promised Sif Roisinan, Fodrun had been thinking only of the battle to come; he had wanted a prince who would be a war leader to his leaderless, all-but-crushed army. What he received was something far bigger than he had bargained for—Fodrun Kingmaker. For some reason it sat ill on Fodrun's ears. But the king he had made was waiting, and his words had been less a request than an order thinly veiled in courtesy. Fodrun drew a deep breath and dredged up a smile from somewhere. "Lead on, my prince."

The guards found Deira almost two hours later. By then she no longer had the document they were seeking; her reputation, so well respected by March, had been richly deserved. When the matter was brought to him, Sif was intelligent enough to realize he had lost that particular battle. The contents of the damnable document must have been the stuff of tavern gossip even as he sat quaffing ale with his general, who would emerge from that particular outing as the Chancellor of Roisinan. Counselled by his newly appointed chancellor, now First Lord in Sif's new council, he did not order the woman killed; after all, he himself had summoned her to Rima's chamber, and if anyone had been to blame for her keeping hold of the parchment, it was him. He had merely asked his guards, in a laconic tone laced with steel, never to let her cross his path again, and by nightfall she was packed and gone, set on the road of exile under permanent ban from Miranei for as long as Sif Kir Hama reigned. She was followed, as an afterthought; it had been Fodrun's idea, and one of his own men who had been charged with it. Deira could conceivably have played them all for fools, and headed directly for Anghara's hiding place. But March's words had been heeded; Deira knew nothing. Fodrun's agent followed her to her brother's house, and, on his return, reported to Fodrun that the lady looked likely to stay there for the rest of her days, intimidating her brother's lady with grim tales of the Battle of Miranei.

The army that took Miranei had been only a fragment of the force that fought at the Ronval. These men had ridden hard and fast, reaching the keep quickly, ready for battle. The remainder of the men, who travelled much more slowly, had been something of an honor guard, their task to escort Dynan's body. Everything had waited upon them, for the return of the dead king. Sif merely held the reins of power, but could not be crowned until his father's body had been properly laid to rest, and these arrangements had been the first order of business Sif attended to. Dynan was given a ceremonial state funeral, which he shared, although it galled Sif to enshrine that relationship even in death, with his queen—and with a casket devoid of a body, purported to contain the remains of his daughter. Sif himself attended the formalities with his mother on his arm, Lady Clera having suddenly become a person of some influence at court. Not a muscle on his face moved during the ceremony, but Fodrun, who was beginning to read Sif's moods by the subtle signals of his flashing eyes, saw how much it upset him to see the grief expressed by the people at the sight of that third, smallest casket. Even at her own "funeral," his half-sister was successfully upstaging him.

But that was the last time. With the past laid to rest, the next ceremony was wholly Sif's. He was crowned in the full brilliance of a royal sacrament, every detail meticulously planned. He would stamp his right to rule in the memory of every man and woman who saw him take the crown. And if a heresy had already taken root, a story of another crowning, which should have been put to rest in an irrevocable manner with Anghara's burial but which only seemed to have been inflamed by it, it would have been a foolhardy man indeed who showed he knew anything about it at Sif's coronation.

And the story did flower in Miranei, and spread beyond. There were those who may have bowed to circumstance and accepted Sif as the new king in Miranei who nevertheless flatly refused to believe Anghara was dead, and spoke of her return as if it was preordained. When Sif first heard the tale, he had merely laughed. When it surfaced to taunt him again and again, he ceased to find it funny.

"I could order the body taken from the vault and exhibited, and put the whole thing to rest," he said to Fodrun one evening, in a particularly foul mood about the story that wouldn't die. He was pacing back and forth in front of the stone fireplace in what had been Dynan and Rima's bedchamber, which he had appropriated for his own use. "I should have thought of that before, however, and provided the body. Finding one now, one that looks sufficiently like her, at the right stage of decomposition—it might prove a little difficult. I laid her in the family vault, Fodrun, and she will not stay. Anghara is a restless ghost."

Sif had been king for almost two months, and only Fodrun and Clera knew just how vulnerable he still felt, part of the reason why the stories of Anghara bit so deep. People tended to forget all too easily, given Sif's considerable abilities and the tenacity and ruthlessness with which he pursued his goals, that the new king was only a few weeks past his twenty-first birthday.

"I wonder what would happen," said Sif rather grimly, "if Anghara rode into the bailey and proclaimed herself queen, with that damned declaration in one hand and Dynan's great seal in the other. I never did find that, Fodrun. If Rima had anything to do with hiding it, she knew Miranei better than any born here. We've been over every conceivable place with a fine-toothed comb." If Anghara should choose to challenge Sif for her heritage, his possession of the throne would count for little, should she convince the people of the truth of her claims. He knew that. Anghara would know it, too.

Fodrun, who knew he had been summoned that night to deal with his king's fit of despondency, as he had done before on previous occasions, eyed a half-full decanter of red wine on a nearby table with longing, but the king had not offered. He swallowed, looked away. "I may have found something," he said diffidently.

Sif stopped pacing, whirled in mid stride. "Tell me!" he commanded.

"There was a sudden flurry of departures in the wake of the first rumors of your coming, lord," said Fodrun. "It's hard to be sure. But I have heard some of those wagons and carts were heading toward sanctuary."

"The priests of Nual?"

"Yes."

Sif rubbed his temples with his hands. "If she is there, the priests will never tell. And I cannot breach sanctuary with a raid. Roisinan may forgive Dynan's son much, but not that."

"But there is another way to find out. Not all who go into sanctuary go there for good. Nual shelters many who go to him for a few weeks, a few days, even; sometimes merely a wife fleeing from her husband's wrath, or a scoundrel evading the law."

"What are you saying?"

"What if a man sought sanctuary, a man who could learn from within who else the priests were harboring? They do not ask to know a seeker's sin if it is not freely told. The man could be in and out within a week. And we would at least know. Later . . . we have time. We could set a watch, if we were sure. She would never leave those walls."

Sif allowed himself a guarded smile. "Do it. And report to me."

"Yes, lord." Fodrun had made it a habit to execute all Sif's orders instantly. People who lagged tended to be remembered. He was already on his feet when Sif laughed.

"Tomorrow will do." There was amusement at Fodrun's alacrity in Sif's voice. Now, finally, he turned toward the decanter. "Wine?"

Fodrun settled back into the chair into which he had been waved at his arrival. "Thank you, my lord."

Sif's back was to him as he poured, and Fodrun studied him, safely unobserved for the moment. Even in the loose house robe, there was no disguising Sif's dangerous build, the breadth of his shoulders, the smooth muscle in his back. This was a true warrior prince Fodrun had raised to power, wild in all warriors' ways—a few words of prudent advice were all too often needed to calm his hot blood. Unpredictable, too; it was hard to gauge the sudden swing of Sif's moods. With all his faults, however, this was where Fodrun's fate had been cast. Why, then, did he sometimes find himself so reluctant to point out things Sif might have missed, especially on the subject of Anghara? Fodrun had thought on her intriguing disappearance, and the convenient amnesia of Rima's deathbed. He had been on the point of discussing these thoughts with Sif many times, yet somehow he could not bring himself to speak. Why? Did he still think he could protect Anghara? Against the power Sif consolidated daily? And what did his wanting to protect his king's only rival for the throne of Roisinan make of his loyalty to Sif?

Some of those thoughts, concealed so carefully for so long, must have showed on his face. Sif paused as he turned, two full wine goblets in hand. The king's eyes narrowed suddenly. "You have something else to tell me." It was a flat statement, not a question. More, it was an order; Sif's silence was expectant.

Cornered, Fodrun grasped the nettle. "I was thinking about Anghara," he said. "She vanished too quickly, too well. They simply did not have time to plan this, my lord; King Dynan's death and your being at hand for the battle at Ronval was not something anyone could have foreseen long enough in advance to produce an entire contingency plan, not one this flawless."

"What are you telling me?" said Sif, stepping forward, offering a goblet. Fodrun accepted it, and took a convulsive swallow. Sif would not like what he was about to hear.

Fodrun said carefully, "Rima must have had help. Anghara did not merely disappear, she was actively hidden from you; and yet there was the document, which implied she had already claimed the crown. I believe she is alive, she holds the original, and she was hidden from you by something more than clever planning. By Sight."

Sif was frowning. "Sight," he repeated hollowly.

"None in Miranei ever saw her use it," said Fodrun, even more carefully, "but it was an open secret that Rima had it."

"Yes," said Sif flatly. "I know." The hand that was closed around the stem of Sif's goblet whitened. Fodrun tensed, waiting for the wineglass to shatter against the wall at any minute. But Sif thought the better of it, and took a large swallow instead, forcing himself to relax into a chair. He looked faintly revolted; he had never liked to traffic with Sight. Sometimes he used it, ruthlessly, if he saw no other way past some obstacle toward a goal—as he had wielded it to wring true memories from the dying Rima in this very room. But Fodrun had seen Sif shy from it several times so far during their short partnership. It seemed to frighten him sometimes; it repulsed him always. He clearly saw it as something dreadful, inhuman.

"Then Anghara could have it too," said Sif, after a pause. "She may well be alive, but she's out there somewhere hiding her time, waiting until she comes into her power. If she doesn't want to be found, I'll never find her."

"She is too young, Sight comes into its own only with adolescence," Fodrun said. "In her own right, I don't think she can be a threat, or even a factor in her own concealment. Not yet. That still had to be done for her, by others, with mature powers. But yes, if she has inherited the gift, she will be able to use it, sooner rather than later. And one day she might well turn it against you. But if she has been hidden with Sight, lord, then she may be found with Sight. Perhaps."

"What do you mean?" The query was sharp, intense.

"There are still Sighted women in Miranei. Set some of them looking."

Sif rose violently to his feet and crossed to the window, staring outside into the thin winter twilight. "I never liked dealing with those witches." It sounded as though he spat the words.

"They may succeed, where all else has failed," said Fodrun with delicacy. He wished he could get rid of the foul taste the words left in his own mouth—he could not seem to rid them of the guilt of betrayal which clung to them like a skin. If Anghara was ever discovered, Fodrun knew he would go to his grave feeling like a murderer. And yet . . . not helping Sif's search was unthinkable.

Sif seemed to have come to terms with his own qualms. "I'll do it," he said, but his voice was heavy. "If it will help, I will do it. But I swear I do not like it. Why is just being human never quite enough in Roisinan?"

With a sudden flash of insight, Fodrun realized part of the reason Sif harbored such an implacable hostility toward Sight. When both Rima and Clera, Sif's mother, had come to Miranei there had been little to choose between them. Both daughters of country gentry, lords of distant manors who laid claim to neither great wealth nor power, all they brought with them had been their youth and beauty. If Dynan had been an ordinary man it might have been different—but he was more than a man, he was a king. Clera had borne Dynan a son, but it was Rima whom Dynan had married, and crowned; Rima, whose single advantage and addition to Dynan's treasury had been Sight—something that Clera, for all the proof of her devotion, could never offer.

3

Anghara had been very quiet during the first part of the journey from Miranei. Lady Catlin, who rode with her in the back of the covered wagon together with their trunks and bags, made no attempt to draw her out and wisely left her to herself for a while. Anghara had stared at Miranei for as long as she could see it through the rear of the wagon, where the flaps of the wagon covering had been tied back. They made good time. The great keep grew smaller and smaller, finally vanishing altogether; it was then that Anghara closed her eyes, sealing in the memory.

Catlin thought that the girl dozed, as their horse kept up its steady pace and carried them further and further into the night. But Anghara was not asleep; her senses, if anything, seemed to have been sharpened by the last few hours to something almost supernatural. She was aware of the way the lantern hanging by the side of the wagon swung and bounced, its wavering light keeping time to the rhythm of the horse's hooves striking the road. She was aware of the stars winking above in a sky deepening from salmon-pink and apricot clouds into shades of amethyst and indigo. She heard the tuneless whistling of the wagon driver on his seat, his back to them, and the dissonant counterpoint of another horse's hoofbeats, March's great heavy beast, pacing the wagon just out of her line of sight. This day's sunset, starrise, swift travel on unfamiliar roads, these things were being burned into her and would stay with her for the rest of her life. Without fully understanding what it was that had touched her and brought her to this dark hour, Anghara tasted the bitter grounds of exile.

They stayed at a roadside han that night, anonymous travellers. The driver would sleep in the servants' wing; for the rest of the party, the han-keeper assumed the obvious and placed March, Catlin and Anghara into a large, spacious family room. They made no protest. March left the room in tacit understanding while Catlin, fastidious court lady that she was, and the girl who had until a few short hours ago been a princess, prepared for bed. Anghara was still mostly silent, and it was only when Catlin became aware of her darting eyes that she realized the child was looking for something. Seeing the turned-back covers of the wide bed she would share with Anghara, Catlin's hands suddenly flew to her face and she gazed at her in blank dismay over the tips of her fingers.

"Anassa! I forgot Anassa!"

Anghara's eyes were strange, both sympathetic and utterly blank at the same time. "It doesn't matter," she said, very quietly, climbing into the bed.

"But you have slept with her ever since you were a baby," said Catlin remorsefully. Tonight of all nights Anghara should have had the comfort of something warm, familiar. But Anassa, the battered doll that had been Anghara's favorite since babyhood, had slipped Catlin's mind when she had been given orders to pack the child's belongings back in Miranei . . . was it really only a few hours ago? And now she stood blaming herself bitterly for the oversight, for the little bit of home she should have thought to bring into banishment for the little girl who had already left too much behind.

Anghara turned away and curled up on her side of the bed. Catlin doused the lights, climbing in carefully beside her; she listened for a while, surreptitiously, but Anghara's breathing was deep and regular, no sound of crying. She seemed to have fallen asleep almost instantly, although Catlin was a little incredulous at the thought—especially after being severed in such a violent manner from a favorite bedtime companion of many years. In the end it was Catlin who shed quiet tears in what she thought was the privacy of solitude with her charge asleep beside her, and it was Catlin who drifted off into sleep first. Anghara lay motionless for a long time, wide awake, staring into the darkness and remembering the way Miranei had faded from her horizon, the odd finality of it, almost as though it had been swallowed by the approaching night, or the yawn of immeasurable time. She was conscious of what was almost terror beating within her, a fear that she was somehow sundered from her home for good. Or that she would only come back after everything had changed, come back to rubble, or a different city altogether, with every street distorted and every tower different from her memory. Should she forget the smallest detail of the place, it would happen, she knew this with a dreadful certainty; this was her nameless fear. She lay in the dark, trying to capture the perfect memory of Miranei, which lived within her heart. And yet, when she did fall asleep, it was only to dream the same dream that had haunted her waking hours—the vision of Miranei of the Mountains vanishing gently, slowly, into darkness.

The darkness also frightened her, for it lay before her as well as behind. She had no idea where they were going, and aside from her mother's vague warnings of danger, no inkling why. She clung to her silence for the first day of their journey, but eventually the thought of leaving her home further and further behind while going forward in no certain direction drove her to March, who at the very least seemed to know where they were heading.

She caught up with him at another roadside han, having followed him into the stables. He had not heard her drift in after him; he had gone to have another look at what might have been causing the increasing lameness of one of the wagon horses. It may have been the intensity of her regard that made him lift his head from his perusal of the gelding's left front hoof and look at her, with some surprise.

He dropped the hoof and straightened, pulling his fur-lined winter cloak, flung back so as not to hinder his examination, down over his shoulders. "And what are you doing

here?" he asked lightly. He had never addressed her conde-
scendingly, adult to child, but always, with a built-in deference that went without saying, as though they were equals.
They had dropped all titles when they left Miranei and Anghara had instinctively understood, it was a matter of their
disguise; but March's unspoken "princess" still hung between them in the small warm stable of the roadside han like
a charm.

"March . . . Mama told me nothing about this journey. It
all happened so fast; she only said there was danger, and she
would call me back when it was over. But why didn't she
come with us? Why couldn't I have stayed?"

March suddenly realized how little she knew. Nobody had
found the time or seen any real necessity to explain any of
the actions of the past days to a child who, royal or not,
would simply do what she was told in the end. But Anghara
was frightened and more than a little lost, crowned in Miranei's Great Hall by her father's council lords one moment
and fleeing madly into the winter night the next. All she had
ever known had been torn from her in a matter of a few hectic hours. She had been sent away from everything familiar
with only vaguely couched words of warning about a nebulous danger, which must have sounded like a dragon of legend and a few even vaguer promises about returning soon. It
was to her credit that in the beginning, while time had been
of the essence, she had obeyed those she trusted without
question. But she was far too intelligent to take obedience
into blind submission. March would have been disappointed
if she had.

"We're going to Cascin," he said, glancing around to
make sure they were alone. "Where your mother was born.
You will be staying there for a while, with your aunt and
uncle."

"Mama took me there once," said Anghara slowly. "I was
still a baby, I don't remember it at all. But Aunt Chella came
to visit Mama at Miranei, when I was five. She had a baby
with her, a little girl."

"Yes. Your cousin Drya. She would be about four now.

There are also the twins, Adamo and Charo, they are only a year older than you. And Ansen, he's the eldest, he's turning twelve this year . . . or is it thirteen?"

Anghara, who had been rendered a solitary child through the circumstances of her birth, suddenly quailed at the thought of all those children, all those unknown cousins. The only one she had ever seen had been little Drya, and even that couldn't really count as any sort of acquaintance. The others, the boys . . . doubly alien, older than her, and male. Would there be any common ground there at all? At least they were kin; that ought to count for something . . .

March subsided onto a nearby bale of hay and patted the space beside him for Anghara to join him. "There are some other things you'd better know before we go much further," he said, and the seriousness of his voice distracted Anghara from her thoughts on kinship. "Now seems as good a time to tell you as any. When we left Miranei, we left a great deal behind—but you left something you haven't even missed yet. Your name."

Anghara stared at him in blank incomprehension.

"When we get to Cascin," said March, "you go there not as Anghara Kir Hama, Princess of Roisinan. You'll be someone else, a little girl called Brynna Kelen, come to foster at the manor. Your aunt and uncle will know who you really are, but not the children; you'll meet them as a new foster sister, not blood kin."

"But why?" wailed Anghara. Even that which she thought immutable in a world of chaos, her own identity, was being taken from her; nothing was left, nothing. She was being forced to take herself apart, and put herself together as a different person. And all for . . . what? She still did not know what the danger was which hunted her, but by this stage it had grown into something huge, incomprehensible, all-powerful—something capable of reaching across half her world and tearing from her the very name that made her who she was.

March gently touched her hair. "There is another who wants what is yours, my princess," he said, very quietly.

"Someone who wants to be in your place badly enough to destroy you, if he knew where you were. Someone who is coming to Miranei to steal your crown."

"But my father was the king," said Anghara, with implacable nine-year-old logic.

"So was his," said March. "You know him. You share the same father, the same name. But it is your mother who is queen, not his, and that is why he has had to take by force what is rightfully yours."

"Who?" Anghara asked, genuinely bewildered.

"His name is Sif."

To Anghara it was as though the great black monster stretching against the wall showing huge, frightening fangs was suddenly revealed as nothing more than the shadow of a kitchen cat yawning quietly by the fire. "Sif? But Sif would never harm me." That, because she knew him, knew of him. The first reaction was to Sif, the person. But then . . . "He would not dare. The lords swore the oath to me." The unconscious arrogance was there, the same arrogance Sif had shown in the army camp by the River Ronval. The same man had fathered these two; they were more alike than they knew. And yet, March had seen enough of Sif Kir Hama to expect no mercy to stay his hand, not this close to the fulfillment of all his dreams.

"Yes," said March, "but oaths can be broken. And even if they held, Sif comes with your father's army, and he will take Miranei if it will not be given. And once he takes it, he will have his own lords. Ones who swore no oaths to you."

"But Mama gave me . . ." Anghara's hand leapt from the straw, and then sank back, slowly, as she had time to think the motion through, even here, with March, whom she trusted. But March was anticipating her.

"The seal?" he said. "It's all right, my lady told me what she intended. I know you hold it. Yes, that might slow him, but not stop him. He can declare it lost and have a new one carved. But unless he can prove it lost or you dead, he will never sit securely on your throne. My lady the queen knows you are too young to resist him now; but if we can keep you safe, in a few years you can face him, and nothing he can do will stand against you. You are King Dynan's true heir, and Sif knows that as well as you. But until then, you must remember you are Brynna Kelen, not Princess Anghara of Miranei—because if he finds you before you are ready, it might go ill for us. Can you do that?"

"Yes," said Anghara. "It won't be for long."

All the same, she glanced back at her bright name with yearning as she laid it gently for safekeeping into deeper recesses of her mind. She tasted the other, the one to be hers for a brief while before she could rise to reclaim her own lineage and name. "Brynna," she said experimentally. It felt foreign, but not unduly so; she started to practice wearing it. "Who is she, this Brynna?"

March impulsively discarded everything Rima might have concocted as Brynna's "history" in her letter to Chella, turning to the child beside him with an air of conspiracy. "I think," he said with a quick smile, "we will leave that to you. Who do you want to be? Nothing too involved, mind; you are trying to disappear. If you draw too much attention to Brynna Kelen you might as well wave a flag to announce where Anghara Kir Hama might be hiding. Do you want to think about it?"

He had distracted her, and there was a gleam in her eyes. Already she was creating a new self, something she would do far better than trying to live up to whatever artificial biography Rima had prepared. March would simply warn Chella in advance of the slight change in plans.

Anghara came to him again when they reached Halas Han, only a day or two's travel from Cascin, and gave the seeds of her new life into his keeping. She had sensibly made Brynna from Miranei. March initially thought it dangerous, pointing an unerring finger to the place from which Anghara had fled; but then he saw the wisdom of it. It would have been nice to have made Brynna an exotic from Shaymir or from some seafaring family of Calabra, but Anghara knew little about either place, and her hesitations would have shown her as a fake within minutes to anyone who cared to probe the disguise. This way, nobody could trip her up on her story; she knew Miranei too well, even for one who had spent most of her short life immured within castle walls. She explained away her knowledge of the court by making Brynna a minor aristocrat, one of the dozens Anghara had observed around the palace, with enough access to the court to have first-hand information of what she "knew." It would also account for the clothes she was bringing in her trunks, rich enough for someone of standing, although Catlin had been warned to pack the simpler gowns and to leave the richest ones behind. Although only nine, Anghara was proving to have a gift for subtle intrigue; she was creating an effective camouflage, allowing just enough truth to shine through to make the lie convincing.

"Very good," March had said approvingly, once it had all been told. "You've done all the right things."

"Then call me Brynna from now on. I suppose I'd better get used to it. You should," she said with a faint air of admonishment, "have done that from the beginning."

This was entirely true and March had already berated himself for not thinking of it before. He agreed immediately, and found it remarkably easy to think of her as Brynna—already she was no longer the Anghara he had known. Catlin was worse. She kept slipping, and Anghara would turn instinctively at the sound of the old name, then a strange closed look would come into her eyes as she caught herself doing it. But she trained herself until it became second nature to respond only to Brynna. At the last, March felt his hackles rise as he watched her raise her head on one occasion at the sound of Catlin's voice, and then glance behind her with a motion as natural as breathing to see who it was that Catlin wanted. It was as though she had turned to look for her own lost soul. But in that moment she had achieved a total victory over herself; she had lived through a moment during which she had truly thought of Anghara as "other." It was what was needed; but March had turned away with something suspiciously like tears prickling at the back of his eyes. He caught himself wondering whether they could ever really give back what had been taken from her on this journey.

Halas Han was one of the bigger hans, more of a small trading town than a simple wayside inn. It had small quays poking out into three different rivers, and there was a constant coming and going as porters bearing mysteriously wrapped bales staggered from quay to warehouse, or from the storerooms to the river boats waiting on the water.

The stables did a brisk trade, and half a dozen grooms were kept on the hop, saddling one horse, unsaddling and boxing another. Glancing into the cavernous depths of the han's stable as he passed his horse into the grooms' custody, March glimpsed two desert horses from Kheldrin. These were rare, usually fabulously expensive, and a badge of someone very highly born or very rich, someone who wanted to flaunt their wealth. He had only seen seven others in his life, and four of those had belonged to Red Dynan's own stables. He felt an abrupt pang of misgiving at the sight of desert horses deep in the heart of Roisinan. Who owned this pair? If the owner had been to the court at Miranei and seen Anghara, she was in danger. They could still lose everything, even here, at the very threshold of safety. He had pondered confining Catlin and Anghara to their room for the duration of their stay.

But Halas Han was a good place to be for someone seeking to stay lost. It was constantly bustling, crowded, new faces coming and going in a confusion of impatient men whose motto, howled unanimously from a thousand throats on every conceivable occasion, seemed to be, "I've no time to waste!" In keeping with han tradition, there was only one hostelry, a rambling building of motley architecture, spreading up and out over three floors and half a dozen haphazardly built-on wings added as and when it seemed necessary. A guest in one wing could go for a week without setting eyes on anyone from another wing, and a week was considerably longer than any guest would be expected to spend in Halas Han. The landlord was a man with a prodigious memory for guests, especially those about to depart and due for an accounting—but even he could hold only so much in his head. Even if March's anonymous lord tripped over Anghara in this bubbling cauldron, the girl who called herself Brynna had taken to wearing her bright hair in two long plaits, and looked nothing like the royal princess spirited out of Miranei several days before. If the lord should think the face was familiar, even so, enquiries with the landlord, if they produced any results at all, would yield only a false name. And Anghara's best protection would be an innocence of danger. Any sign she was guarded in the presence of strangers might jog the memory of a name to go with that face, and could•trigger an unwelcome train of thought.

But fears for their safety proved unfounded. They were only there for one night, and gone again far earlier in the morning than a pampered lord could have been expected to have been astir. They made their departure cleanly, and were certain to have been wiped off the slate of the landlord's memory, making space for new arrivals, as soon as they had settled their account with the queen's gold. Their passing left hardly a ripple in the constant bubble and simmer of Halas Han. And the next stop was Cascin—safety at last, and, for March, home. This was country he knew well, the land of his boyhood. While Anghara travelled deeper and deeper into exile, March was returning from a long one of his own.

Perhaps he had unconsciously picked up the pace, or else he was simply unwilling to stop over for another night so close to the manor. In any event, the last day of their journey was by far the longest they had endured. Catlin was tired and well shaken by the constant jouncing of their wagon, and Anghara had passed through tiredness into exhaustion and was fast asleep by the time they drew near Cascin Manor. The moon was up and most of the house abed, but a messenger had been sent on ahead when Rima had conceived of this plan. Someone had been sitting in the gatehouse ever since word had come to watch for travellers out of Miranei. One of the two men on guard that night hastened ahead to alert the manor's lord and lady as the other climbed onto the wagon next to the driver and directed him into the inner court. Lord Lyme was already waiting as March rode in and dismounted from his horse.

"Be welcome here, all of you," Lyme said. A childhood paralysis had left him the legacy of a withered leg and a carved stick without which he found walking difficult. He was now leaning on this, a man not yet past his forty-fifth year. The illusion of great age was strengthened by pale blond hair, almost white in the light of several small torches burning in the yard.

"Thank you," said March. Catlin poked her head out of the back of the wagon, rubbing her eyes, and scrambled to get down when she saw Lyme waiting. March turned to help her with instinctive courtesy, but his attention was still on Cascin's lord. "Has there been any news out of Miranei?"

"Some," said Lyme. "You travelled slowly; news flies. It filters through the han, they know things there almost before they have happened; I keep a man at Halas constantly, and we hear anything new almost as soon as the han knows of it. Sif is at Miranei, with the army, but at the last count the keep was still holding against him."

March's head came up, his eyes bright in his white face. "Still? They hold still? I thought . . ."

"It can't be much longer now," said Lyme. There was sorrow in his voice; he saw Rima's death in the eventual fall of Miranei, and he was deeply distressed. "The child?" he asked, thoughts of Rima followed almost immediately by thoughts of her daughter, the cause of this desperate journey.

"She is asleep, my lord," said Catlin. "This has been a hard day for her."

"Her room is prepared," said a new voice, and Catlin curtsied lightly to Lady Chella, Lyme's wife and sister to Dynan's doomed queen, who had joined them in the court. "Were you one of my sister's suite, lady? What is your name?"

"Anghara's own," said Catlin. "I am Catlin." Her voice cracked on a yawn she could not quite swallow.

Chella smiled. "Let us bed the child down, and then perhaps you too can seek some rest. It has been a hard day for you all, and a harder journey." Her eyes glittered in the torchlight as she came up to the wagon, clear gray, Rima's eyes that Anghara had inherited. "Tomorrow we will have to think of a plan," she said. "There are few in my household who know who the child is, and it is better not to stir up questions best left unasked. We will find you a place here, Lady Catlin, but she cannot be seen to have a personal attendant, not in the station in which she has been cast, or else people will start wondering. But for tonight, do you wish to share her chamber? She might find tomorrow easier in a strange place if she wakes to the sight of a friend."

"You are kind," said Catlin in a low voice.

Chella, who had reached into the wagon to gather Anghara into her arms, smiled down at the sleeping child. Sudden tears sparkled on her lashes. "Yes," she said softly. "But kindness is a fragile enough cocoon for her, from whom so much has been taken. Kindness I can give her, and a kinswoman's love. I only wonder if it will be enough when the cold winds find her?"

They put Anghara to bed without her offering more than a faint, mumbled protest at the gentle removal of her travelling clothes. Certainly she had no memory of arriving at Cascin, or of being carried into the room in which she found herself when she opened her eyes into the bright light of the next morning. She had half expected to see the close hangings of the wagon all around her, and feel the gently swaying wagon floor beneath. For a moment it was strange to find herself once again in a room that, despite lacking the grandeur of her chambers in Miranei, still had more style and grace than the sparsely furnished and barely comfortable rooms offered by the average roadside han. She was alone, but Catlin poked her head round the door almost the moment Anghara opened her eyes, and the rest of her followed when she saw her young charge had finally roused.

"Good, you're awake. You've slept almost twelve hours; you must have really needed a good rest in a decent bed."

"Where are we?" murmured Anghara, or Brynna as she had learned to think of herself even first thing in the morning, rubbing the sleep from her eyes.

"Cascin. We're here at last. Come now, get up; your breakfast has been waiting for the better part of two hours."

Brynna found herself to be ravenously hungry all of a sudden at the mention of breakfast. She swung her legs out of bed and sat up, pushing her long hair out of her eyes. She accepted, as every morning, Catlin's gentle ministrations—shrugged into a robe Catlin handed her, slid her feet into slippers Catlin brought, sat still at the gentle tug in her tangled hair of the comb wielded by Catlin's hand. But that was a vestige of Anghara, the princess who had always accepted such as her due. Now, coming fully awake and her mind clear and rested from her long sleep, she caught the faint regret in Catlin's eye as the woman moved away to lay the comb on the bedside table.

"I'm Brynna," she whispered, "and you were Anghara's. This will be the last morning, won't it?"

"Yes, my dear," said Catlin, trying to keep the emotion out of her voice. "I'll stay for as long as you need me, and be here for you; but they can't see you being set apart like this. I can only be your friend now, and perhaps, later, in some things, your teacher—but no more than that, not here. Perhaps some day, when we go back . . ."

"Then you'd better let me dress myself," said Brynna. "Go and tell them I'm coming to breakfast as soon as I'm finished." And then, realizing the power of command was hers no longer, not in this place, she lifted her chin and smiled in Catlin's direction with a strange expression on her face. "If you would," she added.

Catlin looked down, a sudden wave of love and fierce protectiveness threatening to overwhelm her. She covered the moment by dropping gracefully into one of the deepest curtsys she had yet offered her young mistress. "Yes, my princess."

Then she was gone. The girl who used to be a princess finished plaiting her own hair, and shrugged into the clean dress left for her. Then she stood before the closed door and tried to still her wildly beating heart and enter this house of kinsfolk whom she must count as strangers. In her whole life as a child of royal blood, sheltered and safe, there had always been someone there—her mother, her nurse, and then, later, Catlin and her other women. Now, when all security had fled, when she needed support as never before, she walked alone. It was a strange new dance. Brynna might know the steps, and it was the Brynna identity to which the frightened child now clung. The princess called Anghara felt the absence of all the familiar props and flailed in nothingness; this was a country in which she did not know her way. But she would find it; in the tracklessness the goal rose like a light—her perfect memory of Miranei. From here, all roads would take her home. It just might take a little time.

She squared her small chin with determination. Anghara retreated into shadows to wait her time; Brynna Kelen stepped out bravely to enter a new and unfamiliar world.

**4**

Breakfast was a rather solitary affair. The only other person who awaited Brynna in the small room where it had been laid out was Lady Chella. Brynna had hesitated at the door, her two personalities both aroused at once: Anghara could not but respond to the stamp of her mother, so clearly etched in her sister's face, and Brynna was nebulously aware she must somehow keep control. Her aunt—her foster mother—had noticed the confusion, and smiled.

"Yes," she said, "it's hard denying something we both know. But even though I would love nothing better than to renew an acquaintance with the captivating little niece I left behind at Miranei almost four years ago, perhaps it's best if you remain Brynna, even here with me. Brynna is someone whom I must still get to know; March tells me Rima's account of her life is mostly wrong. So come, tell me about yourself."

So it had been Brynna who had entered and sat down to breakfast, and it had been both easier and harder to cling to Brynna in Chella's presence than the girl who had been Anghara would have expected. She felt almost guilty, indulging in what must seem like pointless play-acting, with both of them knowing what they knew. At the same time, a gesture, a look, a turn of phrase would remind "Brynna" of the mother Anghara had left behind, and Anghara would cry out with the thwarted need to find something more of her mother in her aunt. On the other hand, she realized juggling Brynna with Anghara at a whim, depending on the company she kept at any given moment, would drive her mad within days. And besides, what if there was someone else with her aunt, a stranger, and she made some silly small mistake? Discovery could follow all too easily. So she clung stubbornly to Brynna's thoughts and feelings; careful, thoughtful Brynna, who considered things conscientiously before she spoke, who would shy away from every unnecessary risk. Her first breakfast at Cascin was something of an ordeal, but at the end of it Brynna, although exhausted, was aware of a feeling of what was almost triumph—she had endured, and she had won. Chella had risen with her and given her a light kiss on the brow.

"You'll do very well," she murmured. "You're strong; you've got potential you haven't touched yet. It's probably just as well, for now. Do you want to go and explore a little? The grounds are quite safe, only don't go falling into any of the wells, they're still pure snowmelt. You might even run into the boys, they're out there somewhere; they know you're here."

Brynna colored a little and Chella chuckled.

"They are your cousins, remember, but even if you take that away, they are now your foster brothers. You're going to have to meet them sooner or later."

"How will I . . ." Brynna began, and then lost herself in the complexity of the question. She wanted to ask, without quite knowing how to go about it, how she was to know them, how she should approach them and win them. Her eyes dropped at Chella's liquid laugh, but it was not unkind, merely amused comprehension.

"They'll know you," she said, "and I hope I have instilled enough manners by now for them to introduce themselves and make a guest feel at home. After that, it's up to you. To all of you. Perhaps I do wrong in not telling them the truth, but maybe it's for the best—it's yourself they will take you as, not a cousin whom they must accept for form's sake."

Brynna wanted to ask what would happen if they didn't like her. She saw months and perhaps years unfold before her in a black tunnel of loneliness as the single outsider, the youngest not counting baby Drya, the only girl in a clutch of boys—but it was a pointless question. There would be nothing Chella could do if those particular fears came true. So she merely gave Chella what she thought of as a brave smile, not realizing just how much of her soul was revealed in those expressive gray eyes, and obediently left the breakfast room to seek a way into the grounds.

She was initially met with silence, with no sign or sound of children at play. The manor was set into a square of level, well-tended lawn which was nevertheless showing the effects of what must have been a recent retreat of snow—there were still patches of it in sheltered corners. The lawn was empty of any presence but that of what seemed to be a gardener skulking around the edges and picking at something—perhaps an early and hardy spring weed or two. What surrounded the lawn looked like wilderness. Brynna chose a direction at random, heading toward a copse of thinly spaced trees. They were still mostly bare, just emerging from winter, but there was a promise about them, a quickening in the not-quite-buds on twigs preparing to wake into spring. A long-tailed bird of a kind Brynna had never seen before balanced precariously on one of the topmost and most fragile twigs and filled the air with liquid song. Beneath the bird there seemed to be a tended path, and Brynna took it, exploring.

Before long she heard the sound of water. She was soon to learn she would never be far from water in Cascin. The manor was set into a lattice of no less than seven streams bubbling down from the mountains at its back toward the River Tanassa at its feet; it was these that had earned its sobriquet of the House of the Wells. They had called Rima that, Rima of the Wells, but only now, here in the place where Rima had been born, did her daughter realize the name's true meaning. In Cascin the streams were called wells, and the particular one Brynna had targeted was one of the smaller ones, clear mountain water rushing over smooth pebbles in its bed. Coming down to the edge, Brynna dipped a hand into the stream and gasped at the glacial water; beneath the surface odd-shaped stones and pebbles littered the stream bed upon a base of striated rock that formed the root of the mountain, interspersed with stretches of pale clean sand. A fragment of greenish rock caught her eye, rough-edged but carved into an intriguing shape by the water. It lay next to a larger stone, damp and slippery but at least partly out of the water and with a precarious possibility as a stepping stone in the middle of the brook. Balancing herself on this, she leaned over to retrieve the fragment, almost falling into the well despite her aunt's explicit warning. She examined her prize with interest, still crouched and finely balanced in mid-stream on her wobbly stepping stone, and then, clutching the treasure in her hand for want of a pocket, glanced around at the glade surrounding the well.

Two massive willow trees grew leaning into one another, directly opposite on the far bank. They were almost naked still, their grayish twigs and branches trailing disconsolately in the water as if they belonged to something that would never wake again. But even here there were signs, and Brynna realized the willows would form an almost completely self-contained grotto, a bell-like space beneath the spreading boughs, once summer put leaves onto their wintry skeletons. Intrigued, she crossed the well and pushed aside the trailing edge of the nearest willow. A few branch-ends caught at her dress but on the whole the barrier remained more visual than physical, and she was rewarded by the discovery of a quiet place, hidden by what would before too long be a screen of spreading branches. The outer edge, away from the well, was hedged by what seemed to be a sort of thorn bush, a guard against unexpected approach from the rear; and toward the stream the ground sloped steeply down to the water's edge. It was carpeted with moss and bracken, and what looked like it might well develop into a clutch of bluebells.

Brynna forgot about the other children she was meant to be seeking, sitting down with a sigh in this hidden place with so much potential for summer magic, letting go of her homesickness and confusion for a moment. She reluctantly abandoned the idea that the spot beneath the willows had been left unknown and unclaimed, as close to the house as it was; but, for now at least, the bracken was undisturbed, and there were no footprints in the soft earth. Not secret, perhaps, but certainly no man's, not now. Hers, then, if she chose. In an act of claiming that was half childish and half pagan, out of time immemorial, she took the stone she had lifted from the well and planted it, sharp end down, into the soft earth on the highest point in the grotto. She worked it in until it looked properly rooted—not unlike a Standing Stone. A shiver of peculiar energy rushed through her, a feeling of having done something right, something she had yet to understand the significance of but which was nevertheless profoundly important in some way. And then, eventually, she left the tree-cave, careful to leave few traces of her passing, and resumed her search for Chella's sons.

They were still lurking in silence somewhere; she thought she heard a faint sound of raised childish voices once and tried to follow it, but it had soon faded. No matter; perhaps it was for the best. Perhaps it would be better to meet all these young strangers, of whose welcome she was far from certain, in an environment made safer by the presence of friendly adults. At least then she would have the advantage of that first instant of acceptance forced by the presence of their elders, in the absence of any of her own. In any event, her thoughts far from Cascin, she had ceased looking for them when she finally emerged into what looked like a small, empty clearing in the woods as she headed back toward the house. When a sudden hissing sound broke the silence of the glade, she looked up—and froze, transfixed by the sight of an arrow heading straight for her. Perhaps it was only the sudden breeze, or the shaft had been sped a notch too high, but the arrow suddenly lost height and fell short, embedding itself in the ground at her feet, where she stood rooted with shock. The arrow was followed by an exclamation with equal portions of anger, dismay and relief, and the sudden appearance of a rangy, fair-haired boy holding a sturdy bow.

She seemed to have found her cousins.

The first boy was followed by another, dark-haired but with piercing blue eyes, and then by two more, obviously twins, their almost lint-white hair an unmistakable bequest from Lyme, their father. Brynna did a swift double take. Four? There were meant to be four children in Cascin, but only three sons, the fourth being a much younger girl, still in the nursery. And Chella had said nothing . . . she had said, the boys might be out there. Her words still applied. But nobody had told her there would be more than three . . .

The oldest blond boy scowled at her darkly from across the clearing. "You thundering idiot!" he said sharply. "I could have hit you! I still don't know why I didn't, you were such a perfect target! Who are you? Don't you know this is our practice range?"

"No," said Brynna, goaded into equal sharpness by the unexpectedness of this second attack. "How could I? I only got here last night."

"It must be the new fosterling, Ansen," said one of the twins, plucking at his brothers sleeve. Brynna, her eyes dancing from one to the other, already despaired of ever telling them apart.

"Yes. It must be." Ansen put down the bow, but the scowl still didn't leave his face. "All the same, you shouldn't wander in our woods until you know where you should go."

"Or where you shouldn't, I suppose," the dark-haired boy said, with a sudden smile. "Lay off her, Ansen, she didn't do it on purpose. We were pretty well hidden; you would have been even more upset if she'd seen right through our hiding place." He stepped forward, the first of them to do so. "I am Kieran Cullen, of Coba in Shaymir. I'm the other fosterling at Cascin."

"My name is Brynna Kelen."

Ansen seemed to remember his manners. "I'm Ansen, and these are my brothers, Adamo and Charo."

"Which is which?" said Brynna, looking from one to the other in almost comic disbelief.

One of the twins giggled. "I'm Charo," he said. "If you hear one of us talk, it's usually me. Adamo only really speaks when spoken to."

Adamo succumbed to a slow flush at this brotherly gibe, but said nothing to disprove Charo's quip. Ansen crossed the clearing and bent to retrieve his arrow. He examined it minutely, and scowled at it again.

"I don't get it," he said. "It's straight and true. By all rights it should have skewered you."

"Give over," said Kieran, his voice suddenly sharp. "Would you have rather it had?"

Ansen made no answer, wiping the point of the arrow clean of forest earth on his trousers and sliding it back into the quiver slung across his back. To say he was upset would have been putting it mildly; he had obviously set great store on the shot he had loosed—and he was right, it should have connected. And yet it had dropped like a stone when it came to within three feet of her.

"Where are you from?" asked Kieran, breaking the awkward silence lengthening between them.

"Miranei," said Brynna.

That earned her a quickening of interest from Ansen, at least. "Miranei? My aunt lives there, she's the Queen of Roisinan." It wasn't entirely unexpected; Ansen looked as if he had already enjoyed plenty of mileage out of his royal connections. Perhaps the best path to his acceptance would have been to tell him outright who she really was; he would likely never have left the house without his "royal cousin" in tow. "My father says there's a great battle going on there right now. Did you see it?"

"No," said Brynna, whose heart had missed a beat. Battle? "We left before the . . . before. There was no battle."

"Miranei," said Ansen. "That's not so near. Why did you come here?"

"I'm from Shaymir," said Kieran reasonably. "That's a lot further."

"Yes, but you're a boy," said Ansen. "They hardly ever send girls far from home."

"Maybe she ran away from the battle," suggested one of the twins ingenuously.

That was getting rather too close to the bone. "But there

was no battle!" Brynna protested. It only earned her another withering look from Ansen.

"You're only a girl," he said scathingly. "And probably a precious and pampered one. They might have heard the battle was coming, and they sent you away as far as they could so you wouldn't be there."

"Little did they know," said Kieran in a tone ripe with amusement, "that they would send her straight into the path of your arrow, foster brother. If it hadn't been for her, you might even have hit your target."

"Of course I would have hit it!" Ansen bristled, shooting another venomous look in Brynna's direction. She seemed to have wrecked a bet; and Ansen's failure, together with Kieran's teasing, seemed to be setting Brynna's relationship with her oldest cousin and, now, foster brother, into a mold of pique and resentment right from the start. She had not begun well.

They started out for home in a sort of unspoken common consent—it went without saying the morning was ruined for Ansen. Kieran's interest in Brynna seemed to have been exhausted by his defense of her in the face of Ansen's rage and spite, and he walked ahead with Ansen, the two of them muttering something between themselves, too low for the other three to hear. Brynna was left to the mercies of the twins, or, rather, of Charo, since Adamo still maintained a grave silence. Charo, however, seemed to want to make up for his brother's sins of omission, for he didn't shut up for a minute during the short walk back to the house. Brynna learned all about the wells, Cascin, Lyme, Chella, and every beast in Cascin's mews, stables and kennels. This last appeared to be the topic of the moment, since one of the bitches in Lyme's prize hunting pack was about to whelp and the twins had been promised a puppy each from the expected litter.

When Charo stopped to draw breath, Adamo startled her by speaking for the first time.

"Father said Kieran might have a puppy too, if he wanted," Adamo said. He had a lower voice than his twin, and spoke in slower, more measured tones; Brynna suddenly knew she would have no trouble at all telling them apart, once they opened their mouths to speak. "I guess you're also our foster sister now, same as Kieran is our brother. Maybe Father will let you have a puppy as well."

It was an attempt to accept her, to make her feel as though she belonged to this family; Brynna suddenly warmed to Adamo. Charo immediately took up the notion and took over the conversation again, but Brynna saw Adamo was the brother who originated ideas in this twosome and Charo was the chatty, bright, social face the twins presented to the world—a kind of a mask.

Ansen, too, had a mask—several of them. It was hard for Brynna to read him. When they reached the house and met Lyme in the hall, it was Ansen who told, in light, self-deprecating tones, of the incident with the arrow. Anyone would have thought he had dismissed the episode without a second thought—anyone who hadn't witnessed his reaction, or who didn't see, lulled by his light banter, the curiously intense look he gave Brynna as he related the story. He lingered only long enough to explain the whole thing to Lyme, as though afraid someone else might beat him to it with a different account, then he was gone, vanishing somewhere with the agility of a mountain cat. Kieran, who greeted Lyme with real affection almost surpassing that shown by his true sons, added nothing to Ansen's tale, and followed him into whatever refuge Ansen sought. The two were of an age, and obviously pursued their own interests when not lumbered by the younger brothers.

The twins, though, seemed to have adopted Brynna, something that seemed to amuse their father. Nothing would do but she had to go with them to inspect the canine mother-to-be in the kennels, and get caught up, which she found herself doing with surprising ease, in speculation about what the impending puppies would look like and which of these phantom puppies each would choose.

The children ate lunch with all the adults in the dining hall, but Brynna had the distinct impression, from the twins' table manners, that this was not an everyday occasion. Indeed, it wasn't long before she was confirmed in her assessment by a whispered aside from Charo.

"Maybe it's because you've arrived, and they wanted everyone to have a good look at you at once, and you at them," Charo had hissed as a footman, bearing a decanter of wine, made an ostentatious detour around the end of the table where the children had been seated. "But when Kieran came they didn't . . ."

"We've probably got a new tutor," said Kieran with a comically doleful face, eyeing an unknown guest a few chairs down from Lord Lyme, in what might have been an indirect attempt to explain Charo's words.

Seeing the man was March, Brynna couldn't help grinning; the smile brought her Ansen's immediate beady attention, distracted from the wine-steward's retreating back. He had been allowed wine for the first time that year, and had developed a taste for it; he had been caught up in wishing the steward had not detoured quite so comprehensively.

"Do you know him?" Ansen asked, after a last disgusted look at the water in his goblet.

"He brought me from Miranei," Brynna answered, truthfully if not completely.

Ansen gave her a measured look. Brynna was instantly on her guard; she backtracked, thinking on what she'd said. Would an ordinary girl from Miranei rate an escort? Did she just plant a seed in Ansen's mind that she might be more than she looked? Thoughtfully, Brynna added a snippet of extra information. "He comes from here," she said. "He was coming home, and I came along."

Ansen still looked as if he wouldn't believe the time of day from her. Once again, unexpectedly, it was Kieran who stepped into the breach. "I don't suppose he looks like a tutor," he said, assessing March with a long, cool look. "Not unless he came to be our Arms Master, Ansen."

Distracted as always when it came to arms and fighting, Ansen's attention wandered from Brynna, and she breathed a surreptitious sigh of relief. All the same, she couldn't seem to uncoil a tense knot somewhere within her. *Avanna!* she thought desperately. *It's not fair! I can't watch him all the time!* It was the thought of a child, but that, after all, was what she still was.

The question of tutors cropped up the very next morning. Brynna had retired to her chamber after breakfast, but it wasn't long before someone came for her and delivered her into a bright, spacious room with several bookshelves along the walls. Any remaining wall space was hung with an eclectic collection of items—mounted sets of twelve-point stag antlers, a large and brightly painted shield bearing Lyme's heraldic arms and several artistic displays of polished swords. A large window looked out onto the open lawn. The weather had turned foul again, the tail-sting of winter, and the window was lashed by sudden slaps of cold gray rain; there was a fire lit in the grate, and four chairs were set around it. One was empty. From another, the tallest, a long, lanky figure dressed in the blue robe of a priest of Nual rose as Brynna was deposited inside the library and the door closed behind her escort.

"I am told," said the priest, "that you are a new student. Come in, sit."

His voice was kind, but Brynna's heart was beating like a drum. In Miranei she had several tutors—but there it had been expected of her, as Dynan's heir, to be familiar with the history and the geography of the land she would rule. This was entirely unexpected, a cold surprise, especially the sight of her co-students in the other chairs—Kieran and Ansen peered at her, not the twins, whose age she was nearer and with whom she would more plausibly have been placed if education had been an issue. After all the talk of concealment, what were Lyme and Chella trying to do here?

The priest studied her as she approached, settling back into his chair, as she took the one he indicated. "We are none of us here what we seem," he said cryptically, and Brynna stiffened in alarm before she'd had a chance to control her reaction. She forced herself to relax, but her hands stayed clasped in her lap, her fingers twisted almost painfully into one another. "For myself, my name is Feor, and I was not always a priest of Nual. I was trained in Kerun's schools, given Kerun's knowledge, but I left the temple when I was of age and sought sanctuary. I have been Nual's, ever since. Hence this." He fingered a fold of his blue robe thoughtfully. "When Lord Lyme sought a teacher for his sons, I heard of it, and he took me," Feor continued. "That's what I'm doing here. As for the others, Ansen is twelve, and has been my pupil for two years; but a scholar's robe is just a disguise for his other inclinations, I very much suspect, and this room is, alas, rather too potent a reminder of what they might be. Even now he would rather be swinging a blade, or training a hawk in the mews, or chasing after some stag to put another set of antlers on the wall." Ansen looked both thunderous and abashed at this, but he held his peace; he obviously had great respect for the priest. "Kieran is thirteen and, like yourself, is not of this house," Feor continued. "He probably has other secrets I have yet to discover. And now there is you. Why would Lord Lyme require you to join us at our lessons, young Brynna? As far as I can gather, you have barely turned nine, and . . . forgive me . . . educating daughters does not seem to be a priority for most fathers in Roisinan."

Brynna had had a chance to recollect herself, and think. When she spoke, it was with a cool logic, offering unvarnished truth. "I'm not just a daughter, I'm an only daughter. An only child," she said, and Feor nodded, interpreting smoothly.

"Ah, not just an heiress, an heir. Your father is grooming you to take over . . . something, after his passing. That does explain the education, of which you have probably had a bit already. But enough to hold your own in this schoolroom with boys three or four years your senior?"

Anghara's response would have been a snap, rooted in the royal arrogance inherited from Dynan and never really discouraged by those who surrounded her. But Brynna simply looked down into her lap, concealing eyes that danced with the challenge Feor had thrown her. "I don't know," she said.

"Well, we shall see," said the priest, settling back into his chair. "Throw another log on the fire, Kieran, and you, Ansen, tell me where we stopped in our history lesson the last time."

"The Interregnum," said Ansen. His inspiration seemed to dry up after naming his subject, and he glanced toward Kieran for support.

"Continue," said Feor, giving him no chance to malinger. Once again, however, Ansen was being forced into a position where Brynna would witness a humiliation, for he sat mute and mutinous, his back straight, his face flushed with more than simply his close proximity to the flames Kieran had fed a smidgen too zealously.

Feor, who had been sitting back and watching Ansen through hooded eyes, sat up again with a sigh, lacing his fingers. "Very well, we will get back to you. Kieran?"

Throwing an apologetic glance Ansen's way, Kieran launched into an edited version of the first Rashin grab for the throne of Miranei. To Brynna, once again almost wholly Anghara at hearing these lessons of her childhood, this was exquisitely painful. It had not been concealed from her where her father had died, how, and why. Sooner or later they would come to the battle he had fought. That he had died in. It was too close, too close to home . . .

"Brynna? What happened next?" said Feor with impeccable timing, stopping Kieran with a gesture of his hand in mid-sentence and turning to face her.

Brynna would have hesitated a little, wondering, waiting to see what was expected of her. But Anghara sat without looking up from her folded hands, not seeing the sudden interest in Ansen's and Kieran's faces, and in Feor's own. She hesitated not at all. She launched into a very soft but errorless accounting of what followed the point in time where Kieran had halted.

"Stop," said Feor after a minute or two of this. He thought for a moment, and his three pupils sat in silence, Ansen and Kieran staring at Brynna with a sort of fascination with which they might have watched a winged horse, Brynna herself watching her teacher, too late, with a wary uneasiness from beneath lowered eyelashes.

The priest's face was inscrutable, his thoughts veiled. But the pause lasted less than a few heartbeats, and then Feor merely smiled.

"Very good," he said. "I can see that Lord Lyme has sent me no undeserving student. We should have a session, young Brynna, where I can determine just exactly how much you do know of what we have done here. In the meantime . . . we'll get back to the Interregnum. For now, let us skip forward a little to the battle where Garen Kir Hama, King Dynan's grandfather, regained his throne. We'll take a closer look at the Kir Hama kings."

There was knowledge in his voice, so solid Brynna could almost feel it settle on her shoulder like a heavy hand. But when she looked up, mortally afraid at the blunder she had just committed, Feor was looking away into the fire over his steepled hands as he began a reckoning of King Garen Kir Hama's return to Miranei after the temporary exile contrived by the Rashin. The two boys, knowing they would be interrogated later until Feor was satisfied they had this latest lesson down pat, had their attention firmly held by their teacher, whose own mind seemed to be focused tightly on his subject matter. All the same, Brynna felt his vivid interest in her, not lessened in the least by the fact that he was very efficiently doing something else entirely. She had met that before, at home, several times, this subtle ability to communicate feeling masked by some quite unrelated activity, except that there it had only emanated from some of the women in her circle, and from Rima. Never yet had she seen it manifested in a man. But in Miranei it had a name. They called it Sight.

5

$B$rynna had the feeling that Kieran, at least, was curious and intrigued by his new classmate, and would have liked to linger and talk to her after the lesson was over. Ansen was, perhaps predictably, in a deep sulk—once again, unhappily, one precipitated by his new foster sister. But Brynna made her escape from both tutor and fellow students as soon as she possibly could, staying only long enough for Feor to demand her presence half an hour earlier the next day in order to assess her knowledge.

The first person she ran into in the corridor, perhaps fortuitously, was March. He was safe, a link with home who knew all her secrets, and she rushed up to throw her arms around him, heedless of who might be watching or what conclusions might be drawn.

"Well, hello," he said, disentangling her small form from his midriff, "how are things going? I saw you whispering with the others at lunch yesterday, you looked as though you might have been talking about me."

Brynna cast a glance back over her shoulder, a look of such panic that March's smile slipped a little and his hands tightened on her shoulders.

"What is it?" he demanded, speaking very softly.

"The tutor," Brynna gasped, glad to have found someone to whom she could blurt out the whole thing and remove the burden from herself, "the priest of Nual . . . he is Sighted, March, I know it, and I think he knows who I really am!"

March looked at her gravely for a long moment, and then reached out to smooth away a wayward curl of red-gold hair.

"Let us find Lady Chella," he said at length. "Lord Lyme said you must have a proper education, but this was her idea. And the Lady of Cascin does nothing without a good reason. She knew what she was about." He was a little uneasy, but he was not worried. Yet. Rima's sister had made this decision. And yet, it was to Rima March had sworn to keep her daughter safe—and now, here, already . . .

The time they took for this exchange in the corridor was enough, however, for Feor to forestall them. When March and Brynna were ushered into the lady's chambers, they found him there already. The priest's strange, luminous eyes met Brynna's briefly, and she went white as she returned his look, again unable to control her reaction. Even if Feor had known nothing before, her chalky face would have condemned her, believing herself to have wrecked what had been a carefully laid illusion by betraying her secret at almost the very first test. Chella and Feor seemed to be exchanging cryptic messages with their eyes, in total silence, and then Chella smiled. "It's all right," she said softly.

At the same time Feor, somewhat unexpectedly, suddenly lowered his long, angular frame onto one knee, bending his head before Brynna as a sign of respect before looking up at her. "Yes, it's all right," he said to her. "You see, Lady Chella was sure of me, and I think she was almost sure of you. Sure of me, because she knew I would guess almost everything within the first few moments I spent with you, and never tell; and sure of you, because she thinks you also have this gift that she and I and your mother share. And if I am your tutor in things like history and geography, I will have occasion to teach you . . . other things you must know. Am I right, Lady Chella?"

"I am truly sorry to have given you such a scare," said Chella, coming over to give Brynna a hug. Then she put her away, her hands still on Brynna's shoulders, her eyes steadily holding the child's. "I wanted Feor to read you unaware—if I had gone to him and told him of a Sighted child at Cascin, we would have had to plot desperately for him to have access to you. This way, you have been placed in his charge by

Lyme himself, the lord of Cascin. And there's another advantage to all this, another layer of concealment for you."

"If Sif comes looking for the female fosterling he may hear about at Cascin, he might think she is perhaps twelve or thirteen, not nine, if he hears of her being tutored by the same man who teaches Cascin's older boys," said March slowly.

"Exactly," said Feor. "And already I see she knows quite enough to stay with us. She certainly knows more than Ansen." Chella grimaced at that and Feor, getting up creakily from his obeisance, could not help smiling. "So we'll have a few private lessons, young . . . Brynna, but not all of them will have to do with history, even though Kieran and Ansen will have to think so." He came up to her and cupped her chin in a gentle hand, tilting her small face up and searching her eyes. Brynna suddenly felt quite dizzy from the hypnotic depth of his look. "But not just yet, I think. In time. You are still so very young," he murmured. "It's astonishing to me that already we have been able to tell. In most children Sight does not show until they are into their teens. But you . . ." He shook his head. "I think you may well be a melding of two very strong Sight lines, my child. It runs in your mother's family, although it seems to have passed by all her sister's children. And by all I can gather from the history I teach, Red Dynan's line had it as well, although they always shrouded it carefully away. I wonder if some of the old kings ever really knew the potential they were leaving untapped . . . but most Kir Hama kings wedded Sighted women. That alone should tell us something. Like calls to like, and you may be more than just a strong melding—you may be a culmination of many generations." Feor let her go, and his smile was warm, full of comfort and support. Freed from the terror of having betrayed herself so easily to a stranger, Brynna found herself smiling back. It was hard to like Feor—he had a distant, other-worldly air that precluded closeness—but he could be a tower of strength to his friends, and Brynna suddenly realized he wanted to be her friend. That by itself was worth a great deal; another layer of safety added to her precarious existence, another ally in the devastating and swiftly emptied world in which the exiled child-queen had been set adrift.

But ally or not, Feor was an odd and rather troublesome companion. He wandered Cascin like a restless spirit, popping up unlooked-for at unexpected moments, liable to come out with barbed double-edged remarks which could pass at face value with anyone who wasn't listening for hidden messages but which would reveal a great deal to those who were. He seemed to take pleasure in this baiting, and while Feor was capable of judging his audience very finely, never actually saying more than was prudent, two days of this was quite enough to completely unnerve Brynna in his presence. It did not help that there was always the menace, all the more frightening because it was shrouded in silence, of impending instruction in arcane matters concerned with Sight. But having told her she had it and that he would help her learn to deal with it, Feor seemed to have forgotten about the whole thing. But Sight does not allow itself to be easily forgotten or thrust aside. It was only a matter of days before it rose to haunt them all.

Less than a week after her first lesson with Feor, sitting once again in her by now accustomed seat by the fire, a shaft of indescribable agony lanced through Brynna's skull and she doubled over with a moan of pain, clutching her head. Ansen glanced up, and Kieran surged out of his chair, but both were forestalled by Feor who, languid though he looked, could nevertheless move with remarkable swiftness and agility. He was already crouching by Brynna's chair, his long, bony hands gentle on her hair.

"It hurts! It hurts!" she moaned.

"Don't fight it," admonished Feor in a low voice. "It will pass. Ride it."

"Are you a healer, too?" asked Kieran, his attention diverted briefly. Feor spared him a swift glance.

"I was a lot of things in my time," he said. His eyes were flooded with a strange sort of compassion, but Kieran could tell that, although Feor had looked directly at him, he'd been very far from seeing him. His compassion was all for Brynna.

His attention was back on the girl, who sat small, fragile and somehow lost in the great chair, with tears streaming down her face. Feor seemed to be observing her with a furious concentration, his hands never leaving her temples. At length Brynna drew a ragged breath and he nodded, straightening up. "Good. You're through it."

"Is she feeling ill? Shouldn't she lie down or something?" asked Kieran, prompted, perhaps, by his memories of his own first days in a strange house as a new foster child—and other, deeper memories whose roots lay in his own childhood.

"I'm fine," said Brynna, wiping the tears with the back of her hand, sitting up straighter. She would not look at him, however. Kieran's acquaintance with his newest foster sister was still very short, but already he had seen how her eyes mirrored everything she was feeling, her emotions revealed for anyone to read. Kieran knew what would have been written in Brynna's eyes if she had looked at him—a residue of her pain; resentment she had succumbed so abjectly and a strange, still sort of fear, whose cause he could not pin down but which was always about her like a faint scent. Ansen, looking at him, suddenly snorted in what sounded like derision; Kieran looked away into the flames in the fireplace, aware that his own face must have been mirroring Feor's compassion.

Kieran would have liked the chance to have lingered, more curious than ever about this strange new classmate. But between them, Ansen and Feor gave him no chance— the former dragging him out of the room at the conclusion of the lesson, and the latter claiming Brynna's attention, excluding the two boys almost before they'd left the circle before the fire. Kieran glanced back from the doorway, but the teacher and the young girl were deep into a softly spoken conversation he could not hear—and then he was out, with Ansen closing the door almost pugnaciously behind him. He turned away, following his foster brother with ill grace.

Back in the schoolroom, Feor was once again by Brynna's chair. "You did very well," he said encouragingly, "very well indeed for one so young. Perhaps I was wrong to wait. Perhaps you are ready to begin to learn."

"But what happened?" murmured Brynna, sounding a little lost, her eyes filling with tears even at the memory of the pain.

Feor, who had stretched his angular features into a rare smile, looked sober once more. "As to that, I cannot say," he said. "Something grave, though, else it would not have caused so much pain. Something very deeply connected to you. I do not know what might be happening in Miranei right now, but something of great importance for you has probably occurred there. If you were a little older, and maybe a little more trained, it would have come to you as an image, a sign. But you still do not know how to interpret these signs, even though you are obviously capable of receiving them. Let me speak to Lady Chella. Perhaps she could give us some answers." He rose. "You look better. But you are likely to nurse a headache for a while longer; go to the kitchens and ask Mariela to give you an infusion of wirrow. It's as well to try and prevent a major . . ."

The door opened behind them, very softly and gently, but they both looked up with a sudden feeling of doom. Lady Chella stood there, her normally serene face drawn and white and her gray eyes dark with tears. Feor stiffened, glancing from aunt to niece, for the first time putting together this shared vision of pain into a picture that made all too much sense. The hand that suddenly dropped back onto Brynna's hair was no longer that of a healer with Sight, instead it was the hand of a friend helpless to shield a child from a mortal hurt. He did not speak, merely giving Chella an awkward little bow before lifting the edge of his blue robe and gliding out of the room. Watching him leave, Brynna had an abrupt, unaccountable vision of Feor guarding the door from outside, as implacable and perhaps far more dangerous than any soldier. Chella came inside and knelt by the chair, taking Brynna's small, cold hands in her own, lifting her face to the child's. There was something subtly different about it today, and Brynna suddenly knew what it was—Chella's eyes, the eyes that had reminded her so of her mother. They were unfamiliar now, eyes which might have had a passing resemblance to those of someone she loved, but nevertheless the eyes of a stranger. Something had vanished for good, a link, a nexus that was there before, binding the two of them into family. The disorientation lasted only for a moment, and then the world changed again, returning to something Brynna knew and recognized. She found herself looking down into painfully familiar eyes once again—and realized it was now Chella's eyes that were familiar and reminded her of Rima, not the other way round. It was as though she had never seen Rima's eyes, except in a distant dream . . . And then, just like that, she knew. "Mama . . . She's dead, isn't she?"

Chella reached out to gather her in a wordless embrace and Brynna stared over her aunt's shoulder into the leaping flames. She felt curiously empty, as though there were no more tears, as though she had cried them all, shed over nothing more than the pain which had wracked her so a moment before. The memory of Miranei, the perfect memory she still cherished and her last thought before she fell asleep every night, was intact. But in this instant it seemed to Brynna that the city and the keep were starkly empty of people and a woman named Rima had never walked its corridors or shared the Throne Under the Mountain with a king they called Red Dynan. There was nothing there, no memory of a face, of a form—nothing except a pair of beautiful and intense eyes which now existed only as remembrances, pale copies in the face of Rima's sister, and that of her daughter.

Chella drew away to look at her. "When it came to me I knew you must have felt it too," she said, "and you had no means of knowing . . . it was a good thing Feor was with you. Come, Catlin is waiting for you upstairs. I thought . . ."

But the thought of seeing Catlin was suddenly unbearable. Catlin was a potent reminder of Rima and the world that had been torn from Brynna, the latest in a series of deep wounds and gashes oozing not life-blood but an even more agonizing and incessant trickle of loneliness, heart-sickness, and a hopeless longing for what was irretrievably lost. Brynna dropped her eyes. "I don't want to go to my room," she said, and there was an echo in her voice of the girl who had known the power of command. "May I go for a walk out in the garden?"

Chella glanced at the window. "But it's raining," she said.

"I know," said Brynna, her voice ringing with equal measures of obstinate need and dull resignation.

Chella reached out to stroke her hair. "You'll get soaked," she said gently. "If you'd like to be alone, that's all right. Only come up to your room. Nobody will disturb you there until you call, I promise you."

It was too much effort to argue. Chella took the now silent child upstairs and left her alone in her room. But it wasn't solitude Brynna craved so much as air; caged, the four walls began to bear in on her. It was open sky Brynna wanted; the manor was too small to contain her pain. In the end she succumbed to this urge, stronger than herself, stronger than the years of obedience instilled deep within her. Leaving her room unobserved, she made her way down the back stairs and let herself out through the scullery door, taking the path through the kitchen courtyard and stable yard and making for the woods. It was a measure of her state of mind that she had not even taken a cloak.

Something took her back to the willows, the place where she had planted her little Standing Stone only days before. The stone was where she had left it and it looked as though nobody had disturbed this place since Brynna had last been here. But the grotto was wet, dripping, uncomfortable; the willows' leaves still only a promise on the graceful branches, far from sufficient to hold off the rain.

Brynna was unused to this soaking Cascin rain—back at Miranei, weather came in a louder, rougher, but shorter guise. The mountain thunderstorms there could be vicious, the winds sometimes strong enough to make burly soldiers stagger and fall on the open battlements, the rain with the feel and strength of wet whipcord—but the storms came, exploded, and vanished all in the space of a few hours. Here in Cascin it had been raining steadily, deliberately, for days.

Brynna had thought her tears cried out. She could recall in vivid detail the sense of emptiness that held her back in the schoolroom in Chella's arms. But whether it was the open sky releasing a grief too huge to be contained between four walls or whether, as March often used to say, the air was only now getting to the wound and waking the real pain, she found there was a well inside her, still untapped. Tears mixed with rain on her face. She knelt beside her Standing Stone, dimly aware that she was exceedingly wet and muddy, and part of her cringed inwardly at the reckoning to come. But another part knew she needed this release, without it the air would never have reached the wound at all—it would merely have been wrapped and bandaged, and it would have festered beneath the loving care. All who loved her wanted her to forget, but before she did, she knew she needed to remember.

Out here Rima was much closer; the color of the sky was the color of her mother's eyes. Leaves whispered in the crisp breeze blowing from the mountains in the exact timbre of her voice when she whispered her daughter goodnight. The touch of rain on her cheeks was the touch of Rima's gentle fingers. The memories woke and raged. Weak in their backwash, she bent over the rain-sluiced little stone she had planted and wept.

And so it was that Kieran found her.

Perhaps it was just the proprietary way Ansen had laid claim to him after the day's lesson, but for some reason Kieran found Ansen's company more stifling by the minute after they left the schoolroom. Within a quarter of an hour things had flared up into a swift, hot quarrel; Kieran was under no restrictions, and stormed out into the stable yard via the scullery door, his cloak carelessly thrown over his shoulders, the hood flapping uselessly between his shoulder blades. A sudden gust of wind flung the fine rain into his face and he lifted his head, closing his eyes for a moment in something like pleasure. He had been born in Shaymir, on the edge of a desert, and even after three years at Cascin he relished the feel of water on his skin as something close to miraculous; rain was all too rare in his small village.

He had gone first to the stables, but the silent companionship of his horse proved as inadequate, for its own reasons, as that of Ansen. He stayed for a few minutes in the dry refuge of the stable, and then, driven by a strange compulsion to seek the solitude of the woods, he emerged again, skirting the waterlogged lawn and plunging into the trees at random.

Whatever effect Brynna's indisposition may have played in this sudden restlessness was debatable; Kieran was certainly not thinking of her when he stepped into the wood. She was the last person he expected to see as he rounded a rain-slick tree and was faced with the spectacle of the crying girl in the middle of the willow grotto he had always thought of as his own.

After Brynna's last visit, he had found the Standing Stone and wondered at it, but left it untouched. Now it seemed obvious to him that only one person could have placed it there, the girl now bent over with trailing strands of loose, wet hair hiding her face and draping her shaking shoulders. Whatever he had expected to find in the woods on this odd, driven expedition, this explosion of passionate grief left Kieran surprisingly shaken. He stopped, nonplussed, searching for something useful to say, but there seemed to be little that would allay the wretched suffering which lay bared before him. In the end he said nothing, simply stepping up and dropping his own damp cloak around her shoulders.

Brynna started, her head snapping around toward him, and he found himself held by the devastation in her face— held, and then flung back into the realm of memories.

If it weren't for the rain and the dripping trees, he could have been back in Shaymir, in his father's house in Coba, when word had come of the accident in the copper mines. If Kieran had been able to call on the powers of logic, he would have realized one of the reasons he had not simply turned and walked away was the grief he recognized in the set of her shoulders, in this instinctive fleeing of people and seeking of solitude. He understood these things, intimately. He had seen Keda, his older sister, run from the house when news was brought of their father's death. He'd run himself, up into the copper-bearing hills, to a place where the warm wind blew in from the desert through a fold in the land, bringing the sweet scent of distant desert sage, a place where he could be alone. That had been four years ago; he'd thought he had buried the past. The freshness of the memory, the pain of it, stopped his breath. But logic was far from his mind, here in Cascin's woods. Without a word being spoken, pure instinct told him Brynna's loss had to have been catastrophic. He reached out almost without thinking, gathering her closer, rocking her gently against him. He still said nothing, but the gesture said much. *You are not alone.*

It was affection freely offered and freely accepted, a bond forged between two lost and exiled creatures far from home. At first sight they were utterly mismatched—a thirteen-year-old boy was hardly fit company for a girl barely nine, their interests and inclinations following different paths. For all that, they accepted one another as natural allies. Brynna, whose initial fears of loneliness at Cascin could have very easily been borne out, would never again be alone. Kieran would still be best friends with Ansen, because that was the way of things; he could hardly take Brynna to archery practice or fencing lessons. Nonetheless, Ansen would never again lay claim to more than this superficial layer. It would be Brynna and not Ansen with whom Kieran would share the secrets of his soul.

But Brynna would not share hers, not all of them, and not yet. She took him then as closer than a brother, yet it was a deeper instinct still that stopped her from telling him everything. To him she was still Brynna Kelen, and would have to remain so until everything changed, until she could speak her name freely. Not even Kieran would know the real story, Brynna's true loss, not yet. Now more than ever, with Rima

gone, the secret of Anghara Kir Hama had to remain hidden
if her sacrifice was to have any meaning.

Brynna was far from ready to go back and face the
adults, but Kieran had a deeply practical streak which
resurfaced almost immediately after the initial shock of
this encounter. He reached over and flipped the hood of the
cloak up over her hair, a gesture as futile as it was affec-
tionate, since both the cloak and the girl were already as
wet as it was possible for them to be. Brynna had enough
presence of mind to stifle a waterlogged giggle and Kieran
smiled in the sudden way he was given to. "It's getting
worse," he said, glancing up at the sky. "A roof is beginning to sound like a good idea."

Brynna, whose first paroxysm of grieving had spent itself,
felt the discomfort of her wet hair and gown. Kieran's words
sounded eminently sensible. She glanced down at the
muddy hem of her dress. She tried to push away a wet strand
of hair stuck across her cheek, opened her mouth to speak
and instead surprised herself with an explosive sneeze.

That seemed to decide Kieran. "You'll catch your death,"
he said firmly, getting up and drawing her to her feet.
"Come on."

At the edge of the trees Brynna checked suddenly, looking out across the lawn. Kieran narrowed his eyes against
the rain. A posse of anxious adults led by March and Feor
was beginning to fan out from the house, heading for the
trees. Kieran glanced down.

"Do you want to . . ." he began, jolted out of his own idea
of taking Brynna back to the house by seeing the forces the
household had mustered to look for her. Now, in the manner
of many a boy cornered by adults bearing retribution for some
childhood transgression, he was suddenly intent on escape.

But Brynna, watching March's face, felt a kind of serenity flood back into her spirit and smiled. "It's all right," she
said. "They're friends."

Kieran looked far from convinced, but when she stepped
out from the concealment of the trees, he followed.

Seeing the bedraggled child who had once been his

princess, March took refuge from his concern in a fit of righteous indignation. "Young lady, you have most of the household hunting for you! What were you thinking of? Look at you! You're absolutely drenched!" He reached down and swept the child up into his arms, cloak and all, turned on his heel and all but ran back toward the house.

"Wait!" cried Kieran, whom March had ignored almost completely, taking a few steps after them and raising a helpless hand to halt March's implacable charge.

The hood fell away as Brynna turned her head back to where Kieran had been left standing in the rain. "It's all right," she called, echoing her own words of a moment before, speaking over March's shoulder; there was something very tender in her face as she looked back on Kieran. That was new. Feor, too, had been left behind, and did not fail to note the subtle change in this relationship.

"Feor, don't let them shut her in . . . they don't understand . . ."

Feor looked at one of the most eloquent pupils of his career grown suddenly and oddly incoherent, with eyes that glittered. "They will do her no harm," he said with a deceptive placidity which in reality had very little to do with his true character. "She is too important to many people, that one."

Kieran did not blink. *She did not tell him*, thought Feor. *He has no inkling of the truth.* "That was your cloak she was wearing," he remarked while shepherding Kieran in the direction of the house, his comment forking into two subtle and quite separate meanings—bland comment on Brynna's apparel, query as to the reason behind it without seeming to ask.

"She went out without her own," said Kieran, not taking the bait, shaking the water from his hair as they came inside.

"I see," said Feor. "It is well. She will need a friend."

The innocuous words rang with the iron truth of a prophecy; Kieran swung around to look at Feor, but already he was alone, Nual's priest knowing how to make a dramatic exit. Kieran already knew any direct questions would be fielded with finesse, and he had as much chance of coaxing anything out of Feor by means of wheedling or blandishments as piercing a suit of armor with one of Lady Chella's sewing needles. The emphasis Feor had laid on the concept of friendship, however, implied that one day much more might be required of Kieran than just a foster brother's cloak.

"So be it, then," Kieran muttered to himself, casting a last glance up at the staircase where March had spirited Brynna. The boy had been sensitive enough to hear the cadence of prophecy in Feor's voice; he seemed utterly unaware of his own, the few short words uttered in Cascin's hall having the force of a vow. They hung in the air as he turned away and clung to his shoulders, content to let him carry them into the future.

**6**

Duerin Rashin, King of Tath and Pretender to the Throne Under the Mountain, had been wounded and defeated in the battle which saw the death of Red Dynan, but he was far from ready to give up his dreams. For him, the kingdom of Tath, once Roisinan's southernmost province, had always been a bone flung to his ancestor while the choice meat, Roisinan itself, had been snatched away. Duerin was clear-headed enough to realize the time to strike at Roisinan was now, while the land was still recovering from the sudden turmoil that had taken her Royal Family and given the crown to Dynan's illegitimate son; now, before Sif consolidated his gains. Barely had Sif been crowned in Miranei when the Tath armies, led by Duerin's son Favrin, began once again to nibble at Roisinan's southern borders. Sif was a fledgling king; his realm needed governing, needed all his attention. He had none to spare for the war being foisted upon him. Fodrun had been a good general but he was now Chancellor of Roisinan and his duties lay elsewhere. So it was an army with a host of newly dubbed generals that rode out to meet the forces of Tath.

It was not that they were incompetent, or foolish. But by the time the main Roisinan force reached the border, Favrin's men had already crossed the Ronval as well as the Tolla, and overwhelmed the garrison left as the Roisinan rearguard at Tollas Han, commandeered from its landlord as army barracks. The Tath forces had also anchored themselves comfortably in the hills above the han, and from this high ground they rode in lightning raids against the larger, slower army of Roisinan, still shaking down under its new command. Favrin's men gnawed irritatingly at its flanks, there and gone before anyone could turn to meet them. The Pellen was too shallow to hold them, and chasing after small guerilla bands into the hills was more often than not suicidal as the pursuers were drawn into artful traps. The southern plains of Roisinan smoldered with a sullen, desultory war; it dragged on for weeks, for months, with no real end in sight.

It was hardly surprising that Roisinan suddenly chose to recall the slights, insults and hurts Tath had been guilty of for generations. The Tath capital, Algira, had been one of Roisinan's jewels before the division of the two kingdoms; it had been not been surrendered easily. Now there were impassioned mutters for Roisinan to take her city back. But that would embroil Sif in a fully fledged war on enemy territory. He was not unaware of the dangers such a course of action would pose for him; his undoubted personal magnetism faded with distance, and going into Tath would mean leaving Miranei. Rather than rush into something he could later have cause to regret, he waited, biding his time, delaying any major decisions until he could be more certain of success.

At Cascin, Feor had abandoned ancient history and now studied the current conflict with his pupils. Kieran was voluble on the subject, but calm; Brynna mostly just listened, holding her peace, aware that whatever she said would be ripped to pieces by Ansen purely for the pleasure of contradicting her. Ansen himself was fired up, as fiery a boy-general as any who ever watched other men's wars from behind the safety of high walls.

"Why don't they flank them?" Ansen would say, fretful at what he saw as delay, poring over Feor's map. His finger stabbed the hills above Tollas Han. "Here! There's a saddle! They could come up and attack them suddenly from behind, and then they'd soon know from which quarter the wind was blowing!"

"It wouldn't work, Ansen," said Kieran patiently.

"I was about to say the same," said Feor, turning to Kieran. "But let us hear why you think so."

"It's too far, for a start; travelling from that saddle to the spit where Tollas Han lies would mean making a long trek through terrain which is much more suited to their kind of loose fighters than to an army. It would be one long ambush, as soon as Favrin Rashin realized what they were doing."

"Quite correct," said Feor. "It would be best for us if Favrin's men could be drawn out from the mountains. They are a natural fortress."

"Sif Kir Hama ought to go himself," said Ansen in a tone close to worship. Sif's military prowess was widely spoken of, especially in the short time since he had become king. His victory at the Ronval not so long ago, turning the battle that had slain his father into a rout for the Tath forces, was already the stuff of legend. A whole new generation saw him as a younger, more powerful incarnation of the legend that had been Red Dynan. And for Ansen the pull of that legend was stronger than for most. Red Dynan had been an uncle by marriage; Sif was, if only technically, a cousin.

Brynna could not help tossing her head at Ansen's words, and Ansen, adept as ever at noticing things not meant for his eyes, glanced up.

"Oh, don't you think so?" he asked, rather nastily. "Do you have someone else in mind?"

The reply came, somewhat unexpectedly, from another quarter.

"Sif Kir Hama is only a man," said Kieran.

"He is his father's son," Ansen said, his head snapping round to face his foster brother.

"Duerin Rashin's army destroyed Sif's father," Kieran said quietly. He had jumped in to deflect the barb from Brynna, and was surprised to see her flinch at his words. Ansen, for whom the remark had been intended, had kept still, staring sullenly at the map. Feor adroitly steered the conversation into safer waters, but it was of short duration. Ansen was something of a bulldog; once he had an idea in his head he hung on to it for dear life, and he was utterly involved in this war, his mind jumping with possibilities.

"Don't they take pages, Feor? Squires?" Ansen asked passionately at the conclusion of the lesson, as Feor sat rolling up his map into a tidy scroll. "I'm good enough, I'm good enough to fight with them right now. You know that, Kieran. You remember what Master Yall said to me only yesterday?"

"Pages don't fight, Ansen, and squires do no more than carry their masters' weapons," said Feor with an almost plodding calmness, so unlike him that both Brynna and Kieran looked up in what was almost consternation. "You can't fight unless you're a soldier, or a knight. And you cannot be either."

"Why not?" Ansen lashed out.

"You have to be at least seventeen to be a common soldier, and eighteen for a knight, after at least a year of gruelling preparation and elaborate ceremony. As you well know. And you, Ansen, can lay claim to only thirteen summers come your next birthday." Feor still spoke in the same serene tone of voice, swatting gently at the ends of his scroll to get them even, peering shortsightedly at his handiwork. He fussed with the cord and the tying of a precise knot until he sensed Ansen was beginning to simmer down. Then he looked up, dismissing his class. "Tomorrow," Feor said placidly, "we will backtrack a little. We will look at last winter's Tath campaign; see if we can discern any lessons to be learned for the conflict at hand."

That was a cue to leave, and the three took it.

"I could go," muttered Ansen, subdued but still mutinous. "Sif would have me, if Mother asked. He was son to her sister's husband. I could go."

"You have to be thirteen to be even a page," said Kieran, spouting the catechism of rank both of them knew so well.

"I will be, in only a few weeks!" said Ansen obstinately.

"You also have to have the permission of your father," said Kieran, "and I doubt that yours would give it. You're Cascin's heir."

"You could go," said Ansen slyly. "You're fourteen, and your father is dead. You're your own man."

"Sif is nothing to me," Kieran reminded him, "no cousin, no friend. And I would rather wait my chance at knighthood, if ever I get one, than spend my life uselessly as no more than some general's errand boy on the field of battle."

"The trouble with you," snapped Ansen, stung into the retort by the implied rebuke, "is that you've absolutely no sense of adventure."

Kieran smiled cryptically, and turned away.

Ansen did ask his father for permission to join a knight's entourage as a page when he turned thirteen, although he did not mention Sif's name, his nerve having failed him at the last instant. In any event, Sif was still not in the field himself when Ansen did the asking. But by the time summer came and brought with it the long-awaited birthday, that had changed; Sif had taken the field to run a swift and determined summer campaign. Ansen, however, was not part of his army. Lyme's reply had been short and to the point, and Ansen was forced to watch the war unfold from the news which filtered through to Feor's classroom, and smolder at his own impotence.

Other things had changed by this time. Duerin was more than a king who commanded an army; while he could not tease out all the details, he saw a dim plot outlined in Sif's sudden accession to power. It was not only with the sharp-edged weapons of war that he sought to undermine Sif's precarious hold on his throne. It was impossible to prove anything, but Sif would have had to be blind and stupid not to see the subtle touch of Duerin's hand in the rumors sweeping Miranei in his absence.

Word reached him while he sat in his tent on the banks of the Ronval and tried to think up a plan to dislodge Favrin Rashin from the strategic high ground he'd been lax enough to let him gain in the first place. Dispatch in hand, Sif's thoughts had been suddenly and forcefully diverted into channels where they had not sojourned for some time, full as his mind had been with the burden of governing Roisinan. Reading Fodrun's carefully worded letter, the prudent euphemisms with which the Chancellor worked round a name which was studiously never mentioned leapt out at Sif; he crumpled the dispatch in his hand, and began pacing the tent angrily. His servitors, all too familiar with this mood, tried to keep out of his sight.

"Anghara!" Sif spat, indifferent to who might overhear, with undisguised hostility. "Will she haunt me forever?" He stopped pacing and scowled, lifting the parchment of the dispatch closer and peering at it again.

> . . . there is talk of Dynan's daughter being alive and well, her burial only a sham to raise you to the throne. We cannot seem to trace its source; everyone we detain appears simply to have heard it from someone else. But I do not have to tell you how dangerous this is. If people start believing it, you might well finish up being accused of murder. So far our Sighted coven has found nothing; it must be as I told you, that she is protected by Sight. I have been pursuing some avenues of my own, but this is not to be talked of lightly in dispatches even though I trust the man carrying this implicitly. Perhaps it would be a good idea if you returned to Miranei soon, for an extended period, to re-establish your presence here. With you away, it is a straightforward contest between believing in you or in a vanished past. There is so much loose talk that I'm afraid . . .

There was always that quandary. Sif was no fool. Given a little bit more time to plan and act, he knew he could overcome Favrin Rashin; but Fodrun's letter made him wonder whether he would still have a throne in Miranei to return to when the fighting was done.

In the end, of course, there was no real choice. The campaign would have to be left to his generals, to carry on as best they might. Sif crumpled the letter in his hand and flung aside the flap of his tent with a quick, furious gesture.

"Ready the horses!" he called out into the night. "We ride for Miranei in the morning. But first, bring me a couple of good archers. There is a plan I want to try at dawn. A parting gift, for Favrin to remember me by."

The plan was somewhat foolhardy, and perhaps not what Sif would have chosen to do, under normal circumstances. But he was maddened by the impasse and the dispatches, and decided to blood Favrin with his own hit-and-run tactics. There were guards posted at the han, but it was built as a hostelry, not a fort, and visibility was limited.

Favrin had done what he could, cutting down one or two large trees which the Roisinan men, who recalled their beauty, mourned and swore to avenge. Even so, Favrin's lookouts were encumbered by the set of their posts, and were not expecting this kind of attack from the usually slow and methodical Roisinan forces. So far, Sif's army had persisted in doing things by the very rules their attackers flouted with such impunity. As a result, in the dim hour just before dawn, the Tath sentries waited eagerly for their relief and never suspected an engagement from across the river.

The han was sturdy, roofed with tiles in the manner of the south, not thatch. This may well have been why nobody had tried something similar before—but the building itself was wood, and the summer had been dry. By the time Favrin's men noticed the fire arrows embedded in the han walls, the fire was already eating at the timber frame. Sif, sitting astride his horse behind the phalanx of mounted soldiers waiting on the riverbank, smiled grimly at the chaos he had wrought. In the early morning stillness sound carried, and voices drifted across the broad, placid, shallow Pellen.

"The horses! Look to the horses!"

"Stand still, fool, your back is on fire!"

"Watch the shore!"

"The beam! Watch the beam!"

And, finally, one with more authority, "Retreat! Into the hills!"

Sif leaned down and whispered into the ear of a squire who stood holding his horse's reins. "Now. Bid them follow. Take back the river."

The squire trotted off to pass the quiet words to a young knight Sif had placed in command. No order was called out aloud. Sif's forces moved in eerie silence, urging their mounts into the river, blades drawn. They looked, for the moment, implacable and invincible, with the first rays of the rising sun stealing over the tops of the hills to touch their armor with metallic fire. Soon the sound of voices from the han was replaced by incoherent cries—some of agony, some of exultation. Sif chose this moment to turn and ride away.

Back in Miranei, events blew no less hot than the flames he had chosen to fan at the River Pellen. Granted, the rumors subsided when he returned to court and publicly laid remembrance wreaths at the graves of his father and the rest of the royal family. It was a foolhardy man who would dare to repeat rumors infringing Sif's rights or his dignity to his face. Nevertheless, the seeds had been sown. There were many who genuinely mourned Anghara Kir Hama. There were others who watched Sif closely, and waited. He would eventually make a mistake. It was only a matter of being on hand to witness and proclaim it.

The summer drew to an inconclusive close. Sif's army had dislodged Favrin's men from their base at Tollas Han, now a smoldering ruin, and established a Roisinan presence in the foothills above. The Tath forces had split, some remaining in the mountains to harry and annoy those parts of Roisinan closest to them, others returning over the Tolla into Tath. Still others, led, for a time by the recovered Duerin, crossed the Ronval lower down, picking their way across the vast and malodorous Vallen Fen which surrounded the Ronval estuary, emerging on the Roisinan side of the river to make a determined bid for the port of Calabra. Sif, still wary of outright war, moved to block them. It would later be recounted in soldiers' tales that the Tath men had been easily found . . . by the smell they brought with them from the marshes. An endless series of jokes at the expense of the new Tath perfume did the rounds in the taverns. The defeat dealt out to Duerin was not so much a military one as a humiliation of the spirit. The men of Tath did not forget it.

The military moves were followed in the Cascin schoolroom as soon as they were known. On one occasion Feor called for an analysis of the key commanders.

"Sif's generals seem to be adopting Favrin's tactics," said Kieran. "They're not an army any more; they're individual units."

"It's easier to absorb the blows if they present a smaller front to hit," said Brynna slowly.

Ansen could never bear Brynna's analysis of strategy quietly. To his mind, her presence in the room became superfluous when the real war was discussed; war games were men's work, a chit of a girl had no place here. "What would you know about it?"

"What I see," said Brynna, goaded, as always, into the defensive. "The last word we had spoke of three raids, all with small casualties on our side. The dispatch before that, there had been ten in the same time period, and our casualties were bigger. The difference is that our army has split up. They're more mobile, and once they draw out Favrin's men from the mountains, it's easier to cut them off from their line of retreat."

"But Favrin is changing too," said Kieran. "He's raiding less, but he's making each foray count now. He knows what they're doing, and he's moved to counter them."

"Who do you think is the better commander, Duerin or his son?" asked Feor.

"Favrin," said Kieran immediately. "Duerin is predictable. Were he in Favrin's place, he would never have changed his tactics. He's the kind to issue orders, and then follow them until death. Favrin, now . . . he thinks. He changes."

"Duerin's cunning. He's more at ease with poison and rumor, a word whispered in the darkness, than with a lance," offered Brynna. Without realizing it, she was repeating things she had absorbed in court circles, laying herself open to awkward questions had any who heard thought to ask them. But there was a certain amount of distaste in her voice and for once, Ansen found himself in agreement; he looked past the interesting mystery of how someone like Brynna would have such intimate knowledge of Tath's king and contented himself with reacting to her words.

"He's too driven by his greed for the Roisinan throne. He's ruled by an idea, rather than reigning over it; he can't distance himself from something he wants for long enough to think about how best to win it," Ansen said, an indictment which utterly disregarded a very similar fault in himself. Brynna could not help a small smile, but wisely chose not to comment.

"Favrin is adaptable, clever, strong," said Feor, endorsing their comments succinctly. "When Favrin becomes king, that is when Roisinan will have the real trouble with Tath. Right now it is easy for Sif to keep the status quo. But when Favrin comes into his own, Roisinan will have to choose: war to the hilt, or some sort of treaty."

"Why doesn't Sif go out there himself?" demanded Ansen. "Now, while he's still got Duerin to deal with?"

"A king," said Feor cryptically, "has many wars to fight. Perhaps Sif is engaged on some other battlefield."

"Do you mean the rumors that Princess Anghara is still alive?" said Ansen.

"Or those which say it was Sif himself who killed her," added Kieran. That was treason, but in this schoolroom nothing was forbidden.

It was Ansen who roused at this, though, his eyes snapping; he would hear no ill of Sif Kir Hama. "That's a foul lie!"

Brynna dropped her eyes and bit her lip.

"Why does he not simply sweep down and clear the plains of these Tath raiders and drive them back beyond the Ronval? He has the bigger army, he could take them into Tath itself and finish it there and then. And he's already routed Duerin once in open battle," said Kieran.

Ansen had no answer, while Feor had one that seemed singularly unsatisfactory at the time. He started rolling up the map, which had lain between them, with a gesture of finality. "Tomorrow," he said. "We'll talk about that again tomorrow."

The war dragged on, and so did the sessions with Feor

and his maps. Brynna soon realized this was no longer an ordinary classroom; these discussions had taken the place of what might have been a council, had Anghara Kir Hama sat on the Throne Under the Mountain. Feor never mentioned Sif by name if he could avoid it; he always talked about what might be the best course for Roisinan to follow. Feor was no longer a simple tutor to the sons of a small baronial keep. He was using those sons, and himself, to prepare Roisinan's queen to take up her inheritance when her time came. It was an unspoken compact between Brynna and the priest—she knew what he was doing, and he knew that she knew, but neither allowed the merest suspicion of the truth to show. Brynna still kept mostly silent in class, allowing Ansen his hot air and braggadocio—but she was growing all the time, growing and learning, changing into something so much more than the child she appeared to be. Feor once surprised her alone by a dying winter hearth, her shadow huge on the wall behind her, and was struck by the aptness of what he saw. Brynna's shadow was Anghara Kir Hama, Princess of Roisinan, already so much more than Brynna could ever be.

Brynna turned eleven during her second winter at Cascin. Feor took all his duties seriously, and already she was adept not just at history and genealogy but also at some of the lesser disciplines of Sight. She still lacked control and stamina for a lot of the work, but Feor had pronounced her more apt a pupil than most. If she could not always tell when a vision would come in the flames or call one to order, she was able to recognize Sight when it came upon her and could report, if not yet wholly interpret, the things she saw. The other children at Cascin remained largely ignorant of her gifts, even Kieran—although Brynna's ability to sweeten Drya's occasional fits of temper was known by the child's minders. Drya was more Ansen's sister in her temperament and disposition than the twins'—but she liked Brynna and would happily spend hours with her without fussing, which meant Brynna was in demand as the child's companion.

For Kieran himself, the spring of the following year brought his fifteenth birthday and something quite unexpected—a visit by his sister, Keda, whom he had not seen since he had come to foster at Cascin. Keda was dark like her brother, but lacked his height; she was small-boned and fragile, and although she was the elder by some three years, Kieran at fifteen almost topped her by a head. The time he had spent fostering at Cascin and being instructed in the arts of war, history and strategy by Feor and Lord Lyme's Master of Arms, Keda had spent in the household of a widowed Shaymir noblewoman at Aymer. She had been taught quite different skills, and now carried with her, in its soft leather case, a small Aymer harp. This was a notoriously difficult instrument, and proficiency earned instant admission everywhere from roadside bans to kings' palaces. Keda had succeeded in mastering it and had travelled from Shaymir into Roisinan as a journeyman singer to ply her trade, stopping off to visit the little brother she had not seen for many years.

She had sent word of her coming to Cascin, but asked that it be kept as a surprise for Kieran. All he was told was that a visiting musician would play at supper, and the children would be allowed to stay up as a special treat. Kieran subsequently surprised everyone when, upon entering the hall where Keda already sat in her dark musician's robes, he let out an uninhibited whoop of delight and descended on the visiting "singer" with such unbridled enthusiasm she was in serious danger of being crushed by his exuberant embraces.

"When did you get here? How long can you stay? What's the news from Coba?"

"Easy, sprig," she said, fending him off, laughing together with Lyme and Chella at his spirited welcome. "There will be time enough. Lord Lyme and Lady Chella have been kind enough to invite me to stay as long as I wish, and there is a lot of catching up for us to do. But there will be time enough." Her eyes were also blue, like Kieran's own, but paler, less vivid, shading almost into gray. They were serious in her laughing face as she gazed on him, with an appraising eye. "How you have changed," she said at length.

"No. Never that. Not with you," said Kieran, his own mood quenched a little by the memory of their years apart.

"But you have," Keda said earnestly. "You left Shaymir a boy. I find a man."

Ansen, hovering nearby to be introduced, heard the remark and it rankled. There was just under a year's difference in their ages, but Kieran and his opinions were always taken seriously while Ansen was constantly dismissed as a mere child. Now his lips thinned for a moment as he stepped up and bent in a gallant manner over Keda's narrow, pale hand.

"I am Ansen of Cascin, Kieran's foster brother," he said, deciding to effect his own introductions. "He has spoken of you, but now I see he has never done justice to a description."

Keda turned her slow, languid smile upon him.

"My oldest son," said Lyme, the faintest of rebukes in his voice.

"I am happy to make your acquaintance," Keda said, with all the warmth and dignity with which, Ansen was sure, she would have greeted the Lord of Cascin himself. "You are very kind."

"I think," said Chella with a smile as she watched Kieran claim the chair next to his sister's, "we had better leave the music until after dinner, else Kieran will have to be gagged and sent from the room. He is bursting with questions of home. Come, Ansen, let us leave them a while."

Ansen, who had meant to press his advantage, followed his parents with ill grace and watched the vivid conversation between the reunited pair from the other side of the room. In truth, his compliment had begun as courtly gallantry; Keda was slim to the point of thinness, her figure almost boyish with narrow hips and small breasts. Ansen, with all the precocious arrogance that went hand in hand with being heir to a great and lordly house and estate, had already tasted the promise of a kitchen maid or two. He had thought his tastes ran more to the fairer, more buxom type. But with the joy and animation of this reunion coloring her pale cheeks with a faint flush of excitement, and her eyes sparkling with love for her brother, Keda was very far from plain. Later, when she took the floor with her harp and filled the hall with complex, mysterious Shaymir airs sung in a smoky, low alto, Ansen found himself revising his initial estimates. By the end of the evening, he would have described Keda's mysteriously slanting pale eyes, her masses of dark hair, the delicate tapered fingers of her long musician's hands and her wide, generous mouth as his ideal of womanhood, and seen nothing peculiar about his sudden change of opinion.

**7**

Keda had meant to be on her way within a relatively short time, but the days of her stay lengthened imperceptibly into weeks, and soon summer was upon her. She had planned to be in a city for the festival of Cerdiad—Calabra, or even Sif's own Miranei—where celebrations of the Harvest Festival revolved more around revelry, music and dancing than the harvest itself. She had hoped to find work there and establish the beginnings of a reputation. But she found it hard to leave; the years of separation lying between herself and Kieran could not be compressed into a period of weeks. Something always cropped up to keep her at Cascin, and Lyme eventually invited her to stay and grace Cascin's own festivities. With a short excursion to the common room of Halas Han, just to test her skills (as Keda put it) on strangers whose judgment would not be colored by the fact that they were family or friends, she agreed.

Returning early from her visit to Halas Han on the eve of the festival, in order to be back in time for Cascin's own celebrations, Keda found the great doors of the manor open wide. The smooth expanse of lawn stretching before the house was aboil with scurrying masses of children, dogs and servants carrying plates or cloths or candles, hurrying in and out of the house. Others tended the great Cerdiad bonfire being kindled on the paved stone circle in the midst of the lawn. Keda, having changed from her singer's finery into more relaxed garb, had meant to come out for a quiet stroll. She hesitated at the door, taken aback at the sudden crowds on the usually quiet lawn. She stood for a moment, then slipped past a manservant staggering under what looked like the legs of half a dozen trestle tables, and along the shrubbery by the side of the house into a more tranquil and secluded area. A door standing ajar at the side of the house should have alerted her to another presence, but Keda's thoughts were far away in distant times and places; she almost blundered straight into the motionless figure of Brynna, who stood alone in the darkness staring intently at the sky. Almost involuntarily Keda's eyes snapped up as well, but all she could see was a clear sky full of summer stars.

"What is up there that interests you so?" she asked with mild curiosity, after a moment of companionable silence.

She could not be sure in the dim light, but it seemed as though Brynna blushed deeply as she looked down. "Oh, it's nothing," the younger girl said dismissively, hugging her elbows close to her body with her hands. "It's just . . . Catlin told me that if I stared very hard at this one star on Cerdiad Eve, and then closed my eyes very quickly, I might see . . ."

Keda could not help smiling. "Oh. I see. Please forgive me for disturbing you, then. But where I come from there are much simpler ways of finding out the identity of one's best-beloved."

Now there could be no doubt as to Brynna's embarrassment at being so blatantly caught out at one of Cerdiad's myriad love charms, but nevertheless she looked up with interest. "Like what?"

"Well, you could sleep with a bloom of the desert sage under your pillow," said Keda, teasing lightly, "but those are relatively rare even in Shaymir, outside of the true desert. A favorite flower would do, I suppose. Just ask it to show you a true dream of your love, and, on Cerdiad Eve, it must obey. Or peel an apple so that its skin stays in an unbroken ribbon, and throw it over your shoulder under moonlight with your eyes closed; it's meant to come down in the shape of the initial which begins the name of your future husband. Do you want to try it?"

"It's all very silly, isn't it?" said Brynna with a self-conscious little giggle.

"We're all allowed a little silliness once a year," said Keda lightly. "I saw apples on the tables and there must be a loose knife in that chaos out on the lawn; wait here, I'll be right back."

Ansen, standing by the main door, saw her as she was returning from the assemblage of trestle tables already groaning under fresh bread and roast beef. She was moving with what seemed swift purpose, with an apple held in one hand and a small paring knife in the other. Everything Keda did was of great interest to him; curious, he followed at a distance, halting just out of sight as he heard Brynna's voice.

"There's no moonlight," she said, recalling part of Keda's charm.

"No matter," Keda said, "the stars are just as good. Here's the peel."

"What do I have to do?"

"Just think of your question, and throw the peel with your left hand over your right shoulder, like so. That's right."

"Where did it go?"

"It's right here. Look, it works; it's made a C."

"But I don't know anyone whose name begins with a C," said Brynna plaintively after a moment.

Ansen heard Keda's low, throaty laugh. "There's time enough for that," she said.

"You do it," said Brynna impulsively.

"The peel's only supposed to be good for one throw."

"Well, we've done it by starlight and not moonlight, and already the charm's changed. Try!"

"Oh, all right, then," said Keda. "How this takes me back! I haven't done it for years."

There was a silence, and Ansen dared to come a little bit closer and peer around a large, leafy lilac bush. He saw the two girls bending over something on the grass.

"It doesn't look like anything," said Keda skeptically. "Perhaps the peel really was only good for one . . ."

"No, but look! If I just move this bit out of the way, it's an A!"

Keda bent a bit closer, and then straightened up with another rich laugh. "I suppose you could say so, with a little bit of imagination."

They linked arms and wandered away across the lawn, each eating one half of the apple, which Keda had split with her knife. Smiling to himself, Ansen slipped into the house through the half-open door they had left behind, closing it carefully in his wake.

By the time he strolled into the great hall again, it was to hear once more the sound of Keda's laughter, this time coming from the dining hall. It was followed by other voices—Kieran, Brynna, the man March who had come down from Miranei with Brynna, Lady Chella, even, incongruously, Feor's own lugubrious tones. Ansen glanced out into the milling throng on the lawn, caught the hot eye of a young maidservant he had bedded a few days ago, less than a week after his fourteenth birthday, and decided against going outside. He remembered the girl's ripe beauty, her round haunches and large pale breasts which overflowed his grasp, the sideways glance of her dark eyes through the curtain of tumbled hair, her breathy little voice . . . *a birthday gift, my young lord* . . . But that was days ago; she had no more secrets. And even then, at the time, while his body coupled with hers and he forgot himself in the ecstasy of his desire, it had been quite a different girl who writhed beneath him in his mind. A girl who was always polite, always kind, whose eyes swept past him without lingering, who seemed to think him no more than a gnat. Again he heard her laugh, and turned toward the sound as though to a magnet, peering into the candlelit room.

Feor was the first to notice him. "Another who disdains the crowds," he said, beckoning him in. "One whom, truthfully, I would not have expected to do so, but welcome nonetheless. Come in, Ansen, take a glass of wine."

Brynna was holding a goblet of fruit punch, but all the rest, including Kieran, had been offered red wine. Ansen came in and accepted his own from his mother's hand. It was not, as she believed, his first that night; and those before had been the robust beverage of the lower halls, with one or two quaffs of strong ale, offered by grinning servants, downed in between for good measure. His color was high, but Chella took it for no more than youthful exuberance.

"Happy Cerdiad," Chella said.

"Did you see the bonfire?" asked Kieran. "It's even bigger than last year."

"They make it bigger every year," said Ansen. "It's almost as though they're trying to burn the house down."

"Really, Ansen," laughed Chella reproachfully. At this instant, though, a servant appeared at the door to request the lady's presence for the Harvest Blessing, and, diverted, Chella put down her wine, smiled at the children and walked out on March's gallantly offered arm.

"That ugly old priestess of Avanna died last winter; there'll be a new Tower Priestess to say the blessing. About time, the old one's face could sour a harvest all by itself," said Kieran irreverently, putting his own cup down. "Let's go and see."

Feor had gone after March and Chella and was already disappearing out the door; Kieran and Brynna were about to follow, when there was a small, sharp cry from behind them. Kieran's head snapped around; Brynna spun on the balls of her feet.

Ansen saw his chance when he observed Keda go off by herself to look at a festive Cerdiad tapestry displayed on the far wall. He had drained his wine goblet and followed her. They were of similar height, with Ansen perhaps the taller by a hair's breadth, and he boasted muscles honed to rock-hardness from years of martial practice. He slid a loose arm round her waist from behind, his hand straying upward to cup one small breast. Startled, Keda half-turned and tried to push him away, but his arm suddenly tightened into whipcord; there was little she could do other than stare in shocked dismay.

Another Cerdiad custom in Roisinan held that if one maneuvered the object of one's desire underneath a sprig of honeyberries, often coyly hung in doorways for this express purpose, one could legitimately claim a kiss. Ansen brought a stalk of crushed honeyberries from underneath his cloak, flourishing it above Keda's head. Her eyes snapped to it, then back to his flushed face.

"Happy Cerdiad, Lady Keda," he said, and the wine could now be heard clearly in his voice. Keda tried to squirm out of the way but found herself firmly pinned to the wall by the whole length of Ansen's body. It was all she could do to utter the cry Kieran had heard before Ansen's mouth came down to cover hers.

Kieran had turned in time to see this. "Ansen!" he thundered, bounding back into the room.

Ansen lifted his head and languidly turned to face his foster brother, keeping a light hand on Keda's shoulder. "I do but wish your sister a happy Cerdiad, foster brother, in a good, traditional Roisinan way," he drawled, tossing the honeyberries into Kieran's hands. Kieran caught them automatically and his fingers closed in a savage grip. "All I did," Ansen said, with deceptive mildness, "was fulfill a small prophecy of a certain Cerdiad Eve apple peel."

"What in the world are you talking about?" demanded Kieran.

"The girls threw apple peels to discover their true love," said Ansen. "Keda got an A; and does my name not begin with A?"

Keda flushed darkly and stiffened; then she rose to her full height and delivered a stinging slap to Ansen's cheek that made him recoil. When she spoke her voice was harsh, devoid of its usual musical lilt. "And if you know that, then not only is your behavior boorish and ill-bred, but you are also crass enough to skulk in bushes and eavesdrop on conversations not meant for your ears, like a prying little boy."

Ansen stared at her with narrowed eyes. "I am not a little boy!"

She lifted her chin and, although almost looking up, managed to give the impression she was looking down on him from a great height. "Let go of me."

"Let her go!" Kieran said in the same instant, through clenched teeth. "Go find yourself another of your kitchen skivvies for your Cerdiad revels, Ansen!"

"But this was only a kiss of greeting," said Ansen, goaded by wine and this lofty disdain from the quarry he had watched covertly for weeks, the quarry he had hoped to conquer with the license of Cerdiad Eve. His thumb brushed Keda's breast again. He felt her flinch and tensed his arm, folding her tighter into his side. "No more than a *little boy* could be expected to deliver. What of gifts to be delivered by a man?"

He kissed her again, this time more deliberately, with one hand dropping down to the small of her back.

Kieran's fists clenched; he tried to dredge something from the years he had spent in this house, to remind him that he spoke to his foster brother and best friend. There was nothing in him, though, nothing but cold rage. He reached out to pry Ansen away from Keda's struggling form. Ansen, whose action had been calculated provocation, instantly propelled Keda away with a sudden push, and even as she took her first stumbling step, a knife glittered in his hand.

Until this moment things seemed to have been occurring in slow motion, but now everything began to happen at once. Feor, who had left the room without hearing Keda's cry, had discovered nobody followed him and, with a pang of sudden misgiving, had returned to see why. Pausing in the doorway, aghast, in a fraction of a second he took in Keda standing with her hands at her throat, watching Ansen raise the knife and Kieran lift his bare hand to block it. But Brynna's scream, and the sudden rush of power that made the air in the room tremble with electricity and his hackles suddenly rise, snapped Feor's attention instantly to where she stood, incandescent in a nimbus of pale gold light.

He flung out a hand, knowing he was already too late. "Brynna!" he called. And then, because the power was not Brynna's, because Brynna was nothing more than a mask, *"Anghara! No!"*

But the bolt was loosed; the nimbus faded, and Anghara slumped bonelessly to the ground. There was a sound of shattering glass, then a scream of agony. Candles fluttered madly as though a wind had suddenly passed through the still, airless room; one or two shuddered and went out. Feor regained some presence of mind and whirled, closing and bolting the doors behind him. He strode into the room, pausing to bend over Anghara, touching her forehead, shaking his head in angry sorrow. Then he looked up to where Ansen sat slumped against the blood-spattered wall, his head tilted back and covered with his hands. Blood oozed from between his fingers.

Feor crouched beside him. "Let go, you fool, let me look," he said sharply.

"My eye . . . my eye . . ."

Beneath his hands Ansen's face was a ruin of slashed flesh, shards of broken glass and puddles of wine all around him seemed to show how he had received his injury—except that no physical hand had thrown the pitcher. One of the sharper pieces had ripped across his eye, biting deep, and Feor sucked in his breath. This night would have dire consequences; and it wasn't over yet.

He looked up at Kieran, who stood pale and rooted with shock, as someone tried the door, banging on it when it wouldn't give. "Kieran! Snap out of it! Tell them at the door to admit only Lord Lyme and Lady Chella. And bid them ask for the healer. Nobody else. Understand?"

"Yes . . . Will he be all right? What happened? In the name of all that's holy, I didn't mean . . ."

"You did nothing," said Feor. "The door!"

Chella was in first, and could not suppress a gasp of horror when she saw her son, who had mercifully passed out from the pain and no longer writhed against the wall clutching at what was left of his face.

"Feor! What in the Gods' name happened in here? I heard a scream . . . I heard you call out . . ." She hesitated suddenly, aware of Keda and of Kieran himself.

"Who else heard?"

"Most of the gathering . . . all the doors were open . . ."

Feor sat back, closing his eyes. "It's over, then. This won't be kept quiet easily. They heard me call out the name of one the land thinks dead. They will soon see the evidence of an inexplicable accident. They will talk. Sif must hear."

Chella glanced at where Keda had gone over to tend to Anghara. "She . . ."

"Yes. Ansen threatened Kieran, and she . . . There is too much power there, too untrained. I am no longer enough, my lady. You must send her to those better qualified than I to teach her what she must learn. Otherwise she will sooner or later destroy herself, perhaps through sheer mischance—without training she is a danger to others. You can see what happened here today. She could have killed him."

There was a commotion at the door as the healer arrived, and was admitted. He paused by Anghara, who was already starting to come round, then came to where Feor knelt at Ansen's side. "The girl will be all right. But this . . ."

Feor and Chella withdrew, giving him space to work, and looked toward the other patient. Both Kieran and Keda were now kneeling at Anghara's side, and she was stirring into consciousness, pressing her palms against her temples with a moan of agony.

"We must get her out of here," said Chella firmly.

"That might prove difficult," Feor said, arching an expressive eyebrow at the muted hubbub seeping through the closed door. "Your entire household is out there, waiting to see what transpires in this room. Nothing can be done without it being in full sight of every man, woman and child in Cascin. Have her carried out of here, and then carry out Ansen straight after, and you will have everyone concocting their own version of events and broadcasting it in the han's beer rooms tomorrow."

"What, then?"

"Wait until she can walk out. It's one thing less to explain. As for Ansen . . ."

The Cascin healer approached them, clearing his throat deferentially. Chella whirled to face him, silent, her whole soul in her eyes.

"There is little I can do, my lady," the healer said in a soft, hopeless voice. "The damage is very great. I have dressed the eye, but it is possible he will lose its sight. We must wait and see."

Chella groaned and buried her face in her hands. "Oh, Ansen, my son!" she moaned softly into her palms, her fingernails pressing into her white forehead. He would be maimed, never whole again, he would never enjoy the life which should have been his. He would still inherit—he was the oldest, and Lyme himself was crippled to a degree—but it would be a bitter inheritance. Ansen would probably end up hating the two younger brothers who could tread roads this night had closed for him forever, brothers who could still gauge distances with two sound eyes and shoot a straight arrow. And Chella knew well Ansen's youthful pride, his . . . arrogance. This wound had not finished inflicting its harm. Ansen's pride would bleed and scar where the shard had taken his eye.

Feor touched her elbow gently. "She is up," he said quietly, avoiding the use of any name at all now that Brynna was sloughed off and Anghara not yet owned. "Go with those three, take them upstairs. Leave me to deal with the rest."

Chella roused, cast a last glance at Ansen's motionless form, and nodded. "Feor," she said, and her voice was cool and solid with decision, "the celebration must go on; I will be down again directly. The Harvest Blessing has not yet been pronounced. But as soon as it can be contrived, come to my lord's chambers. We need to make some decisions, fast. Lord Lyme and I would value your opinion. And . . . if you see Rima's man, March, bid him come with you."

Feor bowed his head in a gesture of assent. "My lady, I will be there."

In the end they thought that it would be less conspicuous if Anghara and the two young Shaymiri left the chamber by themselves. As they supposed, the crowd waiting outside dismissed the two Cascin foster children and the visiting singer as unimportant and waited to learn the substance of the mystery the room concealed. Those who had heard Feor's appeal to Anghara had yet to connect the name with the girl they had known as Brynna for almost two years.

Bringing Ansen out was far more difficult, but they announced the interrupted Harvest Blessing was imminent, and this persuaded many to move out onto the lawn. Ansen, his face roughly cleaned and bandaged as a prelude to more substantial care, was whisked away into his quarters. When Ansen came out of his swoon and began to moan in pain, the healer administered a powerful sleeping cordial; they left him there, with one of Chella's women in attendance. Lyme and Chella attended the Harvest Blessing, but it was a muted affair, with even the children losing their appetite to scramble for the customary handful of gold coins Lyme flung into the crowd. The bonfire was allowed to burn down early, with nobody feeding it more wood as though by some pre-arranged agreement, and the Cerdiad festival, usually so boisterous and joyous, faded quietly into the night.

Upstairs in Lyme's chambers the conclave to decide Anghara's future had come together. Chella was white, with dark circles under eyes puffy with unshed tears. Lyme's lips were drawn together in a thin line. March was still and tense, only a restless hand playing with the hilt of his dagger as though he itched to use it, but his face was curiously blank. Feor alone seemed calm, but this veneer of outward serenity was something they were all used to—it hid many deep secrets. No one in the room was willing to hazard a guess as to his true feelings.

"She was sent to us," said Lyme. "For us to guard. And yet . . . I cannot see her and Ansen continuing to share the same roof, not after this night. One of them must go. And if we are not to fail in our trust, it cannot be Ansen; we must send from sanctuary, instead, the very person we have sworn to protect. I know my son. He would never hold his peace. Do you think he heard the name?"

"I cannot tell, my lord," said Feor.

Lyme turned toward him. "Ansen attacked Kieran? You saw this?"

"Yes. I have spoken to Kieran since, and I also know why. It would seem Ansen was trying to trifle with Keda, and she was not willing."

"Holy Avanna!" muttered March. "Of course she was not

willing! She is a young woman, and Ansen turned fourteen in her presence not two weeks ago! To her, he is a child—he offered her nothing less than a mortal insult. Is that how it began? Did Kieran try to defend his sister?"

"Yes. Ansen was armed. Kieran was not."

Lyme turned his head a fraction. "There is no chance that Kieran might have reached the pitcher, that it was he who . . ."

Feor was already shaking his head. "I tell you, my lord, I felt the power."

Lyme sat down rather suddenly, straightening his game leg as though it pained him. "So. What are we to do with the young queen? This house is no longer a shelter for her—nor a safe foster home for Kieran, whom I have loved no less than my own sons. It seems I must lose two who have been given into my care, and all because of my son's precocious passions." He sighed deeply, casting his eyes down. "And yet," he murmured, "how to blame him—my own son. My blood. Was it I who taught him that everything he desired must be his?"

"It will be an empty house," said Feor, with an unusual touch of sadness in his voice, "but you are right, my lord. They must both go. Kieran is old enough to be given into a knight's entourage, and his training sufficient for him to acquit himself with competency, if not distinction. We must leave that in your hands, my lord. As for Anghara . . ."

"She must go to Bresse," said Chella unexpectedly.

March's head whipped around. "Castle Bresse? Would that not be the first place Sif would keep under observation?"

"He does not know she is Sighted," Chella pointed out.

"He might well surmise. Rima's daughter . . . there is often a bloodline. And if a young girl of Anghara's age and description suddenly appears on Bresse's doorstep . . ."

"She needs training and Bresse is the only place I know that can give it to her. It is the place where I was trained, and Rima also . . ." The memory of Rima was a sharp, sudden pain; Chella fell silent. Chella was no young girl tasting Sight for the first time. What Rima's daughter had still been too young to know, Rima's sister had tasted in full measure. Chella knew how Rima had died. "Yes," she said at length. "It could be dangerous."

"There may be a way," said Feor slowly.

Three heads swivelled as one. Feor steepled his fingers in front of his face, formulating his thought. "Yes," he said at last, "Sif might well be looking for Anghara. But he is not looking for Keda."

"What are you talking about?" snapped March, goaded into impatience.

"The focus," said Feor slowly, "of anyone spying on a young woman travelling with a maidservant is on the young lady, not the servant. If Keda were to enter Bresse, with Anghara wrapped in homespun and carrying her harp, I daresay Sif's spies would consider the girl who trailed after the Shaymir singer beneath their notice. Another girl could leave with Keda when she goes, carrying the same harp—someone who could later return with impunity because her description matches nobody in whom Sif is remotely interested."

Chella never hesitated. "I will speak to Keda tomorrow. Anghara will have letters to my own teacher. And she will be safe . . ."

"Who will she have to protect her in that nest of women?" demanded March, his eyes dancing with what was almost fear. "If Sif should suddenly decide to . . ."

Feor was betrayed into a laugh. "Your loyalty does you credit, March, but I am afraid that smuggling you into the sisterhood of Bresse would cause no small consternation and bring upon the place precisely the kind of unwelcome attention you wish to avoid."

"You," said March, stabbing the air in Feor's direction with a peremptory finger, "you are also Sighted, and schooled enough to have trained the princess in the early disciplines of the art." It was all too easy for him to slip back; Anghara was the princess again without a second thought on his part. "Where were you trained? If a man would cause such consternation at Bresse, who taught you?"

"An old woman, long dead," said Feor softly. "She died before she taught me all too many things. Perhaps my deficiencies were what caused tonight's catastrophe in the first place. No, March, Bresse is all there is. Bresse alone remains, after the Castle at Algira was put beyond our reach." His voice dropped. "Trust me, I would rather die than see the girl come to harm. I am proud to have had the teaching of her, such as my contribution has been. She will be great some day; she will be queen, and Sif will be a memory. I do not send that destiny to its death."

March searched his eyes, and then nodded once, sharply, turning away. "All right. I will accept it. But I will be somewhere close, where she can find me if she needs me."

"Not too close," cautioned Feor. "Sif may not know her, but you are another matter. And where you are, he might well expect to find Anghara."

"I cannot abandon her!"

"You will not," said Feor softly. "None of us can. None of us will. But we can be more useful to her now if we let her go. She tried to fly tonight, and almost broke her wings beyond repair; we must let her go, to learn what she might of survival. She is strong, March; strong enough to doom herself, if we let her."

Unexpectedly, March's warrior's eyes prickled with tears. "She's a little girl," he whispered.

Feor shook his head, rising. "She is a queen," he said, very softly.

# PART 2

## Sif

**8**

It was hard, being adrift again. It had been difficult enough before—leaving everything but coming to what was, after all, still family. Now, going from even this haven into the unknown, a part of Brynna wanted nothing more than to curl up into a tight little ball and cry herself to sleep. But there was another part of her, a part that kept her back straight as she sat on her dappled pony, riding behind Keda on the road to Castle Bresse. Both halves of her shared one thing—the burden of guilt and misery she carried with her from the place she had, for however short a time, called home. She knew she would never forget her last days at Cascin.

She had crept in to see Ansen the morning after the Harvest Blessing, but he was still under sedation, his breathing shallow and uneven in a restless, unnatural, drugged sleep. All she'd wanted to do was say she was sorry, but she stopped and simply stared at the great white bandage wrapped around his head. Only a few wisps of blond hair and the mouth, curled into its habitual, almost supercilious sneer, told her the prone form on the bed was Ansen. Cascin's healer, coming to visit his charge, found her standing mute in the doorway, her hands crossed at her breast in a gesture that spoke eloquently of her shock.

"What are you doing here?" the healer asked, half-annoyed, half-sympathetic. "He should be left to sleep. Are you all right? As I recall, you too appeared to suffer some effects last night. Here, come inside, quietly now. Let me look at you properly."

Brynna was limp, allowing him to drag her into Ansen's room without protest. The healer peered into her eyes, lifting the lids as if to seek some arcane knowledge, and asked her if her head hurt when she made any sharp or sudden movement. Her reply, a quiet no, seemed to satisfy him.

"You'll be fine. It was no more than a swoon," he pronounced eventually, dismissing her. "You must go now, I need to change Ansen's dressing."

The name restored her power of speech. "Will he . . . will he be all right?"

The healer spared her a kind glance. "Perhaps. Perhaps all will still be well. We have to wait and see if . . ." But there was something in the wide gray eyes that gazed at him, into him. The platitudes died. Almost without thinking he spoke the truth, bluntly, not veiling it as he would normally have done, if he were to have uttered it to a child at all. "He will probably remain blind in that eye. Permanently."

The hypnotic gaze was broken as the child's eyes filled with sudden tears and long, dark lashes swept down rapidly as she tried to blink them away. The healer regained his composure, and his facility for prevarication. "But there is always hope. Now go, child, and let me work."

But the gifts that smoldered within the mind of Miranei's lost princess let her winnow truth from lie, without trying, without even knowing she did. The one truth Brynna heard from the healer was that Ansen would remain blind. And it was her fault. Her fault.

She fled with tears streaming down her cheeks, flying out of the main doors and into the woods. Straight to the willows, the place where her Standing Stone spread its small peace in the shade, where she had found solace before against dozens of small household catastrophes.

This time peace was gone, even from here. Instead, she found more guilt. Kieran stood on the banks of the well, leaning against a tree trunk, staring morosely at the bubbling brook. He looked up as her feet found a twig and cracked it, as though he had been waiting for her, and she recoiled from the expression on his face.

"What is it?" she gasped, seeing the hurt smoldering in his eyes. "What have I done?"

She had forgotten that Feor had called her by her true name, forgotten that Kieran had heard. All she could think of was Ansen, something to do with Ansen; Kieran had, after all, been his friend and foster brother for some time before Brynna had recast the equation. But she was not thinking of that other self, the Princess of Miranei, when she searched her soul frantically for the sin she had committed against one she loved with a child's unwavering devotion, for whose sake she had blinded another human being. She was completely unprepared for Kieran's reply, a pain far deeper than any surface wrong she might have done him.

"You could have told me," he said, very quietly.

She closed her mouth on the words that were about to burst forth, and simply looked at him. His eyes slid away, falling again on the water, following a piece of bark that pirouetted along whirlpools in the water and was carried away downstream. He kicked at the trunk of the tree against which he leaned, with barely leashed savagery.

"Kieran . . ."

"What do I call you now? Brynna? Anghara?" He paused, looking up briefly. His mouth was tight. "Your Highness?"

She flinched. "I couldn't . . ."

"Did you think I would run and tell the first spy I found?" he said. "All those lessons . . . all those campaigns we dissected . . . Sif is your brother!"

"He is not!" she flared at last.

"But he is king. And you . . ."

"And I. Yes. I couldn't tell you, I couldn't tell anybody! They made me promise!" It was a child's reaction, instinctively defensive. "Nobody knew except Lyme and Chella and Feor! Even I tried to forget. When Feor found out . . . it was . . . and I knew he wouldn't tell anyone . . ."

"They're sending me away," he said, bitterly.

Her heart stopped for a moment, and then lurched into a wild, jolting beat. "I'll be alone again . . ."

"You were always alone," he said, looking around at last

with something other than anger and pain in his face. Now there was sorrow, a trace of compassion—reluctant understanding. "Even while I thought I was with you."

"You were," she almost wailed, "you're my friend . . ."

"Yes, but whose? Brynna's? Anghara's?"

"I am both of them . . ."

"And I don't really know either, do I?" he said. A breeze brought a strand of his hair to snap across his eyes and he reached out to pin it. "And what is really ironic is that only now do I go, now that I know it all. Now that I am, according to some, the most dangerous."

"You will never tell," she said, all the unshakeable faith of her love for him in her voice.

Kieran looked at her, and, unexpectedly, smiled. "No," he said. "Still, you should have known that a long time ago. You could not trust me when it mattered . . . Anghara." He experimented with the name, rolling it around his mouth as though it were a ripe plum. "That hurts. There is very little you don't know about me." He shrugged. "Granted, my life is devoid of secrets. Yours, it seems, is a labyrinth, full of them."

She was a child, but she was a princess, and royal pride finally rose to the surface. She met his eyes with a look that smoldered. "I did not ask for it."

"No," he said, looking at her as though he had never seen her before. "I still cannot fathom," he said after a pause, "that I sat and discussed Red Dynan's last campaign with his daughter, all unknowing. That must have hurt," he added, even as it occurred to him, an afterthought. "What must have gone through your mind at Ansen's mad adoration of Sif, at my own dissection of your father's death with not a thought for anything beyond the bare facts? I could not have sat there, wrapped in silence, while someone blundered mindlessly over the death of someone I loved." He reached out, hesitantly, to touch her hair. "You should have told me," he murmured. "I would have . . . I wouldn't have been so . . ."

*You should have told me . . .*

The memory suddenly exploded, vividly, of the autumn day her mother had died far away in Miranei, of sharing something that, had Brynna been able to cast her thoughts into adult philosophy, she would have called their souls. Or, rather, Kieran's soul; she remembered how she had given him everything in return—everything except the deepest secret that made her what she was. Yet he had given all. And she had taken it, giving back only that part of her life which had been a lie. Always, always, the wall . . . Others had raised it for her, in her, but she had shored it, buttressed it, strengthened it and fed it with her fears . . . for her life's sake. And while she nursed the spark of her life, so deep within her air never touched it and sun never saw it, she had forgotten what it was like to live in the light. Kieran would have helped her, perhaps, but while he was blundering about trying to find a door, she had walled herself within and cowered alone in the dark. And now, when she wanted to open the door and let him in, he was on the verge of vanishing from her life, for what might well be for good.

*You should have told me . . .*

Kieran hesitated, helpless once again before the sight of her tears but constrained as he had never been before at the revelation of her identity. He could not give the same comforting hug to a Kir Hama princess as he would have given without a second thought to Brynna, his little foster sister. There was a barrier between them now that had never been there before, and he found himself missing the child he had known as Brynna with a passion which surprised him. He had—almost—sworn once that he would always be her friend, but his oath shimmered before him now, the words taunting. He understood why she had never said anything to him, and part of him admired her for it, yet another part was more deeply hurt than she could ever know. It was not a matter of forgiving—he'd forgiven her, both of her, unconditionally and almost immediately—but a matter of healing. And yet—this was not the end of it. There were still secrets. Ansen, lying half-blind in his room, could attest to that. Kieran still didn't understand what had happened after Ansen raised his knife. And that web, too, had Anghara Kir Hama at its center . . .

He reached out to touch her shoulder. "I have to go," he said, his voice coiled, tight.

"When are you leaving?" she managed to stammer out, wiping her eyes childishly with the back of her hand. Kieran's heart turned over at the gesture. How could he be angry with this child . . .

"Tomorrow," he said, instead of all the other words crowding his tongue.

She said nothing. The silence lengthened between them as their eyes held for a brief moment, full of all those things they could no longer say out loud. Kieran broke it; raised his hand in a gesture of farewell, at once too little and too much. Then he dropped his eyes, turned, and walked away. Brynna reached blindly for the tree he'd been leaning on and touched her cheek against the harsh bark, welcoming the small pricks of pain as something telling her she was still alive, still a part of this world.

He was true to his word. The next day he was gone, vanished sometime in the night, even as she stumbled out of the house in the early morning to wish him good luck and goodbye. But his saddle was no longer in the tack room, and his horse was gone from its stall. There was something, though—he had left his cloak, the one he had sheltered her with the day her mother died, on a nail in the stables. It was a message, of sorts, or at least that was the way Brynna chose to take it: *A part of me will always be with you.* She took it almost clandestinely, as though she was doing something wrong, and folded it at the back of her closet, still smelling faintly of the stable, of Kieran's horse, of Kieran himself. A keepsake. Perhaps a promise.

The cloak and its message were soon driven from her thoughts when she was summoned before Chella and Feor and informed she would also be leaving Cascin. Her guilt returned with the force of a blow.

"You're sending me away?" she asked, a little wildly. "I didn't mean to do it, I didn't . . . I'm sorry . . ."

It was Feor who forsook dignity so far as to allow her to

weep on his shoulder. When the storm subsided, he wiped the tear tracks from her cheeks with long, gentle fingers.

"If anyone is to blame, it is I," he said, trying to put balm on her wounds. "Perhaps I taught you too much without also teaching you control. But you must be taught that control, otherwise, what happened here will happen again. And again. You have a gift. It is time you learned to ride it to whip and curb."

"I'm sending you to my own teacher . . . and your mother's," said Chella. "Feor spoke your name out loud . . . the other night. We must try and hide you again, before someone comes to look for you here."

"You will still be Brynna," said Feor. "At Bresse, only your teacher will know. It's safe for you there, it's a nexus of our power; and even if they do not know about you the Sisters will protect you as they protect everyone there against harm."

"Keda will take you," said Chella. "You'll go disguised as her maidservant; nobody will take you for anything more."

"And then?"

"They will teach you what you must—"

"No, I mean . . . I'll be alone . . ."

"Not alone," said Feor, "but in a Sighted Sisterhood. You will never be quite alone in Bresse. But, yes," he continued as she veiled her eyes against him, too honest to fob her off with a nebulous promise, "alone, until you make another friend. There is nobody we can send with you there. Catlin cannot go into a place of the Sighted when she is patently not gifted that way; questions are bound to be asked. And March . . . well, he might be just a little conspicuous. He asked," Feor added, and was rewarded with a quirk of Brynna's lip so small as to be almost invisible. It was, nevertheless, the beginning of a smile. Feor sat back; she would be all right. "March will be somewhere close, he promised us that. He'll find a way to get a message to you."

"And Keda?"

"Keda will go her own way. She's a musician; she's going

to fledge out in the world. She would not stay even if she was Sighted, and she is not."

Travelling with Keda would be bittersweet, because of her link with Kieran and, indirectly, to Cascin. Brynna had not wanted to ask, but the sense of his loss was greater than her resolve. Her mouth formed the words even as she fought against them in her heart. "And . . . Kieran?"

"He's gone to one of Lord Lyme's friends, a knight with a keep near Tanass Han," said Feor. "He's to be a squire in the household."

That was all they told her. That was all she could ask. Perhaps one day . . . but, for now, it was safer for everyone if nobody knew exactly where anyone who had been in that fateful room had gone. Ansen, Brynna suddenly knew, would probably be told very little, if anything at all, about the sudden disappearance of two of his foster siblings in what almost amounted to a midnight flit. Brynna was told to pack immediately; Keda would be leaving within the next two days.

She managed to say goodbye to the twins, who were mystified and fretful at the upheavals shaking their world; she left her dog—given when she had first arrived—in Adamo's care. Ansen was under a strict regimen of sleeping drafts and still asleep, wrapped in his stark bandage, which made him look as though he had no face at all. She whispered next to his ear, never to know if he heard or understood her heartfelt apologies. She did not ask if he would forgive her; she was leaving him much to forgive. When she left him, finally, he looked as though whatever dreams might come in his drugged sleep would be anything but pleasant.

Keda and Brynna left early in the morning, two days after Kieran's departure. Catlin stood crying in the doorway; Feor, beside her, looked like a statue cast in stone. Lyme and Chella had already said their farewells inside, out of sight of prying eyes. March was gone, trying to find a place to watch over his charge; the twins were asleep, Ansen adrift in his drugged dreams and his pain. Nobody else had roused to see them go. The sun had risen, but Cascin's woods were still in deep shadow, and Feor suddenly shivered as Brynna's pony vanished within. He looked up into the promise of a blue summer sky, filling his mind with the soothing image of a pool of clear water as he sent a prayer winging to his God. *Nual of the Waters, protect her, keep her safe . . .*

Keda had bargained for a ride on a flat-bottomed river barge from Halas Han's docks a few hours later, and the boat took them and their horses up the Rada River. Keda was silent and preoccupied; Brynna, afraid of the future, burdened by the past, might have opened up had Keda made an overture, but the older girl seemed sunk into her own thoughts. The camaraderie of Cerdiad, only days past, seemed as though it belonged to another life.

The journey was uneventful, almost tedious, leavened only with rumors of border skirmishes, which were endlessly chewed over by the crew. But even those palled after a while, and the next place for reliable news was at Radas Han, at the far end of their journey. They greeted it with something like relief, the boatmen hurried to the han tavern to wet their throats and re-stock on gossip and Keda quietly took Brynna to their room. The next day they were off again, taking the ferry across the Rada and riding north into the foothills. They both found their eyes drawn to the west, for different reasons, and thought themselves alone in this until they both looked away in the same instant and happened to meet each other's eyes. Keda's face acquired the ghost of a smile.

"What do you see?" she asked, and she did not mean the empty, rolling moors stretching across the Rada toward the distant western mountains, no more than a smudge on the horizon.

"Home," said Brynna almost inaudibly. The perfect memory of Miranei, so cherished, so carefully husbanded, rose almost solid before her eyes. She offered a halting word of description, then; a glimpse of pennant, a swift glance at a battlement, the hewed stone corridors of the citadel, the mountain-buttressed sky that vaulted across the ancient walls. It started as a trickle and ended as an emotional torrent, leaving the girl who had been Anghara trembling in its wake. Keda looked at her with surprise and wonder.

"And I thought I was a poet," was all she said. But that was praise enough; and later, when they rested, she took out her harp and drew out strange, haunting passages evoking the things of which Brynna had spoken.

"It's beautiful," said Brynna, listening with rapt attention.

Keda looked up with a slow smile. "It's the first music I have played which is truly my own," she said. "When I get to Miranei, I'll play it there, tell them it was a gift from one of their own whom I met on the road."

Anghara jumped, her face flushed. "But not . . ."

"No, of course not." Keda put the harp away with a sigh, reaching for one of the younger girl's hands. "I haven't been the best of companions," she said, "not what you needed. I'm sorry; you're hardly to blame. It's just that I'm finding it difficult to come to terms with the last few days. Too much has happened; I came to spend some time with my brother, and I wound up driving him from a place where he was happy, which he was far from ready or willing to leave."

"But it was I who did that," said Brynna plaintively. Her eyes filled with tears again, at the thought of Kieran. "He was the only real friend I had, and now I don't even know where he is . . ."

"I just hope Sif doesn't send his master to the borders," said Keda, thinking aloud, coming to herself with a start at Brynna's sudden gasp. "It's all right," she said quickly. "Kieran is a man already, and knows how to protect himself. I'm not worried he'll die. It's just . . . I would have wished that he came to war a little older. Not at all, if I could help it, but if needs must, not when he is still not properly sixteen. I always thought taking young boys to war is barbaric. Who needs a page on a battlefield?"

But the topic of conversation seemed to agitate Brynna, who had not thought of this horrifying possibility; Keda tried to change the subject, but Brynna worried at it like a puppy at a bone. As she rode, she had waking nightmares of Sif ordering Kieran into the mountains, the woods bristling with hidden spears of ambush as he entered the forest shadows. So wrapped up was she in this bloody fantasy, appalled but unable to shake herself free, she almost screamed aloud when Keda gently touched her shoulder.

"We're here," said Keda. "Look."

Castle Bresse was not a conventional castle, not a citadel like Miranei or the parapets of walled Calabra. Instead it was a tall white tower surrounded by an inner ring of smaller, thatch-roofed dwellings and an outer skirt of stone sheds and outbuildings that faced them across a circular paved yard. There was a gate in the outer ring, closed, with a huge iron ring fastened on the outside. A white pennant flew from the steeply sloping roof of the tower.

"It looks like a Tower of Avanna," said Brynna, who had expected . . . she did not quite know what, but certainly something quite different.

"I think it probably used to be one, before the Sisters took it over," said Keda. "Come on, I think they've seen us."

Sure enough, the gate was opening as they approached, revealing a knot of three Sisters dressed in plain white. They waited in silence.

"Greetings," called Keda as they drew closer. "I am a harper from Shaymir, and I ask for your hospitality for the night."

"You have it," said one of the Sisters with a solemn smile. "Will you honor us with a tune at evenmeal, harper?" Keda inclined her head graciously, slipping off her horse before the gate. The Sisters moved aside to let her pass as Brynna joined her, one of them waiting until the visitors dismounted to gather up the reins of their horses and lead them away in the direction of the stables.

"They will be cared for," said the Sister who had spoken earlier. She walked a little ahead, with Keda at her elbow, her smile slightly quizzical. "Forgive me, but it can't be just the desire to let a few cloistered women hear the heavenly sounds of the Aymer harp that brings you all the way to Castle Bresse," she said. "We are hardly on paths frequented by your kind."

Keda smiled, relaxed and at ease. "I bring a message," she said, "to Lady Morgan."

"And a recruit, perhaps?" said the Sister, glancing back to where Brynna walked behind the other two Sisters, on her own.

"Perhaps," said Keda.

The Sister tucked her hands inside her wide sleeves. "Lady Morgan will see you after evenmeal," she said. They had reached one of the thatched buildings at the foot of the tower, and one of the other Sisters stepped up and pushed the door open. "Our guesthouse," she said. "We hope you will be comfortable. Evenmeal is almost ready; the bell will summon you when it is time. Any Sister will show you where to go."

Keda thanked them, and they withdrew. Brynna's eyes were round with wonder. "Am I going to have to stay here forever, then?" she asked, almost frightened. The Sisters had a disturbing air of permanence.

"I don't think so," laughed Keda. "Not everyone who comes here does, and you of all people are a special case."

"My aunt and my . . . my mother were both here," said Brynna carefully.

"Yes," said Keda, seeing through the logic, "and they both came to leave. All you have to do is stay here until you learn what they have to teach you." She looked at Brynna with eyes that were suddenly shadowed, and her long fingers could not help clenching into a fist for a moment. "Avanna," she murmured, "yours is a gift I am glad I was never born with. Not after . . . what happened at Cascin."

A vision of Ansen's bandaged face flashed across Brynna's mind, and she cried out, burying her face in her hands. "I didn't mean it . . ."

Keda crossed the room in one long stride and took the other girl into an almost maternal embrace. "I'm sorry. You're hardly to blame. He was mad that night, mad! And who's to say that, if it hadn't been for you, it wouldn't have been Kieran lying wounded in his bed? I can pity him, but I cannot bring myself to grieve for what happened to Ansen."

It was absolution, of a sort. In any event, they were not given time for more, as a melodious peal from a high, pure bell echoed through the settlement. It was all they could do to drag a comb through their hair and splash some water on their faces and hands before they joined the company of white-clad Sisters streaming toward the open door of the white tower.

The meal was simple, and relatively short. For Brynna it lasted a lifetime, knowing that all too soon, after Keda had sung for their supper, the harper would vanish up the stairs to the private sanctum of Lady Morgan, head of this community, and Lady Morgan would open Chella's letter. Brynna dreaded the aftermath. They might question her, demand to know what it was she had done to Ansen—the truth was, she did not know, and was in fact almost sure she could not do it again if she tried. It had been instinct, pure and simple, when she had seen the knife raised against Kieran; the rest came . . . from somewhere beyond her. But Feor seemed to think the likelihood of it happening again was not as negligible as Brynna believed. That was why they had sent her here—to blunt the killing edge, to teach her to wield her blade with more circumspection.

But when Bresse came to claim her, it was gently. Lady Morgan came back to the guest lodgings with Keda and bowed her head to Brynna in a gesture as unexpected as it was, in its own way, proud. It was an obeisance to a queen from one who was herself a queen of sorts in this, her small realm. But the queen gave way almost instantly to what might have been a loving grandmother, with Morgan bending down to smile and take Brynna's small hands into both her own brown, aged ones.

"I grieved for your mother," she said, her voice low, husky, rich with her years. "I bless the day I learned I have to grieve for you no longer, my princess. Sleep well, child; tomorrow we will begin the work that is before us. Tonight, Castle Bresse will keep you safe."

9

If there was something out of the ordinary in the fact that the Lady Morgan of Bresse herself undertook the teaching of the youngest novice in her Sisterhood, the girl still known as Brynna never suspected. Brynna was allowed her freedom and Keda's company for as long as the harper was at Bresse. The morning after Keda left, Brynna was deposited, garbed in the ubiquitous white robe of Bresse, in Morgan's chambers and left to cool her heels in the empty room until the lady was ready for her. At first she waited patiently, sitting on the edge of a wicker chair by the hearth, but when the minutes stretched into a respectable part of an hour she began to fidget, kicking the leg of the chair with her heel. Eventually she rose to wander round the room, examining the few objects left lying about for her to see. Morgan was giving nothing away; her room was remarkably free of anything personal by which her nature could be read. The pickings were poor; Brynna ended up standing by the window, one of her hands clutching childishly at her thin wrist behind her back. The window faced west. Unbidden, Keda's question of only a few days ago returned to whisper in her mind.

*What do you see?*

This time, it was different. Perhaps it was just the change of perspective, but it was not Miranei which rose to haunt her so much as its dead queen, herself once a novice here in Castle Bresse.

Her mother's voice, the flushed cheeks of excitement. *They will not forget this.* The crown of Miranei, trembling above Anghara's head. *They saw the crown upon your head.*

*It looked as though it belonged there. They will not forget this, Anghara. When you can come back to Miranei, I will call you.*

But she couldn't call. She was gone. And her daughter was Anghara no longer; she was plain Brynna Kelen, coming to Bresse from the hand of Chella of Cascin . . .

"She does not have to beckon from the battlements to call you home," said a voice at Brynna's elbow, answering the flow of the girl's thoughts. Brynna's eyes snapped up to meet Lady Morgan's serene smile.

"How did you . . ." she blurted, shock wiping all the proprieties she had ever known from her mind. This easy mind-reading was not something even Feor had done.

"That," said Morgan, "is just one of the things we will teach you at Bresse. But first of all, we must see what you already know. Come, sit. Let's talk."

At first they avoided any mention of the Cerdiad festival at Cascin. Morgan explored the little things, the triggers Feor had taught Brynna to use in order to touch her gift, the manifestations he had tried to teach her to control. Morgan muttered once or twice, with a twinge of impatience, that there would be not a few things that Brynna would have to unlearn; but on the whole she seemed satisfied with her new pupil. In the end, inevitably, they came to it as Brynna had known they must—the night when the carefully cultivated control had shattered and power had flooded from her like spilled wine.

It took one mention of Ansen's name, and Brynna closed up like a bruised flower. Morgan, perhaps surprisingly, had not expected a wound this deep; it would have to be healed before it could be explored. The most dangerous of Brynna's gifts would have to be left until last, until the girl had learned enough of the art to forgive herself for what she thought she had done. With a sigh, Morgan left it there.

"We will start from the beginning," she announced instead.

Brynna looked up in something like dismay. "Then is nothing that Feor taught me right?"

"I did not say that," Morgan said. "But if Bresse is to have a hand in you, then it is our disciplines you must learn. And you may as well start afresh. What you already know might make it easier for you—or harder, I don't know. We'll have to see." She paused, looking down onto her hands, folded gracefully in her lap. "What is Sight?"

Outflanked, Brynna blinked in consternation. "Lady?"

"You have seen it, you have experienced it. Now tell me, what is Sight?"

Brynna tried; but there were no words. Sight was the banked glow that told her what Feor was, that told Feor what *she* was, within moments of setting eyes on one another. Sight was her mother's healing touch when Anghara had grizzled over some childhood megrim. Sight was Rima's true dreams; it hid in the way Brynna could tell truth from lie, could force truth by no more than a glance from one determined to slide by on a falsehood. Sight was within a thousand small things, all around her. Familiar; completely unknown. She stammered, mumbled, finally swallowed hard and came to a grinding halt, certain she had failed an important test.

To her surprise, Morgan only smiled.

"No worse than some of the Sisters could offer," she said unexpectedly, her expression almost wicked. "Sight," she carried on in a voice quite changed, sliding almost imperceptibly from the glimpse into the girl she must once have been into the dignified teacher and mistress of her own small domain, "is all around us. They called it that because it was first recognized as something they called Second Sight, when village spaewives predicted next week's weather or the way a marriage would turn out. But we have grown far beyond that. There were things done with you, which were done with Sight no village spaewife would recognize."

"What things?" said Brynna, latching onto the specifics where they had to do with herself. "Like magic?"

"Not magic," said Morgan. "Power. Power ordinary women have learned to reach out and take from the well where it abides. Or, rather, power for which they have learned to allow themselves to become vessels. Those of us born with Sight are no different from any other human being—except there is a knowledge and ability within us to sense and control something to which ordinary people are blind. Your first task at Bresse, therefore, is to learn to empty yourself before you can reach for the power."

Brynna greeted this with a blank stare.

"Every Sister at Bresse has what we call a talisman," Morgan continued, by way of explanation. "I do not know what yours is; you will have to find that out by yourself. Mine is a white rosebud; I watch it opening in my mind, and when it blooms, I am ready to let the Sight in. You are welcome to try that, but the same talisman seldom works twice. Others have chosen a candle flame, a seashell, a butterfly. Anything that you love, that you think beautiful, that brings you a sense of serenity and peace. Anything you can hold in your mind until there is nothing there except your vision, strong enough for you to see it almost solid before you." Morgan's hands moved underneath her gaze until she might almost have been holding the ghost of her rosebud; Brynna swallowed.

"And when I have done it?"

Morgan had to smile again, at the unconscious arrogance of this. "It isn't as easy as it sounds. Other thoughts are loath to leave your head. But this is something you will have to master before we can go any further, and it is something you will have to do alone. Cheating is easy, but pointless, and if you come back to me and tell me you've achieved this task, I will know if you are telling me the truth or not. You are welcome to seek my advice, or any other Sister's, if you need help; but until you have chosen your talisman, and learned to enter it, the rest of the disciplines of Bresse are impossible to master."

"Do I have to tell you what I have chosen?"

It could have been a rhetorical question, but her tone left no room for doubt. "You have chosen already?" said Morgan, lifting her eyebrow. "No, you don't have to tell me. It is a secret useless to anyone but yourself. It is entirely up to you."

She asked no further, but simply pointed the way to a staircase leading up into the Novice Chambers, high in the White Tower. Brynna was to go and claim one of these and wrestle with her talisman, reporting her progress to her teacher the next day.

But she was given only an hour to bend her mind to this task. There were no servants in Bresse; every Sister took her turn at the chores of the Castle, from weeding the garden and feeding the cows to doing laundry, cooking meals and washing the dishes afterward. Brynna was just another novice and the newest one at that, ripe for the plucking. The community at Bresse did not know she had been a princess, was indeed a crowned queen, but even if they had known it would probably not have made any difference. In Bresse, she was nothing until she earned her rank by her skills and talent. When one of the older Sisters came to the Novice Chambers to round up a clutch of girls for kitchen duty, Brynna was one of the haul. Her sleeves rolled up above her elbows, she was set with another novice to peeling potatoes by the kitchen hearth.

In truth, she was far from annoyed at the interruption of her meditations. She had thought Morgan's task would be easy enough, but the talisman she had set her heart on kept slipping from her grasp. Every time she thought triumphantly *I have it!* she was reluctantly forced to admit she did not, else she would not have been able to think about having it. She struggled with it until she was flushed and breathless, with a thundercloud of an incipient headache rousing on the horizon of her mind like the purple storm hammerheads of Miranei. In the end she had to concede that, for the moment at least, her talisman had defeated her. She had almost welcomed the potatoes.

Which is not to say she was making an unqualified success of them, either. She had peeled very few potatoes in her life, and it showed, painfully. In the time her peeling partner had taken to peel three, Brynna was still struggling with her first, gouging out respectable quantities of the flesh together with the peel.

"With those white hands," said the other, breaking the silence that lay between them and pausing to survey Brynna's work with a mixture of amusement and disdain, "I'm not surprised you peel a potato as though with a broadsword. Do you think there's going to be any of yours left to cook by the time you're done with it?"

Brynna looked up, biting back a retort.

"High-born?" enquired the older novice conversationally, as she took up another potato. "Here, for the sake of all our suppers, watch me. This is how you do it." Her hands were deft, fast; the potato gleamed creamily, pale and bare of skin, in her palm in seconds. Then she relented, having shown Brynna up in no uncertain terms. "You don't have to do it that fast, not in the beginning. I have a year of potato peeling behind me in this place. I'm Bly, my father is Sir Machin of Nevan. Aren't you a bit young to be here?"

There was the faintest trace of envy in Ely's words; if young, the new novice must have been all the stronger in Sight for her gift to have been discovered already. And that meant the younger girl would be better than the common flock, destined for higher things.

Brynna bent industriously over her potato. "I'm Brynna," she said, "from . . . Cascin." She could not say Miranei—not here, when Miranei seemed so close. It was too painful to lay claim to a place which had not been home for so long— and perhaps, although this was no more than an afterthought, even risky. Brynna knew of Nevan Manor, close enough to Miranei for its family to have been a part of court life—she did not remember Bly, but that was not to say that Bly, prodded in the right direction, would not come to realize Brynna might be more than she seemed.

But what she said had triggered something almost as dangerous. "Cascin?" said Bly, tossing the second potato she had finished since Brynna had laboriously begun her own into the bowl set out to receive them. "Cascin of the Wells? I seem to remember there were only three sons in that manor."

"There is a daughter, too."

"Oh yes, I do recall. We haven't had much contact with Cascin lately, but one summer, it was a year or two ago now, my lady mother spent quite a lot of time with Lady Chella of Cascin. Still, the daughter would be much too young to be you." Her interest piqued, Bly left off the potatoes, measuring Brynna with a steady gaze.

"I fostered there," said Brynna blandly. She lifted a pitted potato for Ely's inspection. "Will this do?"

"A somewhat lighter hand would still be advised," said Bly, peering at it.

Brynna made a deliberate mess of her third potato; anything to divert Bly from her line of enquiry. It worked, after a fashion, especially after the Sister who was in charge of the kitchen came to cuff them into greater industry, if they wanted to eat that day. Wary of betraying herself with an inadvertent word, Brynna decided her best chance of safety lay in solitude. She fended off Bly for the moment and, after her, one or two other novices who tried to make some kind of contact. Before her first week was out she had acquired a reputation for being withdrawn and aloof; some even said haughty. There were those who resented being rebuffed by someone who was their junior, both in years and in status. The Sisters were kind to her, and gentle, as they were with everyone, but very soon her peers left her to herself. It was safety, in a way.

Morgan, keeping an eye on her newest charge, saw a danger Brynna had entirely overlooked. Isolation made for conspicuousness; if anyone came asking who was the most mysterious, most intriguing and most tantalizing novice in Bresse, the one most likely to hold dangerous secrets, Brynna Kelen would have had no competition. For someone who wanted to stay unobtrusive and unremarked, it was poor strategy. Still, there were no enquiries after her, and it would have made her stand out even more if she suddenly changed tack and began cultivating friendships. Even people who had remained indifferent might have started to harbor suspicions. Morgan decided to leave the matter alone.

Brynna learned quickly how to peel potatoes, milk the

cows, feed the chickens and make vegetable broth for fifty people. Her studies took a little longer, though. It was true she had chosen her talisman without thinking twice that first morning in Morgan's chambers, almost in the same instant she had first heard of the existence of such a thing. Taming it, though, proved to be a beast of quite a different color.

She would start well enough, focusing first on Cascin, then the path she knew so well, leading from the house to the woods and the well on whose banks the willows dreamed lazy summer dreams. Using the same facility that had kept Miranei alive for her in her years at Cascin, Brynna found she could charm up an image of the willow grotto in such perfect detail that she could see every individual leaf on the two old trees in her mind's eye. She could almost feel the softness of the springy moss beneath her feet, and there, on the highest point of the little mound, virtually touch the greenish pebble her own hand had planted there. In Brynna's vision, the little Standing Stone stood in the midst of an aura of . . . something, a pale green light, a shroud of its own small sphere of power. This alone in the picture was strange and unfamiliar, the sole thing Brynna could not remember having seen at Cascin. And it was precisely this aura which proved to be her problem. She focused flawlessly on the idea of her talisman until she came to the vision of the stone; but as soon as her mind reached out to touch the light around it, her concentration would vanish in a shimmer of scattered thoughts, dreams and memories. The stone would disintegrate into motes and slivers, sparkling like sunlight on water, and in the welter of visions that were its gifts, Brynna found it difficult to remember the stone at all.

Some of the things it showed her, she recognized. Kieran holding her as she wept in her pain when Rima had died; herself drowsing against the warm trunk of the willow on a summer afternoon; hunting for Charo's puppy, after it had run after a baby hare and lost itself in the woods. She saw Keda throwing an apple peel in slow motion over her shoulder on a moonless summer night; Cerdiad . . . the Cerdiad bonfire . . . *ah, but I don't want to see this . . .* shattering glass . . . men with scowling faces, smoking torches, eyes full of tears . . . *This isn't Cerdiad . . . this hasn't happened . . . they've come to burn the house . . . no . . . No . . . No!*

She'd cry out loud, coming to herself bent double with pain on the mat in her chamber, with tears streaming down her face. When she calmed down and took a few moments to catch her breath, she'd doggedly try again—and come up against the same vision, or different ones, no less potent. Touch the stone and be swirled into madness, that seemed to be the impasse she shipwrecked against time and time again. And yet . . . she couldn't understand it. The willows had never given her anything but peace beneath the green bower. Now, far away, the place seemed to hold nothing but chaos and confusion.

She struggled with it alone for almost two weeks. Perhaps she would have gone to Morgan sooner if she hadn't been so aware of having given the impression of choosing her talisman so blithely in the first place—but stubborn pride kept her at it until the thing simply defeated her by its sheer persistence. Beaten, exhausted, she sought Morgan's wisdom.

"It's as though it has a mind of its own," Brynna complained. "I can catch it, I can hold it, but then it fills my mind with other things even as I am thinking of it, and it's gone."

"Perhaps you had better tell me," said Morgan, frowning, "what the talisman is."

Brynna hesitantly described the willows, wishing she didn't feel as though she was laying bare a hallowed place to infidel eyes. "I had a stone from the well when I first came under the willows," she said, gazing down into her lap. "I planted it there, in the ground, like a small Standing Stone. That was what I took as . . ."

"A *Standing Stone?*" echoed Morgan blankly.

"Not a real one, just a pebble . . . it was only I who ever thought of it that way," Brynna said.

"But . . . a Standing Stone . . ." Morgan shook her head; realizing only now just how different her charge was from the rest of the girls in her care. "What made you pick that, of all things? Don't you realize you're crossing power with power . . . I don't even know myself what you've done here. It's quite possible you're lucky you aren't dead!"

"Should I choose something else?" asked Brynna queasily.

"You can't," said Morgan, in real perplexity. "The connection has been made already; it's often said that novices don't choose talismans so often as they are chosen by them. For some reason this stone of yours has picked you. But, my dear child, I'm not at all sure just where we go from here. It is unlikely that a Standing Stone will ever allow you the freedom you need for it to be the talisman you require."

"But it's only . . ." began Brynna again.

Morgan shook her head. "It's no longer only anything. Whether or not it is a Standing Stone raised for obscure purposes by those long dead or a pebble planted all unknowing by a girl unaware of the power of naming which lies in the gift of her Sight, it's all the same in the eyes of the Gods."

"You mean I made it a Standing Stone just by willing it so?" said Brynna, a little breathless at the magnitude of this.

"It would seem so—even if it is just for yourself. It may serve a useful purpose for you—from what you said, it appears that many of your stone's visions are concerned with things which are yet to come to pass. But taming this wild beast to be ridden as your talisman . . . I don't know, Brynna. Try again, here, with me. I will try and follow you, perhaps then I will be able to see what to do."

Brynna obediently focused on Cascin again—the house, the path, the trees . . . the stone . . . Her mind brushed it, and dissolved almost instantly in a tower of flames wreathing a column of white stone, an unearthly wail of terror and distress rending the air. Her eyes flew wide, her mouth opened and gasped for air. She was dimly aware that one of the voices in the fugue of fear and dismay was her own, her cry loud in the silence which remained behind after the vision faded. It was the only cry she heard as a sound . . . the rest . . . the rest had cried out in her mind, had been felt there, and had been silenced . . . For a few moments darkness took her, held her, then her eyes cleared. She realized with a start that the grip on her shoulders was Morgan's hands. They were both kneeling on the floor before the fireplace—Morgan's face almost as white as her robe.

"Kerun and Avanna!" Morgan gasped, invoking the protection of almost every God she knew. "You had to cope with this every time?"

Brynna reached up to wipe salty trails of tears off her cheeks, tears she could not remember having shed. "It's not usually . . . this bad," she finally managed to say, her voice oddly hoarse. "What was . . . that place?"

"I'm not sure," said Morgan, very slowly.

*She lies,* said Brynna's mind with cold clarity.

But Morgan was too wise in ways of Sight to be drawn out by the long, hypnotic stare of Brynna's truth-gaze. Brynna was not going to hear from her that she could put an interpretation to the vision the Stone of Cascin had seen fit to give them. It was obvious that Brynna had not recognized the tower writhing in the fire. But Morgan had, having lived in it for almost half her life: the white tower of Bresse. There was no denying the truth in the revelation—with powers of her own Morgan could tell that much. Castle Bresse, which had stood for almost two centuries, was going to fall; and it was beginning to be painfully obvious to Morgan that the oracle predicting its downfall was also the trigger that would spark it. It was something Brynna herself could not but become aware of in the fullness of time, but Morgan did not see why it should be necessary for her to be burdened with the knowledge before it became inevitable.

She steered her thoughts, instead, into more productive channels. The disciplines of Bresse demanded a talisman; it was obvious Brynna's stone would not do at all. And yet . . . there had been the choosing . . .

"Are you all right now?" asked Morgan carefully, reaching out to cup Brynna's chin in her long fingers. When the girl nodded, Morgan let her go and sat back, arranging her robe around her. "I think I may have your answer," she said. "It's only the Stone that is your bane, not the clearing itself.

So let the clearing take its place—or something else within it, something close to but not of the Stone. The moss around it perhaps, or the willow tree. It is much more difficult to hold a pure image of an entire physical space than that of a single object, but I think you're well able to do it." She did not offer to explain the reasoning behind this declaration of faith; in truth she was still reeling from the purity of the images she had seen in Brynna's mind. A part of her found it difficult to believe the white tower was not already in flames around her.

"But the Stone . . ."

"Yes, there is a risk that your new talisman holds within itself this seed of danger; you have to make sure you are warded in your mind against the Stone's touch, unless you are in need and actively seek it."

"Seek it?" echoed Brynna, her eyes haunted with stone-sent dreams.

"You may well have an oracle within you," said Morgan gently. "We might never have known if you hadn't . . . the Gods preserve you . . . decided to pick a Standing Stone as your talisman. The choice is made, the damage is already done; but we can still hope to turn this to advantage. But we must go slowly, and very carefully. The least of my problems right now is that this has never been done before, and I shall be making up the rules as we go along. Ignorance always means danger; and you, of all people, we cannot lose." She reached out to touch Brynna's cheek in an almost maternal caress. "It's you who will be blazing this trail," she said, "I'll just follow, learn, and keep you out of trouble if I can."

But trouble seemed to follow the girl who had once been Anghara Kir Hama, of Miranei under the Mountains, like a shadow. Castle Bresse, protected and secluded, was shelter for a while—but the storms that beset Anghara's young life were far from blown out.

The first touch of the cold wind came early, when young Brynna Kelen of Castle Bresse was only just beginning to find her feet in the dangerous streams and eddies of Sight.

Brynna, with Morgan's help, had succeeded in centering on her substitute talisman—the spongy, yielding moss which surrounded the little Standing Stone at Cascin. Morgan had objected, again, arguing that the stone itself was standing in the midst of the moss and it would be all too easy to touch it by mistake—with consequences which, by now, both teacher and pupil knew well. But it seemed to work, and proved adequate as a basis on which to build. However, the first stirring of coherent power from Brynna whipped up an unexpected wasp's nest.

Brynna, who had turned twelve only the week before, was sitting at Morgan's feet in her teacher's chambers, attempting one of the more difficult exercises Morgan had set for her. In her mind's eye she sat in, was surrounded by, what was almost a nest of the soft moss she remembered from beneath the willows. With a tendril of her mind she perceived the deep green of its presence all around her, feeling its texture with the tips of her fingers. With preternaturally sharpened senses she was following a thread of thought, of Power, retrieving a target set by Morgan. When the alien contact came it was sudden, jolting, and very fast; she was shocked from her cocoon, the moss turning hard and gritty beneath her hand, as though it had transmuted itself into coarse sand. She blinked, shivered, and sat rigid with shock, rubbing the last of the trance's cobwebs from her eyes.

Morgan had felt nothing. "What is it?" she asked, herself startled by the sudden change in her young pupil.

"It felt . . . as though they were looking for me," said Brynna slowly, groping for meaning in what she had just experienced.

A swift vision of a white tower in flames was visited on Morgan's mind, quickly suppressed; she rose, her face grave. Once Brynna had spoken, she had no doubt as to exactly what had happened.

"And they may well have found you," she said. "We still have time for a plan. I think," and she allowed a wintry smile to touch the corners of her lips, "it's time for some of our Sisters to go into retreat."

They gauged it to a nicety. Morgan arranged things in such a way that the patrol came to Bresse in time to see the tail end of a small cavalcade of Sisters and a couple of pack animals vanishing along the narrow track which led up into the mountains. Morgan herself was in the courtyard to greet Sif's soldiers. They were ten, and with them a pair of frightened women, one young, one old enough to wish never to have to sit a horse again, looking anxious and uncomfortable on her placid gelding.

"We have reason to believe you are harboring one whom our lord the king wants taken," grated the leader of the patrol, after observing a sketchy obeisance due to one of Morgan's rank. Behind him, thinking themselves unobserved, four of his men were making the sign against the evil eye.

"Bresse harbors no fugitives," said Morgan levelly.

"We have orders to search," said the patrol leader.

Morgan stepped aside, making a welcoming gesture with her hand. "Search. But disturb nothing."

More men were making the sign; so many Sighted women together in one place was a rare circumstance. Every child in Roisinan grew up with the idea of Sight, sometimes within reach of a Sighted mother or grandmother, and this kind of domestic power was known and accepted. But gathered all together, the little puddles and trickles of familiar Sight pooled into a vast, unknown and dangerous sea. Bresse was not often frequented by common folk. Morgan's injunction was almost unnecessary; not one soldier would willingly touch anything in this place.

But physical searching was not what the patrol leader had in mind. He turned, caught some in the act of making the sign and swore, then beckoned the two women forward. "Well?" he barked.

The older one was sweating, half in fear of her horse, half in terror of the captain of the guard. She offered nothing. But the younger woman was mettlesome enough; she met Morgan's eyes squarely, then allowed her gaze to play on the cottages in the courtyard, the byres, coming to rest finally on the white tower. They lingered there for a long moment, and then she turned her head toward the scowling man who waited for her answer.

"No," she said. "Not here."

The scowl deepened. "By the Gods," he snarled, "if you've led us here on a wild goose chase . . ."

"We heard what we heard," she said, unmoved.

One of the men had been more observant or perhaps less overawed than the rest. "The group that just went into the mountains," he said to his captain, "who were they?"

"Yes, who were they?" the captain asked, leaning forward on his pommel to stare at Morgan. "Where were they going?"

"Four of our Sisters," said Morgan calmly. "They are going on retreat into the mountains."

"On retreat? What does that mean? Where have they gone?"

"Even if I could tell you," Morgan returned, "I would not. Retreat is a calling to solitude, not to be savaged by a mob of angry men. But the truth is I do not know where they have gone. Bresse maintains several small bothies in the mountains; those who go on retreat are not called upon to provide advance notice of which one they will make for."

"This is true," said the younger of the captain's women.

His head swivelled in her direction. "What do you mean?"

"I was trained here," the girl said, keeping her voice carefully neutral and her eyes on the space between her mount's pricked ears. Morgan felt a sudden warmth spreading through her. This was one of their own; Morgan didn't recognize her, but there had been so many novices through the years. This girl was Bresse-trained; she would not . . .

But the captain was speaking again. "Would you know where these mountain huts are, then?"

The girl glanced up at Morgan quickly, almost too fast for anyone to see, and dropped her eyes again. She shook her head. "I never went on retreat."

Foiled, the captain rounded on Morgan again. "How long are these . . . retreats?" he demanded.

"As long," said Morgan beatifically, tucking her hands into her sleeves, "as the Sisters think it is necessary. Sometimes it's only a few days. Often it's weeks, sometimes months. Once, a Sister stayed away for almost a year."

The captain considered this. Perhaps he would have taken a chance and chased after the fugitive Sisters himself, but he knew he would find it utterly impossible to make any of his men do so, even at the point of a sword. Sif could have made them do it, but Sif was far away. "We'll stay until they come back," he decided abruptly, his fingers going to his temples as though he was nursing a particularly violent headache.

"I am afraid," said Morgan, every word oozing with polite regret, "that Bresse cannot offer hospitality for longer than a night."

"What do you mean? We are here on the king's business, and . . ."

"You are men," his captive Bresse graduate informed him.

They stayed in Bresse that night, and it was doubtful if any of them save the women enjoyed a wink of sleep. The captain knew when he was defeated and took up lodgings in Radas Han for almost another month, riding up to Bresse every day to look for the return of the Sisters who had gone on the fictional retreat. He became increasingly bad-tempered. Eventually, losing patience, he returned to Mi-ranei with the two Sighted women and his troop of guards. Even the thought of Sif's wrath at his failure was infinitely more palatable than guarding a castle full of women who set his men's teeth on edge and who, in the captain's own private and considered opinion, had been driven more than a little crazy by their isolation.

The captain would have been in a white-hot, blazing rage if he had realized the Sisters "on retreat" had only gone as far as the first bend in the mountain trail and waited there for his troop to leave. They had returned to Bresse, with him none the wiser, the very next day—via the small postern door, even as the captain was in the process of demanding lodgings from the innkeeper at Radas Han. The object of his search had watched him ride up from Radas Han and back again every day for a month. As it was, he rode away merely furious at the wasted time; he took it out on the two women, whom he made ride at a pace which soon reduced the elder to a quivering jelly of jolted and shaken bones and raw muscles. The younger woman took the punishment, and merely smiled.

Bresse had ways of guarding against accidents. But that gathering of women who ought to have been able to hear a feather fall from an eagle's wing in the mountains on the other side of the world was oddly blind when it came to some things. When the true betrayal came, Castle Bresse lay wide open, unable to turn the blow that came unlooked for, out of the darkness.

10

Ansen recovered slowly from his brush with power. At first he did not question the fact that his only visitors were his parents, the healer, occasionally Feor, and a pair of silent women whose function seemed to be that of sickroom attendants and who came and went in shifts, one of them always in the room with him. By the time he thought to query the continuing absence of Kieran and Brynna, as well as both his younger brothers, his two former schoolroom companions had been gone for almost two months. When he did ask, unfortunately, it was of one of the women, and she did not know any better than to be blunt.

"They were sent away, young lord," she'd said. "Right after your accident."

Ansen, who preferred not to think about his "accident" at all but whose sightless eye never ceased to remind him of that Cerdiad night, sat up in bed, propping himself up on both elbows. "Sent away? Where? By whom?"

"Lord Lyme and Lady Chella," the woman said. "And Feor, your tutor."

The three names rang in Ansen's head, buzzing around his skull like furious bees. He smelled a conspiracy. The woman was obviously ignorant of the real facts, and Ansen pressed her no further, but he waited with angry impatience for one of the three who had been named to come to him, frustrated as he was by his continuing confinement to bed. It was Feor who was the first to arrive, gliding in one morning in his blue robe, trying to arrange his lugubrious features into one of his unaccustomed smiles.

"The healer tells me you're getting restless," said Feor. "That's good. It means you're healing."

"When will I be allowed out of this bed?" demanded Ansen, distracted for a moment by the glittering prospect of a renewal of normal life.

"That isn't up to me," said Feor with his usual adroit verbal sleight of hand.

Ansen's hand rose to touch the bandage which still wrapped his head. It was lighter now than the one Brynna had stared at, aghast, when she'd first come into this room after the accident. The patient was looking a little bit more like himself, his pale hair sticking out at odd angles from beneath the strap holding the bandage in place. "I can hardly wait for this to come off," said Ansen with a sigh. "I feel like half a man with one eye closed like this."

The expression that passed through Feor's eyes was gone almost before Ansen could be sure it was there, but it was such a rare occurrence to catch Feor off guard he was instantly alert. His one good eye narrowed.

"Feor . . ."

Feor spared a moment to frame a choice curse in the privacy of his mind for the healer who had—perhaps out of misguided pity—neglected to acquaint his patient with the diagnosis everyone else in the keep already knew. When he met Ansen's eye, sparking with something that was half anger and half abject terror, Feor had managed to restore a semblance of his usual tight control. When his eyes met Ansen's they were blank, revealing nothing—no pity, no fear.

"There is a possibility," Feor said in the flat, inflectionless tones of a messenger bringing news of defeat in battle to a new widow, "that you might never . . ."

Ansen's cry was that of a wounded beast, inarticulate, inchoate, bleeding. He clawed at the bandage with the sudden and violent motion of a trapped animal gnawing at its own foot to reach freedom. It was as though having heard the bandage was not what was keeping the light from his injured eye, Ansen had decided to tear it away and take his chances without it.

He had decided nothing, of course, not consciously; blind anguish moved his hands, and his strength was such that Feor, who sprang to stop him from reopening his wound, could hardly hold him down. He shouted for someone to fetch the healer, anyone, an extra pair of hands. The healer arrived first, with a potion they tried to force down Ansen's throat. It took three men to do it at last, and even then they were forced to tie his hands together until the potion took effect. He lay there moaning for a long time, and even when he slipped off into a drug-induced sleep he tossed uneasily on his pillow. There was a telltale streak of tears on his cheek, where his pale eyelashes touched flesh pallid from months of illness and incarceration.

Feor did not often give way to rage, but Ansen's pain had distressed him greatly and the sight of futile and childish tears on the face of one so nearly a man drove him over the edge. When he turned on the panting healer, whose forehead shone with the sweat of his exertions, the man shrank from the white fury in Feor's face. The priest's voice, however, was silky, quiet and dangerous when at length he spoke.

"Did you not think he deserved to know the truth?" he enquired, almost conversationally.

The healer, whose eyes had dropped from the other's set face, glanced up hopefully, thinking the storm had passed him by. What he saw made him quickly look down again.

"I did not think," he began portentously, taking refuge in pomposity, "he was well enough to cope with the news. I was waiting until he . . ."

"Until he heard it spilled out without warning?" enquired Feor, still ominously quiet. "Do you consider him well enough now?"

The healer, a rotund, red-faced man with a premature paunch, was far from incompetent or cruel; he had genuinely meant well. He bleated some excuse and stood trembling before Feor, in the silence of a child caught out in some sin by his elders. If Feor had been in a softer mood, he might have pitied him, standing there in abject abasement.

But there was no pity. There was only the glint of the hearth-fire on Ansen's tear-stained cheek.

Feor's voice broke at last, in thunder.

*"Out!"* he bellowed, flinging his arm out to point at the door. "You have done here! If I ever find you in this room again without the express permission of Lord Lyme or Lady Chella, I shall throw you out of yonder window myself!"

There was something faintly ridiculous in the idea of tall, thin, angular Feor lifting the stocky physician and throwing him anywhere, but as Ansen's window was located on the second floor of the Cascin manor the healer saw nothing humorous in the situation. He scurried out of Ansen's door, wincing and ducking a blow which never came, and vanished down the corridor.

Only now did Feor's face soften and his hands drop to his sides. He sat lightly on the side of Ansen's bed and smoothed the pale hair from his face in an unconsciously tender gesture. Ansen turned away, murmuring something incoherent. Feor summoned his attendant, leaving strict instructions that he or one of Ansen's parents was to be called immediately the boy woke, and went in search of Lyme and Chella to tell them of the ugly turn of events.

They were all ready to pamper Ansen when he woke, with Feor aloof as usual but with an odd stoop to his shoulders, which made him look like a wizened old eagle hovering protectively over an injured chick. But Ansen, when he woke, was brittle and hard as obsidian. He wanted no pampering—he wanted the truth. He went back to the accident he had tried so hard to forget, and demanded that somebody help him remember it. All of it.

It was Feor, the only eyewitness still in Cascin, who gave him back the events of that night. The priest tried to blur the outline, pulling ragged edges of concealment where none remained, but Ansen cut through the pretense with a shrewdness that was almost Sight.

"Yes, but who threw the decanter?" he asked again, returning to the one point Feor had skated over. "Keda was right next to me, Kieran had his hands full of me, you were at the door and Brynna was halfway there, close neither to the table nor to me. I would have noticed if she had gone for the bottle, surely, even under the . . . circumstances. I admit I was drunk, perhaps perverse . . ." That was the one concession he made to his role in the whole affair, still arrogant, still haughty. "But . . ."

"Ansen, do you remember taking out a knife?"

Ansen shot him a smoldering look. "Does it really matter? Now?"

"It matters. If you did, you were the reason why two of your foster siblings were made to leave this house."

"Is that all?" Ansen enquired, with sudden nastiness in his voice. His hand rose to touch his bandage. "And what of me?" The hand dropped. There was a goblet of mulled wine on a tray beside the bed; Ansen reached for it, frowned when he misjudged the distance and nearly overbalanced the vessel. "Gods," he muttered, "am I to be condemned to this for the rest of my life?" He looked up again, and there was a flash of rage in his good eye. "They crippled me, damn it, Feor!"

Ansen had experienced episodes of self-pity before, but they were different by far from the fit he was now in the grip of—more innocent, more innocuous, the last vestiges of childish whining from someone who was no longer a child. Now self-pity had congealed into something more brittle, more bitter. It was hard to feel compassion for Ansen when he resorted to mockery and sarcasm; he nursed his misery fiercely, and it colored the way he saw the events of that night. To his mind, he had still done nothing wrong by trying to seduce Keda using the traditional appurtenances of Cerdiad. The knife . . . the knife he could only vaguely remember, a blur in his mind. And there was something else, something he could not put into context, something terribly, terribly important . . .

"Where did they go?" he asked, taking a weary sip of his wine.

"Kieran was placed as a squire," Feor said, abrupt and businesslike. He did not wish to discuss Kieran with

Ansen, not while he was in this mood. Kieran was a living reminder of what Ansen might never be now, a youth on the path to knighthood, to glory. A youth with two good eyes.

"And Brynna?" Ansen frowned into his goblet. It was to do with Brynna, the thought he couldn't pin down. She must have thrown the decanter at him—she must have—there had been nobody else in the room. But that was not it. Although there was something strange . . .

"She has gone to family," said Feor smoothly. Which was true, up to a point; she had gone to a Sisterhood. But Ansen was devilishly sharp that day. Feor made the mistake, imperceptible under normal circumstances, of allowing himself to glance at the door at this point, as though hoping for rescue, or escape. Ansen saw his glance. It was around his odd little foster sister that the whole mystery was woven; and, with terrier-like persistence, he would not let go.

"They did not even say goodbye," he said, sounding aggrieved.

Feor bit back the impulse to ask why, in the aftermath of the Cerdiad incident, Ansen would have expected any of the other actors in the drama to commiserate with him in his plight. "They tried," he said instead. "An . . . Brynna at least came up here, I know that much. She . . ."

But the slip was enough, however swiftly and smoothly patched. It could have merely been the first syllable of his own name, but the sound was different. Ansen suddenly knew with blinding clarity it was not his name Feor had been about to utter. He heard again the echo of Feor's cry in the dining hall of Cascin on Cerdiad Eve.

*Anghara! No!*

"Anghara!" breathed Ansen, putting the goblet of wine down rather unsteadily. "So that's it! She's Anghara, my royal cousin who is supposed to be dead and buried! And Sif . . . Sif doesn't know she is here!"

There was no possible use in dissembling. "No more is she," said Feor tightly, recalling the curse he had formulated for the hapless healer and piling it on his own head with vengeful indignation. *Old. Old. You're getting old. You should be meditating in some Sanctuary somewhere, not cutting the cloth of a world.*

But Ansen, whose intelligence was the equal of Kieran or Anghara, for all that he chose not to apply it in class, was already leaping ahead.

"Where could you have spirited her away to?" he muttered. "She can hardly be easy to hide . . . and if she is hiding, that means Sif is looking. But my aunt must be dead, really dead, else Sif would not be on the throne, not with Sight to help her . . ." He trailed away into a brief silence, his good eye narrowing speculatively. "Sight . . ." he muttered. "Her mother is Sighted; as is my mother. Perhaps . . . Perhaps . . . It was Sight threw that glass at me, Feor, wasn't it? Wasn't it?"

"She has the gift," Feor said flatly.

"Well!" said Ansen, leaning back into his pillows. His eye gleamed in a sly way Feor did not like. "I guess it took this . . ." his hand drifted up in an expressive gesture at his face, "for the truth to come out. I wonder if Sif . . ."

"Ansen," said a cold voice from the door to the room, "that is enough."

Both convalescent and visitor turned to look. It was rescue, but for Feor it was far too late; he could only meet Chella's eyes and give a small, resigned shake of his head. Even this, in his unnaturally percipient state, Ansen caught and interpreted. Correctly.

"You never would have told me, would you," he said. "Just left me to wonder, and to shrivel out here while they . . . Why did you let Kieran out, Mother? Or Keda? Doesn't this knowledge mean death or imprisonment for life? Aren't you afraid they will . . ."

"They, no," said Chella evenly. "You . . . He is your foster brother, and you drew a knife on him. She is your cousin, and . . ."

"She is my cousin and she blinded me," finished Ansen bitterly.

"She was protecting Kieran," Chella said.

"And you are protecting her," said Ansen. "Even now you've managed to secrete her away somewhere. I suppose nobody who was there on that night actually remembers what really happened, do they, Mother? Your doing? Your Sight?"

Chella exchanged a quick glance with Feor. She had also seen the glint in Ansen's eye.

"My Sight, yes," she said at length, after a pause. "There isn't a tongue in Cascin able to speak of Cerdiad Eve to someone outside this house. Except a few who are still free; who can be trusted. Feor, myself. You."

"Yes. Me." There was sarcasm in Ansen's voice. "Aren't you afraid I might . . ."

"You won't," said Chella, softly, firmly, with regret. "If you will not undertake to remain silent—and swear an oath I can trust—then, son or no son, you too will taste the interdict. Either that, or you will never leave this house again."

"I might not anyway," Ansen said, gesturing again at his eye.

"Stop it," Chella snapped, losing patience. "Your father has dragged around a game leg all his life, and he was blameless in the getting of it. Yet I married him, and he is lord of this keep. Show you are deserving of respect, and no one will think the less of you for a disability."

"Mother!" gasped Ansen, caught unprepared by the thinly veiled contempt in his mother's voice. Her face softened.

"We'll talk of this again," she murmured. "You're tired. I will come and see you when you have rested. Feor, come. He still needs a lot of sleep if he is to heal. I'll see the women bring you a draft." She leaned over to brush Ansen's forehead with her lips, just at the edge of the bandage.

Ansen's eyes, much to his disgust, suddenly filled with tears. Or at least his one good eye did. They brimmed on the lower lid, and spilled; Chella reached to wipe them gently away.

"Am I loathsome?" he whispered, very softly.

"Of course not, darling," his mother murmured.

Feor was already outside; Chella followed, closing the door behind her, leaving Ansen alone in the firelit chamber. He squeezed his eye tightly shut, trying to keep the tears back, but new ones came, hot ones, rage and self-pity.

*Am I loathsome? . . . Of course not, darling . . .*

She was lying. She was lying! How could he not be loathsome, fettered in his bed with an eye doomed never to see light again? A sound bubbled into his throat; he swallowed, but it filled his mouth with a taste of mold and ashes. His lips opened almost inadvertently, and it came out, first oozing gently in a soft moan, then building to a crescendo until it peaked in a howl of outrage, horror, thwarted passion. He seized his half-full wine goblet, heavy silver, and threw it with all his strength at the far wall. It struck and spilled, leaving a long smear to trickle down like blood and pool slowly on the wooden floor.

Eventually he found out where Brynna was, or Anghara, as he supposed he must now learn to think of her. He eased it out of his mother, playing her expertly. Once again she had not needed to tell him the whole story, only enough for him to surmise the rest—he knew about her own stay at Castle Bresse. In fact, he did it so well she was unaware she had spilled the secret. It was Feor who, with skill equal to Ansen's own, made the young patient betray himself by an unwary word. When Chella heard of his plan to write a letter to Miranei in which he would detail Anghara's whereabouts, she lost no time in extending the interdict, which, until then, had excluded him. It was with bitterness that Ansen received this new wound. He found himself helpless to utter Anghara's name to anyone but Feor or his parents, and even there the cocoon of silence was tight around him if anyone else was near. His hand would not write the word, and if he tried to wrap it in euphemism or riddle even they were sufficient to confound him utterly. The name of Anghara, and anything that grew from it, were trapped inside his head like the ancient insects imprisoned in amber the children occasionally found in the woods. He raged against it, but he had no gift of his own to break Chella's fiat.

And then he went quiet one day, very suddenly, very deliberately. It was the day he was allowed to leave his room for the first time, wearing an eye patch made from black silk. The long sojourn in his bed had made his legs weak; his knees trembled as he walked, but he would accept no friendly shoulder, no stick, leaning against a wall or a banister when he needed support. It was as though he wanted no further handicap to mar his emergence from convalescence. He insisted in dressing entirely in black for the occasion—saying, in the disturbing tone of voice he had adopted, that he had better learn to match that which would be his constant companion for the rest of his life. It suited him, setting off his pale hair, his white skin; he looked like a tragic prince from a harper's tale, and people he met in the corridors hurried to him to smile and to say how marvellous it was to see him abroad again. Lyme had even allowed the twins to bring Ansen's favorite hound into the house, and the dog nearly flattened him in the initial explosion of its joy—as did his brothers, even the taciturn Adamo finding words with which to welcome his brother back.

And Feor, watching, saw Ansen accepting it all, his head held high. He also saw the instant when Ansen's good eye swept across the hall, pausing only infinitesimally at the closed door of the dining chamber. He also saw exactly when it occurred to Ansen that his confinement in this house and his mind was not permanent. This was his heritage—one day this would be his. And when it was, when his parents were gone, it would be easy to work his will. Until then . . . well, someone else could easily tell Sif where Anghara was, but it was hardly likely to happen in the nest of Sighted women they'd spirited her away to. And as long as she stayed there, Ansen would know where to find her. Would know where to tell Sif to find her. It wouldn't bring back his eye, nothing would, but at least he would have the satisfaction of taking from her something equally precious in return. Certainly her freedom; perhaps her life. Sif was a

king, in name and in deed; Anghara was already dead. It
would cost Sif nothing to meet that condition in truth. All he
needed were a few trusted men. Perhaps, one day, Ansen
would be among them. Perhaps Sif would look past the
missing eye.

Feor shivered where he stood. Oddly, it was not Anghara's face that came to him as he stared at Ansen's shadowy, triumphant smile; it was Kieran's. Kieran, as Feor had
once seen him, dark hair slicked with rain. He heard again
his own voice. *It is well. She will need a friend.*

Kieran. Not March who huddled faithfully in a village
close to Radas Han and kept watch on his hidden princess,
but Kieran. There was a cloud hiding Anghara's future from
Feor's questing mind, a cloud oozing out of the blackness
which draped Ansen's thin frame; and Kieran's name shone
from within it. Feor suddenly knew that when the time came
for Anghara's friends to come for her, March would already
be dead.

Ansen did not return to lessons with Feor. Instead, he
spent weeks and months first trying to get the strength back
into his wasted limbs and then, once he had accomplished
that, trying to regain his mastery of the arts of war. He rode
out to the hunt with his father, carrying his hawk on his
gloved wrist, every inch the young lord. He worked up a
lather in the tilting yard, occasionally partnered by one or
the other of his younger brothers whom he soon taught to respect him since he gave no quarter, and expected none. He
found he had lost his unerring aim in archery, and fought bitterly to regain it, adjusting his stance and grip to compensate
for his disability; but had to come to terms eventually with
the fact that he would never be as skillful a shot as before.
He'd lost the depth of vision essential for accuracy. It was
one more black mark against Anghara Kir Hama. Black was
his color now, in more ways than one; since he had emerged
from his sickroom, he had worn nothing else. Even his mind
was obsidian, black, gleaming and utterly impenetrable. It
was no longer possible for any Sighted person at Cascin to

know what Ansen was thinking or planning behind this smooth facade. Feor had his fears, but they were insubstantial ghosts. The atmosphere in Cascin hummed with undercurrents where before there had been only clear waters; Ansen was the most direct cause for this, of course, but this, too, was a legacy of Anghara of Miranei.

Something irreplaceable had been taken from Chella—a vitality that had been hers, a quiet joy in her life had gone, vanished largely the instant she saw her eldest son with his hand held up to his bloodied face. What remained ebbed away slowly, and the change in her became increasingly obvious as her shoulders stooped a little more each day and she made no attempt to hide the gray hairs which now dimmed the familiar brightness of her hair.

"Are you ill, my lady?" became a mournful refrain for Feor as he watched the dark circles grow around her eyes and her hands tremble sometimes as she lifted a goblet or a spoon.

"There's nothing you can do, my friend," was the customary reply.

When she eventually took to her bed, Feor knew she would never leave it.

Distressed as Lyme and Feor were at the inevitability of a bright life ending, they failed to realize the repercussions of her steadily weakening condition until it was entirely too late. When Ansen mentioned Anghara by name in the presence of a servant, Feor did not realize the implications until much later. He was sitting with Chella in her chambers, reading aloud from a favorite book as she lay back alone and small in the great bed. When he did make the connection, Feor stumbled as the words ran into a sudden blur on the page before him. Chella's eyelids, almost transparent now, fluttered open at the silence.

"Feor?" she whispered softly, her voice lifting in a query.

"Ansen. He spoke her name to me today. He said her name . . . and we were not alone."

Chella's white cheeks suddenly flamed as blood rushed to her face. "The interdict . . ."

"I should have bolstered it months ago!" groaned Feor, in an agony of self-reproach.

"Do not . . . blame yourself. It is I who should have realized . . . sooner." She breathed for a while, very carefully, as though she had need of some deep well of power she had not tapped yet—and as though she was far from sure she had strength for the tapping. Her eyes stared at the tapestry adorning the wall, and the shadows flickering upon it from the fire in the hearth. It was warming up for spring, but a fire was laid every day in Chella's bed chamber; she was so often cold. "Let me see . . . if I can't make it . . ."

"Lady, no," said Feor, coming to his feet and holding out his hand in a gesture that was almost supplication. "You haven't the strength. Let me try."

"Perhaps he hasn't had time. Perhaps . . . it's not too late. Feor, bring me . . . my son."

This was a bad idea, Feor felt it in his bones, but could not ignore the pleading in the dying woman's eyes. He hesitated for a moment, then bowed, turning away and striding out of the chamber in search of Ansen.

He did not have to seek far. Ansen was on the lawn, standing on the stone circle where the Cerdiad bonfires were lit each year. Dressed in his customary black, his feet planted arrogantly apart, his hands folded behind his back, Ansen stood looking up at the house with an odd, crooked smile playing upon his lips. It widened as he saw Feor emerge and hovered for a moment on the edge of a sneer.

"I wondered," he said conversationally as the priest approached, "how long it was going to take you."

"Your lady mother wishes to see you," said Feor, refusing to rise to the bait.

"By all means," said Ansen, with exaggerated courtesy.

Feor walked a step behind him as they climbed the stairs, watching the almost jaunty step of the younger man with deepening misgivings. There was something here . . . but the mind was still closed, still obsidian, if anything harder than ever. Ansen was now close to seventeen; he was fully grown, and his mind had not been that of a child for years. At

Chella's door Feor had a sudden urge to leap into Ansen's path, forbid even at this late stage his audience with his mother—but even as he hesitated it was too late. Ansen crossed to the bed to lift one of his mother's limp, pale hands and kiss it ostentatiously.

"And how are you today, Mother?" he said. "I am told you sent for me."

"Sit down, Ansen." The voice was stronger, firmer, than it had been only a short while ago. Feor didn't know what she had done while he had been out of this room, but it had worked. "There is something," said Chella, her fingers tightening on her son's, "I have to ask you."

But Ansen had already decided a game of cat and mouse was not what he had in mind; the crudest thing to do, the thing that would best retaliate for the years of silence imposed upon him, would be to tell the bald, unvarnished truth.

"Yes," he said, "I know. But you won't like your answer. You see, I sent the letter to Miranei almost two weeks ago."

Chella's fragile strength shattered. Her fingers fell away nervelessly from Ansen's hand, and her face was once again a hectic scarlet blush. She tried to draw breath, and it came out as a dry, labored rattle. Feor sprang forward, pushing Ansen out of the way, hands that had once been a healer's already reaching for the woman who lay rigid.

"Get out," he said to Ansen, his voice cold. "Bring the healers, call your father. I will do what I can in the meantime." A beat later he looked up to see Ansen still frozen at the bedroom door. "Call your father," he repeated. "I hope you loved her at least that much."

Ansen's eye was very bright; it might have been tears, but Feor had no time for him. Ansen murmured something Feor only half heard—it might have been *I'm sorry*. But the time was past when a simple word of regret might have served to heal this kind of wound. In any event, he had vanished when Feor next spared a glance his way. But it was already too late. By the time he returned, with Lyme and the same plump healer who had kept the hard truth from Ansen almost three years ago, Chella was gone, beyond all Feor's efforts to save her.

And so had a treacherous letter, meticulously planned and dispatched. What years of peace and education Anghara had enjoyed were unequivocally and finally over. The hunt was closing in.

## 11

There was a family vault in the foothills behind Cascin, in the fork where three of the wells joined into one stream and went rushing down to the River Tanassa. They took Lady Chella there the day after she had breathed her last. There were few mourners: Lyme, speechless with his grief; Feor, gaunt and pale, standing very still with his hands tucked out of sight into his sleeves; one or two of the oldest servants, who had known Chella since she was a child. Her daughter was considered too young to attend, but the twins were there, Charo looking merely bewildered at the unseemly haste in which his mother had left him, Adamo with a deeper sadness in his eyes, a deeper understanding.

Ansen was not there.

It was a gap none could ignore; by his very absence, he was more firmly present than anyone there. There were those who knew where he had gone but did not wish to speak of it; there were those who did not know, but felt with a fine instinct that it would be better not to ask. Lyme himself looked as though his tongue kept on returning to probe an abscessed tooth; the grimaces of pain that crossed his face every now and again had little to do with the loss of his beloved lady. He was finding it hard to come to terms with the treachery of his eldest son.

Ansen had fled Cascin for more than one reason. When he had entered his mother's chambers to play his game, he had not dreamed it would kill her—he'd known she was ill, but not the extent of her weakness. Her death had hit him hard; the murder-guilt of what felt uncomfortably like matricide weighed on Ansen's shoulders. But that in itself was not enough to make him regret the actions leading to it. If guilt burned his soul, so did resentment, his need for revenge, the darkness that claimed half his sight, his devotion to a king called Sif. In his letter to the court of Miranei he had introduced himself as Ansen of Cascin, nephew by marriage to King Dynan and cousin to Anghara Kir Hama . . . who had spent several years in hiding in Cascin and was now safely in Castle Bresse. But there was a possibility the letter might never reach Sif's hands, some royal secretary might simply toss away a missive purporting to be a sighting of one known to have been buried in the family vault years ago. When Ansen saddled his bay and pointed him toward Miranei, his feelings may have been muddied and confused by his mother's death, but there was, nonetheless, a single burning imperative easily discernible through the chaos of his thoughts. *I must go to him and tell him . . . I must go to him myself.*

His horse cast a shoe in the middle of nowhere, when he was still more than two days' ride from Miranei. Ansen lost valuable time hunting for a smith, then chanced upon one who looked as though he had spent the last week carousing and was only now hitting the full stride of his hangover. The man's eyes were narrow and bloodshot, and he worked very slowly, as though he was infinitely fragile and an inadvertently hard tap of his hammer might shatter his broad, calloused fingers. Ansen could only stand and watch him, fretting uselessly over the hours slipping by.

With good reason, as it turned out. When he rode into Miranei, days later, sweaty and tired and his horse lathered with effort, he discovered Sif had already left the city to ride to an unspecified destination. It was a matter of considerable conjecture on the outskirts of Miranei that the direction he took had not been south, as might be expected, given the news of Tath and near-constant border skirmishes, but east.

The news greeted Ansen as he came wearily into the common room of a Miranei han. All he had wanted was to pass through on the way to his room, to try and find supper, a bath and a bed—whichever presented itself first—but he was brought up short by a stray tendril of conversation.

"Shaymir? What would the king want with Shaymir? It's Tath that's the troublemakers, anyone could tell you." The voice was scathing in its contempt.

"Perhaps he's gone to try and get them to help against Tath," someone else hazarded.

The first voice returned, preceded with a snort. "Shaymir? As allies? That's a nation of copper miners and pampered princelings, with nothing in between except a couple of crazies who live out in the desert and pretend to be Khelsie abominations. What would Roisinan want with the likes of them? What would the king want with them? One Sif is worth an army of Shaymir."

Ansen agreed with the principle, where Sif was concerned. He had misgivings, however, about the other's terse dismissal of Shaymir as a source of fighting men—he had sparred for years with Kieran, and there was nothing soft about him. An army of Kierans might well prove a formidable proposition. But Ansen knew Sif had not gone to Shaymir. There was more to the east of Miranei than the Brandar Pass. There was the river Rada; and beyond it, Castle Bresse.

For a moment he considered interjecting and telling the assembled company where Sif really was, and who had sent him there. But the knot of people on whom he'd been eavesdropping sat close together in a tight bunch and looked as if they would not welcome insolent intrusions from a stranger. Especially one claiming intimate knowledge of Sif Kir Hama's itinerary less than an hour after he'd ridden in from the nether regions of Roisinan. Instead, Ansen turned away in pursuit of his original goals. These had now assumed urgency; he would stay in Miranei only as long as it took him to give his exhausted horse a few hours' rest and to organize provisions for another journey. Then he would be out again, following Sif. It had been Ansen who had started this ball rolling; and Ansen meant to be at Sif's side when they brought Anghara to him. Only that, in his mind, would wash the guilt from him—it was not Ansen who had killed Chella of Cascin, it was Anghara! Only that would pay for his ruined sight. He paused to glance once more at the crowded common room. The stories he could tell! He'd have them all hanging on his every word . . . but there was no time. The han-keeper was at his elbow, and Ansen turned to pin him with a smouldering gaze from his one good eye.

"Supper in my room," he said crisply, "and a bath. Have someone tend my horse; I'll be leaving at sunrise tomorrow."

"But my lord said . . ." the han-keeper began, seeing his chance of profit slipping away.

"I changed my mind," said Ansen, turning away.

This particular han-keeper had not had many occasions for entertaining visiting nobility, his particular establishment being too far from the gentry's beaten path. That did not mean he could not recognize aristocratic arrogance when it was thrown in his face, and Ansen had more than his fair share. The han-keeper did not argue. He simply sketched the obeisance which seemed to be called for and departed to fulfill his orders.

Ansen was true to his word; the cook, who was the han-keeper's wife, had to be woken to prepare his breakfast in the morning, as Ansen was astir even before the hardworking han proprietors. It was still dark when he rode out, although the sky was beginning to brighten in the east. Ansen caught himself grinning like an idiot at one point, watching the slow birth of the sun, pinning down a stray thought like a talisman: *It's a good omen. I'm riding into the dawn.* The horse was fresh after a substantial feed and a night's rest, and Ansen made good time; but Sif still had a considerable head start. But soon they would meet, the acolyte and his hero, the knight and his king. Not that Ansen was a full knight, not yet, but others had been knighted for valorous deeds while they were still a few months' shy of their final coming of age. Ansen allowed himself to slip into a daydream, in which he knelt bareheaded before Sif and the king leaned forward, grasping Ansen's arm and bidding him rise . . . *Rise, my ally and my friend . . . Sir Ansen of*

*Cascin* . . . If Ansen still had two good eyes in this dream, he closed his mind to that. Anghara and Bresse were to be his price. After that . . . who knew but that miracles might still happen.

Sif and Ansen weren't the only ones heading to Bresse. Feor, driven by a sudden premonition of disaster, had packed a few meagre belongings, accepted Lyme's blessing and one of his horses, and was himself hurrying to the Sisters' castle. Cascin was considerably closer to Bresse than was Miranei; Feor had the shorter way to go, and should have been at Bresse long before any of the hunters. But his journey seemed to have been conceived under an unlucky star, and he met with delay after delay. All the while he tried to reach the white tower with a mind call, a warning of danger; but either he was getting old and his gift was fading fast or there was a cocoon of silence around Bresse he didn't know how to break. By the time he got to the village where March had made his home, he was drawn and exhausted—and March, from what he could gather when he inquired after him, was gone.

The village was far too small to rate a proper han, but Feor came to an agreement as to lodgings with the village miller. The miller provided his unexpected guest with a modest supper and a clean pallet before the fire. Feor wrapped himself in his blanket and tried to sleep, but a vision burned in his brain and would not leave him alone. There was a cloud before him, a black cloud, and many of his friends were either trapped inside or rushing toward it. Beyond that dark cloud Feor's Sight could not go, except in flashes that seemed to presage death and disaster, and perhaps a proud young king, drunk on power or victory, stabbing a shining sword into the black billows which hid the sky. Anghara was in this. March had gone rushing in. Sif was coming.

By morning, as merely the last in a long series of troubles, misfortunes and plain bad luck, Feor had developed a high fever and lay shivering on his pallet, almost incoherent. His host summoned the village healer, who prescribed a regimen of hot herb tea and complete bed rest. Feor was far too ill to protest; by the time he had come sufficiently to his senses, it was already too late.

The arrival of Sif and his entourage had reduced the hankeeper of Radas Han first to incoherence and then to stark silence. Sif had in effect taken the han over almost completely. Guests who were staying in parts he had not occupied quickly found that urgent business called them elsewhere. Sif was not pleasant company. Some of his men, grim-faced and well armed, had parted from the main body and commandeered two flat-boats, upon which they had drifted downstream on the Rada River. It was worth a man's life to ask where they were going, although there were rumors that one of the boatmen had overheard the name of Halas Han and, from thence, a place called Cascin. Sif selected patrols from those who remained; they came and went in shifts, departing mysteriously up the Rada toward the foothills and coming back when another had taken their place. There was nothing up there except Castle Bresse. That was hardly an object of siege to draw a king from a southern border beset with brewing war. People watched and wondered.

The rumor of Cascin had gone out, though, and it was this that greeted Ansen a day's ride from the han where Sif waited. Given the choice, Ansen would have ridden the entire distance right then, but he had already driven his horse hard that day, and his only reward for such an effort might have been a cold camp midway between two hans. He was close enough now, he could afford to take a brief rest. His faithful bay had foam around its muzzle and stood with its head drooping with exhaustion. Ansen had tossed the reins to a willing stable boy and strode into the common room of the village han, only to look around sharply as a familiar name caught his attention.

"Cascin, is it? Are ye sure?" The voice sounded uneasy. "I've got kin there; my sister married a good man, he was a wizard with horses, Lord Lyme took him on at Cascin a few years hence."

"Cascin they said, I'm positive," said another voice, more gravelly. Ansen focused on the speaker—a big man, broad shouldered, his face all but smothered in an explosion of red beard. He had brawny arms where corded muscles rippled like ropes; a river-man, gnarled and pickled by his trade. Ansen sidled closer. "I've been doing that run for years. That's where they were headed, and they didn't look like they were goin' for pleasure, either."

"How many?"

The river-man glanced down at his hands, his short fingers jerking resignedly once or twice. He was no scholar; Ansen had grown up on the river and had been in and out of Halas Han often enough to know his type.

"Dunno, for sure," the river-man said at length, after some deliberation. "More than ten."

Ansen, quite pale, moved away and gestured for wine. It occurred to him for the first time that his actions may have brought ruin on his house and family. Sif may not have taken kindly the news that Anghara had been sheltered in secret at Cascin. It was warm in the room, but Ansen shivered violently beneath his cloak. He was suddenly torn: home to Cascin, to see if there was something evil happening, or on, to Sif, to the fulfillment of his dream? There was no chance that going to Sif might also stop any planned act of retaliation on his behalf—orders had already been given, the soldiers, if this river-man's story was to be believed, already on the river. Riding cross-country at breakneck speed, Ansen might be able to forestall them . . . and then what? Would they stop if he stood before them and told them nay? The twins . . . his father . . . his little sister . . . the house that was his inheritance . . . had he gambled them all, and lost?

The night that Feor shook in his fever and Ansen agonized over his dwindling options also saw March take what was to be at once his first and final step into the black cloud Feor had foreseen for him. He had been to Bresse before—not so frequently as to cause comment, but often enough to satisfy himself of Anghara's continued well-being. He'd been there far too often for either comfort or safety during the last few weeks, as word of Sif and his foray started to filter through the village grapevines. His passionate pleas to both Lady Morgan and to Anghara herself seemed to be ineffectual.

Anghara, at least, had the sensitivity to fear Sif's anger, and suggested that the community relocate, at least temporarily, into the mountains. As far as Anghara knew, only Morgan and perhaps her second in command knew Brynna Kelen's true identity; it was hardly fair to throw every Sister in Bresse to the wolf who was coming for the changeling in their midst, of whom they had known nothing. But Morgan, with a strange, almost supernatural calm, had insisted the project in hand had to be completed. The two were working on an important and entirely esoteric purpose March was incapable of understanding, which seemed to render them, or at the very least Lady Morgan, completely unable to comprehend the danger looming for them all. What neither March nor Anghara realized was that Morgan had told the community of the real reason behind Sif's coming in good time, leaving the Sisters free to choose whether they wished to go or stay. Some of the younger novices, still ignorant of the truth, had been spirited away before Sif's arrival, but most of the Sisters turned down the chance to leave, aware of danger but refusing to confront it by fleeing their tower. For the ones who were ambivalent, it soon became obvious they had waited too long. By the time some thought to try and play it safe, to flee or retreat into the mountains, it was too late. Sif's patrols were already in position.

But there were some who wanted to go, and March snatched at the idea. "Would they take the princess with them?" he had asked of Morgan at their last meeting. His loyalties were still pledged first and foremost to Anghara and the true Kir Hama line; he was ready to do his utmost to help Bresse in any way he could, but only after he saw Anghara safe. March would have been willing to take any Sister who cared to go into the mountains and lead them through the back ways down into Shaymir. Perhaps the prince would offer them shelter there. But only if Anghara was with them, if Anghara was safely out of Bresse.

Morgan gazed at him steadily. "Nothing could get from here into the hills unobserved," she said. "Sif has learned from his captain's failure. The area between the tower and the mountains is the most heavily patrolled." She hesitated for a moment, then gave March a secret kept for many years. "There is a secret way. But it comes out close to the han, and that would be crawling with Sif's men. There also the patrols would be thick. And if they discovered a secret entrance into the tower . . ."

"I could take care of one patrol," March said. "Until the next one came, the path would be open. If any want to leave, I will help them. But I must try to get the princess out of here somehow. Kerun and Avanna! If Sif comes upon her penned in this place, you must know she would not live to see another day! And you . . . you would do well to consider going with them, lady. All of you. Sif will never forget what you have done."

"If there are those who would go, and if there is a chance for them to make it, I would be happy to see them succeed," said Morgan. "I will even make sure Anghara is with them. I know she can expect nothing but doom at Sif's hands; for him, she is already dead—did he not watch her laid in the family vault in Miranei years ago? If he were to kill her here it would be no more than putting the seal of truth onto something long accepted as fact. If you can get her safely away, you have my blessing. But as for myself . . . I stay."

This was why March was out alone on this moonless night, waiting for the patrol that had drawn the midnight shift. It was a last chance—let one patrol go missing, and Sif would react swiftly and violently. But if they could ensure Sif did not know of the patrolless shift until it was time for a changing of the guard, it might still be possible to evacuate into the mountains. March had been studying the pattern of the patrols since their inception; the guards were due to meet and change directly in front of the copse in which he crouched. March planned to eliminate the three who took over the new shift, quickly and as soundlessly as possible. Bresse would be waiting for his signal; it would be their last chance.

Except that Sif had made an unexpected change of plans.

When March saw the relief shift arrive with only two men, he had little time to think of anything other than that his task had been made easier. Perhaps it was this premature relief and the urgency to complete the unpalatable job—March had always been a soldier, a knight, never an assassin in the dark—which combined to make him careless. The arrival of a further two men, just as he was pulling his knife from between the ribs of his second victim, caught him completely unaware. He had no time to do anything but give a grunt of surprise—the hand which already held his bloodied knife made an instinctive motion of defense, but the small blade could not parry the downward swing of the bright sword already in the soldier's hand. It was over quickly. One of the men loped back the way he had come, to make a report and bring reinforcements; the one who had wielded the sword knelt in the grass and peered dispassionately into his victim's face, where life was fading quickly. The soldier bent forward when he thought the dying man whispered something, very softly, but he was too late; March was already gone. The words he had spoken hung in the air, unheard. *Rima . . . my queen . . . I could not save her . . .*

There was no signal to Bresse that night. Morgan, who had known there would not be, gathered the Sisters of Bresse into a last council. Anghara, who was not a part of this but who had known of March's plan, watched on the walls, alone, until dawn began to paint the mountains to the east pink and gold. When Morgan summoned her at last, she went slowly, almost in a daze, beginning to comprehend the only thing March's silence could mean. Her eyelids were swollen, her eyes bloodshot; she had never looked less like a princess, more like a child driven past the edge of endurance.

Morgan met her at the doorway of the white tower, arms tucked into wide sleeves in a characteristic gesture.

"There was no signal," Anghara said dully.

"I know," said Morgan. "Follow me, and do exactly what I say. Do you understand?"

"Yes, my lady." The voice that acquiesced to Morgan's command was flat, exhausted, almost automatic.

They went into the tower, Morgan unlocking a small door in the side of the spiral staircase, which Anghara had never seen open before. At first sight, what lay inside was no more than a small storage cellar, piled untidily with odds and ends, empty barrels, a clutch of bald brooms leaning drunkenly against one another in a cobwebbed corner. Morgan entered confidently, going straight to the far wall and pulling aside a massive barrel, with too great an ease for it ever to have been anything more than clever camouflage, to reveal a narrow doorway. Sturdy oak planks were set fast into the stone of the tower. Morgan produced two small keys, which had hung suspended on a cord inside her robe, fitting one into the hidden door. The key turned with a grinding protest; the door, heavy and solid, yielded to Morgan's hand and swung slowly inward. Darkness gaped inside. Morgan reached for a torch, which stood ready in a bracket just inside the door, and lit it. In the flickering light of the dancing flames another staircase was revealed, a twin to the one spiraling upward above their heads, this one twisting down into deeper darkness where shadows overwhelmed the insubstantial torch. The walls were raw stone, rough to the touch; the stair treads were dusty and looked old. Anghara stared into the dark depths, her eyes clouded.

"What is this place?"

"Follow me."

Morgan moved away, her white robe glimmering as though silver in the dim, reddish glow of torchlight. Beyond the narrow circle of light darkness encroached again. Anghara, who had stood unmoving, suddenly shuddered as the last of the light began to vanish round a bend in the twisting staircase, and hurried after it, keeping just a step away from the edge of the robe which swept the stairs in Morgan's wake. The Lady of Bresse walked in silence, making no move to acknowledge Anghara's presence.

The stairwell seemed endlless, but finally bottomed out in a landing of cold, damp flagstones. This was empty of everything except, almost incongruously, a small travelling pack and a folded cloak beside yet another locked door, this one small, round and stout, with bands of iron reinforcing the sturdy wood. It looked like an entrance to a mountain troll's den. Morgan produced the other key, twin to the one that had opened the door at the top of the staircase, and fitted it into the lock. Then she turned for the first time to look at Anghara, her eyes full of love and compassion.

"I would send half of Bresse with you if I thought it would help, but the presence of one of our own with you out there in the world might do far more harm than good. From here you walk on your own," Morgan said quietly. "This leads into a tunnel which comes out at the river, just above Radas Han. Be careful there, Sif's men might still be prowling around. After that, trust to water. If you will take my advice, seek a Sanctuary, and wait there until you are strong enough to claim your own."

"You're sending me away?" said Anghara, her voice muffled; her words an uncanny echo of the ones she had spoken in Cascin on the eve of her departure to come to Bresse. Was there never to be an end to running? "And what about Bresse? What about all of you? If Sif knows I'm here . . ."

"It's you he wants," said Morgan. "He will leave us alone. We have done nothing to him. And what he does here today will make it easier for you to return to Miranei. People will remember."

"He will . . . he will . . ." Anghara's agitation robbed her of words. She reached out with her mind, unravelling her thoughts too fast . . . the clearing by the water . . . the willows . . . the Stone . . .

The small dark antechamber exploded in a shower of sparks as the vision took her. Flame. Rivers of flame. Down the river, Cascin, the house waking to a dull gray morning with the promise of rain. Men coming up the long avenue from the gate, some with drawn swords, some with lit torches. The house was quiet. Too quiet. A male voice, too loud in the silence: "They're gone." A brawny hand round a torch. *Burn the place. Burn it.* Sif said. Sif said. And then . . .

the mind blurs . . . there's a protection on this place . . . pulsing blue light by the river . . . the soldiers stand, uneasy . . . one brings his torch down with an uncertain motion . . . the others seem to have forgotten why they have come. The rain comes down at last. The torches go out in a hiss of smoke. But in the minds of the soldiers as they turn to leave, bright and brave, a vision of a house in flames. Behind them, the house stands unharmed in the rain . . .

"This is happening . . ." Anghara heard a voice moan from a great distance. It sounded like her own. "Cascin . . . they went to burn Cascin . . ."

"You protected it." Another voice, familiar, far away. Morgan's arms around her. "You raised a Standing Stone in Cascin."

But the smoke was still there, billowing black and ominous. The vision was not done. Smoke . . . black smoke . . . black horse, man in bright armor, bare-headed, red-haired, bright sword in his hand . . . white tower . . . black smoke around a white tower . . . rising into the morning sky . . . voices . . . screams . . . *felt, unheard* . . . dying, dying, they were all dying . . . a solitary girl, watching from a distance . . .

Anghara struggled out from beneath the vivid pictures cascading and tumbling through her mind, gasping for breath, her eyes wide and wild. "He'll kill you! He'll kill you all!" she cried, finally able to interpret the vision she had never clearly understood before.

"He may," said Morgan calmly, her arms still around the younger girl, protecting, sharing strength.

Anghara raised wide gray eyes awash with tears. "He'll kill you all," she repeated with conviction. "And you . . . you're sending me away . . . I can't go, I can't leave you. None of them even know why! It's because of me . . ."

"They all know," said Morgan. "It will all have been for nothing if you do not leave. Everything has its appointed hour. That of Castle Bresse has come. And you, you must go out and keep the part of Bresse we have given you alive in the world. Dark days will come for our kind, and you will be their light, Bresse their beacon. But if you do not go, then darkness claims it all. Bresse has done its duty—the price was high, but it will be paid. I do not know what the price will be for you, but part of your debt is to keep the memory of this place alive when it is no more."

"You knew," said Anghara slowly. "You knew all the time."

"I have known for a long time that this would come," said Morgan.

"And still you took me . . ."

"I was in the path of the Gods," said Morgan. "So are you." She bent to plant a kiss of blessing on Anghara's brow, holding both the girl's hands between her own. "Go now, Queen of Roisinan. May the Gods watch over you."

"Morgan . . ." Anghara was not even aware she had omitted the honorific it had been second nature to use, but Morgan didn't fail to notice. She merely smiled and folded Anghara's cold fingers around the stem of the flickering torch. She lifted the pack she had prepared for her, shaking out the cloak and settling it around Anghara's rigid shoulders. It looked familiar; for a moment her mind was blank, then her hand brushed it and memory came flooding back. The cloak was Kieran's, the one she had worn when she had ridden into Bresse for the first time.

"Go," Morgan said, and the word was a command from Lady Morgan of Bresse to the youngest of her novices. "Go, and remember us."

Anghara obeyed as though in a dream, ducking through the low doorway. She heard it being closed and locked behind her. The tunnel before her was narrow and claustrophobic, but dry; the dust of many undisturbed years lay at her feet. Slowly, moving as if she were in pain, Anghara began to inch forward into the unknown.

Morgan climbed the twisting stairway in the dark, sure-footed as a cat. She stood for a long time on the top stair, looking down into the shadows from which she had just come with an odd expression on her face. This secret way was something each matriarch of Bresse bequeathed to her successor, along with the power to obliterate it. Morgan would be the last Lady of Bresse. After generations whose task had been to preserve, it fell to Morgan to be the one to destroy. With a soft prayer, Morgan reached for a stone in the lintel, which her predecessor had pointed out so many years ago. Her eyes were full of tears, but her hand was steady as she grasped the protruding stone and pulled it forward.

She only just had time to close and lock the door and haul the concealing barrel into place before she heard a muffled roar behind her as the secret staircase tumbled into ruin. She paused for a moment, sparing a thought for Anghara, to whom the noise must have sounded like the coming of doom. Then she took the cord which held the two now useless keys and dropped it behind one of the barrels before meticulously slapping telltale dust from the folds of her white robe and coming out into the tower proper, closing and locking the door of the "storage cellar" behind her. Even as she turned to leave, she heard the sonorous sound of steady blows upon the barred outer gate; and accompanying them, more an echo in her mind than sound that carried to her ears, a voice calling out:

"Open! Open in the name of the King!"

12

It was Sif himself who rode into the inner court of Castle
Bresse when they opened the doors to his knocking. He
wore armor, but no helmet, and his red-gold hair flew free in
the cool breeze drifting down from the hills. His sword was
naked in his hand, resting gently in the crook of his left arm;
above it, his eyes were two chips of blue ice. Sif was dangerous, bright, finally within reach of sitting unchallenged
on the ancient throne at Miranei. Feor would have recognized him easily, his Sighted vision cast in mortal flesh.

Morgan waited for him at the door of the white tower, her
hands tucked in her sleeves, completely calm in her knowledge of what was to come. She stood immobile, making Sif
come to her; and he did, stopping his great black war-horse
barely two paces away. His eyes bored into her and she met
them levelly, head held high. A slight shiver of light danced
down his blade—his hand may have trembled, perhaps—but
his voice was steady enough when he spoke.

"Give me what I seek," he said softly, pitching his voice
for her ears alone, "and I might forget where I found it."

"Bresse holds nothing that is yours, King Under the
Mountain," Morgan answered, using his ancient title. "We
can give you nothing. Not even absolution."

That struck home. The naked blade twitched as his hand
closed harder around it; his mouth thinned into an angry
line. "We can take by force what you choose to withhold,"
he said, and the voice was edged with threat. "I can order
this place taken apart stone by stone."

"You can," said Morgan, admitting to no more than the

king's undisputed ability to destroy Castle Bresse. "You will not find what you seek, and you will leave only rubble as your monument. People remember such monuments for a long time."

It had been a long while since anyone dared speak to Sif like this. His patience snapped at last, and the sword came arcing up from its resting place. Three men, summoned by the signal, immediately peeled away from the detachment waiting by the gate to gallop to his side. Two wore the insignia of a captain.

"Gar, Hury, take the sheds. I want every man to know this place better than the house of his birth by the time you're done. Insel, post a guard on the gate and on the postern—nothing leaves this place but that I hear of it." Sif sheathed his sword in a swift, violent motion and swung down from his horse. "Then get ten men and come with me. We'll take the tower."

Morgan simply stood aside and let him pass. If he had suspicions before that the searching would be in vain, they now coalesced into knowledge—Sif was suddenly utterly certain Anghara had been here, and just as certain she no longer was. There was something in Morgan's eyes, a telling glitter, which required no spoken word to let Sif know Morgan knew exactly what he was thinking. The perception that she was mocking him, letting him show off his empty power, suddenly unleashed a red rage in his brain. With his foot on the first step of the spiral staircase, Sif turned. "Insel!"

"Yes, my lord?" His captain, halfway across the yard already, turned in a fluid motion, alert, awaiting further orders.

"Bring all the women into the refectory. Everybody. Have a guard at the door until I can deal with them."

Insel sketched a salute and loped off to obey. Sif threw a challenging look at Morgan, but she merely smiled, bowed, and came toward the staircase with a graceful, gliding step.

"Where do you think you're going?" snapped Sif, goaded into ungraciousness.

"Following your orders," said Morgan gently, as though explaining something very complex to one too young to be expected to fully understand. "The refectory is just off the first landing."

She was making him feel like a child again, him, a crowned king. Sif turned and took the stairs two at a time, his fists tightly clenched underneath his royal cloak.

He and Insel searched the tower with a lot more force and roughness than strictly necessary, the men taking their cue from their king, who in his turn had given way to an impulse of angry destructiveness the white tower seemed to feed into a frenzy. There was nothing here of the barely concealed anxious fear the first expedition had shown, waiting to be stopped or crossed at any moment by invisible and potent forces of concentrated Sight. With Sif, fear had long been subsumed by his anger and loathing; he would have almost welcomed an intervention so he could pit himself against it, and win. But nothing stopped them, nothing stood in their way. The men's heavy booted tread echoed eerily in passageways which had never known anything but the gentle whisper of women's slippers; they kicked open doors, tore down curtains in alcoves, slashed at rugs to hammer bared floors for secret trapdoors or places of concealment. They turned Morgan's room upside down, leaving a mattress bleeding straw from savage sword-thrusts and naked windows with russet curtains pooling beneath them like blood.

The women penned in the refectory could hear the dull roar of the soldiers' passage through the kitchens; there was the occasional crash of shattering crockery or the metallic ring as a clutch of kitchen knives spilled against stone, the sound of cooking pots clanging hollowly on flagged floors. Men swept out the fires laid on the cooking hearths and climbed in to peer up into the chimneys, with spilled embers glowing dull red amidst pale ash on the scrubbed kitchen floor. By the muffled remarks which drifted through, someone had even speared the carcass of the calf they were to have butchered for tomorrow's supper. "Nobody hiding in here," a half-facetious voice was heard to say. At least one kitchen cat, by the sound of a pained and abruptly stilled yowl, met an untimely end. Some of the younger Sisters, now that the consequences of the choice they had made were beginning to be borne in upon them, were clinging to each other and crying, or simply sobbing softly on their own, hugging their shoulders with pale trembling hands, in fear and confusion. Morgan sat apart, erect and dignified, her hands folded in her lap. She looked as though she were praying.

At last the men had had enough. They were tired, hot and bad-tempered; they had spent hours on a futile search, which had turned up precisely nothing. Sif, his rage far from spent, called a halt. He was breathing hard, his eyes narrow slits of blue fire. Thwarted, by the Gods! Thwarted again by Sight, and the Sighted! The first slight he had risen above—Sight had not been enough to save Rima, after all, or prevent him from claiming a crown. It took a loyal army to do that, and to raise his own mother, who could have been queen but for Sight, into her own rightful place. But the child of Dynan's Sighted and lawfully wedded queen moved on paths eased by Sight, where Sif could not follow. Anghara, whose claim, by virtue of that Sight, was more valid by the laws of Gods and men than his own, had once again slipped through his fingers. And the women of Castle Bresse had done it—taken her, sheltered her, and then, in the instant before his nets closed, somehow set her free.

"Enough," Sif growled, deep in his throat, softly enough for Insel, the man closest to him, to turn his head sharply in his direction, unsure if his lord had just issued a command. Sif had not, but the movement drew his attention to the small knot of men surrounding him and something crystalized in his mind in that instant, a thought terrible in its clarity of purpose. He straightened, squaring his shoulders.

"Insel," he snapped, "torches."

When he flung open the door to the refectory, dishevelled and dusty but with a fierce glow of emotion wrapping him like a cloak, he stepped into a spreading pool of silence, with even the youngest Sister stilled by the sight of this avenging king.

He sought Morgan's eyes again. Somehow, it had become

personal. If he had planned murder, she had planned sacrifice; Sif knew, in a part of his mind that was still rational, that martyrs live forever, but he was too far gone to care that his hand was giving them eternal life.

"This place," he said in a voice which was steady with incandescent and savagely ridden rage, "has fostered treason against the Throne Under the Mountain—fosters it still, sheltering what the king seeks. So speak I, Sif Kir Hama, King of Roisinan. You forfeit your sanctuary, your status, and your lives. Castle Bresse dies today, and with it all that it stands for. My father's line has been royal—and human— for many years before the taint of Sight seeped into it. It was enough for Roisinan, once. It will be enough, again. I will rule human in Roisinan; when I am done, Sight will be a memory, a legend to frighten children. Sight dies, here, today, with you." He turned his head, gestured to Insel and Hury, the other captain, who were standing behind him with lit torches. The faces of the two men reflected their thoughts clearly—there was a sort of terror there, at Sif's sheer audacity and at the bloodthirstiness of his revenge; there was also a blind devotion. If Sif decreed death, they would deliver it.

"Bar the doors," said Sif in a voice made all the more terrifying by the very softness with which it unleashed catastrophe, "and put this place to the torch."

He strode out without looking back.

He had half expected cries to follow him, entreaties for mercy, for clemency, for pity. There was silence. Pleas might have swayed him, even then, in his extremity; but nothing came. Out on the cobbles of the inner yard, he paused, glancing over his shoulder, his face a rictus which was hard to read—his teeth bared in what might just as easily have been a feral smile as a snarl. One of his men ran past with a sketchy obeisance in his direction, arms full of kindling. Suddenly sick at heart, Sif turned away; but it was only a moment's weakness. He thought of Rima, and of his mother. Of the lives that could have been. Human. He was *human*. The witches had done enough.

The man who was king, mounting his restive horse in the yard of the castle he had condemned, closed his heart; his eyes as he turned the beast's head toward the gate were bleak, but hard. The decision had been made, and he would stand by it. Something changed in him in that instant, and the man he might have been was lost in the wind. He fully realized that what he did now at Bresse would haunt his reign until the day he died—and could not bring himself to care, if he could but achieve his goal of clearing Roisinan of the treacherous witchcraft which tainted his land's blood.

And yet . . . the first wisp of smoke came drifting out of the doorway of the white tower as Sif was riding away. There were no regrets in his mind, but his faithless body would never forget the acrid smell of the black fumes which curled around him to sting his nostrils and hang before his face like a curse.

Away on a hillside above the river a girl sank to her knees with a cry, the hood of her travelling cloak slipping back to reveal hair almost the precise shade of the man who had just passed the death sentence on Bresse. He could not hear them, but the voices of the women dying in the flames echoed in her mind, their death, however freely chosen it had been, a bitter reproach. It was darkness, something that descended on her and wrapped her like a skin; a sadness, a yearning, something that would always be a part of her. She lay as though lifeless on the ground, her eyes open but unseeing, her mind filled with the vision of the black smoke and the white tower crumbling, writhing, falling within it. Dying. Dying.

Feor felt it, deep in his fever, and called out incoherently, struggling to rise, his cheeks wet with tears. Along the length and breadth of Roisinan women with Sight crumbled into a black swoon. Some keened the death of sisters they had never met, tearing their hair and pouring ashes over their heads; others stood in silence, gazing unerringly in the direction in which Bresse lay from their own threshold, with welling eyes and tears which carved their passage down salt-stiff cheeks. They did not know yet of Sif's decree, and what it would mean to them. Instead they mourned the passing of something powerful and precious which would probably never come again in their lifetime.

Ansen, pale with the toll that his guilt at not running to Cascin's succour had exacted, had the misfortune to be waiting for Sif in the han when the king returned from Bresse. Sif's black mood upon his return could perhaps have been predicted, but Ansen had no way of doing so—as far as he knew Anghara was still at Bresse, and already captive. Not gifted with Sight, he had not felt Bresse's dying; he waited for Sif, torn between anxiety and excitement, ready to present himself as the man who had led the king to his quarry. He was a little nonplussed to see Sif riding in alone, unaccompanied by Anghara, but he had not paid much attention to the grimness on Sif's face, believing it to be merely the result of a distasteful campaign. He could not know, when he came to kneel before Sif and announce he was Ansen of Cascin, that Cascin was a name which could be counted on to prod the barely cool embers of Sif's passion and fury back into leaping flames.

Ansen had missed all the signals, but he could not fail to read the message written in Sif's eyes as the king looked down on the kneeling young lord at his feet. Far from the friendliness and joy Ansen had expected, Sif's cold gaze seemed to convey nothing but an ominous distance and cold loathing.

Sif never spoke a single word directly to Ansen. After that first baleful look, the king's eyes focused somewhere beyond Ansen's shoulder and he swung his cloak aside, almost as if he did not wish it to touch Ansen as he passed him by. "Confine him," was all he said, over his shoulder, to one of the captains who walked behind him.

"My lord . . ." Ansen called, aghast, as two brawny soldiers laid hands on him and hauled him upright. But he spoke to the king's retreating back. The captain gazed at Ansen with something resembling pity.

"You picked the wrong moment, lad," he said, in a voice that was almost friendly. "What possessed you to accost him

now, of all times? And just how in the world did you get past
the wretched guard anyway? I'll have to have a word with
the officer in charge before the king thinks of that. Come on,
me lad. With a bit of luck, my lord will have forgotten that
you . . ." But then his eyes clouded suddenly, and he lapsed
into silence. To Ansen, this was even more ominous. His
earnest request for information went unheeded. The captain
marched in silence beside the two men who half-led, half-
dragged Ansen between them toward a room with a stout
wooden door and sturdy iron lock. Then he simply turned
abruptly away to walk off in another direction with his head
bowed in what seemed to be troubled thought. Cascin's heir
was thrust, none too gently, into the room and the door
locked behind him. There was a window, but he discovered,
when he crossed to it almost automatically in what might
have been an instinctive urge to escape, that its wooden winter shutters were firmly locked and barred. He was a prisoner.

The injustice burned him all the more because he knew
Sif was a matter of a few rooms away, all the while unaware,
perhaps, of the truth of things. All right, so it had gone
badly; but surely he could not blame Ansen for that? It
looked as though they hadn't found Anghara, somehow she
had managed to get away. But if it hadn't been for Ansen, Sif
wouldn't have known where to look for his vanished half-
sister in the first place. Surely, once he'd had a chance to
cool down and think about it, he would send someone for
Ansen, to talk to him, perhaps to ask him if he had any idea
where she might have gone. Ansen sat bolt upright in the
room's only chair for hours, clutching its arms, waiting for
the sound of approaching footsteps—someone coming, at
the king's command, to set him free.

No one came.

Sleep eventually overcame him and he slept where he sat,
slumped uncomfortably in the rigid-backed chair, his hands
slipping off its rough arms to dangle limply just above the
rush-strewn floor.

It was, in the end, the sound of the key in the lock which
roused Ansen. The cold light of early morning was seeping

through the closed shutters, and at last somebody was at the door which stood between him and Sif's approbation. They had come for him. Ansen still believed with unshakeable faith that Sif had sent for him at last. He straightened his aching back with a soft groan, rubbing life back into his stiff shoulders; his muscles were tight and strained, his clothes rumpled, and, he thought as he rubbed a hand ruefully over his chin, it seemed as though he needed a shave. They simply had to let him have a few moments to make himself presentable for the king, he could hardly be expected to go into Sif's presence looking as he did.

"By your leave," he began, even as the door began opening, wincing as he stood on a foot where a fierce tingling was only now beginning to restore life to a limb numbed by a night's uncomfortable sleep, "I would appreciate a few moments to make myself a little more . . ."

The captain in the doorway, the same one who had escorted him here the previous night, stood watching him in silence, and the pity in his eyes stilled Ansen's words. Ansen swallowed convulsively.

"What is the king's will?" he managed to ask at last, through a throat tight with incipient panic.

"Eh, lad," said the captain, his voice oddly gentle. "Many died yesterday at his order. He was inured to death." He shook his head. "It was an ill fate that sent you to him yesterday, lad. I am sorry."

"What . . . what did he . . ."

"We leave for Miranei in a few hours," said the captain, his voice changing to the official tone, brisk and abrupt.

"We leave . . ." echoed Ansen, color flooding into his face at this restoration of hope.

The captain shook his head. "Nay, not you, lad. You'll be staying behind. You'll not be leaving this place again."

The color, quickly risen into Ansen's cheeks, fled just as quickly, leaving him white with shock. He was only just beginning to understand the depths of his folly. Swaying, he reached out behind him blindly and sagged very slowly back into his chair.

"You're to be hanged this morning," said the captain abruptly. He was all soldier now; his eyes veiled. Not for him to question his master's word. "Come with me."

"But . . . but . . . now? Right now?"

The captain nodded.

Ansen fought the urge to howl like a child. Inured to death . . . what had Sif been doing up at Castle Bresse? Just what had Ansen unleashed?

"Do you want a moment?" asked the captain, after a pause. The pity was back in his face. His thoughts were mirrored in his eyes. *He's so young . . . it's too cruel to tell a man he's to die just as he wakes from a night's sleep . . . and this one . . . he's just a boy . . . what could he have done that Sif destroys him this easily?*

Ansen could only nod, mute. The captain withdrew, shutting the door behind him. Ansen heard the lock snick home.

When they led him out, he walked with his back straight and his head held high, but his face was that of a boy being punished for a misdeed of which he has no knowledge. He raked the han anxiously with his good eye, hoping to see Sif somewhere, that the king's presence would lend dignity and pride to at least his death if not his life—but even this was denied him. The only witnesses, it seemed, were a kitchen maid who watched him pass with her eyes suddenly brimming with tears and the few soldiers who were the execution detail. They did not ask if he had a last request. He died early that morning, in silence—it seemed, in vain—just as the sun was beginning to pour itself upon the waters of the nearby river.

Perhaps the burden would have been lighter if he had known that Sif had indeed watched him walk to the tree, from one of whose sturdy branches they had hung the rope. Watched him walk every one of his last steps, and watched him raise his face to the sky only just beginning to be gilded by dawn.

"What was he, lord?" one of his captains asked as Sif turned away from the window.

"Nothing," he said abruptly.

Nothing, and yet everything. This was the death that paid for all the other deaths, the throttling of the snake which had poured the first poison. It was Ansen of Cascin who had set Sif on this path—his feet were now too firmly on it for him to turn back. But Ansen's death was almost an act of expiation for what he had done. It did not work—entirely. Sif would always be haunted by his actions at Bresse; Morgan had been right when she said the Sisters could not grant absolution. But Ansen was, in a strange way, a personification of the guilt Sif would never acknowledge again—would never think of without adding, silently, *I did what had to be done.* Killing Ansen was killing the guilt. What Sif felt when his eyes slid away from Ansen's dead body dangling from its tree was not the burden of another death upon his conscience, but a sense of peace.

The king's men rode away within the hour. The han was quiet for a brief while, and then life returned, like water pouring through a breached dyke. The gossip eddied in the common room, batted from one man to the next, wild stories growing wilder with every retelling; the king's visit soon assumed the status of a legend from another time. Now and then someone would glance outside where the body of the strange one-eyed young man had been taken down that morning, or fall silent remembering briefly the smoldering remains of Castle Bresse. But already the whole thing was almost a dream; when a slightly built young girl with dark circles under her gray eyes passed through like a shadow, most people paid her no mind, and nobody thought of her as someone who had lived the horrors and bore its tracks. She passed by, and was gone, into oblivion. Country life shook itself free of tragedy like a wet dog shedding water, and took up where it had left off.

Feor recovered slowly from his fever; when he felt strong enough to rise from his bed he made the short journey to where Castle Bresse had stood. It was almost enough to kill him. Not the journey itself—he weathered that well, with the miller's youngest son and a placid gray donkey along to help. But the blackened ruin that was Bresse was imbued with such a potent power that Feor came close to succumbing. Only the vivid life force of the boy and the tranquil living warmth of the donkey against which he leaned prevented him from accepting freely the death which hung around the Castle. For those who could hear, Morgan had left a message no edict of Sif's could ever erase: *We died here, the Sisterhood of Bresse, for the sin of Sight.*

"Are you all right, Master?" the miller's boy asked him with a careful, self-effacing wariness; there was something profoundly unnerving about this old man.

The youthful voice, waking echoes of other young voices which had crowded his schoolrooms over the years, made Feor draw back from the brink. He opened his eyes and managed to smile at the boy. "I will be," he said. "Will you take the donkey and wait for me, there in those trees? I need to be alone for a moment."

The boy did as he was told, with considerable alacrity.

Feor cast his mind into Sight, groping for trace of Anghara. If she had died here . . . but there was nothing of her, nothing except . . . very soft . . . beneath the words of Morgan's epitaph . . . *We died here, the Sisterhood of Bresse, for the sin of Sight . . . The young queen lives.*

The young queen lives.

Hope woke in Feor's breast. Perhaps March had managed a miracle and Anghara was safe somewhere, in hiding again, waiting.

He hobbled back down the hillside to where he had sent the boy; he found him pale and shivering outside the trees, keeping the body of the donkey between himself and the copse.

"What is it?" asked Feor, disturbed by the boy's face.

"There's a dead man in there," the miller's son said.

"Wait here," Feor said, picking up the skirts of his robe and turning to enter the copse. The thorns of a black premonition had already begun to prick the bright bloom of his hope.

The body was several days dead, buried cursorily under a shallow layer of soil beneath one of the trees. A hand encrusted with the black scab of dried blood had slipped free of concealment, with a strange pale band around one finger where a ring might once have lain. Feor knew the vanished ring: a signet bestowed by a queen of Roisinan on a faithful knight. Anghara might have escaped, but March was not with her. She was alive, but she was alone.

"Ask your father to have someone bury him decently," Feor said quietly to the boy when he came out of the copse. "He was a brave man."

He left the village that very day. The owner of the boat he took down the Rada toward Halas Han could have told him of a quiet girl who had asked for passage down-river only days before, a girl whom he had been obliged to point to another southbound boat leaving sooner than his own. But Feor did not ask, and the boatman had long ceased to give the solitary girl a second thought.

The first rumor that Cascin might have been razed to the ground reached Feor as he disembarked on the pier at Halas Han. It was immediately contradicted by another, quite at odds with the first, and then he heard a third, differing from both. It was obvious people didn't know what had happened at Cascin, and were loath to go and find out for fear of what they would discover. Someone recognized Feor as belonging to the Cascin household, and ventured to ask the truth of him. Feor told the questioner, rather more brusquely than he intended, that as far as he knew Cascin stood and lived as always; but the brusqueness was born of fear. He did not tarry at Halas Han, as he had planned, to rest bones which had suddenly grown old over the past week, but saddled his horse and rode at once toward the manor.

The house was ominously quiet as he approached it. Nothing stirred in the stables or the kitchen yard. The mansion itself was whole and unharmed, but it had an odd, derelict air, as though it had been abandoned for years.

Feor dismounted and crossed to the kitchen door, giving it a desultory push he did not expect to yield much reward. To his surprise, the door gave, and he stepped inside. The kitchen was clean, but cold and empty, with no fire on the cooking hearth, no stirring of steaming pots or bustle in the scullery. His heart like lead, he passed through and into the house proper. It had the echoing air of a mausoleum. There was dust on the usually gleaming wooden banisters. A striped cat usually confined to the kitchens darted warily across the hall into the dining chamber and seemed to be the only life stirring in this place.

"Sif," murmured Feor through bloodless lips, "Sif, what have you done?"

He turned on his heel, suddenly acutely aware of his solitude and aching to get to his horse again, to try and track down, if they were still alive, the family who once laughed and loved and lived in this place.

A tall youth wearing bright armor stood squarely in the arched doorway leading through to the kitchens, filling it with his presence, barring Feor's way.

His first stab of panic was replaced, almost instantly, by a rush of recognition and relief. Feor clutched at the banister of the main staircase for support, closing his eyes.

"Kieran! By all the Gods, Kieran!"

Kieran pushed back the cap of mail covering his head, releasing his familiar dark hair, and crossed the hall in two long strides to offer a strong arm in support. He noticed with some surprise that he was of a height, perhaps even marginally the taller, with Feor, whom he had always thought to be so tall. Feor clutched at his arm with long bony fingers which suddenly belonged on the hand of an old man.

"I was never so grateful to see a face in my life," said Feor. "Do you know what happened . . ."

"They are fine. The family is fine," Kieran hastened to reassure his old tutor, painfully aware of the naked need in a face which had always been so firmly controlled. "They fled when Sif's soldiers came, but they are all right. Adamo says the soldiers came to burn the house; he isn't sure what made them change their minds. They took the horses with them when they left, and killed most of the dogs. They aren't likely to come back, but Lord Lyme doesn't think it's safe to return just yet, and I agree. Where Ansen is, I don't know; nobody will speak of him."

"He went to Sif," said Feor. "I fear he may have met with a reception that was far from the one he imagined."

Kieran hesitated. "Is he . . ."

"He lost the eye," said Feor curtly. "And he went to Sif to exact a kind of revenge. He thought he might have the coin to buy Sif's favor—news of Anghara."

Kieran's fingers tightened on Feor's arm. "Is she all right?"

"She's alive," said Feor tiredly. "It's all I know."

"Where is she?"

Feor met Kieran's troubled eyes with a steady gaze. "I am too old a hunter," he said. "She's lost in the wilderness, in exile in her own land. She has been to the brink of death and survived, but Sif will not rest until he has taken her. You are all I can wield against the king, Kieran. You are the hawk I will loose to search for her."

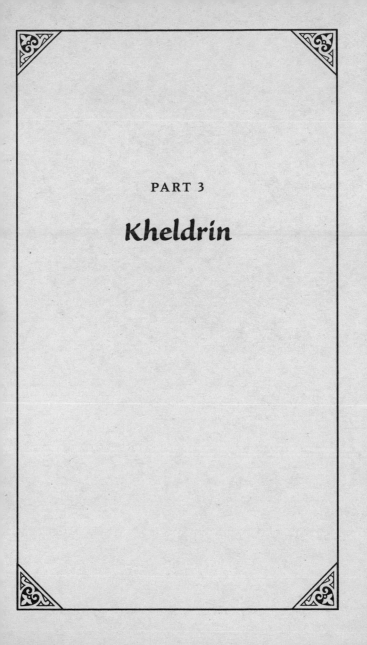

# PART 3

# *Kheldrin*

13

The only rumor which reached Anghara's ears when she had passed through Halas Han on her way down-river was that Cascin no longer existed. Both her visions of the fall of Bresse and the sparing of Cascin had been equally vivid; one had come to pass almost exactly as she had seen it happen in her mind. There was no reason not to trust the other. Cascin must be standing, and safe. But she paused a moment and cast a longing glance up the road which led across the bridge of Halas Han toward the house where she had spent what now seemed the golden days of her childhood. Even if Cascin was as it had always been, it was the one place Anghara could not go. Sif knew everything. He knew all about Cascin. It was no longer sanctuary—and, worse, it was entirely possible that even if it had been spared so far, Sif might decide to destroy it as he had Castle Bresse, for the simple reason of having given her safe haven. No, Morgan had been right. Her only chance was to seek Sanctuary with Nual, at least for another year or two. There was little a girl of fourteen could do to stand against a crowned king with loyal armies.

But Nual was a small God. There were temples to Kerun in nearly every village; and most people could find a Tower of Avanna somewhere within a day's ride of their home. Nual's Sanctuaries were scattered and few, and always on or near water. Anghara knew of only three. One was on the Mabin Islands, south of the Tath border, too far away to be of any practical use, even if it wasn't in what was technically enemy territory. Another was in Shaymir, near the source of the River Shay which fed their great lake. It could have been a good choice, if Anghara hadn't fled south and, more to the point, if she didn't have to creep almost under the shadow of Miranei to reach the Brandar Pass, which would itself doubtless be under guard. The alternative was making for the eastern passage and then having to face the length of the barren Shaymir plains or trying to trek through the mountains. Without friends or supplies such a venture would be doomed from the start. That left the third, on the promontory beyond the port of Calabra. It was a long way from Halas Han, just like the others, but it had the distinct advantage that it could be reached simply by keeping to the River Tanassa. All Anghara had to do was keep a low profile and catch the right river boats.

She boarded the first one at dawn of her second morning at the han. She had no way of knowing that Kieran, who had arrived late the previous evening, was asleep in a room in another wing, almost close enough for him to hear if she called his name. Feor was already on the river and due to arrive at the han the next day. Morgan had sent her off with a tidy sum of money which would be sufficient to keep her for a short while, as well as a little set of pipes she had been learning how to play. She would never be Keda, but her small talent at the pipes, together with the blessing of a good, clear soprano might prove a help in securing an occasional meal or lodgings until she could reach sanctuary. She was a vagabond queen, after all; it was not entirely inappropriate for her to sing for her supper. But she did not much feel like making music in the first few days after Bresse, and the boatman at Halas Han seemed content enough with her coin.

He did not go far, merely until the first landing in Bodmer Forest, where several stewards of forest holdings waited to pick up cargo bespoken from Halas Han. Anghara disembarked together with the bales, ignored by nearly everybody; she was the only thing left unclaimed on the pier when everyone had loaded their consignments onto carts and traps and trundled away on narrow forest roads. The home of the man who plied the ferry across the river and doubled as landing overseer could not be called a han, by any stretch of the imagination. But the ferryman's wife served a hot stew for which she would accept no payment and, seeing as there would be no boat down-river until the next day, allowed Anghara a small pallet by the hearth. She was a quiet woman, who did not ask where this strange solitary girl was going; but she did come out the next morning, wrapped in her faded shawl, and watched as Anghara boarded a narrow river-runner bound for Tanass Han. Anghara gave her a grateful smile for her unquestioning hospitality, and the tired face of the river woman was transformed as she smiled back and waved her on her way.

Anghara was one of two passengers on the boat, and had to share cabin quarters with what looked like a lapsed priest of Kerun. His hair was suspiciously coarsely chopped, as though his priest's braid had been hacked off not too long ago, with a rather blunt instrument. She tried keeping her distance with silence, but he became increasingly persistent in his attentions as the days wore on. She even went so far as to approach the skipper of the small boat, asking if there wasn't somewhere else she could sleep.

"Sorry, little love," he said apologetically. "If I had a spot to myself I'd offer it you, but there's three of us crew sleeping on top of each other as it is. And he paid his dues, just as you. But if he tries anything with you, you call me, you hear? I'll see that he stays decent."

"I'd almost rather take my chances with the crew," said Anghara, with some desperation.

The skipper grinned, showing teeth that were green with decay. "Believe me, little love, one or two of us crew aren't much of a substitute. I'm nice enough, but that Squint-eye . . . I wouldn't trust him closer'n an arm's length if I were you."

No sooner had he left her than the ex-priest was at her side in the prow. "Telling tales?"

"Just insurance," she said, looking at him coldly and stepping away.

"Now, don't be like that. We've still days to go before we

reach landing, and we've only each other to talk to. You can't seriously think you'd find more in common with that yob of a river rat than you would with me? I can see you've had something of an education, just by the way you speak . . ."

"Leave me alone!" cried Anghara. "I mean it! The last time someone tried to harm me or someone I loved I . . ." *I put one of his eyes out.* But she could hardly say that. For one thing, it was not something she was proud of; for another, the priest would probably laugh at her, in which case . . . she might well have to put her words to the test. Her eyes were hooded, opaque. "Leave me alone . . . or take your chances."

"Dangerous, are you?" he said, the tone of his voice mocking her dire implications, and laid a hot hand on her arm. He jerked it back in an instant, as though he had laid hold of a burning ember. "Ouch! What was that?"

The aura flared and died around Anghara's head, almost too fast for the priest to have seen it. She smiled at him coolly as he snatched up his hand to stare at his unmarked fingers.

"Just a sample," she said. "Stay away from me."

He did, for two nights; then the temptation proved too much for him. Anghara woke on the third night to feel trembling fingers fumbling with the laces at her throat. Her first impulse was to protect not herself, but the king's seal which she still wore beneath her bodice; as her eyes flew open she could only think of exposure for Dynan's daughter and not of profane fingers reaching to cup the curve of her breast. She cried out, lashing out with power that was barely controlled, even as she brought up her hands to physically ward off the assault. The lascivious priest only had time for a strangled yelp of surprise before he was flung away from her as though by a blow, colliding with the opposite wall with a thump and fetching up crumpled against the far side of the cabin.

The commotion brought the crew, one with a burning torch, the skipper with a drawn dagger glinting in the flickering light. He surveyed the scene with something like disgust, but he was not too far away from sympathy as he glanced at Anghara's fellow passenger, who lay groaning in a heap where he had fallen. His eyes glinted as he turned and took in Anghara's slender hands fumbling to retie the laces around her throat.

"What in the Nether Hell did she hit me with?" the priest kept on repeating, rubbing his tender jaw. At least one tooth appeared to be loose.

"Do I have to post a guard outside this place?" demanded the skipper gruffly, not in the best of tempers. "What'll it take for you to mind your own business? I run a river boat, not a whorehouse; the lady paid to be taken down-river, just as you, and she's under my protection as long as she's on this boat. So are you, so far; don't try any more tricks, else I withdraw it and dump you in the river to cool off. Am I making myself clear?"

"Very," muttered the other passenger venomously.

The skipper sheathed his dagger in the knife scabbard at his waist, which obviously never left his side, even when he was asleep. He crossed to where Anghara sat huddled in her cloak, wide-eyed, her hands still at her throat, and bent over her, reaching out to cup her face in one calloused hand—it was a gentle gesture, but not an entirely friendly one. The palm was too hot and damp on her skin. "I'll be just outside," he said, and the voice was caressing. He patted her cheek in a manner that was almost possessive, and went out, signalling with an abrupt jerk of his head for the other two to follow.

"Is that it? Are you his piece?" hissed the ex-priest from across the cabin, making no move to approach Anghara again.

She fought the impulse to scream she was no one's "piece" and simply lay back, wrapping herself into Kieran's cloak as though seeking strength. It was obvious this boat was no longer safe; she had taken it because it had been the first one leaving, but it had been a mistake. She needed the anonymity of crowds, not the concentrated attention she was getting in this situation. She would have to find a way to get off the boat, at the next stop for water, perhaps, and try to find alternative transport for the rest of the journey.

It wasn't going to be easy. The ex-priest left her alone in that he didn't try to lay hands on her again; but now the skipper made her the focus of his attention. It was becoming increasingly clear he could well succeed where the other had failed, if only because he was the absolute law on his boat and there would be no recourse to a higher authority. At the next forest pier, Anghara stepped off the boat and lost herself in the mercifully dense crowd. Three or four boats had arrived more or less simultaneously, some larger than her own and laden with cargo which was being briskly unloaded without regard to any kind of order. The result was considerable confusion as stewards squabbled over what belonged to which estate. Anghara made enquiries at the other boats, but as luck would have it every single one would be continuing upriver, of no use to her.

"There's another landing on the next bend," one of the skippers said to her. "It's quite busy; the next one down after that is Tanass Han, and there's always boats in and out of there. You don't like the look of yours for another day or two until Tanass, do you, eh?" He grinned, revealing teeth every bit as green as her own boat's captain. It might have been something they all chewed, because the man spat something green and noxious into the water. "I don't blame you, lass, the *Sanda*'s master's a shifty lot. What made you pick him?"

"But how can I get to the other landing without a boat?" asked Anghara, ducking the question by asking one of her own.

"It's not too far if you're not averse to a little walking," the captain said. "And you can always try and get a lift with one of them nobs, if they ever untangle themselves." He gave a gleeful chuckle; one could easily conclude that the chaotic unloading was not entirely by accident. The river men took amusement where they could, their sense of humor notoriously unpredictable. "I could fix that for you, if you like. I know one or two of them well."

But Anghara thought she had better arrange her own lifts. She was beginning to be wary of these river connections. If the captain intimated she might have something worth taking, it wasn't inconceivable that an outwardly upright steward of a noble estate might be persuaded to deliver his "passenger" into the hands of someone whose acquaintance he would later deny to his grave, for a share of the anticipated loot. Many noble houses were notoriously loath to provide a decent wage when it came to household staff.

As it happened, an elderly steward who had only two small bundles to collect had the room and the inclination to offer some of his extra space to a paying passenger. He was leaving almost immediately and Anghara managed to give her particular skipper the slip without too much trouble, especially as she was leaving him in possession of full fare for an incomplete journey. She paid her passage with the steward both with good coin and with the obligation to listen to his long and often rambling discourses and moans about his family and master, both of whom, it would seem, had a lot to answer for. The journey to the next landing wasn't long, but it seemed endless, and Anghara was profoundly grateful when she eventually reached the place. She scrambled down from her perch with her head aching violently, thanked her escort with as much graciousness as she could muster under the circumstances, and went down to the water.

For once, luck was with her. No less than three boats were leaving in the morning, and she could take her pick. On one she would have been the only passenger, but she had learned the senselessness of this the hard way. She opted instead for boatful of river farmers and their buxom wives, screaming children and squealing livestock in the shallow hold. Comfort was minimal, but it would do until Tanass Han, and if this was anything like Halas Han, she would have a rather larger choice when she got there.

"Where are you going on your own, and so young?" one of the farmers' wives, with a wriggling toddler on her lap, asked the next morning as Anghara took an empty seat next to her. The woman didn't mean to pry, but gossip was life's blood to the farm folk, and Anghara was a new face.

"To family," Anghara replied, rather rudely, but she really didn't want to be the object of too much curiosity.

But her companion would not be deterred. "Is it far?"

"A village, near Calabra," said Anghara, inventing. This was nothing new, she had already had at least two different lives. More, if she counted the tales she had spun while on this latest odyssey. Anyone trying to follow in her footsteps could hardly be blamed if he thought that not one, but at least five or six solitary girls had been seen travelling down-river, all going to different destinations.

The woman clicked her tongue against her teeth. "Far. Have you come a long way? Was there not someone who could come with you? Times are not as they once were; it can be dangerous now for a young child to travel alone."

Anghara could have answered that she'd already found that out, but bit her lip.

"Where do you come from, then? How come your parents allowed you to go alone like this?" persisted the young mother, bouncing her own progeny vigorously in her plump lap.

"My parents are dead," said Anghara, quite truthfully. "My father was killed in battle against Tath."

"Poor child," the woman said instantly, reaching to touch Anghara's cheek in compassion. "War. Leave it to men to mess things up. Look at what happened to you. I wonder how many other families . . . Is someone expecting you at Calabra?"

"Yes," said Anghara. That was a lie. But the woman swallowed truth with falsehood and made no distinction.

"They should have come to meet you," she said decisively, "at least as far as Tanass Han. It's criminal, letting a child travel by herself in these times. I've a good mind to ask my Rogan . . ."

Anghara made a mental note to get as lost as possible in Tanass Han, lest the woman ask "her Rogan" anything at all and Anghara find herself prisoner of these well-meaning people to whom meddling was in the blood. Quite aside from being found out in her lies, others might pick up the trail, and quite soon Sif's soldiers could be paying an unwelcome visit to Rogan and his family.

She managed to escape without major trouble, from Rogan as well as other familiar faces. One night she had a narrow squeak when she resorted to her pipes in one of the han's lesser common rooms and had to step out quickly when she recognized the skipper of the boat she had abandoned on the forest landing above Tanass Han. She waited until his boat had gone before emerging from hiding to try and find a boat to take her on to Calabra, finally trading one of Morgan's silver florins for passage on a large cargo vessel carrying skins and furs in addition to a handful of passengers.

She was wary of attracting attention by asking for a cabin for herself, although she ached for some time alone. The old woman she was sharing with had a passion for reading fortunes, and was appallingly bad at it; she read Anghara's palm and prophesied marriage within the year to a "nice young man with a bit of land—nothing too grand, mind, just a little plot." There would be five children . . . no, six. And as for her past, Anghara was cast as one of three children, her mother was a Shaymir woman, and she had lived all her life in Bodmer Forest, this being her first trip out into the world. The old lady even had the gall to foretell shipping disaster for the captain, who threatened, entirely good-naturedly, to have her thrown off his ship at the next landing. She was a nuisance and an old fraud but she was likeable enough. Even though she snored abominably at night, at least she was a safe travelling companion who often found business—and clientele—on other parts of the ship, thus affording Anghara some of the privacy she craved. Then, at least for a brief while, she could drop her guard and relax into being herself.

They were clear of the forest by now, and after a short stretch where the wide central plains of Roisinan spilled flat as a sheet on either side of the river, the land slowly changed. First it began folding itself into gentle hills, and Anghara could see occasional emerald squares of small vineyards on the slopes. Then the hills grew steeper as the river plunged into what was almost a shallow gorge. A few stretches of the river, foaming fast and treacherous with underwater rocks, were quite tricky to negotiate.

"I told him he'd have a disaster!" cackled Anghara's companion knowingly as she felt the boat lurch and thud against some invisible obstruction. The captain had little time for frivolity, having his hands full trying to get his boat through undamaged. It was a tense time for the crew, which could not help but spill onto the passengers, and when they came out into gentler country again, the river rolling silky and placid between low hillsides, it was as if everyone let out a collectively held breath. The captain steered his vessel into the next landing stage and decreed they would stay there that night and most of the next day.

"We'll leave tomorrow at midday," he said. "Take the chance to give your legs a good stretch. There are not many landings we can stop at between here and Calabra. It will be a long journey."

Anghara's cabin mate wrapped a knitted shawl around her head and stepped gleefully onto dry land as soon as she was given the chance.

"Don't really like boats," she confided in Anghara. "Never have. Unsafe things, boats. And they seem to have a nice little han here; maybe I'll set me up in a corner and tell a few nice fortunes, that will keep me in coppers until we get to Calabra." She patted Anghara on the arm. "You enjoy yourself. I heard one of the gents say there might be a dance later. It's not every day they get this many new faces. You enjoy yourself."

Anghara said she would, but stayed behind on the boat after her cabin mate had departed, staring first down the quiet river toward Calabra and then up at the dun-colored hills which embraced the few houses which had sprung up around the landing. The captain, emerging from his cabin not much later, found her standing alone on the prow of the boat.

"I was serious, take a walk on dry land," he said to Anghara, to whom he'd taken a paternal liking on the journey. "There's a Dance up on that hill," he added after a moment, following her gaze up the grassy slopes. The way he said the word made it patently obvious he was not talking about the same dance as the old lady. "You've plenty of time to go and see it if you like. It's probably the best-preserved one in Roisinan. I'd take you, but Gramin tells me we hit something up river and there might be a weakened strut or two in the belly of this beast. I'd better have that seen to before we go any further."

"Thank you, I will," said Anghara. She had not seen many true Standing Stones in her life, despite the ease with which she had "recognized" one in the pebble she had planted at Cascin. A dimple suddenly appeared on her cheek as she remembered her cabin mate's parting words as she'd hurried to the han where she meant to make her fortune. "You're the second person to tell me about dances since we got here. Old Selina just told me there might be one tonight in the han, the common-or-garden variety."

"Perhaps you ought to go," said the captain, smiling at her gently. "They're a pleasant clan out here, and they're said to be mean fiddlers. It might be fun for you young folk."

She almost didn't go to the village dance. Apart from one or two court balls, at which she had made a fleeting appearance before being bundled off into the royal nursery, and a few festivals in Cascin where she danced a simple step or two with Kieran or one of the twins, Anghara's experience of dancing was severely limited. Still, the distant sound of spirited music which drifted across the pier toward the boat soon proved too great a temptation.

Old Selina, safely ensconced on a chair near the hearth, spotted Anghara as she sidled into the common room of the han, and waved her over; the old lady's feet were tapping in time to the music, and her face was wreathed in a smile.

"You wouldn't believe it, looking at me now, but I used to be quite a dancer in my day," she said complacently. "Young men used to queue to dance with me. Why don't you join in?"

"I'm . . . not sure I know how . . ." said Anghara. She felt an unexpected reluctance all of a sudden, and only part of it was due to the prospect of making a complete fool of herself in front of all these strange people.

"Rubbish," said the old lady peremptorily. "Go on. You'll soon pick it up."

The crowd on the dance floor were involved in what was a complicated measure involving a large number of people dancing in a huge circle which seemed to wheel faster and faster as the music kept speeding up. Selina almost shoved Anghara toward the dance floor, and she staggered onto it to have the circle open up immediately and swallow her, each of her hands grabbed by dancers on either side of her without their missing a beat.

"I don't know how to do this!" she yelled apologetically to the young man to her left as she lurched into him, thinking the circle was moving in the opposite direction. He grinned good-naturedly.

"Just do what everyone else is doing!" he called back over the music and the high-pitched whoops of other dancers across the floor.

A couple of dancers, a girl from one side of the circle and a young man from the opposite end, seemed to drop spontaneously out of the circle and gravitate into the middle where they wove a short burst of an intricate dance pattern around one another before withdrawing back into the circle. Another pair followed them; then a third. The circle spun furiously, faster and faster, then the music swirled to an abrupt crescendo and ended on a prolonged wailing note as the sound of violins was allowed to die gradually away. There was a moment of silence and then everyone began clapping and shouting their approval at the small knot of musicians who had been precariously packed together on a raised podium above the dance floor. They smiled and nodded, bobbing their heads in pleased acknowledgment.

"You did quite well," Anghara's neighbor said, a few decibels lower now that the music had given him a lull of relative silence, with another slow smile. "You're from the boat, aren't you? Bound for Calabra?"

"Yes," said Anghara warily.

"Well, you don't do a bad roundel for an outsider. My name's Brem, my father owns the han. Are you from Calabra, or up country?"

"From the mountains," said Anghara, and fought down a sudden lump that rose in her throat at this reply. She was far from the mountains now; the Gods alone knew when she would see them again. Brem's words had invited her own name in exchange and she hesitated, if only briefly, between giving her alter ego or her true name. But caution had been bred into her too deeply by this stage. Granted, Sif must know all about Brynna Kelen by now, but it was still safer than announcing a solitary traveller who bore a royal name. "I'm Brynna."

"They're going to play something simpler now," said Brem. "Will you dance with me?"

Anghara blushed violently. "I really don't know how . . ."

"That's what you said just now, and you did fine. But it's easy, I'll teach you. There they go, come on. Give me your hand."

They stumbled about for a bit, but he was so nice about all her mortifying blunders she could not help but laugh at herself and by the end of the tune she was doing passably well. Better, it seemed, than one of the fiddlers, who was good enough to cover his occasional slip-ups but not entirely good enough to stop making them. He kept on wincing and offering apologetic little smiles in the general direction of the dancers; but, much like Brem with Brynna, they seemed to be taking it in good part.

"He's been co-opted," Brem felt impelled to explain to Anghara, defensive of the honor of his clan, as he whirled her around. "He's not a regular member of the group, and they didn't have time to practice before tonight. But my mother just doesn't seem to be able to play any more. Not since . . ."

His face was suddenly bleak. Anghara knew that good manners mandated changing the subject, but there was something about his words that struck a cold chill of premonition into her.

"Your mother is ill?" Anghara asked carefully, keeping her voice sympathetic but neutral.

There were three of them, apparently, in this small village who were similarly afflicted—all their Sighted women. They had simply collapsed one day, fainting clean away, and they hadn't been themselves since. Brem's mother had walked around like a wraith for days. One of the other two had still not left her bed. And the day . . . the day was the same day on which Bresse had perished under the hammer of Sif's wrath.

The echo of the tower's dying, which Anghara had needed to smother away under a layer of practicality necessary to survive her river journey, was a familiar specter which now suddenly rose bleakly to haunt Anghara once again. *How could I? How could I come dancing? And they less than a month dead?*

The vivacious spirits of a fourteen-year-old who had only just begun to find delight in her first dance faded as though they had been so much vapor. Brem's dance partner metamorphosed in his arms from a bright-eyed, pretty young girl to someone who suddenly withdrew deep into herself, retreating into the impregnable walls of some private castle, pulling up the drawbridge behind her. Brem, bewildered and full of completely unjustified self-reproach, did his utmost to try and repair the damage, but it was a task far beyond his powers. Anghara would not dance again, and when he left her to run and bring her a mug of elderberry wine she slipped out of the hall and into the night, in desperate need of solitude and darkness.

A few whispering, giggling couples had crept outside as well, to take advantage of the cold brilliance of the full moon hanging low in the sky like a gold coin. Anghara avoided them, detouring round to the pier where her boat was tied. Within reach of the boat, hanging back in the shadows, two things made her suddenly pause in her intent to gain her cabin. One was the unmistakable figure of old Selina stepping on board. The other was the captain who, after having helped the old lady on, stood squarely in Anghara's path, talking with a group of his crewmen and another man who, by the size of him, could only have been the vil-

lage smith. Anghara would have to pass by this handful of
men, and quite possibly have to answer the captain's well-
meaning queries as to why she had left the dance so early.
Then, in her cabin, she would have to endure Selina's questioning until the old lady fell asleep—which, given her gar-
rulous curiosity and the impossibility of it being satisfied by
Anghara's inadequate explanations, could prove to be uncomfortably long.

She hesitated, biting her lip, her eyes welling with tears
she could not hold back. Through the sudden veil of tears the
moon blurred into shapelessness, the sharp shadows it cast
vanishing into trembling darkness. Turning away and blinking rapidly several times to clear her sight, Anghara found
herself looking straight into the black silhouettes of the hills.

The other Dance.

Part of her mind told her she was insane to even think
about negotiating an unknown hill path alone in the darkness, not knowing what she would find at the other end. Another part knew, with equal conviction, that her grip on her
reason depended on finding the Dance this very night. Pit-
ting herself against physical darkness, and winning, would
be the only thing that would bar the flooding of that other,
more dangerous darkness of her soul.

Pulling Kieran's cloak closer around her against the
evening chill, Anghara resolutely turned her back on the
boat and struck out on her own on the pale, glimmering road
which led up into the hills. The illuminated han, the bobbing
lights of the boat reflected on the water, everything faded
from her mind as though it had never been; every step she
made took her deeper into a trembling vision, weaving her
into the hillside and moonlight, taking her further and further from the world of the common man and, once again,
into the paths of the Gods.

14

She opened her eyes to light. The sun was slanting oddly, too gold; this was not morning. Anghara sat up, jolted fully awake, and rubbed her eyes, looking around her.

The Dance of the Tanassa Hills rose up above and around her, the stones glowing in the sunlight with a pale, golden gleam. She was quite alone, and had been curled up, wrapped tightly in Kieran's cloak, in a bracken-filled hollow by a fallen lintel, one of only two which had succumbed to the hollow tooth of time and toppled to mar the perfection of the Dance. She could pin down fleeting fragments of dreams, never enough to make an entire and coherent picture—but how could she have allowed herself to fall asleep? How long had she been here? Slowly, the memory of last night came trickling back, so tangled with dreams and visions that Anghara had to fight to separate truth from fantasy, if indeed the division existed. The memories were oddly fragile—brittle, delicate things with wings like butterflies, they fluttered in her mind, uneasy, yet with a sort of preternatural clarity of recall.

She had climbed steadily, smoothly, as though she had known this particular hill path all her life. There was nothing around her except the whisper of wild grasses in the breeze and soft white moonlight pouring over the hillside; in that silent night she was the only thing that moved. Her sense of time fell away from her, pulled back into the human world she left behind and of which it was such a fundamental part—but she had no need of it, not up here. She fell into the rhythm of her stride, and after a while could not have said if she had been climbing for minutes or for hours. And then, very suddenly, the hill flattened out into a level space, and the Dance was there, ghostly in the white light.

Anghara felt her hackles rise as she stepped into the circle, under a massive archway with the great lintel stone spanning the two uprights far above her head. There was an ancient power here, a power which sang to her—something achingly familiar in its sense of strength and of danger, a feeling she knew very well, having wrestled with it at Bresse for long months. She had never been this close to a true Standing Stone before, but she had known instinctively what they were like when she had plucked a pebble from Cascin's well and named its nature. Her own little stone had defied her, giving visions where she had sought only inner peace—but there was something here in the Dance which she could learn, could master. It was far more ancient, perhaps, than the Sight which was in her blood but the old magic called to it in a language which she could almost—almost—understand . . .

Again, time slipped from her like a discarded cloak. She sat touching eternity, her back against the cool stone of one of the uprights and her knees drawn up into the circle of her arms, and simply stared wide-eyed into the empty circle flooded with light.

There were things there which perhaps only she could have seen—and accepted without courting madness; the wraiths of the dead whom she had loved rose to speak with her. Morgan, with her strength and her gentle smile, Morgan with the message she had left in Bresse and which Feor had already discovered: *The young queen lives—that's you, my child; one day you will return to Miranei, and it will be yours again.* And Anghara, still bowed under the agony of her betrayal that night, would have cried out—*Already, already I have forgotten you!* The touch of the night breeze on Anghara's cheek might have been Morgan's fingers: *They all chose to stay in the end, knowing everything, and none need be on your conscience.* Morgan had never said these words, but her spirit was saying them now, giving her young queen the absolution she had withheld from Sif. *There was nothing you could have done, except die with us. Live for us instead, Anghara.* March, sturdy and dependable, turning to what was still a little girl—ah, but it wasn't so long ago— soon after their arrival in Cascin: *Remember this place. This is where I will leave the second copy of the document witnessing your coronation. One day this will take you back to your throne.* Rima, smiling through tears in the throne room of Miranei: *They will remember this.* Her father, Red Dynan of the battles—a true wraith, wordless, passing by with a distant smile and a gentle touch on her hair with the calloused sword hand of a warrior king. Ansen . . . can he be dead? . . . Ansen, an angry boy stepping forth from his concealing shrubbery, impatient and brusque with the interloper who had wrecked the shot which was to prove his superiority over his foster brother . . . Ansen slumped unconscious, with rich blood welling through the fingers of the hand over his eye . . . Ansen, hands bound, glancing up with pride and pain at the sky gleaming with dawn, and in the background, ominous, the shadow of a swinging rope that was waiting . . .

And then others crowded in, the living, visions of things which she knew as true deep down in her bones but which had played out far away from her, visions running down one another like water . . . *Sight dies here, today, with you*—Sif's rigid shoulders, then only the icy blue eyes . . . *I will rule human in Roisinan* . . . Kieran, no longer the boy she remembered, kneeling breathless in a trampled, bloody field with the hood of a chain-mail shirt thrust back and his head held high—the bright flash of a descending sword . . . Anghara cried out, flinging an arm out in an impotent attempt to shield him from the death which was plunging toward him, but the sword landed gently, on his mailed shoulder . . . *Rise . . . be a valiant knight, Kieran of Shaymir . . .* but Kieran's eyes were suddenly troubled, and the voice he was listening to was different, familiar, old: *I am too old . . . you are the hawk I will loose to look for her . . . you are all I have . . . you are all I have . . .*

Anghara could remember, through all this, the moon sailing with graceful purpose across the sky which showed the stars of midnight and then, slowly, those of morning. It was not quite dawn yet when her eyes closed in what was utter exhaustion, both of body and of spirit, but a pale golden glow was stirring in the east, and the morning star was bright above her.

And now the morning was done, and afternoon shadows lengthened on the grass.

Anghara scrambled to her feet with a sudden muffled cry. The boat—when did the captain say they were leaving? How long did she spend up here? How long would it take her to get down? Would they even notice she was missing?

Most of the river was hidden from this hilltop by the fold of the hills, but a snatch was visible, gleaming bright gold in the sunshine. Anghara peered at it, shielding her eyes with her hand—was that black speck a boat which had left without her? But it was too far, and the sun was too bright, making her eyes water even as she gazed.

"Oh, dear Gods . . ." she moaned softly, aloud, as she shook out her rumpled cloak and lifted her hands to her tangled hair even as she took the first rapid steps toward the road which led down to the village. And then she froze, feeling eyes upon her back, acutely aware that she was no longer alone. Her heart climbed into her mouth—this, after all, was a Dance of Standing Stones where only hours before ghosts had walked in the moonlight. Letting her hands drop to her sides, very slowly, she turned her head and scanned the empty archways. Nothing. And yet . . . The power stirred in her, unsummoned, the faintest nimbus of gold haloing her head.

"Peace," said a strange, low voice. "I mean you no harm."

She could have sworn there had been nobody underneath the arches at her back when she'd looked moments before, but there was now—a slight figure, shrouded in a dusty, dark cloak which seemed at least three sizes too big, its face hidden behind a white mask. Anghara knew such masks; beggars with disfiguring disabilities or scars used them sometimes on city streets, to spare the sensibilities of those of whom they begged a few coppers for their next meal. They were far more common in the south than they were in Miranei, but there had been enough for the young princess to notice them. This particular mask had its eye slits filled in with white clay; this beggar was blind.

A blind beggar? Alone on a hilltop, in a ruined Dance?

"Who are you?" said Anghara, in a voice which was commendably steady given the rapid beating of her heart. There was something uncanny about the cloaked figure—as though it had truly been dreamt into existence, a product of Anghara's own visions of last night. "How did you get here?" she asked, after a barely perceptible hesitation. There was a lot of courage in the question. Some things one had to ask; this did not necessarily mean one wanted an answer.

The woman reached with uncanny accuracy for a white staff which leaned against the closest upright. "I walked, of course," she said matter-of-factly, as though the very question was absurd; Anghara thought she might even have smiled beneath the white mask. The mask was turned in Anghara's direction, and she was uncomfortably aware of a piercing scrutiny which should have been entirely impossible. "I watched you, and over you, last night, this morning," the beggar said, her voice oddly foreign in its accent and cadences, in the choice and order of words. "There are few in this land who would willingly spend a night in this place."

This was true. The builders of the Dances were long forgotten in Roisinan, as were the original purposes of their handiwork—what was left were the dregs of power, strong enough to touch someone far less sensitive than Anghara, and the rumors of old magic, blood magic, practiced upon these ancient stones after nightfall by those who invoked the dark and hungry aspects of the Elder Gods. While many Roisinani would come to see a Dance in the bright light of day, none walked willingly under the shadows of the Stones after sunset—some of those who had tried had been found dead or mad with unspeakable fear.

If she had not been in the grip of something far stronger than herself, it was doubtful if even Anghara, doubly armed

with Sight and the ancient royal blood which bound her to
her land, would have considered spending the night here
alone. By her own admission, the blind woman had not only
done so as well, keeping the same vigil as Anghara, but she
had also had the presence of mind to "watch over" Roisinan's lost princess as she wrestled with her visions.

Anghara felt for a brief moment like a vessel filling with
light, on the verge of understanding—the Gods who had
driven her here last night . . . was it for this? Then it faded,
leaving her empty and frightened and very much aware of
every one of her fourteen years—too short a lifetime for all
that had befallen her. If she'd had the life she should have
had, if the arrow hadn't taken her father and her father's son
had not slain Rima of the Wells on his road to power, Anghara would have been waking this morning in her own bed
in Miranei to light and laughter, a few more years of un-
clouded and sheltered childhood behind the impregnable
battlements of her father's castle . . . but Sif walked those
battlements now, death in his eyes, and the beautiful fantasy
shattered even as her thought lingered lovingly on it. That
was all gone, vanished, torn from her. Her childhood was
here and now, facing the unknown in a ring of power raised
by hands which had been dust and ashes for a thousand
years.

*This land.* The slender form, the foreign voice. *This land.*

Once, a long time ago, a man from the desert country of
Kheldrin had come to Miranei, bringing four matched
dun'en to the king—worth a king's ransom, the dark, glossy
horses of the desert, with their grace and power and the spirit
of the open desert in their eyes. Anghara had been barely
five years old—old enough to feel the electric excitement
the arrival of the animals and their handler had produced in
Miranei's halls. She had wheedled, cajoled, and finally commanded her nurse from the full height of her rank to take her
to the stables.

She would never forget the first sight of them, their gleaming coats and slender legs which looked infinitely fragile, as
though made of glass. Beside a desert dun, all other horses

were heavy, awkward and clumsy. Dynan's great stallion, his head poked out of his stall, was snorting furiously as though in derision at these new inhabitants of the stables he ruled. But he was vanquished at the start, nothing but a great lumbering brute next to creatures who looked as though they had been dreamed up in a bard's vision.

Now, on a hilltop above the River Tanassa, the memory came flooding back to Dynan's daughter. Not because of the horses, although it lingered on them with a delight undimmed by the years, but because of the man who had been standing at the head of one of the beasts—the man who had brought them all the way from their desert home. He had been small-boned, slender, his head barely reaching Dynan's shoulder. His skin was a deep bronze and his hair, straight and worn long, sprang from high on his forehead and was the color of beaten copper. There was nothing on his face that was not found on the face of any man—but every feature was achingly different. His chin was too pointed, his mouth thin-lipped, narrow, folded into itself; his nose impossibly narrow and sharp, nostrils mere slits, and his profile was almost a straight line down from his prominent forehead. His eyes were a dull gold, with black pupils huge in what must have been dim mountain light after his desert sun.

*This land.*

The rest could all mean nothing—there were wasted old women enough in Roisinan who would have looked no different from the beggar woman who stood before Anghara if wrapped into the beggar's shapeless cloak and muffled into anonymity behind the white mask. But the voice was not of Roisinan, had never been, and neither was the courage to brave a nightfall in the presence of Standing Stones. Anghara suddenly knew beyond any doubt that what lay behind the concealing mask was the bronze skin and cat-like eyes of a woman of the desert country.

"Kheldrin," she said, out loud.

For a moment the woman—whatever she was, she was almost certainly no beggar—seemed startled by the name, blurted so abruptly; then she bowed her head slightly in acknowledgment. Anghara once again heard a hidden smile in her voice as she spoke.

"Yes. I am of Kheldrin."

"Here?"

It was a thoroughly incoherent way to ask a dozen questions which milled in Anghara's head.

"You are surprised?"

"Yes!" That was torn from her. "I have lived all my life in this country, and have only ever seen one . . . and that was with the horses . . ."

"Dun'en. Yes. Sometimes we travel with them. But I am no horse trader."

Anghara felt oddly chastened. She fought to collect her thoughts. When she spoke again, it was as a Kir Hama princess. "Your kind . . . are not common in this land." This land. Now the phrase had popped naturally into her own mouth. And then the child which that princess still was, the impatient child who had too many questions and too few words to ask them, spoke again. "I know that people don't . . . I mean, that Khelsies . . ."

The moment the word slipped out she would have given worlds to unsay it. That was what the frightened and the prejudiced called the people out of the desert, odd and shocking in their differences. She had heard it a hundred times, always denigratory, slighting, insulting—Khelsie, Khelsie abomination. And now she had flung it, without meaning to, without thinking . . .

But the Kheldrini woman merely gave a small nod. "Yes. I know. You do not expect to find one of us this deep in your land, alone. But this is not the first time I have been deep in Sheriha'drin."

"Sheriha'drin?" echoed Anghara, distracted by the name.

"That is what we name your country in our tongue, Sheriha'drin, River Land, Land of Running Water. There are things here which are meaningful for us; and many things that are holy."

"Holy? To you?"

"If nothing else, then the water alone," said the Kheldrini woman softly. "There is no water that is not holy to us; every one of your rivers and lakes is a place of worship. Your people have never understood us—and never trusted us, unless for simple trade. We have many things they covet, and they are happy to give us grain in exchange for our horses, or jin'aaz silk. But often there are times when some of us must come—call it a pilgrimage—and when we do we come as shadows, and you never know. But I have been as far as the river you call the Rada, and never has a Sheriha'drini eye seen me pass." She reached up to the mask and took it down, very slowly, with the measured and deliberate dignity of a queen. "Until now."

She was old; that was the first thing to strike Anghara as she gazed at the face thus revealed. The bronze skin had darkened to chestnut, a deep golden brown, and her hair was no longer copper but a palely gleaming silvery-white. Her eyes were filmed over with white, with no iris and no pupil, and yet they were resting on Anghara with sight which was all the more compelling because it was so patently not of the physical world.

"My name is ai'Jihaar ma'Hariff," the unmasked woman said. Her words were simple, but her tone was high pride, and Anghara had no doubt that in Kheldrin the name meant something. Here, in the land she had named Sheriha'drin, the words were just words—except that a great trust had been shown by the very fact that ai'Jihaar had chosen to unveil both her nature and her name to one who had still not returned the honor. And there would be no half-truths here, no Brynna Kelen could stand before this scrutiny. Anghara drew a deep breath.

"I am Anghara Kir Hama of Miranei," she said, taking her name back for the first time in years. Her heart leapt to hear it.

"Kir Hama is a royal name," said ai'Jihaar. "And you are very far from Miranei."

"My mother was Rima of the Wells; my father Dynan, King Under the Mountain," said Anghara, in response to the

questions which had been so skillfully disguised as simple
statements. "He fell in battle, and the son he begot in his
youth seized the throne. He reigns now in Miranei." It was
bitter, this confession, her vulnerability and helplessness exposed for all eyes to see—especially these eyes, so penetrat-
ing, so swift to understand.

"Against your law."

"Sif is king. He *is* the law."

"And you are the terror that stands between him and true
kingship, the thorn of unease lying deep in the heart of his
reign."

The words had the lilt and the cadence of a bard's chant,
hard truths wrapped in the velvet of metaphor and poetry.
Anghara shivered at them, but stood silent.

"How is it that you live, and are free?" asked ai'Jihaar unexpectedly.

That lanced at pitiless memories, and drew blood. It was
a moment before she could speak. "They hid me from him.
And every place that hid me has had to pay for that sin."

"Where are you headed now?" asked the Kheldrini
woman, unexpectedly gently. The tone of her voice made the
question one of concern, not mere prying.

"Calabra," said Anghara, "and Sanctuary, with Nual." She
turned her head almost instinctively to peer again at the visible snatch of river, still golden in the sun.

"They have gone, your companions," said ai'Jihaar with a
precision that was eerie—it was as though she saw Anghara's gesture and responded to it, as any ordinary person
would do, despite her handicap. "They came here to look for
you, but it was as if they were unable to see where you lay."

Anghara's head whipped around again. "You were here?"

"Yes."

"You could have shown them, then . . ."

"No," said ai'Jihaar regretfully, shaking her head. "Not
without revealing myself. And let them see me here I could
not." Again, the oddness of her speech, the strange order of
her words, the inescapable sense that this creature had come
from elsewhere . . .

"But you showed yourself to me," said Anghara slowly.

"I," said ai'Jihaar enigmatically, "have my own Gods. And, if you will recall, I had little choice at the last. To reveal my presence to one who obviously already knew I was there would be breaking no rules." She paused to fit the white mask back on her face. "I am bound for Calabra," she said, once again in that matter-of-fact voice with which she had answered Anghara's first question. "If you would come with me, you are welcome."

Anghara spared another brief cheerless glance for the river, blazing more golden than ever. "I cannot take another boat," she murmured, "all I owned in the world was on that one, and I do not know what became of it. I will walk with you."

It was rather a graceless acceptance, but ai'Jihaar merely nodded with a degree of rather unsettling complacency, as though this had all been meticulously planned months ago, and the meeting in the Tanassa Dance preordained. "Come, then."

She moved with an uncanny skill and speed, so much so that Anghara, taken a little by surprise at the suddenness of her departure, had to scramble to catch up to her. The woman's outward frailty was deceptive; she was built for stamina and endurance—much like the fragile steeds which hailed from her homeland. She found paths where Anghara could see only trackless waste—for the back slopes of the Tanassa Hills were different from those which faced the river. No smooth meadowland here, it was all tussocks of wiry grass rooted in long expanses of naked stone, soft and crumbling, and loose rocks, which rolled treacherously beneath a foot and could turn an ankle with effortless malice. Anghara followed where ai'Jihaar led, but even so she was breathless with exertion when they finally reached the grassy plains. Looking around, ai'Jihaar paused, waiting for her. "It becomes easier from here."

"You climbed that? Alone in the dark?" panted Anghara, coming abreast of her companion.

"There are far worse things in Khar'i'id, where I have walked at night," said ai'Jihaar softly.

"What is Khar'i'id?"

"The Stone Desert of Kheldrin," said ai'Jihaar, "where nothing thrives except se'i'din and diamondskins, and both of these are death."

Anghara was suddenly overwhelmingly curious about the strange land of which she had heard little that was not legend, fable, or simply malicious fabrication of small and frightened minds. "Tell me of your country," she said, and she was quite unaware of a tone of ringing command which had crept back into her voice as she had taken on again the mantle of the Kir Hama name.

While ai'Jihaar did not miss it, neither did she bow under it. "In time," she said. A light breeze swirled around the walkers, twitching the ends of their cloaks, tousling Anghara's hair—ai'Jihaar lifted her masked face into it, as though listening to tidings, or asking for them. And so she was, in a way. *Oh, ai'Shahn al'Sheriha, bright messenger of my people's Gods, was it for this that you sent me to seek when you sent me into holy Sheriha'drin?* The wind was silent, but the quiet excitement that coursed through ai'Jihaar's blood at the bright aura of the girl who walked beside her was answer enough to her prayer. And yet . . . it had been many ages since one of the sheriha'drini was taken into the heartland of Kheldrin. Many ages; the world had been broken and remade at least once since that time. There was pity in the old woman—for the child who was running, for royal blood cast adrift to survive on the wind, sustained only by the hope that one day she would reclaim what had been taken from her. But pity must not sway her decisions. She was *sen'thar,* chosen of her Gods, and it was their voices she must heed. She walked in silence, listening to the whisper of foreign winds in the grass of Roisinan's plains.

It took them many days to reach Calabra, days in which Anghara learned to respect ai'Jihaar's silences. She learned much more, as well, for there were times when ai'Jihaar was quite ready to talk, and the strange, enigmatic land of Kheldrin began to take shape before Anghara's eyes. A shape more real than her own country, for all that they moved beneath familiar skies—for ai'Jihaar had a mesmeric power with words and Anghara had no other companion to dilute their impact on her mind.

Just how strange and alien her own land could become in a short space of time was borne in upon her only when, after avoiding every habitation in their path, they finally plunged into the outskirts of Calabra and Anghara saw for the first time the consequences of Bresse.

Because ai'Jihaar seemed to know where she was going, Anghara, who had never been alone in a big city before, was content to let her lead the way. She had taken Anghara's arm, and although it looked like an able-bodied girl was helping a blind woman cope with the crowds, it was in fact very much the other way around, with ai'Jihaar leading and hanging on to Anghara lest they be swept apart by the jostling people in the broad main street.

"I'll have us down one of the smaller streets in a moment," murmured ai'Jihaar very softly, so that Anghara barely heard her. "It should be easier then. There should be . . . oh, *al'Khur!*" The sudden recoil came an instant before something slammed at Anghara's own mind, a dark madness which pulsed in their direction from somewhere . . . somewhere above them. Anghara echoed ai'Jihaar's gasp of pain, snapping her watering eyes upward.

It was bad. Very bad—ai'Jihaar felt the black silence of shock as it descended like night on Anghara's bright presence beside her, even if it hadn't been for the sudden tight, bone-crushing grip in which the girl had her arm. But it was something that escaped ai'Jihaar's own senses, blurred them into dangerous fuzziness. For a moment she had known what real blindness meant.

"Go," urged ai'Jihaar softly, for they had stopped dead in their tracks. "Take the next turning. Get us out of here."

Anghara obeyed, but she moved jerkily, slowly, her breathing uneven and harsh. In the quieter atmosphere of the side street ai'Jihaar recaptured some of her composure, but under her hand Anghara was still rigid. Reaching up toward Anghara's face, ai'Jihaar touched her cheek very gently.

"Tell me," the Kheldrini woman said, and although the voice was very gentle the words were a command.

"A cage," said Anghara, expressionlessly. "They have strung up a cage above the street. There are three women inside. One may be dead, or unconscious—she lies there, unmoving, and the other two trample her in their madness. And they *are* mad . . ." She shuddered violently, and then again.

Taking both of Anghara's hands into her own small-boned ones, ai'Jihaar squeezed them with unexpected strength. "There is more," she said. "Tell me."

There was a moment of silence, and then ai'Jihaar became aware that Anghara was weeping. "They had no eyes," she said at last, and ai'Jihaar understood.

"They were Sighted," she said flatly.

Anghara's hands were cold, her palms clammy. "Sif," she forced out through stiff lips.

"Come," ai'Jihaar said, taking charge. "I know a place of safety where we can rest. Tomorrow, we look for a ship to bear us across the sea."

She felt Anghara grow very still. "We?" she asked softly.

There was no more doubt in her mind—ai'Jihaar's Gods had spoken. Her voice was very gentle when she spoke again.

"Sheriha'drin cannot shelter you any longer," she said. "There is no place in this land strong enough to offer you sanctuary in this hour. Sometimes love alone is not enough."

## 15

It was a Kheldrini ship they boarded in the morning. It stood out from the other ships in the harbor in much the same way a Kheldrini face would stand out in a crowd of Roisinani. The ship from the desert country was smaller and narrower than its Roisinan counterparts, built, much as everything else from that land seemed to be, for endurance and speed. It was crewed by a handful of Kheldrini men, clad in narrow sand-colored trousers that fitted them like a second skin, their bronze torsos bare, their long hair tied back out of their way with thongs while they grappled with the complexities of wind and sail. Still, for creatures born and bred in oceans of sand, they seemed to be quietly efficient upon the water. The ship, with its cargo of grain from Roisinan and two passengers, glided out of Calabra at mid-morning.

Anghara had spent most of the previous night weeping quietly and, it seemed, quite inconsolably for the sight she had seen in Calabra's street. Things were worse even than this; in the place where ai'Jihaar had taken them they received other news, and it seemed that the cage was only a small part of the whole. All over the land the countryside had been scoured, helpless Sighted women run to ground by armed men demanding they renounce Sight. Often, the wretched women could not do so. How could they renounce something they had been born with? They would be killed on the spot, spitted on lances or laid open with a sword or, if they were really unlucky, they died slowly under torture, before witnesses, so that Sif's message could be brought home. Sif, or his advisors, had concocted a brew which his inquisitors and his soldiers administered to their victims, too often by force, that purported to "purge" the Sight from a mind which harbored it. That it had an effect was without doubt; it was very seldom, however, the effect that had been anticipated. Not a few of those who took it died. They were the lucky ones. Those who lived sometimes lost their minds, becoming less than idiots; some found its dulling effects were temporary, and were fed more and more until they became bitterly addicted. Others, like the ones in Calabra, had been senselessly maimed and exhibited as an example. Concealing a Sighted woman, or helping one flee Sif's avenging soldiers, was a crime almost as great as Sight itself, and scores of husbands, fathers or brothers paid for their women's gift with their own heads.

Something wild was riding Sif. He had unleashed a pogrom, made all the more horrifying because it was unexpected. Sight had been a part of Roisinan for hundreds of years—now Sif seemed intent on rooting it out within a single generation. He would rule human, as he had vowed, but more than that—he would rule a human people.

Anghara, to whom Sight meant so much more than her own wild gift, who had grown up with her gentle mother, venerable Feor and the Sisters at Bresse, could not comprehend so much hate. Sif could not hate an entire people this much, it was impossible, it was insane, and in her anguish Anghara even asked, lapsing into a childish logic which tore at ai'Jihaar's heart, whether he would stop if she surrendered herself to him.

"He would not stop, dear heart," murmured the Kheldrini woman compassionately, sitting by the bed where her young companion lay, stroking her hair with a gentle hand. "This has gone past the search for one girl, although he may hope to crush her together with the rest."

"But the babies, ai'Jihaar, the babies . . ."

And that, perhaps, was the worst. The babies of Sighted women, children who had the possibility of Sight in their future, were dealt with just as ruthlessly. The tale of one particular village in the north, which had more than its fair share of Sighted women and to which this had been a source of some pride, had filtered southward, spoken of in fearful whispers. Soldiers had scourged the place; infants had been torn from their mothers' arms and slain before their eyes. Children barely toddling had tasted the sword. When Sif's men left, the place which had been so proud was left weeping, its streets red with innocent blood. The land reeled from the blows the king dealt them, noble and commoner alike. They had not yet had time to recover or react.

"But they will," ai'Jihaar had said, with quiet certainty. "Sif believes he has started a crusade, but he has only sowed the seeds of his own end. Now they are afraid—but soon, very soon, they will start to hate him."

Anghara had thought her tears cried out at last, boarding the foreign ship of her exile, her dry eyes red and swollen. And yet it was still not over, for more tears came, salty as the ocean which was widening between her and the shore of her land, as she felt herself physically torn from Roisinan. Her heart was breaking, but she stood straight and proud, her gray eyes locked on the shore until it faded from her sight.

"I will come back," she murmured as the shape of her land sank beneath the sea, and it was not, after all, a vow of revenge. But it was a vow nonetheless. *I will return. I will not abandon you.*

By the time she returned to where ai'Jihaar had been installed in one of the small cabins, the Kheldrini woman had undergone a remarkable transformation. The travelling cloak and the mask were gone; there was no further need. Instead, she wore a loose robe of gold jin'aaz silk and over it a white djellaba; a necklace of yellow amber set in silver lay around her neck. Her hair was gathered in a delicate net, sprinkled with amber beads.

She seemed completely unaware that anything was different, sitting cross-legged on cushions before a small table bearing a tray with tea things. In that uncanny way she had, she turned toward the door as Anghara opened it, and smiled. "Tea?"

Anghara wrinkled her nose at the unfamiliar, rather pungent aroma that arose from ai'Jihaar's small handleless cup. "That is tea?"

"Lais," said ai'Jihaar, gesturing at the small teapot on the tray. "Try some."

Anghara poured out a small measure into a second cup and came to sit beside ai'Jihaar. Her face was disciplined, but her gray eyes were swimming with loss. Once again, impossibly, ai'Jihaar responded to things she could not have known.

"Do not think of it as exile," she said unexpectedly, as though answering the unspoken thoughts that roiled inside Anghara's mind.

But Anghara was becoming used to these sallies, and simply continued the conversation from that point, without pausing to wonder anew at ai'Jihaar's sharp perceptions.

"I am grateful," she murmured, "but it *is* exile . . . and it's hard . . ." She swallowed convulsively. She would not, *would not,* start crying again. "Why did you show yourself at the Dance?" she asked, a question she had asked before. "You could have let me go and I would never have known that you were there."

"I could not," said ai'Jihaar, patiently repeating an answer she had already given. She was indulgent in this, because she was herself intrigued by their meeting. "Do you not remember? It was you who sensed my presence, before I spoke. Never before has a Sheriha'drini known me, as you did then. The choice was taken from me in that moment."

"Have you been to . . . to Roisinan often before?" It was deliberate, that; the land was not Sheriha'drin, not to Anghara.

"Many times."

It was suddenly very important to Anghara that she find out. "Why?"

"I am *sen'thar,*" said ai'Jihaar simply, as though that explained everything. And it would have, had Anghara been of Kheldrin. But there was much still for her to learn, and ai'Jihaar knew it; she went on smoothly, "There are those amongst us who are bound to our Gods. It is not with us as it is in your land, where a priest serves one God alone. *Sen'en'thari* know every God, serve every God, and when a voice speaks to us we obey. There are many reasons for making a pilgrimage."

"And this time?"

Turning her uncanny eyes on Anghara, ai'Jihaar said, "This time . . . this time it was different. I was sent to seek for something."

"For me?"

"Your Gods and mine, how can we mortals fully know their minds?" she said slowly. "It was only in Calabra that I was sure. And after that, it would have been a hard God who would have me leave you in Sif's path. If you want to know why I was sent to seek for you, the answer is that I do not know. Yet. Certainly it was to spare you from the holocaust; but I do not think the Gods of Kheldrin would have sent me on a mission whose purpose was only that. This is why I tell you: do not think of it as exile. You were meant to come to Kheldrin; that was written before you were born, else you would not be on this ship. The true reasons will become clear to us in time."

The cabin door opened softly and one of the crew bowed low in ai'Jihaar's direction from the threshold.

"The winds are good, *an'sen'thar.* We make good speed. Is there anything you require?"

Lifting a slender arm weighted with silver bracelets, ai'Jihaar gestured gracefully. "No, that is all. Thank you."

He bowed again and withdrew.

The lais tea was making Anghara drowsy, her eyelids drooping already as her gaze, drawn to the visitor, came back to ai'Jihaar—but she had a quick ear, and she could not fail to note the deep deference shown to her companion by the Kheldrini crew. *"An'sen'thar?"* she murmured, her eye still bright. "What are you, ai'Jihaar?"

"The chosen of the Gods," said ai'Jihaar, "their instrument and their servant. A vessel for their visions, a seer, a dreamer of true dreams. And now, your teacher, and your friend." Anghara's eyes closed at the last word, as though ai'Jihaar had spoken an invocation, and she lay back, asleep. Producing a woollen coverlet, ai'Jihaar laid it over her, very gently. "Sleep, my child," she whispered. "May ai'Shahn bring you good dreams."

If the messenger of the Kheldrin Gods obeyed, Anghara could not say—she remembered no dreams when she woke. But she rose refreshed, and although her heart was still heavy at what had transpired during the last day or so she was in better spirits and seemed to have retreated from the narrow edge she had walked in Calabra. While ai'Jihaar had named herself Anghara's teacher, she made no move in that direction on the voyage to Kheldrin, other than occasional information about the place where they were headed, leaving space for Anghara to find her equilibrium again, to calm her soul. When land appeared on the horizon before them, and the captain announced imminent landfall, Anghara was looking forward to setting foot in Kheldrin. Dressed in a white robe which the Kheldrini woman had procured for her, Anghara stood on the ship's prow and eagerly awaited her first sight of ai'Jihaar's country.

Which, when it came, was not at all what she had expected. "It looks much like the land around Calabra," Anghara said, strangely disappointed at the pastures she could glimpse beyond the harbor. "I was somehow expecting . . ."

"You will see plenty of desert soon enough," said ai'Jihaar, who had come to stand beside her, in mild rebuke. "There is very little green in Kheldrin once you go beyond those mountains. We treasure these grasslands; they are all we have."

A glint of sunshine on water that was not the ocean drew Anghara's eye, and seemed to find an echo somewhere in ai'Jihaar's own exotic senses. She made a gesture that was at once a ritual of obeisance and a sign of pure, quiet love. "Sa'ila," she said. "Our one river. The only flowing water west of Sheriha'drin." And then her head turned a fraction, toward a city of slender spires amongst a profusion of low roofs tiled with oddly golden stone. "And that," said ai'Jihaar, "is Sa'alah. Look closely; I do not think you will find much that will remind you of Calabra there." There was both light teasing and an unexpected compassion in ai'Jihaar's voice. She understood that in spite of the anticipation of her arrival in Kheldrin, Anghara must be feeling bereft of everything familiar. There had been disappointment in her voice a moment before—and the disappointment was deeper than even she knew, deeper than surface frustration at not seeing what she had expected to see. Yes, parts of the coastal plain near Sa'alah did look like the land around Calabra in Roisinan—and there was a part of her which would have been happier if it had not.

The captain himself handed ai'Jihaar down from his ship when it tied up at the main dock; Anghara followed, feeling not unlike her father's stallion amongst dun'en. Less so than most Roisinani, perhaps—she was, after all slight and small boned, and her hair was bright enough to match any in Sa'alah, even if it didn't have their pure shade of copper. But her face was pale-skinned, her cheekbones too high, her lips too full, her eyes gray and wide. This was a trade city, though, and people from Roisinan were not entirely unknown. There were a few bemused stares, but not enough to make her feel uncomfortable.

"Come," said ai'Jihaar, adjusting her djellaba to her satisfaction and reaching a hand out to her young charge. "Tomorrow will be soon enough. It would be best if we stayed this night at the serai and tomorrow I will procure ki'thar'en."

"Where will we be going?" asked Anghara, falling into step beside ai'Jihaar, finally asking a question she could not believe she had not asked before.

"Home," said ai'Jihaar, not looking around.

Anghara recognized the following silence from the long days they had spent walking the plains to Calabra, and kept her peace as they walked down the pier. When that abruptly ended, ai'Jihaar turned into the city's narrow streets, moving with the same singular assurance which had threaded her through Calabra. The serai, much like what Anghara would have called a han, was a low, rambling building on the outskirts of Sa'alah, fronting onto a narrow white beach. The man who came to meet them bowed from behind a brightly woven curtain hung in the doorway, as ai'Jihaar spoke to him in her guttural native tongue. He ushered them inside and along a small corridor, then through another set of curtains into a low, wide room full of soft pillows in shades of red and gold. Another curtained doorway, from which the curtains had been drawn back, opened onto a short stretch of lawn, which dropped away abruptly into the white sand and the ocean. Anghara crossed over to look outside.

*"Dhim ki'thar'en ka'hailam, an'sen'thar?"*

*"Dai, saliha."*

There was a rustle of fabric. Anghara turned her head; the man had gone, and ai'Jihaar stood alone by the curtained entrance.

"There will be two ki'thar'en for us tomorrow," said ai'Jihaar, on cue as always. "The man is called al'Sayar, and he says there is a small caravan leaving in the morning; we can travel with them until they turn south to Beku." She crossed over to where Anghara was standing, looking out to sea. "It is a great thing that you will be doing tomorrow," she said slowly. "It lies not in my memory when Arad Khajir'i'id was last seen by any who were not its children. It is harsh and unforgiving to those who do not know it. There are laws in the desert you must know and follow if you are to survive."

"You have spoken of some," said Anghara, picking up the solemn mood.

"Water is precious, and costly," nodded ai'Jihaar. "It may be bought, but not taken. Those who live in hai'ren and in the cities guard their water fiercely. They are not vindictive, but neither are they merciful to those who make mistakes. Guarding against mistakes is your task, not theirs. But there is more. You are marked out there, a stranger of no clan— not even through my protection, for *sen'en'thari* are a clan unto themselves and you are not . . . *sen'thar."* She paused, her voice thoughtful. "Not yet," she amended at last, very softly. She raised her head slightly. If she had not been blind she would have been looking deeply into Anghara's eyes. She softly invoked her Gods with an air of what was almost revelation, "ai'Dhya and al'Khur! Perhaps I begin to understand."

But she would say no more on this.

"Tomorrow," she said. "Tomorrow in the desert. We shall see."

Having only softly stirring curtains between herself and the world was only the first new and strange thing Anghara would have to learn to accept, for Kheldrin seemed never to have heard of the concept of a door. She wondered for a moment, before she fell asleep on the banked cushions that served for a bed, how people indicated a desire to enter a room without having a door to knock on. But then sleep claimed her at last and the thought fled, only to be resurrected vividly as she woke to a soft voice beyond the curtains an hour before dawn.

*"Sa'hari, an'sen'thar?"*

She heard ai'Jihaar reply, and the man she had called al'Sayar entered, keeping his eyes decorously down and his hands, wrapped around a small flat package, folded neatly against his stomach. Anghara propped herself up on one elbow and watched ai'Jihaar and the serai keeper—for that was what he seemed to be—talking quietly between themselves. When their business was concluded, al'Sayar bowed again and turned to leave. Just before he slipped out into the corridor he looked up and stared at Anghara dispassionately for a long moment, returning her scrutiny, and then he was gone.

"That was not very polite," said ai'Jihaar without turning round. She seemed to be paying out a few coins into her palm from a pouch at her waist.

Anghara could not restrain a light laugh. "It probably wasn't. I'm sorry."

"No matter. He was hardly the epitome of courtesy and decorum himself. And there will be others who will find you equally fascinating before we go much further. He brought you something. Come, let me show you."

The "something" was a complicated head cloth which, once in place, could be worn either thrown back or tucked across nose and mouth in such a way that only the eyes showed through a narrow opening.

"There are few things in the desert," ai'Jihaar said, lifting a hand to rub the sides of her narrow nose reflexively with slender fingers, "but what there is comes in many different guises. What you know as sand we might name soft sand, hard sand, dune sand, quicksand—and some are to be sought, some avoided. What you know as wind we may call iri'sah, or khai'san. And when you get caught in a soft sand desert with a khai'san blowing in your face, you die." These were harsh words, but they were truth, and truth on which lives depended. Anghara listened with careful, concentrated attention.

"We of the desert have ways of breathing through storms of sand," said ai'Jihaar, tapping her nose again. "It is something you will have to learn—if you are able. But for a little time, at least, wear this over your face; we do not want the desert to put an end too soon to something hardly even begun. Let me show you how to put it on. You must know this instinctively, you must be able to do it in seconds when someone wakes you from a deep sleep. We have an hour yet or so before we must leave to join the caravan at the Desert Gate. Practise."

Anghara watched ai'Jihaar deftly wrap the burnoose about her head and tried to do it herself under ai'Jihaar's critical hands. The older woman corrected one or two errors, supervised another practice run, then left her to it while she went to arrange their animals and supplies.

It seemed as if she had been gone for hours; Anghara, alone in a strange place where everything was new and a little frightening in the intensity with which it was approached, was on edge, shying at every rustle outside the doorless room. But she practiced, as instructed, the mechanics of donning the burnoose. It was as well; the first thing ai'Jihaar did when she returned was to approach and run swift exploring hands over Anghara's head and face. She tugged at a slightly loose fold, then nodded.

"Good. Are you ready? The ki'thar'en are waiting for us."
Anghara followed her without a word.

They had similar beasts in Shaymir, and Kieran, when he talked to her of his home, had described them to Anghara, long ago in Cascin. Their large, ugly snouts with disconcertingly long-lashed eyes, their faintly supercilious expression, their splayed feet adapted so well to sand and the huge hump on which a rider's saddle was perched were not entirely unexpected. The way the animals were caparisoned, though, was—Kheldrin, it seemed, enjoyed its trappings, or else it was something ai'Jihaar drew to herself. Either way, the two animals on which they were to ride were decked out as if for a royal procession. Their tack was not new, but the bridles were soft, tooled red leather. Their saddles were laid upon rugs good enough to be set in pride of place in a noble house. Anghara knew ai'Jihaar sensed her surprise, and seemed to be enjoying it.

"Hold fast when they rise," she warned, as they were mounting the animals which knelt awaiting them. "Keep a tight grip on the pommel."

Anghara squealed in surprise as her ki'thar began lumbering to its feet with a bored-sounding grunt, and she thought for a moment she was about to make a thoroughly ungraceful head-over-heels descent down the animal's curving neck. She dropped the reins, but held on, and the animal stood placidly in the gray pre-dawn light, waiting for further instructions. A handler, who had been standing by as they mounted, handed her the trailing rein, his face wearing an expression with equal parts of surprise and apprehension— it was as though the spectacle of Anghara seated upon his ki'thar stirred a deep feeling of unease. Anghara wasn't entirely insensitive to this; she would have probably felt the same if he had been mounting her father's stallion, about to gallop off into the moors of Roisinan.

Seemingly oblivious to the undercurrents, ai'Jihaar continued with her instructions. "You urge him forward with your heel, and you make him stop, just like riding a horse, simply by pulling on the reins. But these are trained to verbal commands as well. To make him advance you call *akka;* to halt him, *sa'a.* Gently, though; if you tell him to *akka* vigorously enough, he is liable to run away with you entirely." The diminutive woman, who looked even smaller perched on top of the ki'thar's hump, swung the heel of a delicate chamois leather riding boot against the monster's side and said, softly, *"Akka! Akka! Akka!"*

The ki'thar began walking ponderously, with ai'Jihaar swaying in her saddle to the rhythm of his pace. "Try!" she called over her shoulder. "We have a little time. You will learn as we go, but we can take a few moments to make sure you can exercise at least a little control over your mount."

Anghara kicked at her beast obligingly, calling *akka* in a soft voice. For a moment it looked like it would ignore her completely, wrapped in its own august thoughts. Then with a snort of what sounded suspiciously like exasperation with this idiotic rider, the animal shambled into a slow stroll, managing to give the impression its decision to move had nothing at all to do with the pesky parasite hanging onto its hump. Anghara laughed. So, after a moment, did ai'Jihaar, who nevertheless did not forget her duties as instructress.

"Now make him stop," she called from where she had halted her own beast.

Anghara hauled at the reins, calling *"Sa'a! Sa'a!"* in a voice which, while authoritative enough, still managed to sound unconvinced that it would have any effect whatsoever. For a wonder, the animal cocked an ear and came to an obedient stop.

She would have rather died than admit it, but she had been thoroughly terrified at the prospect of having to battle wills with this animal out in the unforgiving desert. She still wasn't sure she was equal to it, but at least she had told him what to do and he had done it without too much fuss. She might still be disgraced out amongst the desert nomads, but she would not be totally humiliated—and she would not be the utter liability she had feared she would be.

"Try it once or twice more, and then we should be on our way," said ai'Jihaar.

It went smoothly enough, and after another few attempts at starting and stopping ai'Jihaar pronounced herself satisfied. They moved off, ai'Jihaar in the lead, toward the place she had called Desert Gate. The handler remained behind, staring after them with brooding eyes.

They were soon free of the city of Sa'alah, and riding on the road which led toward the mountains ringing the coastal plains. Anghara could not have said when it had begun to rise, but there came a moment when she looked back and the city by the sea was already behind and beneath them, presenting once again a vista of golden roofs. Up ahead, the mountains were suddenly very close; on the green meadows, some of which now had perceptible slopes, she could see sporadic groups of sheep, and occasionally a shepherd watching over his flock, standing still as a statue. And then they had arrived. A loose knot of ten or fifteen people, some mounted on dun'en every bit as beautiful as Anghara's father's had been and others on ki'thar'en, stood waiting for them at the point where the road plunged into the mountain pass. Six heavily laden ki'thar'en waited patiently, carrying burdens which seemed hopelessly huge and heavy. The caravan leader urged his mount forward a pace or two and bowed to ai'Jihaar from the saddle. He wore his burnoose tucked up desert-fashion, leaving only a pair of golden eyes showing in his face, and touched his fingertips to his heart, his lips beneath the concealing desert veil, and his forehead, in the graceful salute of the desert. He murmured something in his own language; ai'Jihaar responded. The leader glanced at Anghara, and, from the set of his shoulders and the sharp glint in his eyes, he seemed far from happy; then he wheeled his ki'thar and urged it to the front of the cavalcade at a shambling trot. There, he raised his right hand and brought it down, very suddenly.

*"Akka! Akka! Akka!"* came softly from the riders around Anghara, and the ki'thar'en, not without a few grunting comments of their own, all began moving slowly toward the pass.

Anghara urged her ki'thar into a slow trot. She had not developed the right rhythms yet, and felt like nothing so much as a sack of loose bones, all of which were protesting furiously and unanimously at being shaken about. Except for the riders leading the beasts of burden, Anghara was last in the caravan until ai'Jihaar quietly assumed a position behind her. They plunged into a narrow, winding canyon, deep in shadow, riding silently in single file. The ki'thar'en were the only ones who grumbled loudly—at the hard stone beneath their feet, at their riders, at the acrid smell that emanated from each beast to the delicate nose of the one that followed.

But very soon the floor of the canyon began to change. First there was just an occasional flurry of pale sand disturbed by the infrequent breath of a breeze which came and went intermittently as they threaded their way through Ar'i'id Sam'mara, the Desert Gate. Then, gradually, the bare stone began to disappear beneath soft sand drifts. The sounds of the caravan's passage grew softer and softer, even the endless litany of complaints from the ki'thar'en ceasing slowly as their feet began to find the sand for which they had been wrought. The breeze grew warmer, steadier, the breath of the desert blowing into their faces.

They began approaching the massive rib of a mountain buttress, so huge it almost spanned the width of the canyon and very nearly closed it altogether—only a narrow corridor remained, where a passing ki'thar almost scraped the towering stone on either side of him. Except for its prodigious size, it was no different from many they had already passed, but even as the leader of the caravan vanished behind the barrier of stone Anghara's heart seemed to stop for a breathless instant. She felt poised on the brink of something extraordinary, standing at a crossroads with myriad paths unravelling from her feet. It was a moment in which she could feel her life change, become something quite different from what she had imagined it would be.

And then she was out of time, all choices cast in stone, and her own mount was edging past the last obstacle and over the threshold. Ar'i'id Sam'mara opened up with a startling suddenness, and the mountains fell away to the sides.

Ahead of them, as far as the eye could see to the flat and shimmering horizon, stretched an expanse of yellow desert, blown into smooth ridges at their feet by the ever-swirling winds of the Desert Gate.

Anghara had known it would be a flat and largely featureless ocean of sand, drifting and deadly. She had known it would be overwhelming in its silence and its immensity. But she had not known it could wring a heart, that it was beautiful.

*Arad Khajir'i'id,* said the voice of ai'Jihaar in her mind. The *sen'thar* had never done this before, but somehow it was not surprising that this should be so, not in this hour, not in this place. *The Southern Desert. This is Kheldrin, Land of Twilight, not seen by alien eyes for a thousand years.*

16

If that first sight of Arad Khajir'i'id had been wine which had gone to Anghara's head, her first day in the desert sobered her up very quickly. It was still beautiful, and had lost none of its power to touch her soul—but the surface beauty was delicate skin stretched over fine bones, and if the bones themselves were beautiful it was the razor-sharp beauty of the purity of death.

It was not yet mid morning when they set out across the sands, but the heat was already overwhelming, the sun a living fire overhead. They had travelled for only a few hours before the caravan leader signalled a stop; a semicircle of black tents was up almost before Anghara could scramble down from her ki'thar. One had been raised for herself and for ai'Jihaar, the first sign Anghara could see that anyone in the caravan acknowledged their presence. She noticed the ki'thar'en had been tethered in the meager shadow of the tents, and she led her own behind her tent, hammering in a clumsy peg to hold his hobble. The *sen'thar's* was already there, and ai'Jihaar was standing by the entrance to the tent; when Anghara rose and looked in her direction, ai'Jihaar simply nodded her approval in that uncanny way she had of knowing when she was being watched and ducked inside. Anghara followed. The tent was small, the air inside it close, but somehow less torrid than out in the merciless sun.

"Try to get some sleep," advised ai'Jihaar. "We leave again late this afternoon, and we travel during the cool hours of evening. It will be midnight before we stop for rest again."

It was indeed a pleasure to close eyes which hurt from the brightness of sun reflected from yellow-white sand, but sleep eluded Anghara—it was too hot, and there was a thin film of sweat on her skin which seemed to make her clothes slide and chafe uncomfortably. All the same, it seemed all too soon when a quiet voice called from the tent's entrance: *"Sa'hari? Sa'hari, an'sen'thar?"*

When ai'Jihaar murmured a response the summoner departed, his chamois riding boots rasping softly over sand as he walked away.

Anghara remembered the serai keeper outside the curtained doorway of their room had used the same soft word to rouse them on the morning they had left Sa'alah. Only now, here in the desert, was she beginning to understand the lack of doors in Kheldrin.

*"Sa'hari.* . . . what does that mean?" she asked ai'Jihaar as they made ready to emerge from the tent.

"You would knock on a door in your land," said ai'Jihaar. "There are no doors in the desert. The sense of *sa'hari* could be translated as *are you there?* It is your answer to this which either invites the one who asked into the place where he seeks admittance, or bids him wait outside while you come to him. Come, they will wish to strike the tent."

Theirs was one of the last, the rest having vanished as though they had never been. For a moment Anghara gazed back the way they had come, to where the mountains shimmered like an illusion behind a wall of heat. It was already difficult to believe anything existed beyond them. When she finally turned away to claim her ki'thar, it was with a start that she found herself face to face with a Kheldrini man, his eyes gleaming from his desert-veiled face, who stood holding the reins of her ki'thar in his left hand. He hissed a word of command at the ki'thar, waited until it had knelt on the sand, and then offered the reins to Anghara in silence. Another word came back to her, one she had heard ai'Jihaar use in the serai.

*"Saliha,"* she said. Thank you.

He bowed—heart, lips, brow—and after a slight hesitation she did the same. Leaving her in possession of her mount, he withdrew. Anghara stood looking after him for a moment, not sure what just happened but aware it had been deeply significant in some obscure way. She climbed into her saddle in silence and made her mount get to its feet, which the ki'thar did with the same rebellious commentary he'd already expounded once in the yard of the Sa'alah serai. Another ki'thar approached her, and the smile on ai'Jihaar's unveiled face was unmistakable.

"That was well done," she said. "Your instincts serve you well."

Beneath the burnoose Anghara flushed with the pleasure of a just praised child who had solved a difficult problem, and the pride of a queen who proved that royalty lay in her more than just skin-deep or conferred by the touch of a jewelled circlet on her brow. She even caught herself wondering, with what was almost venom, whether Sif would have done as well, for all he claimed he was Kir Hama, and royal-born. And then she veered away from that road. Sif's name, and what he had done with his crown, was still too raw a wound.

They rode for the rest of the afternoon and, it seemed to Anghara, most of the night. She was bone-weary when the leader finally called a halt, and it was almost more than she could manage to do her duty by her ki'thar, settling it with ai'Jihaar's for the night with a portion of coarse grain. Then she returned to the center of the tent semicircle, where a blaze had been kindled and several of her co-travelers were busy over a steaming kettle.

The air was cool, even chilly, on Anghara's first night in the desert. Too tired to even attempt to sleep, every muscle shrieking in agony, she came and sat close by the campfire, wrapped in the woollen djellaba ai'Jihaar had given her, holding out her hands to the cheerful blaze. She had removed her burnoose, after a momentary hesitation, and the thick braid in which she had confined her hair fell over her shoulder to pool in her lap, with the usual wayward curls framing her pale face. Others who moved in the circle of the firelight had also removed their burnooses in the quiet,

windless night. Bronze skin and bright copper hair caught
glints from the fire and gleamed in the desert darkness beneath a translucent sky wreathed with bright, cold stars.
Anghara could not see ai'Jihaar anywhere.

It was only now, without the concealing burnooses, that
Anghara was able to discern there were women in the group
with which they travelled. One of the women kept glancing
toward her with an expression that was difficult to read. It
might have been curious fascination and, perhaps not entirely unexpectedly, much the same instinctive wariness and
mistrust with which Roisinani stared at "Khelsies" when
they crossed the sea in the other direction. But at length curiosity seemed to win, the woman left her task by the fireside and disappeared briefly into one of the tents. When she
came out carrying something in her hand, she made directly
for Anghara. She squatted down beside her, reaching out
hesitantly to touch the bright rope of hair, and then smiled,
taking Anghara's hand in her own small warm one and
pressing something into her palm with a murmur. Anghara
looked down, far from sure what to expect, and saw a small,
carved bone comb.

She was momentarily nonplussed, but then she smiled
with real pleasure and nodded her thanks. But the woman
seemed to want something else, and kept on darting a timid
hand toward the bright braid. Anghara glanced around for
ai'Jihaar, but she was still missing; the woman who had
made her the gift of the comb murmured something, and
Anghara grimaced her frustration.

"I don't understand," she said helplessly. She picked up
the end of her braid in one hand and stared at it for inspiration. It seemed to have been an enlightened move, for the
woman nodded eagerly, her lips curling into one of those
odd, narrow-lipped Kheldrini smiles. Understanding suddenly dawned. Anghara lifted her hair in one hand and the
comb in the other. "Now? You want me to comb it now?"

The golden eyes were bright. Anghara felt a little self-
conscious; it was one thing to quietly remove her burnoose,
quite another to perform an act which was so intimate in the

focus of several interested pairs of eyes. By this time others had been drawn to the strange encounter by the fire. But it was such a little thing, after all. She hesitated for another brief moment, and then slid off the knotted thong holding the braid, and began unweaving the strands of hair. When it was done, she shook her hair loose and it spilled over her back and shoulders like a cloak; she ran her fingers through it, tugging gently at one or two tangles.

*"Hai haddari!"* breathed the woman who began it all, sounding impressed. Anghara smiled at her—vanity was not one of her faults, but it was hard not to preen a little in the light of the open admiration in the other's eyes. She reached for the comb, but the woman, suddenly shy, said something else, making a motion toward the comb herself.

Either Anghara was learning the language fast, or it was just a question of being able to extrapolate the meaning of this new question from what had gone before. The request was more than humble—it was clear, from the set of the narrow shoulders and the downcast eyes, that the woman almost expected the reply to be a blistering reprimand, and not necessarily from Anghara but from her own people. She had evidently not been able to help herself, but this was a breach of both etiquette and privacy; and Anghara was a stranger of whom none of them knew what to expect. Anghara hesitated, this time because up until that moment only a select few had been allowed the privilege and duty of caring for her hair. When she had been very young, it had been her mother; later, it had been her nursemaid, then Catlin. Since that first morning at Cascin, she had dressed her hair herself. And the last time it had known the touch of anyone else's hand had been in Cascin, a few days before the terrible events of Cerdiad which would cast her out. And that had been Kieran . . . He had come upon her in the garden, combing her wet hair in the sun. He had taken the comb from her, untangling with a gentle hand the damp knots which she had been furiously yanking at, spinning for her a tale of his own childhood, of the times he had done just that for Keda, back in Shaymir.

It was an oddly potent memory, Kieran's voice echoing in her head as though he was close to her, speaking to her in this strange place from which he was so desperately far away. Anghara sat very still, but part of her wanted to run alone into the desert, leaving the camp and its bustle behind and going into the silence of empty desolation under the stars. There she would be better able to hear the remembered words of one whom she had loved. Instead, and the move was so rooted in pure instinct that it took even Anghara herself by surprise, she held out the bone comb to the one who had given it. The woman took it almost reverently, hesitating now that her request had been granted. Then she sank its bone teeth gently into Anghara's curls and drew it downward, very slowly, along the length of her bright hair.

But Anghara was already far from that place. She was sitting very straight, legs crossed beneath the demure folds of her robe and the woollen djellaba, hands folded in her lap; her gray eyes, wide and unblinking, pupils dilated and fixed with vision, were staring into the campfire which blazed before her. And the voice in her ears was still Kieran's . . .

He was white and troubled, blue eyes bleary with fatigue, dismay and apprehension. Anghara did not recognize the room he was in, nor the old man upon the edge of whose bed he was sitting . . . but no, she knew him, it was Feor, Feor broken by his own grim burdens into a premature old age . . . Feor, whose transparent white hand trembled as he reached out toward the young man at his side . . .

"It's been almost two months since Bresse was razed," Kieran was saying, voice a little unsteady with sheer desperation. "And she's vanished, Feor. Vanished. I found a boat captain or two who think they may remember taking her down the Tanassa, and one who is equally convinced he took her *up* the river; and then there is one who says a young girl travelling on his ship simply disappeared in one of the villages they stopped at for repairs—swallowed by the night. They even organized a search party—but there was no trace . . . Feor . . . I don't know where to look any more."

"But she is alive," Feor said.

Kieran's head came up fiercely. "Yes, I believe that. I have to believe that. But she is out in that chaos, and Sif could already have killed her without even realizing he had done so. Or worse . . ." he shuddered convulsively, looking away. "I saw one woman after Sif's inquisitors had finished with her, *purged* her . . . she had been lovely once. And when I think that could happen to Anghara . . . I . . . I almost rather wish . . ."

He glanced at Feor, met the other's eyes, and quickly looked away again, clenching his teeth. "No. No, never that." He paused. "Adamo is back," he said, his tone quite changed. "We may not have found Anghara, but he's found Ansen. Or, at the least, his grave."

Feor's eyes closed briefly, and a grimace of pain and what might have been regret crossed his face. "That, I expected," he said quietly. "He went hurtling headlong to his own destruction, ignorant to the last of what he was getting into. I wonder if he ever truly realized what he was precipitating?"

"He was hanged, so the people say," said Kieran, leaping to his feet to prowl the room restlessly like a young wolf caged for too long in a confined space. Ansen, whatever his sins, had once been closer than a true-born brother.

"Sif?"

"Yes. It was at the han, and Sif was still there."

"Do they know why?"

"They guess," Kieran said. "There is nothing else left for them to do. But they took him down, and buried him, although the stone they put on his grave bears no name."

"Perhaps," said Feor, and the words were wrung from him, "it is best so."

Kieran gave him a bitter, strange look, half rebellious, half compassionate. He bit back whatever he had been wanting to say and simply nodded. "Perhaps."

Feor raised himself in bed on both elbows and turned toward Kieran, catching the younger man's eyes with an in-

tense gaze. Kieran crossed back to the bed in two long
strides and laid him back down onto the pillows with an extraordinary gentleness.

"Do not exhaust yourself," he said.

But Feor was still looking at him with eyes far too bright,
a world of pride, sorrow, trust and anguish in his gaze.
"What now?"

Kieran straightened. "I go back," he said. The words were
plain, shorn of every embellishment or frill; this was the iron
from which a sword is yet to be forged, all latent strength
and power. But within, already, it was possible to glimpse
the flames in which that sword would be made. He was
young, but already, perhaps, he had seen too much of a
tragedy which should never have been; at the beginning of
this conversation his spirits had been flagging—but he was
through the valley now, and out on the other side, and he was
the stronger for it. "As long as Sif searches, so do I. And
there are many back in Roisinan now who know that she
lives. I will find her, Feor. However long it takes."

"What do you see, *sen'thar?*"

And suddenly, too suddenly, there was nothing there in
front of her except the leaping flames of a campfire in the
desert, and she looked up too fast, and the stars swayed in
their moorings, falling, falling around her in a shower of
bright sparks which vanished as they fell . . .

*I will find her* . . . and then nothing . . . nothing . . . emptiness . . .

Anghara choked suddenly, her vision swimming; overcome with a wave of nausea she retched with a dry, gagging
reflex which brought nothing up from her empty stomach. A
small hand pushed gently but authoritatively at a point midway between her shoulder blades, making her bend forward
over her lap, laying her cheek against one of her knees.

"Anghara."

A familiar voice; a sudden smell of lais tea. Anghara
opened her eyes again; a bowl of it was set on the ground beside her, and familiar hands, ai'Jihaar's, rested one on the

nape of her neck over her foaming hair and one gently on her forehead.

"It will be all right," murmured ai'Jihaar. "Drink the tea."

Anghara tried to turn her head away, but it was as though her muscles had ceased to obey her. The thought of taking anything at all into her mouth made her stomach turn dangerously. But ai'Jihaar, who had felt the tensing underneath her hands, was inexorable.

"Drink the tea," she repeated firmly. "Trust me."

Anghara struggled to sit up and ai'Jihaar let her, but not too fast. She was beginning to come round, but still felt very weak; her stomach was starting to settle, slowly. The thought of the tea became marginally more welcome. She sighed deeply, pushing back the curtain of tangled bright hair, and reached for the lais cup as ai'Jihaar passed it over. The older woman sat back on her heels beside Anghara. The expression on her face was ambivalent.

"There was something in the fire," she said levelly, in a voice of knowledge.

Anghara, color beginning to flood back into her white face, glanced up from her tea—first at ai'Jihaar and then at the woman who had brought the bowl, the same one who had made her the gift of the comb. If the bronze skins of Kheldrin could be said to go pale, then this woman's face was ashen, terrified at the turn of events. She crouched close by, tensely, balanced on the balls of her feet so that she could flee at a moment's notice if necessary. Anghara lowered the cup and gave her a wan little smile.

"Please tell her," she said to ai'Jihaar, "that it wasn't her fault."

"I already have," said ai'Jihaar, her voice brittle, but it was only after Anghara's smile that the nameless woman from the caravan had relaxed a little, lowering a knee onto the sand. "The fire," ai'Jihaar prompted, unusually insistent. Reflections of the firelight danced in her blind white eyes.

*What do you see, sen'thar?*

"But I am not," breathed Anghara, seemingly entirely arbitrarily.

"I am raised to the gold," said ai'Jihaar without missing a beat, very softly. "That, you are not. But *sen'thar* you are, Anghara. And no longer novice. Any of us who saw what you did tonight would raise you to the white circle without a single qualm. But after . . . why does it sap you so?"

"I don't know," said Anghara frankly. "Unless . . . unless it was that it came unasked, that I did not seek it, did not center, did not try first for the talisman—and then you spoke to me and I came out of it too fast . . . if that was Sight . . ."

But ai'Jihaar frowned at her words. "What is this talisman you speak of?"

Anghara drained the lais cup and put it down, steeling herself. This was going to be hard. Talisman lore belonged to Morgan, to Bresse, and they were both gone. She had never given ai'Jihaar a complete account of her life before she had met her, and now that came home to roost. Any point where she began to explain came either too early in the tale or too late. It took a while to circle round to the subject at hand.

At first ai'Jihaar seemed to find the concept hard to grasp.

"Everyone uses this to control the Sight? Everyone? Who teaches the technique to those who would never come to a place like Bresse? From what you say, and from what I know, Sight is common enough in your land, found in croft and hold as well as great halls—and somehow all these women manage their Sight—have they all a talisman of their own?"

"I . . . don't know," said Anghara. "I don't, really. The reason I was sent to Bresse was twofold—because they needed a place for me to hide, after . . . after what happened at Cascin . . . and the second was . . . exactly that, exactly what happened. Feor thought it best that I be taught to control what had slipped from me that night, before I did . . . any more damage."

"And that is all they did," snapped ai'Jihaar. And relented, when she saw Anghara bristle at this harsh judgment against Castle Bresse, which had been martyred at Sif's hands. "Child. Sight is more than control. All they have ever done in that place is learn to open their minds to their power—and then close them again as soon as they have finished using it."

"It worked," said Anghara defiantly.

"Of course it worked," ai'Jihaar's voice was infinitely gentle. "But it is not enough, and they never—not one of them—ever knew the true potential of what they were. And if these were the best in Sheriha'drin, then there are none who can stand against what Sif is doing to them now."

"None of them can!" said Anghara, and her voice was a lash, shaped by her guilt and sorrow. "It was a gentle art . . . although Morgan said . . ." The name was a white pain. "Morgan said that there were things done with me in Sight that were done in power."

"They managed to hide you from Sif and his own Sighted cohort whom he gathered to look for you," ai'Jihaar agreed. "That was a bright deed, and woven of many strands—your mother, Feor, Morgan of Bresse. But even that . . . even that was done with half the power, and it was only because they sought you with half the power that you slipped through their fingers for so long."

"Then," said Anghara, throwing back at ai'Jihaar the first question with which Morgan had tested her at Bresse, "what is Sight?"

"If it is indeed the same well from which we are all drinking . . . glory," said ai'Jihaar softly, answering with a promptness and certainty which the young Anghara would have given worlds to have been able to control years ago in Morgan's chambers. "Power and glory." She reached out with a small hand and Anghara laid her own in it, mesmerized by the vibrancy and intensity of ai'Jihaar's voice in that moment.

The touch was electric, a shaft of lightning; Anghara heard herself cry out, her own voice sounding very far away, and then ai'Jihaar was in her mind again, passionate and powerful, just as she had been at the Desert Gate.

*No! You are stronger than this! Do not turn away from your birthright!*

And ai'Jihaar's soul was a pillar of white fire, and something in Anghara leapt to meet it. She knew that, by all the tenets of Bresse, she should have been writhing on the ground in agony, victim of one of those wild visions triggered by the touch of Cascin's little Standing Stone that Morgan could do nothing about but offer comfort and her own strength which, often, had not been enough to keep Anghara from paying for the experience in dizziness, disorientation, sometimes racking pain. But a bridge had been forged across a gulf which Anghara had not known how to cross before; and her own soul fire was gold to ai'Jihaar's white, the same fierce aura which had blazed from her on that Cerdiad night of grievous memory. If Feor could have seen her he would have recognized it for what it was—and he would also have believed that, for once, Bresse had failed in what it had set out to do.

But there was nothing deadly, nothing uncontrolled, in the golden flame of Anghara's mind.

*This,* said ai'Jihaar's voice, white flame weaving with gold, *is Sight. True Sight. And I name you sen'thar, here, tonight. I name you to the white circle, Anghara of Roisinan, stranger of Sheriha'drin, first to walk on the sands of Arad Khajir'i'id in a thousand years. May the Gods walk by your side.*

When ai'Jihaar released Anghara's hand the flames died, first the white, then, a fraction of a second later, the gold. There was no trace of sickness this time; on the contrary, Anghara still tingled with the molten power which had coursed through her veins. Somewhere in her mind echoed a lost voice of Morgan of Bresse, and Anghara saw, for a fleeting moment, an image of her old teacher and gazed upon it with love and respect, and, finally and at last, with pity. Then it was gone, and she was looking upon ai'Jihaar instead—ai'Jihaar, who sat smiling inscrutably and looking straight back at her through eyes which could not see. The woman who had brought the tea was still crouching nearby, her expression unchanged, and Anghara realized that nothing of what she had just experienced could have been visible in the physical plane, else the entire camp would have been in uproar by now.

"Eat something, and then you should sleep," said ai'Jihaar gently, naming what seemed such an utter impossibility that Anghara wanted to laugh out loud. Sleep? After this night? But ai'Jihaar, as usual, was quick to respond to the unspoken. "We ride again in only a few hours, Anghara. Try. You will find it easier than you think. Remember what I said about being responsible for your own mistakes in the desert. Lose your chance of rest tonight, and tomorrow will be a day of endless suffering for you. And you will need all your strength." The smile widened imperceptibly. "I named you to the white circle, because you are more than deserving to be there—but your peers are much advanced in their knowledge of the Way, and there is a great deal for you to learn before you can call yourself their equal. And tomorrow, we begin."

And, because she would have done anything ai'Jihaar asked in that hour, Anghara accepted a chunk of flat waybread baked in the embers by the women, and another steaming bowl of lais tea; and then she rose and went into her tent, her hair rippling around her. She stretched out on the thick rug that was her bed and wrapped herself in a light but warm woven blanket ai'Jihaar had given her in the serai in Sa'alah. Her mind was still sharp—bright and burning in the desert night like a candle—as she began to think back once again on the events of that night . . .

. . . And woke, blinking, into the pearly light which came just before dawn, at the whispered summons at the tent flap and ai'Jihaar's softly murmured response.

"Wake," said ai'Jihaar to her companion. "It is time."

And Arad Khajir'i'id was also waking with the heat, watchful and full of purpose as a living thing, waiting for the rising of the sun to release it into the yellow sands.

By the time the first long fingers of the sun touched the place where Anghara of Roisinan had been raised into the ranks of Kheldrin's *sen'en'thari,* they were already too late to find anything but cold campfire ashes half buried in the sand and a trail of splayed ki'thar'en tracks leading west. And the desert heat, freed from the shackles of the night in a silence a thousand times louder than any roar, uncoiled and stretched, and sprang to follow.

## 17

Nothing she had ever known could have prepared Anghara for the life she was plunged into in the desert of Arad Khajir'i'id. The caravan rolled on relentlessly, resting through the hottest hours of the day and travelling, to compensate for lost time, into the night. During the night camps, while the women prepared the evening meal, ai'Jihaar never failed to snatch an hour or two to drill Anghara in what she called the Way. And if Bresse had been a hard school, the Kheldrini Way was infinitely worse. It had to be absorbed with a tired mind and a body aching with the unaccustomed punishment it was being subjected to every long, desert day as the sun pinned them down for the heat to hunt them.

But there were reserves in Anghara she had never needed to tap before. She did, now, and held her own—only once, as she had slid off her ki'thar in an evening camp, did she wince at a twinge of liquid agony in a strained muscle, and remember something of the softer world she had left behind.

"Kerun and Avanna!" she breathed, her hands at the small of her back, trying to stretch the knotted muscle into quiescence and back into the obscurity it usually dwelt in. Near enough to hear, ai'Jihaar turned with a ghost of a smile hovering around the edges of her mouth.

"They cannot hear you here," she said. "Ours are the older Gods, jealous of their dominion."

Even that exchange, innocuous as it sounded, had thrust them into the Way with an inevitability Anghara had come to accept as inexorable.

"Older? The Elder Gods?" Anghara queried, her mind winging back to the Dances in Roisinan, where the Elder Gods were said to be summoned with offerings of blood by those acolytes left unfulfilled by the worship of Kerun and Avanna.

And, once again, ai'Jihaar answered both the spoken and the unspoken. "The same Gods have ruled in Kheldrin for a thousand years," she said. "Perhaps longer. They existed when the Dances were young. Perhaps it was to them that the Stones were raised. But the knowledge was lost long ago, when the builders of the Dances passed away, and the Elder Gods withdrew into the Twilight Country where they had been born."

"Why?" Anghara asked, skating off at a tangent. "Why the Twilight Country? I have never seen a place where the sun shines more brightly than it does in Arad Khajir'i'id."

"But not beyond it," ai'Jihaar murmured.

And Anghara suddenly understood. "It is hidden," she whispered. "A shadow on the edge of night . . ."

The older woman nodded. "What did you know of Kheldrin ere you came here? Only that it was a desert country, which bred swift horses and strange people. And on those people your countrymen always looked askance, partly because they were . . . different, and perhaps, as they might say, inhuman—and partly because there is an old belief that there are witches in Kheldrin with powers equal at the very least to those of the Elder Gods."

This was ai'Jihaar's own brand of brittle humor, but it was a dangerous joke; Anghara gave a small dry laugh. "I have heard of them," she said. "But they are rumor, legend, every tale about the Kheldrini witches always begins with 'it is said,' never 'I have seen . . .' "

"Faith needs no proof. They knew enough to think that they never wanted to know any more," said ai'Jihaar. "And Kheldrin, to Sheriha'drini, shrank to the plain around Sa'alah, where some, a brave few, came to do trade for those things only Kheldrin could give them. There, and no further—and even that, for some, was too far. Beyond the mountains was another world, one which was guarded against them by their very fear of it. And so we were content, also, for the twilight is the essence of the Way."

"Then how can it be right for one not born of it to take the Way?" asked Anghara, suddenly troubled.

"You are *sen'thar*," said ai'Jihaar evenly. "Kheldrin is an old land, the oldest, perhaps; it is your own Gods who have called you home."

And Anghara learned of the Old Gods: al'Zaan, Sa'id-ma'sihai, Lord of the Empty Places whose realm Kheldrin had been from the beginning of memory, the God who could not be worshipped within any constricting walls but who lived in every grain of sand in the open desert; al'Khur, who wore the head of the desert vulture on his human body and vulture's wings springing from his shoulders—al'Khur, Lord of Death, but also, in gentler guise, Lord of Little Death that was sleep and of the dreams and visions which were its gifts; ai'Dhya of the Winds; ai'Lan of the Sun, with her bowl and her crooked knife, and the power and protection bought by bloody sacrifice; gentle ai'Shahn, the Messenger of the Gods, who was also ai'Shahn al'Sheriha, spirit of the waters, holiest of them all. *Sen'en'thari* were not bound to any one God but served them all—and knew every invocation, every sacrifice, every word of power that was ever sacred to any God. Every God spoke to them, and they had to learn to understand them all.

Kheldrin was not, never had been, a populous country; even had their version of Sight been as widespread as it was . . . had been, Anghara had to remind herself bitterly . . . in Roisinan, there would have been relatively few who had the gift. But there were even fewer *sen'en'thari* than this, fewer than Anghara could have imagined. The white circle, to which ai'Jihaar had named Anghara, was the first rung in the *sen'thar* hierarchy, just above the novitiate, and it consisted of no more than perhaps two hundred people in all of Kheldrin. The second circle, the gray, boasted less than eighty initiates—for not all of the whites would go on to take the gray robe. And the third, the highest, circle was the gold—ai'Jihaar was one of only five *an'sen'en'thari,* the High Ones, and the oldest of them. And the only one—Anghara trembled with pride and with a strange fear when ai'Jihaar made this confession—to have never taken a novice since she had become *an'sen'thar.* Not until her path had crossed with a lost princess in the Land of Running Water.

Four days out from the Desert Gate, beside the pahria palm-fringed pool of a small hai'r, the caravan met up with another, larger one, also on its way south. Waiving the usual night-camp session of Way lore, ai'Jihaar had released Anghara to watch the dancing around fires built in the space between the two camps. Anghara saw her teacher draw aside the leader of their own caravan and stand speaking with him quietly for some time. When she was finally done, ai'Jihaar turned to pick her way delicately and unerringly to where her pupil sat with her back against one of the huge palms, and Anghara scrambled to her feet. There was a tranquillity on ai'Jihaar's unveiled face, the tranquillity which comes in the wake of having finally made a difficult decision.

"The caravan leaves us tomorrow," she said without preamble when she reached Anghara, offering the first tangible information concerning their destination since they had left Calabra. "They are to join with this other and turn south, to Beku. And we have still a long way to go before we see the dunes of the Kadun."

Kheldrini geography was still hazy in Anghara's mind. She frowned, trying to remember if she had heard the name before. "Kadun?"

"Kadun Khajir'i'id. The Northern Desert."

Anghara was abruptly reminded of a street in Sa'alah, just off the pier. A ship newly arrived from Roisinan; two passengers disembarking, one rooted deeply into the land they had just stepped upon, the other a leaf adrift on a storm. *Home,* ai'Jihaar had answered when Anghara had asked where they were going.

There had been something in ai'Jihaar's voice when she had named the Northern Desert which was very similar to the way she had answered Anghara's question back in Sa'alah.

Kadun Khajir'i'id was home. But patience had not been amongst the least of things which ai'Jihaar had taught Anghara; she waited, in silence, until ai'Jihaar was ready to go on.

"I had thought to make it easier for you," ai'Jihaar said after a pause, "to take the High Road and cross the Kharg'in'dun'an into Kadun. Even the Arad has made you suffer; I did not want to make you face the Khar'i'id before you must. But in Beit el'Sihaya, the Empty Quarter, where the Stone Desert sunders the sands of Arad and Kadun, there is a place which waits for you, and the only way to reach it is the hard way. It might mean nothing at all, and yet it might mean everything—and something is telling me the time to find out is now."

"Where?" said Anghara. It was all she could do to say even that much; a great silence had bloomed in her at the name of Beit el'Sihaya, a silence broken only by what seemed to be the whisper of a distant wind in her mind.

"Gul Qara."

And of course that was where they had been meant to go. Anghara knew as soon as she heard the words spoken. The white flame and the gold, that first night in the desert; all the questions that had arisen, clamoring for answers; and the Gods had been silent.

Silent also, for years uncounted, had been the Oracle of Gul Qara. It had once, so the legend said, spoken with a human voice—but it had been haunted by nothing except the desert winds for almost as long as the Records could remember.

*I know this . . . how do I know this . . .*

But the white flame was twined in the gold; these were ai'Jihaar's memories. And now she withdrew, leaving the Oracle in Anghara's mind.

"Perhaps it is for you," said ai'Jihaar. "Perhaps it will wake for you." She suddenly lifted her face into the still night air, as though she were scenting something. Anghara could see her mood flow into something different, less solemn, more quicksilver. "Pahria nuts," she said, correctly. There were four around Anghara's feet, one cracked open by the little woman—her name, Anghara had learned at last, was ai'Sahli—who had once offered the gift of a carved bone comb. She had come over to Anghara when she'd seen the Sheriha'drini girl was alone, but had prudently withdrawn when she had seen ai'Jihaar approaching. A thin streak of milky juice was oozing out into the sand from the split nut, overturned in ai'Sahli's strategic retreat. "Has ai'Sahli been bearing gifts again?"

It was a light moment, leavened with laughter, one Anghara would recall with something like nostalgia in the days which followed.

They parted company from the caravan the next morning, and Anghara watched it meander away southward toward the city called Beku. The night before ai'Sahli had been the only one to offer some kind of farewell, but nobody, not even she, had turned to wave goodbye at the caravan's departure. During the short duration of their shared journey, theirs had been a quiet, gracious, if rather distant acceptance which Anghara could not see Roisinani offering a solitary Kheldrini traveller, no matter whose protection he travelled under. The caravan leader had voiced his unease at Anghara's presence back at the Sa'alah end of the Desert Gate, and after that had bowed to ai'Jihaar's superior judgment and never, by word or deed, offered any objection to Anghara's presence. In fact, he had paid her the highest compliment of treating her no differently from one of his own people; and if one or two of them chose to make overtures to her, offering the gift of a comb or helping with readying her ki'thar, that was their own concern and no business of his.

But he was gone, with his people, and Anghara and ai'Jihaar turned their own ki'thar'en west once again. Later, after a day or two, ai'Jihaar angled a little more southwest, back into the Arad, when the ground began to change into a thin layer of yellow sand over stone which marked the beginning of the Khar'i'id—not yet, the gesture seemed to say, not until we must. Later still they came upon a tiny, deserted hai'r. Although it was only mid afternoon ai'Jihaar called a halt, no more than an hour or two since their midday break. With new-honed senses she would not have known the existence of only a few short weeks ago, Anghara looked through the solitary pair of pahria palms flanking the little pool of brown water, and saw the air was different in the direction in which they were headed. Heavier, somehow; where the heat of the Arad was a swift wildness released by the sun every morning and confined again at sunset in the cool cage of the desert night, the heat that shimmered ahead was solid, smothering, and had a disturbing air of permanence.

Warned by a sudden stillness in her companion, ai'Jihaar came to stand beside her. "You feel it?" she asked quietly. "That is Khar'i'id. That is where we are going tomorrow. We must make sure all the waterskins are full; this is the last water from here to the Kadun."

"You said water must be bought," said Anghara, glancing around for any sign of this small hai'r's water-keeper, to whom payment had to be made.

But ai'Jihaar shook her head. "Not here. This is the Shod Hai'r, the Last Oasis; this water is a gift from the Arad."

"There are still a few hours of light left," said Anghara. "Why don't we fill the skins and go on? We can make a start, at least, in the cool of the evening, and tomorrow . . ."

"That is Khar'i'id," said ai'Jihaar again. "There is no cool in the Khar'i'id night. And no one walks the Stone Desert in darkness. Not when there is a choice."

And the rich golden light of an afternoon by a Dance of Standing Stones in a different land came pouring into Anghara's memory, and within it, the first instant when she had heard the name of the desert at whose threshold she stood.

*The Stone Desert of Kheldrin, where nothing thrives except se'i'din and diamondskins, and both of these are death.*

She turned away abruptly, back toward the small muddy pool in the midst of Shod Hai'r. Tomorrow would be soon enough.

The ki'thar'en were more reluctant than usual to move the next morning; beasts of the desert, they were even more finely tuned to the atmosphere around them and knew Khar'i'id held nothing good. It was blighted land. The only thing that grew there was thorn-spurred se'i'din, a poison from which there was no reprieve. It was hard to obtain in Roisinan—if Kheldrin traded for it, it was not on the open market—but it was not unknown; a number of feuds had been settled by means of what the Roisinani knew as rosebane. There would be nothing wholesome for ai'Jihaar and Anghara to eat or drink in Khar'i'id until they emerged on the other side except that which they carried with them.

And yet, Khar'i'id held one of the holiest places in Kheldrin, and the journey to Gul Qara was simply the penance required to set foot on hallowed ground. The ki'thar'en were overruled, and pointed into the cauldron.

There was a boundary between the Arad and Khar'i'id; Anghara sensed when it was crossed. Between one breath and the next it was as though she suddenly had to gulp air through a hairy blanket. The burnoose felt as if it was choking her; she was already lifting a clawed hand to release it, her reason dulled by the solidity of the heat around her, when she felt ai'Jihaar's urgent touch in her mind, no less sharp and clear in this place than it had been in the open sands of the Arad.

*Resist it. It can be resisted. It must be resisted. This place kills without trying. Do not let it force you into doing something foolish.*

Anghara's hand dropped. She squared her shoulders to endure; but in that moment she would have given anything for one breath of the high, clear air of Miranei.

All too soon ai'Jihaar's repeated references to walking the Stone Desert became painfully clear. They had started out on the sand-covered stone shelf, which they had encountered before, no more than a condescension toward metamorphosis of the one desert into another. But as the last of the Arad's yellow sand faded away, the true face of Khar'i'id unveiled itself—a black stone plain of loose sharp rocks the ki'thar'en would have trouble enough negotiating while led, but which they had no chance at all of walking with a rider.

The ground was hot beneath the two women's feet as they dismounted, and even the animals, ready under normal circumstances to grumble and complain at the smallest things, were grimly silent at the spectacle of the purgatory which awaited them. Anghara exchanged an eloquent glance with the blind, white eyes of ai'Jihaar, which had been turned toward her—and stepped forward first.

They didn't stop at midday—there was no point, as there was no peak to the heat, it just seemed to burn on and on at the same impossible, blistering, eternal high. Soon it seemed as though they had been walking forever, Anghara having turned into a plodding automaton whose only tasks in life were to remember to breathe and keep putting one foot in front of the other. When ai'Jihaar eventually called a halt, she had to do it twice before Anghara responded, looking up in surprise to realize the sun was already well on the way to setting. She tried to speak, but her dry mouth could not seem to form the words.

*Do not,* said ai'Jihaar. *Khar'i'id is the place Sight was made for.*

After a moment Anghara managed to frame her thought, looking up with gray eyes already limned with exhaustion. *How long?*

*Long enough.*

The one time she had made a concession to her pain in the Arad, it had been no more than a trivial groan at seized muscles responding to the punishment of long hours riding an unaccustomed mount, swiftly put aside and overcome. It had lasted only long enough to be turned into something comical, and, from that, into the basis of one of ai'Jihaar's lectures of the Way. Aside from this, Anghara had never, with word or gesture, expressed the merest hint of a complaint. But now, looking out over the black plain which still shimmered with heat to the oddly blurred horizon behind which a large red sun was slipping slowly, she lifted a visibly shaking hand to press her fingers to her temple, over her securely fastened burnoose.

*Don't let it be too long,* she said quietly into the pain that beat rhythmically inside her skull. *I don't know how much of this I can stand.*

But she rose on the second morning, and walked again.

There was no other sign of life in this place except the two women who moved with weary courage, leading animals whose heads drooped on their necks. Once, it was true, Anghara raised her head to the pitiless sky and saw the huge black wings of a desert vulture riding the thermals far above them—and something stirred in her as she bowed down in the presence of al'Khur, come to them in his deadliest avatar. Another time she had checked her stride, freezing in place moments before ai'Jihaar's warning exploded in her mind, watching as a gray lizard, his skin mottled with black diamond shapes, slid unhurriedly away from her and into the rocks. This was a beast of Khar'i'id, and from poison sacs behind snake-like teeth oozed a venom which was, if anything, more potent than se'i'din. A trickle of cold sweat born of sudden fear ran down Anghara's spine, where her robe already clung wetly to her skin. And then she had squared her jaw and walked on.

Khar'i'id took everything. A traveller was stripped to the bone, and then beyond; endurance had to be sought in the deepest places of the self, delving into chasms whose existence the spirit in which they had been riven had not known until the appointed hour on the black plain. Here, there were no secrets. Khar'i'id found steel in a soul, or destroyed it utterly—with the Stone Desert there was no middle ground.

But the deepest abyss hides the greatest treasure. Khar'i'id had its own gifts to bestow on those who stumbled and cried *I cannot!* only to get up and carry on. In the midst of this, the country whose every face was death, lurked a kernel of resurrection. What ai'Jihaar had not told Anghara was that a night walk in this desert many years ago had forged her own soul, and won her the gold robe of the *an'sen'thar.* But the desert gave nothing that had not been suffered for, and there were times when its only reward was suffering. It was not given to those who braved it to know whether the place found them worthy. As ai'Jihaar watched the gently reared child of Sheriha'drin gallantly take on the worst hell the Twilight Country could try her spirit with, she saw her change to meet the challenge, and grieved for the remnants of childhood which would be irrevocably lost in this place. She could not know that this time Khar'i'id held one of its greatest gifts, poised against the hour of ultimate need in which it was to be given.

It was late on their third day in Khar'i'id that the land changed with a startling suddenness, rising into serried ranks of steep hills whose slopes were covered with a loose scree of small, sharp fragments of the same black rocks which covered the plain. The path Anghara and ai'Jihaar had been following—only now did it become obvious that, in the trackless waste, they had indeed been following a path—plunged between these knolls, forming a narrow twisting passage, where their way seemed barred, again and again, with huge tumbled boulders. The air was stale, hotter and more close than ever, trapped in these convoluted passageways where no wind ever stirred; if it had been thick and dense on the plain, here it was almost a solid wall. Anghara fought for every step against an invisible barrier, which seemed to have been placed there for the express purpose of keeping out unwelcome visitors.

*It was,* said ai'Jihaar. *Gul Qara lies in the next valley.*

Her voice, her presence, were enough to remind Anghara that she was not alone; stifling a sob born both of absolute exhaustion and blessed relief that their goal was almost in sight, she found strength for yet another effort, the last. And then, so suddenly that she almost tumbled headlong down into it, the black hills sloped sharply down into a wide, deep valley with a floor of fine, pale, crystalline sand. Down the very center of the valley marched a double row of closely spaced tall gray pillars. The colonnade began and ended in emptiness, but there was no sign that this place was a remnant or a ruin unless everything else that had ever been here had already crumbled away into the dust and sand at their feet.

There had been something in the sight which had brought

Anghara to an abrupt halt at the edge of the slope, and now ai'Jihaar stepped up beside her.

"Gul Qara," said ai'Jihaar, speaking out loud for the first time since they had entered Khar'i'id. Her voice was rough with the dregs of that silence, and with other things—she had other, older memories of this place.

"The air," whispered Anghara as though she couldn't believe it, drinking in her first breath in many days that was somehow not oppressed by Khar'i'id's heavy heat. There was even—a forgotten luxury, almost—something of a breeze.

"It is said that ai'Dhya of the Winds loves this place," said ai'Jihaar, pausing to let the clean air of Gul Qara clear away the cobwebs with which Khar'i'id had muffled her mind. "Come," she said at length, pulling at her ki'thar's rein and taking the lead down to the valley. "We have tonight, and tomorrow. And afterward, we have two days to cross what is left of the Stone Desert before we reach the Kadun."

Anghara's eyes went to the waterskins the ki'thar'en carried. It suddenly looked as if there was no more there than would satisfy the need of another hour, let alone three more days. "How much is there still to cross?" she asked, almost reluctantly. Just as it had been difficult to believe in Sa'alah in the yellow vastness of the Arad, so it was suddenly difficult to believe in the desolation of the Khar'i'id in this gentle place—and Khar'i'id had to be faced again within hours. Anghara had to forcefully remind herself that Gul Qara was waterless, and all the more deadly for the lull of its unearthly beauty.

"Others have made it," said ai'Jihaar in response to Anghara's question. As an answer it was unreassuring; but they were now close enough to the pillars to see their true scale. All other thoughts fled as Anghara, with a gasp of awe, tilted her head to seek the top of the smooth, towering column which dwarfed them as they approached. She reached out with all of her power, the gold aura flickering eerily around her head, but this place was ancient beyond words, and empty. Dead, except for the whispering wind which had been the first to greet them, and wove in and out of the pillars and stirred the sand around the massive plinths. A wind which sounded oddly familiar, even though she could not quite remember where she had last heard its like.

"What are we seeking here?" she said at last, turning back to where ai'Jihaar had tethered their ki'thar'en a little way off.

"You do not seek in this place," ai'Jihaar replied, without lifting her head. "Even in the days when it still spoke, the Oracle gave what answer it wanted to give—and it was hardly ever something that matched what had been asked of it. But if the supplicant came here open to whatever the Oracle offered, he would often walk away with wisdom to satisfy all the questions which had never been asked." She paused, her small hands stilling for a moment at their task. "If it gives, it will give freely. Be ready, and be near . . ."

"But you say it has been silent for so long . . ."

"Yes," said ai'Jihaar. "But that was before you came."

Anghara looked at her sharply. "You said our coming here could mean everything—or nothing," she said, reminding her of words spoken in an Arad Khajir'i'id hai'r only a few short days before.

"That is true," said ai'Jihaar with the insufferable calm of the seer waiting for the unravelling of a double-edged prophecy which would come to pass whatever interpretation had been placed on the words in which it had been couched.

"But . . ." began Anghara again, rebelliously.

The older woman lifted a peremptory hand to silence her. "Be ready, and be near," she repeated. "All I know is that it was important for you to come. But first, let us eat."

Despite all her protestations, Anghara had been standing on the threshold of the colonnade in deep fascination ever since they had dismounted from the ki'thar'en. Now she tore herself away somehow and helped ai'Jihaar set up a makeshift camp.

Night fell quickly. They had lit no fire, but did not lack for light—there was a big, soft moon and the stars were as clear and close as they had been on her first night in Arad Kha-

jir'i'id. The pale sand on the valley floor seemed to pick up
the light and diffuse it, with even the black slopes of the hills
of the Khar'i'id glowing with a faint, reflected lumines-
cence. It was as though the two of them lay in a bowl of
moonlight, the shadows of the pillars, etched long and sharp,
falling away from them toward the head of the valley.

Judging by her even breathing, ai'Jihaar seemed to have
fallen asleep quickly but Anghara was an empty chalice,
drunk dry of everything but the bitter dregs of her exhaustion by the pitiless desert beyond this hidden valley. She lay
wakeful, and almost preternaturally alert. The maddeningly
elusive wind sighed in and out of her memories, finding no
place to rest there, and at last she left her blankets and
walked barefoot across the cool sand toward the first pillars
of the colonnade.

If she stood precisely midway between the two rows of
pillars, she could reach out and brush them with the tips of
her outstretched fingers; the stone was as smooth and silky
as skin to her touch, worked in some ancient way which had
long been lost. The floor of the colonnade, underneath a thin
layer of sand, was also smooth and cool beneath the soles of
her naked feet; it felt like polished tiles. She stood poised for
a moment on the edge of the colonnade, fingers of each hand
resting lightly on the pillar on either side of her, and then the
wind, seductive and compelling, made her take a step into
the empty corridor between the mighty pillars. And another.
Her mind was clear; a patch of tile lay revealed, free of sand,
at her feet, and she knew she would remember its pale,
pearly gray color for as long as she lived. And it was as Anghara stood there in the moonlit silence, bright hair spilling
loose over her shoulders, that the miracle happened.

There, in the middle of the desert, the wayward, eerily familiar breeze she couldn't quite remember, brought her a
sudden and quite unmistakable breath of the sea.

Now she knew the soughing wind—she had first heard it
as ai'Jihaar had named the Empty Quarter in the Arad hai'r
where the paths of two caravans had crossed. It surged into
a rush of air and blew through the narrow slits between the

pillars of Gul Qara like a deep note of music, whipping the sand at Anghara's feet into small spiral dust-devils. Almost, almost, she thought she could hear a word whispered into her ear as the wind lifted and swirled her hair around her face . . . And then, in the next moment, it was gone—gone utterly; and Anghara stood in a pool of spreading silence. The same silence she had felt inside her under the pahria palms in that small oasis lost in the yellow sands of Arad Khajir'i'id.

Anghara let her hands drop to her sides, and a curtain of hair fell over her face as she bowed her head. She was trembling all over; it would have been easy, all too easy, to back away from this experience and deny it had ever happened. Easy, except for two things. The vivid, strong, salty tang of the sea was still in her nostrils and came so unequivocally from a place other than the empty, brooding desert waiting on the other side of the sheltering hills; and the triumph blazing upon ai'Jihaar's face. It was the first thing Anghara saw as she turned, very slowly, to walk back toward the camp along the cold, silent colonnade of Gul Qara.

18

The air was still as Anghara stepped out of the colonnade. Still enough that every breath she drew was loud in the silence. There had been something oddly different about the columns as she'd walked past them on her way back toward ai'Jihaar and the camp, tugging insistently at the fringes of Anghara's thoughts, sliding just past the edge of focus. But it was the stillness which held her mind. The wind had been the only living thing about this place when she had first seen this valley. Now it was gone. Her mind was slowed, drifting, sinking into this hush; there was something very important she was missing, and she could not grasp it. She felt the first slow beat of panic rouse within her.

Anghara paused for a moment at the edge of the colonnade, briefly leaning on the last pillar for support as she stepped away. The column was cool and rough underneath her palm; she felt a flake of stone crumble at her touch, fall into silky dust over the skin of her hand. As she came closer, ai'Jihaar reached out for her hands and Anghara placed her own into them, obediently, almost mechanically. The *sen'thar* squeezed them; whatever exhilaration Anghara was failing to feel, ai'Jihaar felt for both of them.

"For this," she said, "for this alone I can raise you to the gold, Anghara, and there would be not a single voice against it."

*A flake*

"I did nothing," she murmured.

*of stone*

"But you did," said ai'Jihaar.

*crumble*

"What is it, Anghara?" ai'Jihaar's voice sank into apprehension, sudden concern.

*at her touch.*

The panic exploded, passion, sorrow, fear; Anghara snatched her hands out of ai'Jihaar's and covered her face, unable to restrain a cry of pain. Familiar pain.

"I destroyed it," she moaned, feeling hot tears spring to her eyes. "I destroyed it."

"Anghara! That is not true!" said ai'Jihaar, reaching out to grasp her shoulders.

Anghara flung out an arm with a tight, savage motion and pointed to the colonnade with a hand which shook. "No? Look at it!" And then, with a brittle little laugh, remembering whom she was addressing, "Feel it, then. When I walked in, this place was ageless, eternal; I touched stone which had been smooth for a thousand years. Touch it now!"

Stepping up to the colonnade, ai'Jihaar laid both hands, palms flat, on the stone.

*"Ah."*

The single word brimmed with understanding and ai'Jihaar stood motionless for a long moment; behind her, Anghara slowly sank to her knees. Her eyes were dark with tears, with guilt, with memory; once again the ghosts of Bresse danced in the moonlight, ghosts of another place of power which had invited Anghara of Roisinan inside and then crumbled in her wake.

"Anghara." There was no response; ai'Jihaar reached deeper. *Anghara. Gul Qara was dead, long before you came. If there was a shadow of life, then it lingered here waiting for you. For you. You could not destroy this; all you did was come for that which was yours, and then you freed the spirit of this place to its rest.*

*Every place that was ever a help or comfort to me . . . I have paid back with death . . .*

*Here you did not kill. You resurrected. I heard Gul Qara speak to you, Anghara, as it has spoken to no other in living memory, and beyond. Death has lived in this valley for longer than you can imagine, and it fell to you to reach through it and touch a power of the Elder Days. There is pride in this; not sorrow, not anguish.*

But Anghara was gazing once again at the pillars of the oracle, and in her eyes was fiery pain. "If I had known that this was what I was coming here to do," she whispered, out loud, closing her mind to ai'Jihaar at last, "I would never have come."

For now, in the moonlight, she could see the ravaged pillars with pitiless clarity. The weight of all the years that had passed it by settled upon Gul Qara in a single moment of time. The gray stone was scored and pitted as though from centuries of sandstorms, cracked from empty decades of merciless sun. Dust seeped from deep seams. The intricate carving around the pillars' massive bases had vanished, worn into shapeless nubs within seconds. Anghara, who remembered the timeless beauty which had existed here barely minutes before, felt as though she had been stabbed to the heart.

The smell of the sea was only a lingering memory; the word . . . the word she had almost heard . . . She searched desperately in the recesses of her mind, her memories, but that was gone too, if it had ever really existed. Anghara felt fresh tears well up behind the ones that had dried on her cheeks.

"And it was all for nothing," she murmured.

"You cannot know that. Something that came to you this way, across the yawning gap of so many years, must have meaning. Somewhere. What happened in there, Anghara?"

"You said you heard," said Anghara, dropping her eyes onto the pale sand at her feet.

"Only the wind, at the last," said ai'Jihaar.

"It could have been anything," said Anghara. "How could you know that it was . . ."

"I knew," said ai'Jihaar, very softly, "because you were a creature of light and power standing in a place out of time. I knew you had touched the oracle long before I heard the wind call your name."

Anghara's head whipped round so fast that she had to

reach up and push a swatch of hair out of her eyes before she could see again. "Is that what you heard?"

"I heard the wind blow a clarion call," said ai'Jihaar. "It was a sound not of nature, never before heard in this place, unless in encounters which took place so long ago they are legend by now. What words Gul Qara had for you, I do not know."

"Nothing," said Anghara with barely leashed violence. "A half-formed whisper, gone before I could grasp it. And then nothing. Unless . . ."

"Unless . . ." prompted ai'Jihaar after a moment of lengthening silence.

"There was . . ." began Anghara, not quite sure how to begin describing this, and then settling for blunt truth, "I smelled the sea."

"The *sea?*" repeated ai'Jihaar blankly, caught completely off guard.

Anghara, who had been watching her with almost pitiful hope, looked away again. "You don't know. You see, it means nothing."

"I do not know everything," ai'Jihaar said gently. "But meaning will come to you, in time."

Anghara made a sound halfway between a laugh and a choking sob. "Yes. And perhaps it won't," she said, when she had her voice back under control. There was a flatness in it which, for the first time, gave ai'Jihaar a twinge of fear. They had Khar'i'id to face again—sooner than she had expected, for there was no reason to linger in this place any longer—and Khar'i'id showed no mercy to the wounded. The strength that had taken Anghara to Gul Qara was spent—it died this night; and without that strength, the grim passage through what remained of the Stone Desert would be a gamble, with Anghara's very life at stake.

And ai'Jihaar knew well what lay at the root of this new burden—Bresse, always Bresse, the place Anghara would always think she had abandoned to a revenge which should have claimed only herself. Morgan may have chosen a martyr's death with a very good idea of what she was doing, but she was a persistent ghost. She could not have imagined the side-effects her deed would have—her act of self-immolation to ensure her chick freedom to fly may have crippled the young bird's wings forever. Sif may have been the one to give the order to destroy Castle Bresse, but Anghara had taken the guilt of its ruin on her own shoulders.

"Bresse chose what it chose, Anghara," she said, knowing that she wounded but willing to try even pain to shock Anghara back into a semblance of normality. There was a fey quality to her that night, something that would hand Khar'i'id the key for her destruction unless ai'Jihaar could break it quickly, here. "That is not on your conscience, no more than this. The only thing you did at Gul Qara was set free a spirit which may well have longed for release these many centuries—after calling it back, one last time, to offer you what gifts it could in return. I promise you, Anghara, for this night there is no one who could deny you the gold robe of the *an'sen'thar.*"

"No," said Anghara. "Not for death."

"Not death," ai'Jihaar said, quietly insistent, stretching out her hand. "Come. You need rest."

"No," said Anghara again, more softly. "Leave me be. I need to watch. I need to remember this."

For a moment, ai'Jihaar hesitated and then, unexpectedly, offered a silent gesture of acceptance and respect with the graceful desert salutation Anghara had seen for the first time at the entrance to the Desert Gate. Its meaning was suddenly augmented by many other nuances: heart—the love and pride of a teacher for her pupil, a mother for her child; lips—a giving into silence of all the words that became unnecessary, already woven into that love and pride; brow—the salute of an equal to an equal, to someone who, although still learning, could rise to be greater than her teacher.

If ai'Jihaar thought she had succeeded in taking some small part of Anghara's pain away, it had not been enough. The wind had abandoned Gul Qara, and the valley was hot and airless as they arose the next morning, but Anghara's hand was cold in ai'Jihaar's as the *sen'thar* reached to cover it where it rested on the ki'thar's bridle. Now dusty and scorched by the harsh desert sun to a faded pink, the bridle was but a distant memory of the brave, royal red of the Sa'alah courtyard.

Anghara felt her concern.

"I am all right," she said, but her voice was oddly lifeless. She had slept at last, by the colonnade of Gul Qara, and when she had woken it was to see two of the great pillars leaning drunkenly against their neighbors. It was a matter of time. Anghara had thought the pain had been deep enough the previous night, but the sight of this new ruin, still perfect in a grotesquely sterile, beautiful way, had showed her there was yet life's-blood to be had from her. It would take days, perhaps only hours, for the place which had stood everything time could throw against it to crumble in the wake of Anghara Kir Hama's passing.

"We could spare the day, if you need it," said ai'Jihaar quietly.

"Here?" asked Anghara.

Silently ai'Jihaar's hand dropped away. Anghara was right, of course; anywhere, anywhere but Gul Qara, was where she wanted to be. She did not want to see the moment when the first column fell.

"Anghara. Be careful; be vigilant. Khar'i'id cannot understand mistakes, and will not forgive them."

"I do not forget," said Anghara.

It was not enough. But it was all Anghara was giving, and after another moment ai'Jihaar sighed and turned away. "Go," she said. "I follow."

And so Anghara led them out of the valley and back into the black hills, through the twisting passages with their pockets of still, empty air, and finally back onto the black, stony wasteland of Khar'i'id.

What had come to pass in Gul Qara was nothing to the Stone Desert—praise or punishment, it had not been in its own power to offer. It had been content to relinquish the travellers into the hidden valley in the heart of the Empty Quarter—and waited with implacable, inhuman patience until they emerged. Now, even as Anghara stepped back into the shimmering heat of the barren plain, Khar'i'id gathered its forces for the moment of destiny, readying the double-edged gift which was to be the desert's own price for her passage—and her reward.

When the appointed hour finally came, it burst upon them without warning.

Despite ai'Jihaar's repeated urging, neither was vigilant that morning. Anghara found herself lost in dark thoughts of her own, waking up into the reality of Khar'i'id every now and again with a sense of what was almost surprise. Walking behind her young charge, ai'Jihaar could sense her doing this—and knew how deadly it could be, in this of all places. It was during one of these periods—when the desert, which ought to have been the only focus of every waking thought had become no more than a backdrop against which they moved—that Khar'i'id struck.

With Anghara turned inward and ai'Jihaar focused on Anghara, the two diamondskins sunning themselves directly in their path went completely unnoticed until Anghara's ki'thar snorted suddenly and bucked sideways with a sudden furious strength. Taken wholly by surprise, Anghara felt the rein jerk from her fingers as she stumbled onto her knees. Equally startled, ai'Jihaar cried out and dropped her own ki'thar's lead rein—only for the animal to pick up its mate's alarm, and plunge forward directly into her path, forcing her to step back to avoid being trampled.

The two diamondskins in the front, the cause of all the consternation, had long since fled, slipping into the shadows of the black rocks.

The one behind ai'Jihaar, which none had yet observed, was still there. Her heel came down on its tail; the lizard twisted with uncanny speed and sank its poisoned fangs through the soft, thin leather of her riding boot and into her ankle.

With the lizards which had sparked off their own alarm now out of the way, the ki'thar'en had regained their equanimity and come to a placid stop only a few steps away, trailing their reins. Anghara scrambled up from the scorching ground, her hands tingling with the heat as though she had just passed them through a fire, and ran back to where ai'Jihaar had collapsed almost without a sound, her breathing sharp and shallow, her blind eyes closed.

"No!" Anghara sobbed, coming to rest on her knees beside the *sen'thar.* "Gods, no!"

At her voice, ai'Jihaar's eyelids flickered open. "Take all the waterskins . . . and head north . . ." she said, her voice rasping in her throat, concerned even in these, her last moments, about the welfare of one who was not born of the desert and for whom the loss of her guide and teacher may well mean death. "Find . . . a hai'r . . . a caravan . . . show them my *say'yin* . . . Someone . . . will take you to Al'haria . . . to the *sen'en'thari* . . . tell them I sent you . . . they can . . . take you home . . ."

Anghara had seen the telltale puncture marks; undoing ai'Jihaar's burnoose with hands that trembled, she had seen the pallor of her skin, the white rim around the *sen'thar's* thin-lipped mouth. She could feel the white flame flickering erratically, fitfully, dying away.

She knew what a diamondskin bite meant.

The knowledge could not prepare her for the surge of rage and anguish which flooded into her as ai'Jihaar's slight body went limp in her arms.

But Khar'i'id's double-edged blade had been thrust home. The first edge had cut—the price was paid. The other only now sliced to release the reward.

Sliced along the thin skin that held in a sleeping power.

And through this incision it poured out, cold fire, wrapping Anghara in a blaze of golden light that rivalled the sun beating down on Khar'i'id empty spaces. A rustle of huge wings mantled at Anghara's back, and shadows shrank from where she stood cloaked in the glow of power—power born of the utmost depths of love and fear and fury, released from a dark place deep within her, the last where Khar'i'id had not yet been, where she herself had never ventured before.

But that which had been hidden there was free now, and it was mighty.

*No,* Anghara said, and the words were a power within the power, uttered only to be obeyed. Her eyes were the eyes of a goddess. *No! I will not have it. I will not have it!*

But even as she was bending over the lifeless body she held in her arms, feeling the great white wings of Khar'i'id's gift spread and begin to fold over the shell that had been ai'Jihaar, there came a sound like distant thunder. The descending wings were met and held back, with a crackle of electricity, by something adamant and implacable. Anghara looked up and saw a muscled bronzed body too immense to belong to any mortal, tapering to the naked neck and smooth, dangerous head of a vulture whose beak was bloodied and whose eyes gleamed with something ageless and eternal. The creature's massive black wings had stopped Anghara's own, and their wingtips, black and white, now rested against one another with the infinite gentleness which is power restrained.

And Anghara straightened, looking the Lord of Death in the eye.

*This is not her hour.*

*That,* al'Khur said gravely, *is for me to decide.*

*No,* said Anghara, and there was no supplication in her tone. She was not asking for this, she was taking it. *Not this time. Not this woman.*

They stood thus for a moment, wingtip to wingtip, eye to eye, and then al'Khur's great head bent infinitesimally.

*You do not know yet what you are, Changer,* he said. *You know that you may bind me, but you do not know why. I must obey you, but because you ask this before your time, it is given to me to bind you in return.*

*For this life, I accept the binding.*

*Very well. Then this is what I lay upon you. You will remember what you have done here today, but not how you achieved it; yours, the memory of resurrection, but not the paths which lead to it. And also, because I must—you will forget the name by which I called you, until it is time for you to claim it. This balance I am not permitted to disturb.* And something like compassion gleamed in the vulture's bright eye as he looked upon the being who held death's wings at bay. *And this I tell you freely, little sister, and ask no price: this is not an easy geas. At least one whom you might have wanted to save will come to me before you and I shall meet again. I see suffering.*

Anghara looked at him steadily. *For this life,* she repeated, *I accept.*

The god stood for another moment in silence, holding her eye, and then the great black wings were furled with a soft rustle of feathers as he stepped back and bowed his majestic head.

*She is yours, then,* he said. *Until we meet again, little sister. Go; remember what you can, forget what you must— al'Khur's own blessing be upon you.*

Then he was gone, as suddenly as he came, and Anghara was only Anghara again, the hot black stone of Khar'i'id searing her legs through her robe as she knelt with ai'Jihaar's head cradled on her lap.

The seer's eyelids flickered open in this instant, the familiar blind eyes beyond them ranging out with Sight that was beyond sight. She lay quite still for a moment, and then drew a deep, shuddering sigh.

"Did the diamondskin not bite me, then?" she murmured; and then, as an impossible, incredible memory came flooding back, her eyes widened with cold shock. "I died," she whispered. "*I died.* I remember it."

The white flame that was ai'Jihaar's psyche leapt up, stronger than ever, reaching for power, for answers that it held. And was met with a gentle, so gentle, flicker of the gold.

*"Hai haddari!"* ai'Jihaar breathed. For a moment she had ceased to be *an'sen'thar,* was simply an old woman of the desert who had been a part of a miracle. The desert nomads' superstitious phrase of awe and wonder had been a visceral response torn from a younger, more vulnerable self. "You brought me back. *You brought me back!*"

A bringer of life, not death. Brief visions of Bresse, of

Gul Qara, flickered across Anghara's consciousness, and then they were gone. Paid for. She dropped her desert-veiled face into her hands and wept for it all, the first clean tears of mourning untainted by guilt and remorse.

Rising to her feet, ai'Jihaar's every gesture was one of purest wonder, taking a moment to refasten the trailing veil of the burnoose Anghara had undone. And then she reached out with both hands, placing them palm down on Anghara's bent head in a gesture of blessing which cut across untold ages and civilizations, and the white flame poured down through them, weaving through Anghara's gold.

*Anghara of the white circle, I raise you to the gold, and name you an'sen'thar.* The words were formal, all ice and dignity, and then ai'Jihaar's voice softened into warmth and gentleness that was the purest love and pride. *Once before I offered the gold, and you refused.*

*Not for death.* Anghara had looked up, her gray eyes a gleam in the shadows of her burnoose. There was a ghost of a memory in them, but its sting had been drawn—there was regret at Gul Qara's passing, but no guilt, not any more.

*Will you accept it now, for life?*

*There is so much that I still do not know . . .*

*There is time enough to learn,* said ai'Jihaar. *When you come to Al'haria, you will be ready.*

*Then . . . if you will it . . .*

*Not I. Greater than I have written the chronicle of your life.*

Such had been the power of this moment that even Khar'i'id had faded into insignificance for a brief while. But now it reasserted its presence, and the solid, choking heat descended upon them like a blow. Khar'i'id had given what it had to give; from now until the moment they left it, it would be neither more nor less than an implacable enemy.

As she turned toward the ki'thar'en, ai'Jihaar reverted to her practical survival mode. "It is time we were on our way," she said. Anghara, still caught up in the wonder of it all, turned and looked into the vast expanse of black desolation which still lay before them to be crossed, and laughed.

They made good time, taking just under two days to traverse what remained of the Stone Desert. It was under a sun already low in the west that Anghara had her first glimpse of Kadun Khajir'i'id.

The red-gold light picked up the colors of the desert, not flat and yellow as the Arad had been but sculpted into breathtakingly magnificent dunes of coral pink sand, streaked with bands of ochre, purple, red and gold. It was beautiful, like a work of art; they passed into it as they had left the Arad, through the same eerie and almost physical line which divided the Stone Desert from the sands. The oppression that was Khar'i'id fell away from them. As they stepped into the reddish sands, there was even the first faint stirring of a cool night breeze.

Better still, Anghara swept her eyes across the near horizon and saw, almost disbelieving, the unmistakable tall fronds of a pahria palm catching the last long rays of the sun.

"A hai'r," she breathed.

"Shod Hai'r," said ai'Jihaar.

Anghara turned to her, puzzled. "Did we not leave that behind in the Arad?"

"It is also known as Fihra Hai'r, the First Oasis," said ai'Jihaar. "As is the other. It depends from which direction you have come. It is also, like the other, a gift from the desert. Come, we will find water there."

There was no pool here, under the solitary palm tree, as there had been in the Arad. Instead, there was a stone-rimmed well, and skins for drawing the water, and shallow stone troughs where water could be poured for animals to drink. It was that which Anghara did first, emptying out three waterskins into the trough and leading the two ki'thar'en, magically revived enough to begin a litany of grumbling, snorting complaints, to drink. Then she hauled out a fourth skinful for herself and ai'Jihaar. After they had sated the first raging edge of their thirst, Anghara poured what remained in the well-skin into one cupped hand over the animal trough, so the run-off would not be wasted in the desert sand. She let it trickle down her fingers over her face and throat with a feeling of blessed relief. While ai'Jihaar seemed to have weathered the Khar'i'id well enough—the desert was, after all, her natural environment—Anghara's fingers were sunburned, in some places quite painfully. Her face was caked with dust, even through the concealing veil of the burnoose, and her hair was tangled and matted from sweat and the close wrap of the burnoose. For a newly created *an'sen'thar,* she looked bedraggled, and knew it.

"In Miranei," she said conversationally, standing with her eyes closed and her face lifted into the breeze, "there is a pool in the mountains, just outside the keep. It's mountain water, icy cold, but there is one part fed by a hot spring, and it's warm enough to swim in. We often used to go there in the summer . . ."

Something stopped her, even the memory cut in mid-image. Her eyes opened wide to see ai'Jihaar standing a short distance away, and next to her, kneeling on the sand, three strange ki'thar'en whose riders had not yet dismounted. They wore black burnooses, fastened desert fashion, and their eyes were turned toward her.

She had been speaking her own language; its liquid syllables warm and familiar, but suddenly she heard them with the ears of the Kheldrini and realized how outlandish they sounded in this solitary oasis.

When ai'Jihaar said something in the guttural accents of her native tongue, the three turned to listen. Then one, the leader, slipped gracefully from his ki'thar and, undoing the burnouse to give them sight of his face, offered formal greeting first to ai'Jihaar, and then, more slowly, to Anghara.

Her heart lurched when he spoke—in accented but flawless Roisinani. The dialect was more Shaymir than Miranei, but the language was unmistakably her own.

"Greetings," he said. "Your paths, as usual, are unfathomable, ai'Jihaar. I did not look for you on this journey, and yet it is far from unexpected that I should find you standing on the threshold of Khar'i'id as I prepare to enter it. My companions and I would be honored if you will share our fire tonight."

"It will be welcome, after Khar'i'id," said ai'Jihaar. "But first we ask, of your courtesy, that you withdraw and allow us our seclusion for a brief while longer. The *salih'al'dayan* has not been performed yet."

The man's head came up with a movement that was too swift. He was obviously no stranger to ai'Jihaar; he may have taken her presence in this place serenely enough, but whatever she had conveyed in the Kheldrini phrase she had just uttered had startled him. He glanced at Anghara, his face impassive but his eyes oddly speculative. Then his lashes dropped, masking his surprise. He made an imperious sign, and his companions slid off their ki'thar'en and vanished into the desert at their backs with almost uncanny speed. The leader bowed again to both of the women and followed them without another word.

Anghara turned to stare at ai'Jihaar, her mind seething with so many questions she was rendered completely mute, and ai'Jihaar answered the most pressing one.

"*Salih'al'dayan,*" she said. "Thanksgiving. There are rites for setting out, and rites of thanksgiving when one arrives. I performed the former, both in Sa'alah and in the Arad Shod Hai'r. Now you are gold; now you must learn them also."

A fleeting memory of a vision flitted through Anghara's mind—al'Khur's great head bowing, the quiet thunder of his voice: *She is yours then.* Thanksgiving.

She lifted her chin. "What must I do?"

"Child," said ai'Jihaar, very gently, "remember, these are the Elder Gods. Theirs is the blood magic. It is usual for an animal to be the sacrifice, but when *sen'en'thari* set out from desolate places, it is permitted to defer the proper rites. But only until you find yourself in a place where they may be performed—and you must give blood to the god in token of your willingness to offer them a more appropriate sacrifice thereafter."

"Kerun is content with gold and incense, Avanna with the fruits of the harvest . . . Nual with flowers in the water," murmured Anghara thoughtfully.

"And they are the Younger Gods, who rule a gentle land," said ai'Jihaar succinctly, taking a thin dagger from the sheath at her waist. "This time, watch only, and learn. There may come a time when it will be up to you to offer *sali-h'al'dayan* to al'Zaan and al'Khur."

She bared a slender arm and placed the point of the dagger in the small valley where her wrist met her palm. And then she spoke, and her voice was suddenly the voice of power. She did not raise her voice in the slightest; she did not need to. She uttered her few lines of invocation almost like a lullaby, and yet the small hai'r was suddenly charged with something which raised the hackles on Anghara's neck. There was a pervading sense of the unfriendly emptiness around them, and of a presence that was in it and of it, who watched over the travellers who moved across it: al'Zaan the One-Eyed, Lord of the Empty Places, come down to accept the promise that was this sacrifice. Anghara watched, both fascinated and repelled, as the dagger drew a small drop of blood from where it pressed into ai'Jihaar's arm; ai'Jihaar allowed it to well up, and trickle into her palm. There was a long pause as the *sen'thar's* voice faded into silence, and then the power faded also, the hai'r sinking back into sleepy tranquility. The *an'sen'thar* plunged her dagger into the sand at her feet, and drew it out clean, scoured by the desert, before restoring it to its sheath.

The blood had already stopped, and when she had washed the traces of it from her palm by rinsing her hand into the beasts' drinking trough Anghara could not even see where the cut had been made.

"We heal," said ai'Jihaar. "It is given to us to heal. This is not a wound, it is a god-gift, and there are no scars."

"I don't know . . . if I could do that," said Anghara, very slowly.

"But you understand it," said ai'Jihaar. "You felt what happened here tonight. When the time comes . . . it will be in you. You know these Gods; they are soul-deep within you." She dried her hand against the skirt of her robe. "Now let us call back the others."

"Who are they? You seemed to know each other."

"Yes, we know one another," ai'Jihaar laughed softly. "The man who spoke to us is al'Jezraal; he is Lord of Al'haria, where one day you will go, when you are ready, to stand amongst the *an'sen'en'thari* of Kheldrin . . . and he is my brother."

## 19

At ai'Jihaar's summons—a high, almost shrill ululation which sliced through the night air like a bright blade—al'Jezraal returned with his two young companions in his wake.

"My son, al'Shehyr ma'Hariff; my nephew, al'Tamar, of clan Hariff also," said al'Jezraal with economical gestures of his hand.

"*An'sen'thar* Anghara of Sheriha'drin," said ai'Jihaar in turn, with the utmost serenity.

It was full dark now, except for the bright desert starlight and the remnants of the Gul Qara moon, but even in this dim light Anghara could see al'Jezraal's head jerk up; his eyes fastened on her, very briefly, and then he had himself in hand again. He had filed the startling information away. Now was not the time.

"By your leave, al'Shehyr and al'Tamar will make camp," he murmured.

Making camp had been, at least partly, Anghara's responsibility for a long while—ai'Jihaar was not truly blind in so many important ways, but there were some physical things she simply could not do without someone lending a hand. Anghara stirred now, uneasily, but both a subtle gesture of ai'Jihaar's hand and a soft mental word stayed her.

*It is not for you. Not in this company. You are an'sen'thar.*

The two young men built up a small fire from dried ki'thar dung, and then busied themselves with provisions. One of them—it had been dark when they had been introduced, and Anghara could not remember which was which—came to kneel by his lord in silence, offering a decorated leather flask.

When al'Jezraal had unstoppered it, he presented it to ai'Jihaar with a sudden grin which, had he not been so conscious of his dignity as the Lord of Al'haria, could have been called mischievous. His sister sniffed delicately in its direction and rewarded him with an eloquent grimace.

"*Pa'ha,*" she said, with almost comical distaste, obviously something of a family joke. "Water for me. For both of us, if that noxious pahria juice is all you have to offer."

Betraying his dignity so far as to permit a short, barking laugh, al'Jezraal revealed that his youth still lived in him. After taking a delicate sip from the offending flask, he stoppered it and put it away.

The two members of his entourage prepared a modest supper, slipping in and out of the circle of firelight like two wraiths—pieces of silent shadow torn from the desert night. Neither could help casting sidelong glances at Anghara every now and again as they worked. There was a silence, also, upon the trio who sat waiting by the fire. It was al'-Jezraal, at last, who broke it. "I would know, ai'Jihaar," he said, his voice once again that of Al'haria's lord, "how your companion came to the gold."

It was his prerogative; it was in Al'haria that *an'sen'en'thari* were confirmed, and by his hand. It was to him that Anghara would have, eventually, come to have her own new status blessed and verified. But it was to have been later, much later; a shiver of fear brushed her, like spiders' feet on bare skin.

"For that," said ai'Jihaar, whose own silence had been neither more nor less than a patient waiting for just this question to be asked, "we must go back to the time when she and I first met. I was on pilgrimage, to Sheriha'drin, to the river they call the Tanassa."

"This I know," he said. "I had word from Sa'alah when you took your leave."

"But you do not know that this time it was not entirely the

call of running water that drew me there. I was sent to Sher-iha'drin, to find something. Someone. To bring that which I found back."

Very softly, al'Jezraal said something in his own tongue, his eyes glinting in the firelight. His sister was silent for a long time, turning away from him, and then stirred, lifting her head to flash a brief sad smile in Anghara's direction.

"Yes, it has been forbidden for a long time. I know it. But she is who she is, and I am what I am—there are times I obey higher laws than those of the People, my brother. I introduced her to you as *an'sen'thar*, but she is more than this—she is the rightful queen of the land they call Roisinan, al'Jezraal, and it was not I who sought her out but she who sensed me in the Great Dance in the hills. And then, later, there was death at our heels in the port of Calabra, and there was a Kheldrini ship waiting."

"Even so," he murmured. "The desert has been shielded for so long . . ."

"From enemies, brother. Not from one who is coming home."

He dropped his eyes. "Perhaps I judge too quickly. Proceed."

As ai'Jihaar described Anghara's vision in the desert campfire and her raising to the white circle the old *sen'thar's* voice was strong, measured, vivid, and al'Jezraal bowed his head in thought when she had finished. "That which they call Sight," he said at last, "is that not common amongst Sheriha'drini?"

*It used to be,* thought Anghara with a sharp stab of pain, remembering Sif and the cage which had been hung in the Calabra street.

But ai'Jihaar was nodding. "More so than with us," she agreed.

"And this that she did . . . was this not Sight alone?"

"Nothing she does is Sight alone," said ai'Jihaar. "And what she did was leave her body by the fireside while her mind winged far away. This is not something that comes easily even to the Sighted in Roisinan, where visions, if they come, are too often cast as dreams. They are rarely, if ever, a true reflection of what is happening at the same instant many miles away. Besides . . . this is not something that is given to you to do, my brother, but had we been in Al'haria any of your *sen'en'thari* could have sensed and verified the power within her."

For another brief while al'Jezraal was silent, then he lifted his head to look at Anghara. "I confirm," he said. This should have been done in the Great Hall of Al'haria, but his face and voice were just as proud and dignified here under the canopy of the desert stars. Anghara had not known how tense she was until she looked down at hands she had just relaxed out of a tight fist and saw the deep half-moons her nails had dug in her palms. And then, remembering what was still to come, she clenched her hands again, hiding them in her lap.

"Even so," said al'Jezaar after a pause, "I confirm the white. But to gray, to gold, in the space of only days?"

When ai'Jihaar turned her blind eyes toward him, he subsided. She would not be hurried. "It was for the Kadun that we were bound," she continued, unperturbed, from where she had left off in her narrative. "I would have gone across Kharg'in'dun'an, but there was something that told me to take her . . . to Beit el'Sihaya. And to take her now."

While al'Jezraal's face was impassive, Anghara could see his shoulders tense. There could have been no real surprise here, not after this encounter in Shod Hai'r at the edge of the Stone Desert, but there was nonetheless bewilderment inherent in the fact that ai'Jihaar had chosen to take this route with a *fram'man*. A stranger.

"You once said to me that you would never again brave Khar'i'id alone," said al'Jezraal, and his words were oddly jarring, apparently irrelevant to what ai'Jihaar had just said; his voice too even. There was something here, then, deeper than even Anghara's intrusion into the Empty Quarter.

*"Hama dan ar'i'id,"* ai'Jihaar said softly. "You are never alone in the desert. Have you forgotten our oldest saying?" And then her hand rose in a graceful motion, indicated Anghara, who sat straight-backed and silent by the

fire. "And I was not. I had an initiate of the white circle with me. One whom you yourself have just confirmed in her standing."

"You named her *an'sen'thar*," al'Jezraal reminded his sister, his eyes on Anghara. Under this steady scrutiny, she lowered her gaze briefly in a token of respect, but then lifted her eyes again and met his, squarely—al'Jezraal looked away again, at his sister. "Proceed. Why, ai'Jihaar? Why the Empty Quarter?"

"Gul Qara."

It was the obvious answer, and yet its effect was electric. Even al'Tamar, the nephew, younger than al'Jezraal's own son, turned his head with a snap at the name.

The Oracle was a holy place. To take a *fram'man* into the desert was bad enough. To take a stranger into hallowed ground . . .

"My sister . . ."

The *sen'thar* had no time for this. "It spoke to her, al'-Jezraal! Let the councils debate this until their bones turn to sand, but I brought into Gul Qara a *sen'thar* who heard a voice stilled these thousand years!"

It was clear that al'Jezraal was seriously shaken, enough for his disquiet to show through cracks in his composure. If it had not been ai'Jihaar who spoke, his own sister whom he knew and trusted and one his own hand had raised to the gold, he would have flung her words back into her face and called her a liar.

"The Oracle is dead!" This from al'Shehyr, close enough to have heard, and under no constraints such as those that bound his father. Nonetheless, al'Jezraal shot him a swift glance of silent rebuke.

"It is. Now."

They all turned to Anghara, the one who had spoken; ai'Jihaar wore an expression of what was almost apprehension for a moment, and then her face cleared, flowed into pride, love, compassion. "It is yours to tell, Anghara," she said.

And Anghara drew a deep breath, and told.

She did not know she did it, but her voice was an instrument of the Gods that night—she wove a tale which rose as a vision under the desert skies. The two youngsters who had still been fussing with camp chores laid down whatever they happened to have in their hands and drew near, enthralled, while al'Jezraal sat still as a carved statue. He was not *sen'thar* himself, but the gift was in his blood—he was sensitive to nuances of speech and gesture enough to open himself to a charge of mind-reading when he chose. He could feel the wonder, ai'Jihaar's pride and exaltation, Anghara's own guilt, the pain and the sorrow.

When Anghara was done, the tableau sat without moving for one brief moment, then al'Tamar sighed and al'Shehyr turned abruptly away—but not before Anghara saw his eyes gleam with what looked suspiciously like tears. While al'- Jezraal looked at her steadily, when he spoke, it was to his sister.

"For this, the gold?"

"I refused it," said Anghara in a low voice.

"That is right," said ai'Jihaar. "Not for death, she said."

Weaving his long fingers together, al'Jezraal brought his chin down to rest upon them. He said no word, waiting for ai'Jihaar to continue. His sister had turned her face toward Anghara, but she was also silent—ai'Jihaar sighed and bowed her head.

"It was not for death that she accepted the gold. It was for life. Mine." She shifted where she sat, stretching out one booted foot toward her brother. "Do you recognize these?" she asked, pointing with unerring accuracy to the twin holes the diamondskih's dagger-like teeth had left in the chamois of her boot.

When he saw them, al'Jezraal sucked in his breath sharply, lifting his head. In the flickering light of the campfire Anghara thought she saw his face go pale. In answer to his sister's question, it was obvious that he did, indeed, recognize what he saw.

Clearly shocked, he breathed, "*al'Khur!* Did the fangs touch you . . . Are you truly all right, ai'Jihaar?"

"They touched me," said ai'Jihaar. "They pierced me. You

are right to call upon al'Khur, for he came for me this day in Khar'i'id . . . and it was Anghara who denied him."

In the same moment ai'Jihaar said this, al'Shehyr, who had been kneeling by the embers and extracting the way-bread which had been buried there to bake, uttered an inarticulate cry as his hand closed convulsively on a live ember.

*"Huma dan ar'i'id,"* murmured al'Tamar, huge black pupils, dilated with shock, almost entirely swallowing the golden irises of his eyes.

"How?" said al'Jezraal huskily.

"One of Khar'i'id's gifts?" ai'Jihaar said. "I do not know. It happened."

"How?" repeated al'Jezraal, turning to stare at Anghara.

She gazed back helplessly. "He . . . was there. He gave me back the life. Or I took it. I don't know. I remember that I did it, but I do not remember how."

As al'Jezraal raised a white face to the sky his hands were shaking. *"Hai!"* he whispered. *"Hai Haddari!"*

In the meantime, al'Tamar was bent over al'Shehyr's reddened, blistering palm; now he thrust al'Shehyr's hand toward Anghara. "You resurrect; can you heal?" he said abruptly.

Anghara had accepted the hand automatically, and now her eyes flicked down to it from al'Tamar's face, and back again.

"I have never healed," she said simply, her heart pounding painfully.

Their eyes held, gold and gray, for a long moment—his challenging, intense, almost angry; hers a little frightened, but steady, and utterly innocent of arrogance or guile. And then, just as she became aware that ai'Jihaar was about to say something, Anghara's dropped again to the burned hand which she held. "I will try."

In truth she had no idea what to do. She stared at the burned hand, feeling its tension through her own fingers; it was obvious al'Shehyr himself was not entirely happy with what was happening. But then she emptied her mind of everything except a vision of that hand, whole again. She closed his stiff fingers over his blistered palm, her own hand lingering gently for a moment over his as she did so. And even if she had not felt the sudden brief dislocation inside herself, as though a great wing had briefly cast its shadow over her spirit, al'Shehyr's sharp gasp would have been enough to tell her.

It was done.

The young man almost jerked his hand from her own, opening his fingers to stare at the unmarked skin, as al'Tamar's lips moved soundlessly. Anghara sat still with her head bowed, feeling utterly drained.

"That was unworthy, al'Tamar."

The voice was al'Jezraal's, a subtle weapon. Anghara lifted her head, in time to see the lord's nephew hang his own in shame as al'Shehyr came to kneel at al'Jezraal's feet, offering his hand.

"Father . . ."

"Yes. I know," said al'Jezraal, as he closed his son's fingers without looking down into his palm. His eyes were on Anghara. "All the same, you do not ask for proof of a miracle." He rose to his feet in a single fluid motion, and made a deep desert bow to Anghara. She rose instinctively, and could only stare as the Lord of Al'haria removed a necklace of amber beads in delicate silver filigree from around his own neck and crossed with a light step to where she was standing.

"I confirm," he said, and his voice was commendably steady. "Had we been in my hall in Al'haria, you would have worn *an'sen'thar* gold, and this would have been your own *say'yin*. That will still come, *Sen'en Dayr*. But, until that day, I confirm you, here and now, to the place where ai'Jihaar has raised you. Will you, in pledge, accept this *say'yin* from the hands of the Lord of Al'haria?"

She did not kneel, but bent her head to allow him to place the necklace on her neck and then stepped back—right hand touching heart, lips, brow, and then falling away into a graceful bow, an obeisance deep enough to set the necklace swinging. When she looked up again, al'Jezraal was smiling.

"But lord," she said in a low voice, "I still don't know what I did . . . or how I did it . . . or if I will ever be able to do it again."

"But you have done it," he said. "And I have seen it. The rest is with the Gods."

A moment later, when he came to offer Anghara her supper, al'Shehyr's eyes were opaque, twin gold mirrors. But it was al'Tamar who approached her with a deep obeisance, and begged her pardon for what he had done. And it was al'Tamar who hovered at her side, bringing her things before she asked for them—even, at last, touching her sleeve and informing her that her bed was ready just as she was finally beginning to give way to the exhaustion that was the legacy of Khar'i'id. She left the fireside, and was asleep almost before her head touched the pillow al'Tamar had prepared.

In the morning, the three men were gone; they left no trace of their passing, and if it weren't for the *say'yin* which still hung around her neck Anghara would have been inclined to believe she had dreamt the entire encounter.

Drawn by the change in Anghara's breathing, ai'Jihaar was suddenly beside her.

"It is late," she said. "I did not have the heart to wake you, but it is time we were on our way."

"Where are we going?" Anghara sat up in her bed, stretching the stiff muscles of her back. This was a question she seemed to be asking constantly.

"Home. My home. There is peace there, and quiet, and all the time you need before you face al'Jezraal again in the Great Hall at Al'haria. It is the last journey, for a while. A place to rest. None of this has been easy on you, Anghara."

"I dreamed of the Oracle last night," said Anghara slowly.

"And the dream?"

"Only what was, nothing more."

There had been disappointment in her voice, but that soon quickened into something else as she saw ai'Jihaar's expression. But all the *sen'thar* would say in response to her questions was as cryptic as anything the oracle itself might have uttered.

"It might be a beginning," ai'Jihaar said. "Remember these dreams."

The dream did not recur, at least not during the final lap of the journey to ai'Jihaar's home. This proved uneventful, except for the scenery—Kadun Khajir'i'id showed itself to be infinitely versatile. The wind-shaped dunes would change form and color almost minute by minute, and as Anghara and ai'Jihaar moved north they were broken more and more often by jutting buttes and flat-topped mesas of reddish stone.

It was tucked in the lee of one of these that they finally found ai'Jihaar's home—a small hai'r, consisting of a tiny pool hedged with a thicket of lais thorn bushes. Beneath a trio of pahria palms, a large nomad tent, rose-red like the desert, stood pitched and anchored with an air of permanence at the water's edge. An elderly ki'thar chewed lethargically on something in a small pen at the back; and an equally elderly woman was at the tent entrance to greet them, babbling away in a torrent of guttural Kheldrin which went over Anghara's head. Anghara's arrival into this simple household caused relatively less upheaval than the introduction of two new ki'thar'en into the pen. The sole occupant, obviously used to having the pen to himself, proved loath to surrender his absolute sovereignty without a fight, so that by the time the three animals had been persuaded into peaceful coexistence, Anghara's presence in ai'Jihaar's tent was largely a fact of life. A section of the tent was curtained off for her use with a minimum of fuss, and by the time Anghara first thought to tot up the days that had passed since she had arrived there she was astonished to discover it had been almost a month.

And then the months themselves began to slip by. Riding roughshod over all the tenets of Bresse, ai'Jihaar taught Anghara how to become a part of her gift—not an empty vessel waiting to be filled, but a deep lake whose every drop was power. There was a much greater potential for disaster here than at Bresse, but together with the potential came the safeguard of total control. Never again could Sight lash from

Anghara as it did in Cascin; but only here in Kheldrin did she truly receive that which Feor had hoped for from Bresse.

So deeply was Anghara into her life and training in this place that even Khar'i'id faded from her memory—Khar'i'id, and that which lay hidden in the Empty Quarter. It was with a sense of shock that she woke one morning with a memory of a dream so vivid she could still see its shape on the folds of the rose-red tent which surrounded her. And smell, as once before . . . the sharp, salty, vivid, well-remembered tang of the sea.

And remember something else.

"I dreamed of Gul Qara," she told ai'Jihaar when she found her, out by the pool. "The sea again. And this time . . . there were two words in the wind. It was still unclear, but the first one sounded as though it might be *Gul.* And . . . it was a year ago last night that we were in the Empty Quarter."

Nodding slowly, ai'Jihaar said. "The Oracle often worked in threes."

Anghara stared at her teacher in dismay, quick to comprehend. "Three years?" she asked.

"Perhaps only two. This is the *second* dream."

And Anghara fingered thoughtfully the *say'yin* she had been given by the Lord of Al'haria on another desert night almost a year ago, and was silent.

If she had to, she would wait.

But, in the meantime, there was something she could do to try and hurry things along. The little Standing Stone she had raised in Cascin, the talisman which had chosen her at Bresse, had not been required in ai'Jihaar's disciplines and Anghara had not returned to it for a long time. Its chaos-raising potential was still fresh in her mind; but together with that memory came another—the visions of Bresse in flames, of Cascin spared Sif's vengeance. True visions. The stone had shown a predilection for prophecy long before Anghara had heard of the Empty Quarter or the place called Gul Qara. Fully accepting the possible consequences, Anghara came back to her talisman and asked for another vision.

The results of this exercise were strange. The chaotic edge

of the stone seemed to be dulled—there was none of the explosive welter of images and revelation Anghara had come to associate with her talisman. Perhaps ai'Jihaar's training had given her a measure of control—either that, or her gifts had grown mature enough to deal with it on her own. Or perhaps it was simply too far away from her, the essence of Roisinan weakened by the distance between the queen and her land. Whatever the case, the stone did not take her for its usual wild ride. Instead, it offered a single image—a single Standing Stone, raised in a dimly glimpsed desolation. It was high, for that which was below it was lost in an odd, coruscating mist. And the light around it was not the bluish-green aura that clung to the Cascin Stone, but gold—the bright gold of her own soul fire.

It didn't help. If anything, it was another mystery on top of those still-to-be-unravelled tangles which had already landed in Anghara's lap.

Several times during this first year the flames of ai'Jihaar's hearth had given Anghara quick and scattered glimpses of Roisinan. Once it had been a vision of the arrival of a body of Sif's soldiers into yet another village which had offended. Unable to break away, Anghara had been forced to watch, sickened, as they took their revenge on a Sighted woman and her husband, who had defied Sif's edicts in order to protect and hide his wife and their child. A group of mounted men had come galloping into the village while the soldiers were still finishing the job—but they were too few, and too late. Seven rode in; three survived to be taken back to Miranei. The bodies of the dead were left unburied in the village square as the soldiers rode away. Anghara had come out of this one white and shaking, crying that it was time she returned—to which ai'Jihaar could only reply, "Your time is not yet." This the *sen'thar* knew; there would be a time, and she would recognize it, but what the signal would be she still did not know, and it was hard to watch Anghara suffer over something she was powerless to change.

On another occasion Anghara had floated unseen in Sif's

private quarters in Miranei—the same rooms that had once belonged to the king who had fathered them both. Sif was not alone; his mother, Clera, watched him from within a deep armchair by the hearth as he paced back and forth like a caged tiger.

"I can wait no longer, Mother," he was saying. "Tath is still a thorn in my side, and a problem it is imperative I solve quickly, before the whole thing festers on me—I am not sure it hasn't already, for that matter. And then there's . . . the other campaign. I need an heir, Mother, and if Colwen cannot give me a child I must find a queen who will. It's been almost six years. It is too long."

"She is a loyal and loving queen, Sif. There is still no real hurry . . ."

"There is," he said violently. "Anghara is still out there."

"She is buried," said Clera in a level voice, "in the family vault."

Sif shot his mother a glance that was a distillation of impatience and something like pity. "You and I know she is not," he said, "and too many others do, as well. There is the document . . ."

". . . which you destroyed . . ."

Sif chopped his hand downward like an axe. "A copy. An original exists. And there is the seal. We both know that, even now, if Anghara were to walk through the gates of Miranei there would be many who would flock to her. Too many."

"That is still no reason . . ."

"Mother." Sif's voice was flat, royal; there was no query in it, no hesitation, merely command. "I need an heir. I am putting Colwen aside; the proclamation is already drawn up. And I need you to help me find my next queen."

Clera hesitated. "But who? There are one or two daughters of noble houses still unwed, but you passed most of them over when you chose Colwen."

Sif stopped pacing and stood staring into the leaping flames in the great hearth, his hands gripping the mantle so tightly his knuckles stood out white and sharp. "There is one whom I have not."

"Who?"

"Senena. Senena Shailan."

And Anghara seemed to pass through the suddenly two-dimensional image as through a curtain even as she heard Clera's shocked, fading voice: "But she is not fourteen yet! She is a child . . ."

It was Senena herself who waited beyond the curtain, gowned lavishly for her wedding, her eyes luminous with tears of terror behind the diaphanous veil Clera was adjusting for her. Somewhere in the rows of waiting dignitaries Anghara could see the bitter, resentful eyes of the queen Sif had ruthlessly discarded; and Clera's voice was a hiss in Senena's ear as the child stood trembling and rooted to the spot.

"Go; he waits. In a few minutes you shall be queen, child. Do not fail to remember your duty to your king and your country when the crown is put on your head."

And then, at the last, just before the vision faded into darkness, the sight of Sif's brown, capable hands gripping the small childish ones laid quivering within them. Anghara heard Sif's commanding, intense voice, "I want a son, Senena . . ." And then, fading, fading, the heart-rending scream of a terrified child who had been crowned queen only a few hours before but who did not rule even her own bedchamber.

Another time the vision had been brief, but no less affecting. It came on the eve of Anghara's fifteenth birthday: Kieran, sitting watchful by a campfire, surrounded by a small band of men who looked oddly similar to those who had ridden in against Sif's *cheta* in the village she had seen before. He'd lifted his eyes to the stars, over the rim of the rough cup out of which he was drinking mulled wine, and for a heartstopping moment his eyes seemed to meet Anghara's—but then she realized he could not see her as she saw him. There was a strange sadness in his eyes, a loss that tore at her because she knew . . . she felt . . . she was its cause.

*Kieran . . . Kieran, I am safe . . .*

His head turned a fraction, as though he had heard a step behind him . . . or a voice . . . and then he sighed, putting down his cup.

"Happy birthday," he murmured, soft enough that not even his closest neighbor heard. "Wherever you are."

## 20

Anghara's second year at ai'Jihaar's hai'r was almost up when the *sen'thar* decided her pupil was at last ready to make an appearance at Al'haria. Anghara was now sixteen, and trained as far in the Way as ai'Jihaar could take her. She spoke the language as one Kheldrin-born, although with a stubborn and ineradicable accent; she knew her sacrifices, her invocations, her Gods . . . and her limitations. The blood sacrifices of Kheldrin sat ill with her. She had to be proficient in these, as *an'sen'thar;* she watched ai'Jihaar closely when her teacher performed them, but somehow, for a long time, she managed to avoid doing any herself. She had to, in the end—there was no escaping it. But she had wept for the thing she had slain. During her two years of training she performed the ritual of the sacrifice only twice; both times she did it flawlessly, but at a cost. This worried ai'Jihaar—but in all else her pupil was painfully ready. It was time to take her to al'Jezraal, to claim her own *say'yin* at last.

Finally ai'Jihaar had Anghara ready the two ki'thar'en which had accompanied them through Khari'i'd almost two years before, leaving ai'Jihaar's old servant in charge of the hai'r. The two animals had since become very attached to the reigning king of their pen, the elderly ki'thar which had been there when they had first arrived. Just as, then, there had been much uproar when they had been introduced into the pen, there was mayhem now when they were taken out. Riding away, ai'Jihaar and Anghara could still hear the faint trumpeting of the old ki'thar even after the hai'r itself had vanished out of sight behind red Kadun dunes.

Anghara's brief sojourn in Sa'alah had done nothing to prepare her for her first sight of a true desert city. Al'haria lay against a massive red mesa; the red stone of which the city had been wrought made it look as if it had not been built by mortal hands but grew there in the desert, living rock shaped by wind and sand into the semblance of dwellings and spires. It was a walled city, roofed in obsidian and glass, its low silhouette broken every so often by soaring towers which spiralled toward the wide sky. These were pierced by tiny windows, built to limit the entrance of the desert sun but facing in the direction of the prevailing night winds, so that the coolness of the night could be gathered into the rooms beyond. It was breathtaking, even more so for one who had spent months in a simple tent in the desert . . .

*Not all of us choose to be solitary nomads,* said ai'Jihaar rather whimsically into her mind. *Remember, here we are an'sen'en'thari, chosen of the Gods.*

And ai'Jihaar had made sure they dressed for it. Beneath the black djellaba that was her travelling cloak, Anghara wore a robe of gold jin'aaz silk belted with one of ai'Jihaar's own silver belts. Except for her bright hair, braided and coiled like a crown, al'Jezraal's necklace was her only jewellery beneath the blue burnoose. Clad in a similar gold robe but with silver bracelets on her wrists, three amber and silver *say'yin'en,* and an elaborately worked amber bead belt underneath a white djellaba, ai'Jihaar was more impressive. Anghara cast a swift appraising glance over the two of them, and smiled.

There were only five gold-robed *an'sen'en'thari* in the whole of Kheldrin, and only one of those had a *fram'man* for a pupil—they were recognized immediately. A deputation was there to meet them, bowing, almost before their ki'thar'en had passed through the city's gate. People they passed in the street stopped to offer them obeisance as they were led at a stately, regal pace to one of the towers; at their destination, the soft voices of their guides urged the ki'thar'en to kneel. Anghara slipped off hers with what was now a practiced grace and stood waiting, staring at the huge red doors before her. She had been *an'sen'thar,* confirmed by al'Jezraal's own hand, for almost two years, but claiming that title had been all too easy in the solitude of ai'Jihaar's hai'r. Now, for the first time, she would meet others of ai'Jihaar's ilk . . . and her own, she reminded herself forcefully. All the same, there was less of a Kheldrin God-spoken priestess in the high pride with which she held herself than a resurgence of the Kir Hama blood, quiescent for so long. She had been a gifted young student in the desert; here, within the walls of a city, she was a queen again.

It was ai'Jihaar, however, who effortlessly pushed open the massive but magnificently balanced doors and led the way inside, with Anghara at her heels. They entered a large airy hall; it was empty except for a wealth of beautiful, richly patterned carpets strewn on the floor. At the far end, a stone staircase spiralled upward out of sight, and at its foot waited a trio of Kheldrin women. All were bareheaded, the two bringing up the rear clad in white and looking very young. The one who seemed to be the leader was dressed in gray, with a simple amber *say'yin* around her neck. She bowed to the two newcomers.

"Your presence honors us," she said. "Your rooms are ready . . . *an'sen'en'thari.*" She had hesitated for a fraction of a second before the title. Just long enough for Anghara to notice. But her eyes were downcast, and in all other respects she was the epitome of humility. Anghara looked at her with slaty eyes, but said nothing.

*She will never attain gold,* ai'Jihaar spoke in Anghara's mind. *She knows it. There are some who could well resent you. There are others who will be more inclined to worship you. Your name is known in the desert.*

Their rooms—Anghara was given her own spacious chambers—were not opulent, but they were filled with understated comfort; mountains of soft cushions lined the walls, the floors were strewn with thick, soft rugs, and there were means to summon servants if required. Heavy curtains, desert-fashion, did the duty of doors, but Anghara had long ceased to miss them. Anghara's had been the first doorway they had come to, and the entire group had paused there as both *an'sen'en'thari* stopped.

"Tomorrow, early," said ai'Jihaar cryptically. *It is custom not to keep the temple waiting—or al'Jezraal. And the Great Hall will be packed.* "Rest now."

Then ai'Jihaar waited impassively until the gray *sen'thar* had offered a small farewell bow to Anghara before leading off again. One of the two white-robed *sen'en'thari* remained at Anghara's right hand, and bobbed her head as Anghara turned to look at her.

"By your leave, *an'sen'thar,*" she said in a high childish voice which had awe in it, and curiosity, and fear. "I am assigned to you while you stay in the tower. If there is anything you need . . ."

"Thank you," murmured Anghara.

The white *sen'thar,* hearing a note of dismissal, bowed again and left her alone.

Outside it was getting dark. The little *sen'thar* had lit the lamps in the room, but Anghara doused them all except for a single small one in the corner, and stood for a long time at her window staring out into the sky. Something shimmered in the air that night, a feeling of latent power, a closing circle, but it was a feeling she could not pin down, and presently she sighed, turning away. There was al'Jezraal to face the next morning. He had confirmed her to the gold, precocious but untried, and she had a lot to prove when she came into his presence again.

Sleep claimed her almost as soon as she subsided onto the pillows that were the desert bed. But she woke, suddenly, just as the pearly light of dawn was beginning to filter into her room, and sat up wide-eyed.

"Gul Khaima . . ." she whispered. "*Two* oracles . . ."

The fresh, sharp scent of salt spray off wind-whipped ocean waves clung to the walls and the rich, soft cushions of this room high above Kheldrin's red desert. Two years ago on this night the full moon had shone brightly on the colonnade of Gul Qara.

For a moment she sat motionless amongst her pillows,

frozen, remembering every nuance of the dream which had just left her. And then, pausing only to pull on the cowled golden robe she was to wear for that morning's Confirmation and thrust her feet into open sandals, she hurried down the corridor to ai'Jihaar's room, her unbound hair having to do with only a cursory pass of the comb. She called softly at ai'Jihaar's curtained doorway, but there was no reply to her hail. With the liberties allowed a student with her teacher, Anghara pushed aside the draperies and entered anyway, but ai'Jihaar was not there.

Anghara stared around the empty room, biting her lip. There were loose threads to this dream that Anghara could still not entirely weave together; she sensed its importance, but this was Kheldrin lore—much of it she had absorbed during her two years under ai'Jihaar's wing, but she still needed ai'Jihaar's insight when it came to fine-tuning the interpretation of a Kheldrin vision. But ai'Jihaar's cushion bed was cold; she had left a long time ago, and she could be anywhere. But a sense of urgency was upon Anghara, and it refused to go away just because her teacher was not available to explain and assuage it. There was a second oracle, Anghara knew it as surely as she knew her own name; was, or would be . . .

It was suddenly clear, as though a veil had been torn from her eyes. She gripped her elbows with her hands with sudden ferocity, leaving imprints of her nails on the skin through the thin silk as she made the elusive connection. The image her talisman had given her . . . the Standing Stone. There was, would be, a second oracle, waiting only to be found, or raised; a new place for an old spirit to come and inhabit. Gul Khaima. Gul Khaima by the sea . . .

She suddenly recalled ai'Jihaar's voice: *an'sen'en'thari* have access to al'Jezraal, always; they are his advisors in need, his confidants, his link to the land's soul. Access to al'Jezraal. She would see him soon, anyway—ai'Jihaar had timed their arrival impeccably, with a ceremony of Confirmation scheduled for that very morning, one where Anghara's own title, attained at al'Jezraal's hands in a desert hai'r, would be ratified before all Al'haria as witnesses. But that would be an occasion of stiff protocol and formality; there would be no chance of private communication. And Anghara could hardly announce this in open forum, not yet—not before she had a chance to find out more, to talk about it with people she trusted. And al'Jezraal . . . he had not been entirely happy to accept her in the beginning, but when he had done so he had done it unreservedly. He would listen; he needed to know. An'sen'en'thari had access to al'Jezraal, always. And she was *an'sen'thar*. By his own word.

She whirled and ran out of the room, lifting the golden cowl of her robe over her hair as she did so.

She knew nothing about the city, but instinct took her across the open square before the *sen'thar* tower, where the morning was already gathering itself to fulfill the hot, brooding promise of another searing desert day. Instinct led her into a broad avenue, where the few people abroad at this hour stopped to turn and peer after the slight, alien figure garbed in gold. Another tower, more massive perhaps than even the one she had left, waited for her at the far end; she pushed open the doors without hesitation, and found herself inside a huge cool cavern of a room. On another occasion she would have stopped to stare at the paintings of red Kadun dunes on a background of pale jin'aaz silk—the material alone would have fetched a king's ransom in Roisinan, and here they used it as a canvas—but she had not come here on a sightseeing trip. A staircase spiralled upward and out of sight at the hall's far end, just as in her own tower, except that at the foot of this one stood an unusually tall Kheldrin man, dressed in black and carrying a naked curved blade thrust into his belt. His eyes were a warmer gold than most Anghara had yet seen—the color of the Kadun sand, red-gold, just as beautiful, and just as deadly.

She tossed back her cowl; her hair spilled free. His eyes, perhaps, narrowed infinitesimally, but not a muscle on his face moved otherwise.

"*An'sen'thar* Anghara . . . of Sheriha'drin," she said, with a slight hesitation over the latter name. Not because of the unfamiliarity of the name—on the contrary, it was a pause born of a sudden realization of just how dangerously familiar it had become. "I am here to see Lord al'Jezraal."

The red-gold eyes stared at her impassively for a moment, but it was obvious her name was not unknown to the guard. After a pause he bowed his head, his motions oddly jerky, like a puppet's, and indicated the stairs with his hand, saying nothing.

It could have been taken as disrespect; if he had done this to ai'Jihaar, she would have flayed him—the old *an'sen'thar* could lay claim to a store of colorful language quite unexpected in one of her status and standing, and all the more potent because of this. But Anghara was not al'Jezraal's sister. She was not even Kheldrini. What respect she commanded amongst these people was still based only on hearsay, even if some of that hearsay was al'Jezraal's own. A gold robe alone was not enough to warrant anything but the barest minimum of attention when worn by one who, in many opinions, had no real right to it; anything further would have to be earned. Anghara passed by the black-clad guard without comment, not looking at him again.

At the top of the stairs there was another, like enough to the one below to be his twin. Anghara repeated her introduction and he bade her wait as he vanished behind a thick curtain screening a doorway some way down the corridor. He was back in less than a minute, with a bow somewhat deeper than his downstairs counterpart had offered—here, al'Jezraal's status rubbed off on his guests, especially those he called on the guards to admit at once.

Just outside the curtained doorway waited a young man whose face was oddly familiar. Anghara hesitated, trying to place it, but the young man bowed deeply and then straightened, a half-smile softening an expression of profound respect.

"I am al'Tamar ma'Hariff, *an'sen'thar.* From Kadun Khajir'i'id's Shod Hai'r. I was the one who demanded that you heal Sa'id al'Jezraal's son." He reached to lift the heavy folds of the curtain with his left hand, motioning her inside with his right. "My uncle is expecting you."

There was a flicker in him, something that kept plucking at the edges of Anghara's Sight—a vision she could not quite pin down. She thanked him and entered, and it was only as he dropped the curtain back into place behind her, severing their physical contact, that she realized just what it was she had sensed. A pale flame, silvery-blue. A thin aura around the burnished hair. He had it. He had the gift himself.

The realization confounded her just enough to make her stop in her tracks for the barest instant, blinking at the implications—here, even more so than in Roisinan, the *sen'en'thari*, those gifted with Sight, were predominantly women. *Sen'thar* men were rarer than water in Kheldrin. And here was one with the unmistakable aura of the gift, not in the *sen'thar* ranks but serving as usher to Al'haria's lord . . . But she suddenly remembered where she was, and her eyes focused on the figure of al'Jezraal, his hair lightening to gold with the passage of the years, but still supple and erect as any youth, waiting just a few paces away. She swallowed convulsively, realizing just where she was and what she was doing, not sure if ai'Jihaar would approve of this intrusion into al'Jezraal's private quarters, alone, at this hour—but it was done. She gave him an obeisance, every bit as deep as the one she had offered in the desert two years before, and he returned it gravely.

"Welcome to Al'haria, at last," al'Jezraal said. If he had been surprised by her appearance, he did not show it. There was respect in his mien, but not deference—she may have been a queen, but she was an exiled queen, and if he was only a lord of a desert city it was also true that she was in that city right now, and under his authority. He looked upon her as an equal—and Anghara, Queen of Roisinan, had taken enough measure of this man to take that as a compliment. "I was expecting to see you a little later this morning, though, in the hall." There was a soft question there, couched, in ai'Jihaar's own subtle way, in a rather obvious statement of undisputed fact.

"So you shall, my lord," Anghara said, answering it. "But *an'sen'en'thari* can see you at any time—so ai'Jihaar told me."

"That is correct," he said, unable to hide a small smile. "I suppose that for you my part of the Confirmation ceremony is indeed little more than just that—a formality to put an official seal to something concluded long ago. Will you sit, Anghara? I have to start preparing soon for the Confirmation, but there is still time. Will you tell me why you have come?"

"Do you recall the story ai'Jihaar and I had to tell when we emerged from Khar'i'id?" said Anghara without any further preamble, after she had settled into the proffered cushions and waited for al'Jezraal to subside with a cat-like grace next to her.

"It would be a hard tale to forget," murmured al'Jezraal.

"Then you will remember that all I brought away with me from Gul Qara at that time was the sea-scent in the wind, and the memory of a whispered word."

His gaze sharpening, al'Jezraal nodded silently. He had passed what remained of Gul Qara not long after Anghara had left it, and it had already been difficult to believe it had ever been anything but a wretched ruin. If anything had been salvaged out of that . . .

"What you do not know, *Sa'id*," Anghara continued, more softly, "is that it did not end there. There have been . . . dreams, one on the very night that you and your companions left us in the hai'r. Another, on the first anniversary of that night at Gul Qara. A third, last night . . . and it was two years ago today that our paths first crossed in Shod Hai'r."

His eyes glinted, "Yes, ai'Jihaar has told me something of this." And then, as she hesitated again, he performed one of those feats which had gained him his reputation as a mind reader. "She is at the temple," he said, "making her own preparations for the ceremonies. Shall I have her summoned?"

And Anghara, looking up into the golden eyes of ai'Jihaar's brother, suddenly found all her doubts falling away from her. While ai'Jihaar had taught her what she could, her work was done; Anghara had, indeed, run to her teacher for help in that first instant—but it had been her own under-standing which had interpreted this dream. Anghara squared her shoulders and lifted her chin, finally sure of herself and of her vision—sure enough to take responsibility herself, for the first time, for her own decisions in this, her adopted land. "No," she said. "It isn't necessary. I come to you as one of the *an'sen'en'thari* of your House, al'Jezraal ma'Hariff, with a true dream. I dreamed of the voice of Gul Qara, and at last it spoke to me clearly. There is a new oracle in Kheldrin, waiting only for a word of power to be found, to be born; a sister oracle to vanished Gul Qara—a place near the ocean, a place which is called . . . or will be called . . . Gul Khaima. It lives, *Sa'id* al'Jezraal, Lord of Al'haria. Gul Qara is dead. Gul Khaima lives."

"Change follows in your wake, Anghara of Sheriha'drin," al'Jezraal said, after a moment of charged silence. "Gul Qara had been silent to our own invocations for centuries, yet it responded to you freely when you reached out to touch it—and then it crumbled. There have been some who held the fall of Gul Qara against you, despite the oracle's passing of its last vision into your keeping. And now—now you come with another gift of life where they would lay a death at your door."

Anghara flushed, looking down for a moment, but the sting of Gul Qara had long been drawn. As to Gul Khaima . . . "There is a danger . . ." she said swiftly, glanc-ing up at al'Jezraal's face again, but he lifted a narrow hand to forestall her.

"Of course there is. You were right to bring this to me first. We will seek this place; but I think that its finding is your task. For now it is as well that its existence is not more widely known. Not yet. There would have been those who would have gone seeking, as an adventure, and even if only one of them had gone for the wrong reasons it would have been one too many. After the Confirmation, come back to these chambers. You, ai'Jihaar, ai'Farra . . ." he hesitated for a moment over that name—ai'Farra ma'Sayyed was

Al'haria's own *an'sen'thar*, Keeper of the Records, and a hard woman of whom ai'Jihaar had already warned Anghara. To put it mildly, ai'Farra had not been pleased at ai'Jihaar's doings; if anyone could be counted on to object violently to Anghara's status as *an'sen'thar*, even now at the last, it would be ai'Farra. It was just plain bad luck that this woman, a fanatical zealot of the old school, ruled this particular *sen'thar* tower. But she was here, and in Al'haria she held power; in some matters, more than the city's lord himself—al'Jezraal squared his jaw and continued. "We will speak then of what needs to be done."

It was a gentle dismissal, and Anghara rose to her feet. "I will be here, *Sa'id*." Even as she turned to leave, her hand strayed to the *say'yin* she wore around her neck and she was abruptly transported to the desert oasis where it had been bestowed. *"Sa'id,"* she said softly, "Lord, you gave this once as a pledge . . . today you will redeem it, as you promised. The *say'yin* that you lent . . ."

"Is yours, Anghara," he said. "You named yourself *an'sen'thar* of my House; I accept your vision, as coming to Al'haria, and to clan Hariff. In token of that, the pledge of the *say'yin* remains between us. And here, in Kheldrin, if you will bear it I will give you my clan's name."

"I will bring it honor," Anghara said, her eyes unaccountably filling with tears.

*"Sen'en Dayr,"* said Sa'id al'Jezraal, Lord of Al'haria. *Gods willing.* "Until we meet again, then, Anghara ma'Hariff."

As he held the curtain for her to pass al'Tamar's eyes were shining; he had heard most of their last exchange, and it looked as though he approved.

"It is well," he said to Anghara with a bow. "You need kinsfolk here, and in the desert you need a name that is of the desert. The Hariff will be proud you have chosen theirs. *Sa'id* Al'haria, and now two *an'sen'en'thari! Hai!* They will be proud!" A sudden glint of triumph tinged with a hint of gloating touched that pride in his eyes—he was Kheldrini, after all, and rivalries were everything. "But ai'Farra will not be happy!"

Already ai'Jihaar had spoken to Anghara of these age-old feuds and squabbles between the Kheldrin clans—and new ones were springing up almost every day. Anghara had just set the Hariff against the Sayyed—subtly enough, with no more than a few words spoken in the spirit of the occasion—and for a moment she felt a pang of uncertainty. Was she doing the right thing, involving herself as directly as this? *Sen'en'thari* were traditionally neutral, clanless, although in practice it was hardly ever thus—but in practice none of them could help being of the clan in which they had been born. As a solitary stranger, Anghara had been more exposed than she would have wanted, despite ai'Jihaar's standing—but now she had become a part of an extended "family" which would be expected to rally behind its newest member, despite her strangeness, at the first sign of any slight or attack. And there could be any number of those, simply because of that strangeness. A whole new hornet's nest of trouble could be stirred up. But it was done, and al'Tamar at least thought it was a good idea. For now, that would have to do.

The Confirmation was now imminent, and Anghara hurried back to the *sen'thar* tower to look for ai'Jihaar—it was custom for the confirmation candidates to enter the temple and, later, the Great Hall together with the senior *sen'thar* who had raised them to their new status. She found ai'Jihaar waiting patiently in Anghara's own room. Once again ai'Jihaar did not ask where Anghara had been; she seemed, with that unnerving facility of hers, to already know exactly what had passed. All except for the dream itself. This Anghara related to her as ai'Jihaar helped her prepare herself—taming her unruly hair, finding the correct sandals—and ai'Jihaar listened in silence, merely nodding at the end.

"You did the right thing," was all she said, and it was no longer delivered as teacher to pupil, but rather as one *an'sen'thar,* albeit a senior one, to a younger colleague. She no longer gave lessons, only advice. From today, from the moment al'Jezraal repeated in the hearing of his people the words he had first uttered in the silence of a desert hai'r,

Anghara would become, for all of her inexperience and youth, ai'Jihaar's fully fledged equal.

But before the hall, before al'Jezraal and the people, there would be the temple, there would be the gathered *sen'en'thari* . . . and their Gods. And there would be ai'Farra.

Running delicate fingers over Anghara's face and hair as a final check, ai'Jihaar reached to pull the golden cowl over the younger girl's head.

"You are ready," she pronounced. "Come, child of my heart. There are four who serve for the first time today—two whites and a gray of ai'Farra's, and you. Come; they will be waiting at the temple. It is time."

The temple was a great ziggurat in the center of Al'haria, its stone a shade redder than the rest of the city, as though in acknowledgment of all the blood that had been spilled here before Kheldrin's Gods. It had been built to house thousands with ease; the few *sen'en'thari* who now walked its corridors could, if they had wanted, stake their claims to entire suites of rooms—and they could have done so even had every single *sen'thar* in Kheldrin been living here. But they weren't—this was the largest *sen'thar* tower in the land, but still it held less than half the professed *sen'en'thari*—just under a hundred whites, a handful of grays, two (now three, if one counted Anghara) golds.

All of these were gathered on the flat, open roof of the ziggurat that morning, waiting for the Confirmation Service. There was room enough for half the city to be present as well, and frequently the people did attend, especially if they had a special interest in the offered sacrifices. But those were ordinary services. This one was one of confirmation, new hands taking up the burdens of ministry and sacrifice, new minds offered to the Gods. This service was between the Gods and their initiates; some mysteries were not for profane eyes.

Two white-robed girls and the one clad in gray, who were all being accepted into their respective circles, waited with ai'Farra on the broad landing at the top of the staircase. A stone doorway opened onto the roof; quick glimpses of the hushed, monochromatic gathering of cowled figures dressed in white and gray could be seen on the pyramid top, which was paved in huge slabs of pale stone. But ai'Farra's back was to the doorway, and her eyes, hot and brooding, watched as ai'Jihaar and Anghara ascended the last few steps to join the Keeper of Records and her clutch of new initiates upon the landing.

When ai'Farra opened her mouth to speak, ai'Jihaar lifted a hand.

"The sun moves, ai'Farra. Let us begin."

Biting back whatever it was she had been about to say, ai'Farra flicked her eyes over Anghara like a lash—her features melted into what might have been a smile, but it was not a pleasant smile. It was as though she was anticipating something dreadful, and glorying in it.

"Very well," she said. "Let us begin."

They walked out together, side by side, the two women of Kheldrin robed in gold. Behind them, cowled and muffled, came their candidates for this Confirmation Service. Around them was silence; the roof was not walled or fenced in any way, and beyond the ranks of the assembled *sen'en'thari* it simply dropped away into a chasm at whose foot lay the city. The early morning sun poured across the rooftop, except where a carved altar-stone stood in the shadow of a small squat structure, a windowless cube about the height of a man. As the only human-sized thing in this entire building, it looked small and insignificant. It was as if its entire purpose was devoted to reminding the worshippers just how they compared to the Gods they had come to venerate. There was a door in this building, facing the altar; a gray-robed *sen'thar* stood beside it, belted with a massive silver girdle bearing a long stabbing dagger with a dull black handle, a large key in her hand.

Anghara had been drilled in the ceremonial procedures. Together with the other three candidates, still cowled, still silent, she moved away to the right of the altar while the two *an'sen'en'thari* went up to the carved plinth, bowed and touched their foreheads to the red stone.

"We bring you life, al'Zaan, Sa'id-ma'sihai; al'Khur; ai'Lan; ai'Dhya. We bring you life," said ai'Farra, her voice ringing with authority as the lady of this tower.

She and ai'Jihaar both unsheathed the thin daggers they wore about their waist, the same which Anghara had once seen ai'Jihaar use to draw her own blood in absence of other sacrifice, and laid them upon the altar. Then ai'Farra nodded to the doorkeeper, and the gray unlocked the door of the stone cube and plunged into the shadowed darkness inside, to emerge almost immediately with a white ki'thar lamb. Its legs were hobbled about the knees; it let out one pitiful bleat as it was carried out, a pathetic parody of the endless complaining grunts its elders never ceased uttering, and was then miraculously silent as it was lifted and laid on its side upon the altar. The gray *sen'thar* took her black-handled knife and offered it to ai'Farra, hilt first. The *an'sen'thar* took it, and lifted it so that its wickedly sharp edge glinted in the sun.

"We call your eyes down upon us, your blessing upon our works; we bring you life!"

Anghara made herself watch as the knife plunged downward, a clean slash across the lamb's jugular; only now did she notice the blood pooling into a shallow bowl scooped into the one end of the altar. The god-presence, the same one she once felt in a desert hai'r was back, surrounding her, as though all the Kheldrin Gods were reaching for her soul—and yet her eyes were full of unbidden tears.

There was a God's hand in these sacrifices, because no matter how the blood leapt from the cut the sacrificing priestess remained pristine, with not a mark on her. Once again ai'Farra nodded to the gray, and she came to the altar bearing a scarlet silk shroud which she cast over the lamb. Wrapping it around the small corpse she lifted it very gently, as if it were a sleeping child, and, bowing to both priestesses, bore it away, back into the cube.

The two young white circle initiates now stepped forward, with their own invocations—an oath to their Gods, and the gray *sen'thar,* the cube guardian, produced two young chicks whose blood was to seal it. One of the young priestesses performed the feat flawlessly, as ai'Farra had done, effortlessly avoiding the spurting blood; the other, who from her size and build was really little more than a child, was not so lucky. When her dagger was withdrawn, it was seen that the edge of her sleeve was bespattered with three scarlet drops. A swift sigh like a sudden wind ran along the silent ranks of the assembled *sen'en'thari*.

Her face set in an expression that was both sorrow and cold anger at once, ai'Farra stepped forward and took the dagger; from the hunch of the young one's shoulders, it looked as though she was crying quietly.

"You are not yet ready," ai'Farra said. "Return to the novice chambers. You will not serve the Gods again until you are a year older than this day."

The girl withdrew through the stone doorway; gathering what scraps of dignity she could, she walked while in the sight of her sisters, but Anghara could hear the swift patter of her feet as she broke into a run as soon as she stepped onto the landing. The disaster was swift, the tragedy ruthless, and Anghara was left breathless. The other white, now proved into her circle, stood with her mouth open and her fingers clenched tightly around her dagger. Gently ai'Farra pried her hand open and removed her sacrificial blade, leaning forward to give her a ceremonial kiss on the brow.

"Welcome, sister," she said. "Go, take your place."

The white gathered her wits, and, bowing, withdrew into the waiting ranks which opened to receive her.

The gray now stepped forward, with her own oath, and was presented with her sacrificial beast by her sister at the cube door. Anghara could sense her aura—blue and cold, effortless, ruthless. No blood touched this one. The sacrifice was perfect, and yet . . . Anghara felt the Gods turning from this servant just consecrated to them. She had power, unleavened by pity. She was proud, but she would never gain the gold. The Gods would not let her.

And then it was her turn.

It was ai'Jihaar who called her up to the altar, her teacher and guide.

*Courage, child,* she said beneath the ritual words. *Remember, you have healed, you have raised from the dead . . .*

*But not killed,* Anghara returned as she stepped up to the bloody altar. *Not willingly. Not willingly, ever. Not for death, ai'Jihaar, remember? Not for death.*

Suddenly ai'Jihaar woke to an odd note of determination in Anghara's voice. *Bow to tradition, at least here! Anghara, what are you thinking?*

The animal keeper had made her foray into the animal house, and emerged with a bird. Its back and wings were burnished gold, its breast soft white, its feet coral like the Kadun sand. Silkseeker. One of the most precious living things in Kheldrin, leading men to lairs where wild jin'aaz spiders endlessly spun their soft, strong silk. Wild silkseekers had long, thin beaks with which they dug the spiders' silk-cocooned larvae from their lairs; tame birds had their beaks docked, so they could find the spiders but not reach them to feed. Tame ones were sometimes offered to the temple, usually when they were wounded, crippled or old. But the one which was handed to Anghara had the terrified eyes and the long beak of a wild silkseeker. This was no sacrificial animal.

Anghara heard ai'Jihaar, who suddenly seemed to have picked up the threads of some malevolent plan from ai'-Farra's mind, draw in her breath sharply; looking up, she saw the tense, expectant expression on ai'Farra's face. Her own jaw set.

Holding the bird very gently, Anghara lifted her arm and bared it to her elbow; with her free hand she picked up ai'Jihaar's own slim sacrificial dagger.

"This is not the Gods' blood," she said, her voice low but carrying. "This is captive sacrifice. I give blood to the Gods, but if they wish to take this bird it is for them to call its hour, not I."

With a swift, sure motion she drew the dagger up along her forearm from the elbow toward the wrist in a long, shallow cut. The blood welled out even as she opened her hand and threw the bird up into the hot, high sky. The assembled *sen'en'thari* gasped, and then the sound rose into a murmur, into a cry. Above their heads the small bird had vanished into the blue but high above it, where nothing had been a moment before, they could suddenly see the massive open wings of a circling desert vulture, and the God-presence thickened around them on the roof. One white *sen'thar*—Anghara thought it might be the one newly initiated that morning—collapsed into a dead faint at her sisters' feet; ai'-Farra's face was cold and set.

The door-warder gray came hurrying up with another scarlet cloth, and Anghara took it and laid it on her arm. When she took it away, there was no sign of a scratch or a scar on the white skin; there was no blood on her golden robe.

While ai'Jihaar could not see these things, she felt the power Anghara had drawn down.

"The sacrifice has been accepted," she said, stepping around the altar to Anghara, who suddenly felt drained, weak. With her own hands ai'Jihaar bound a narrow scabbard on Anghara's belt, and slid her own dagger into it.

*But this is . . .*

*Mine no longer. Do you think I could have done with it what you did?* "Welcome, sister," she said. "Come, take your place."

In stony silence ai'Farra came to stand on her other side—a new gold had been called to serve. But her face was closed.

"She broke tradition, ai'Jihaar," was all ai'Farra said as the three of them walked from that place side by side.

But ai'Jihaar did not even turn her head, and her voice, if anything, was even more implacable than ai'Farra's own. "And you set a trap in a holy ceremony, ai'Farra; you mocked the Gods themselves today. She broke tradition?" ai'Jihaar paused, a pause which lasted less than a heartbeat and an eternity all at once. "So did you, my sister. So did you."

**21**

Clearly ai'Jihaar had been right in her prediction of the night before—the Great Hall of Al'haria was packed to the rafters as Anghara entered. Perhaps for the last time she walked at ai'Jihaar's heels, much as ai'Farra's new gray and the surviving white trailed their own *an'sen'thar* sponsor into the hall. The cowl of her robe was still raised over her hair.

Al'haria was a city of scholars, where the Records were kept, where the biggest *sen'thar* tower and the oldest temple were. It was also a city of artisans and craftsmen, a center for the production of artifacts and jewellery, both secular and sacred, from sea-amber gathered on Kadun Khajir'i'id's coastline and silver from the northern mines. It was easy to tell the two castes apart in the Great Hall that morning, even closing one's eyes. The bulk of the *sen'en'thari*, fresh from the roof of the temple, had come into the hall well in advance of their two *an'sen'en'thari* to take up their positions in the *sen'thar* galleries. They fixed their attention as one on the slight girl who walked behind *an'sen'thar* ai'Jihaar, making Anghara the center of a widening circle of spreading silence. The rest, those Al'hariani who came here to work with their hands, had their attention fixed on much the same spot, but for different reasons. From the stories that had filtered down to them, they knew a different Anghara to the one the *sen'en'thari* had just seen in the Confirmation Service; they gazed and murmured to their neighbors behind concealing hands, leaving a wash of whispering which lapped at the edges of the pool of *sen'thar* silence.

There were others there, too, not of the city—nomads who lived in tents in the desert hai'r'en tending their livestock, hardly ever venturing into the cities. Unused to these gatherings, they alternated between awed silence at their surroundings, the red stone pillars of the Great Hall so very different from their tents, and being the loudest of all, excited by the atmosphere, the crowd, the occasion. It was these people who, by means that were almost magical, obtained news of everything that went on in the desert—it was as though they could listen to the sand, and hear conversations taking place a thousand miles away. They were the ones who had picked up and blazed Anghara's story across Kheldrin; it was the nomads to whom ai'Jihaar had been referring when she told Anghara her name was "known in the desert." They knew of her, and what she was supposed to have done, and in their hands the story had already gained momentum—Anghara was already larger than life in many a campfire tale. They believed every word, utterly; to them, the Gods were real beings who walked the land, and the desert tribes were ready to fall at the feet of one who was said to have spoken with one, demanded something, and won it. If anyone had roused to speak against Anghara in that hour, they would quite possibly have revolted—and, by the set face of ai'Farra as she walked beside ai'Jihaar, she was aware of it.

Except for the fact that Anghara had not envisaged so many of the colorfully clad nomads, the scene was not entirely unexpected—ai'Jihaar had described many times, in great detail, what this morning would be like. She looked for the confirmation seat, a long stone bench apart from the galleries set aside for the *sen'en'thari;* ai'Jihaar and ai'Farra walked up to it, leading their three new initiates, leaving them seated there as the two older women turned away smoothly to make their way toward the galleries and their own seats.

*For you, this is a formality,* ai'Jihaar's caressing thought lingered. *Especially now. Especially after the temple.*

As though the arrival of the confirmation candidates had

been the signal for the ceremonies to begin, a conch shell was blown invisibly somewhere above them, followed by the deeper, brassier note of a ram's horn. There was a rustle of silk and homespun as the assembled people rose to their feet. Even the chattering craftsmen had fallen silent, and into this silence, resplendent and almost unrecognizable as the man who had sat across from Anghara at a desert campfire, walked al'Jezraal, Lord of Al'haria. He wore scarlet, robes of jin'aaz silk under a flowing cloak, his pale gold hair held back with a wide circlet of beaten silver set with a yellow stone at his brow. The belt around his waist, which occasionally gleamed free through the scarlet billows, and the handle of the dagger it held, looked as though they had been wrought from solid gold.

He sat down on a massive chair, carved from the city's own red stone, set at the far end of the Hall, against a stone wall draped with woven hangings. The three men and two women who had entered the Hall behind him, the council of Al'haria, disposed themselves comfortably in lesser seats set in a semicircle around al'Jezraal's great chair. One chair remained, empty—ai'Farra's usual seat; on this day she sat amongst her own. A gray-robed *sen'thar,* carrying a copper box, so highly polished it was almost painful to look upon, glided into the Hall in the wake of the council, taking up position at al'Jezraal's right hand.

"We are here," al'Jezraal said into the absolute silence which still wrapped the Hall, "to Confirm the Circles. One enters the white circle of the *sen'en'thari* today; one enters the gray; one is raised to the gold." There was a low murmur at that last; it rose, and then burst like a bubble into silence again. This particular gold was the reason most of them had come.

The *sen'en'thari* had done all the work here. They had chosen and trained their candidates, and what the criteria were for passing from one circle to the next no one outside the *sen'thar* tower knew. It was the temple which conferred the passage, and the temple confirmed it, by its own laws, with such services as had been performed on the temple roof that morning. But it was the secular lord's law which had to confirm the initiate's new status—only once he had done so did the promotion become irrevocable. This is where, for Anghara, danger could lurk.

"The lord will ask if anyone contests the confirmation," ai'Jihaar had told Anghara when they had discussed the outline of the ceremony. "In the Hall, anyone with a valid reason can raise an objection. It very rarely happens, but I recall an instance where al'Jezraal himself raised a voice of dissent, for the candidate had murdered in cold blood and al'Jezraal would not, for all her gifts, countenance her raising into the *sen'en'thari*."

It did not happen often, but when it did it always involved circumstances that were highly dramatic—at the time al'Jezraal had refused confirmation, the ceremony had been spiced with murder. Anghara was no murderess, but her own particular circumstances were unprecedented in the history of these ceremonies; the people scented major drama in Anghara's case. They were here to watch.

The form of the ceremony itself was simple enough—al'Jezraal called upon the *an'sen'thar* directly responsible for promoting the respective candidates to name them before the witnesses of council and Great Hall. This always started from the lowest rank, and so it was ai'Farra who rose and called first the white, then the gray *sen'thar* from the Confirmation Seat. Bidding the candidates themselves to approach, al'Jezraal asked for dissenting voices to their confirmation and waited a few beats for the silence that was his usual reply, then conferred upon each the appropriate amber and silver *say'yin* from the copper box held by the gray-robed *sen'thar* at his side. Each in her turn, they bowed their thanks and retreated to the *sen'thar* galleries to take their places there, sanctioned by both their Gods and their secular lord.

The murmur arose again as the gray candidate received her *say'yin* and drew back, leaving only Anghara, her cowl still covering her hair and shadowing her face, on the Confirmation Seat. The protocol should have been the same—

call upon the patron *an'sen'thar,* ask for dissenting voices, confer the *say'yin*—but al'Jezraal remained silent for an instant longer than was necessary, and it was obvious protocol was going to be left by the wayside. The anticipation bore fruit as al'Jezraal rose and took a few paces into the hall. There was a long, drawn-out sigh from the nomads' ranks.

"Two years ago," he said, and his voice had little of ceremony in it but was rich in memory and wonder, "I met *an'sen'thar* ai'Jihaar ma'Hariff in Shod Hai'r at the edge of Rah'honim Ar'i'id. I met a sister who had died in the Khar'i'id, for I saw the marks of diamondskin teeth upon her—and who lived again. And I met one whom she had raised to *an'sen'thar* gold; a *fram'man,* a stranger from a land we hold holy, who was able to defy al'Khur in his hour and take back a life he had claimed. I saw the signs of death, and the truth of life where life should have been extinct; I did not ask for dissenting voices, for there could have been none. I confirmed ai'Jihaar's word in Kadun Khajir'i'id Shod Hai'r."

He lifted a hand and suddenly held a *say'yin,* heavy and complex, with large amber beads interspersed with globes of tarnished silver and what looked like gold—it was ancient, not one from the copper box of the gray *sen'thar* but something else, something bestowed for a great work. He was giving it for something not yet happened, for a vision still to be born—and the gift of it was a sign of his faith that what Anghara had spoken of would come to pass. To ai'Farra, who still did not know about Anghara's dream, it must have seemed as though al'Jezraal had already heard about the Service at the temple, and was rewarding the way Anghara had slipped her trap.

"I ask for no dissenting voices again today," al'Jezraal said firmly, and his eyes locked briefly with those of ai'-Farra, up in the stands. Anghara could not see the Al'hariani *an'sen'thar's* face, sitting as she was with her back to the stands, but she could sense the gathering thunder in ai'-Farra's soul fire; however, the *an'sen'thar* kept her peace under this challenging look. Once again al'Jezraal's gaze swept outward over the galleries. "I know there would be some; perhaps many. I also know already all the reasons they would put forward. It is true that Kheldrin has been hidden from strangers' eyes for hundreds of years; it is true that Kheldrin's newest *an'sen'thar* should never have seen the desert, had tradition been followed. But this is a stranger who speaks to our Gods, and can rule them; a stranger who heard the last words of Gul Qara before the oracle succumbed to the weight of its centuries; a stranger who walks in our holiest places and takes from them miracles forbidden to their own children. This is a stranger no longer. Today she took clan Hariff as her own, and even though she wears the gold and thus has no clan, my kin will accept her as one born amongst us, and take pride in what she has done, and will yet do. I confirm you *an'sen'thar,* Anghara Kir Hama ma'Hariff of Sheriha'drin and Kheldrin, child of two lands; may the Gods look upon you with favor, and smile upon your life."

Anghara came and stood before him, tears once again bright in her eyes; he pushed down the golden cowl, and there was a low murmur as the light caught the silver circlet, now revealed for the first time, with which ai'Jihaar had bound her brow that morning. It was a statement—no other wore such insignia save al'Jezraal himself, but no one else in that hall bore both royal blood and the gifts of the Gods. Lifting the heavy old *say'yin* over her head, al'Jezraal laid it beside the other he had placed there in the desert two years before. Their eyes held for a moment, and then she bowed to him and walked, as the other two had done before her, toward the galleries where ai'Jihaar and ai'Farra sat on either side of an empty seat left for her. While ai'Jihaar's face was disciplined, her thoughts were smiling; ai'Farra stared at Anghara for a long moment, her eyes almost hostile, before she looked down at the folded hands in her lap. Anghara sat down carefully, still trembling with the emotion of the last few minutes; in the interval, still in the cocoon of silence he had raised, al'-Jezraal had returned to his own great chair and reclaimed it. The gray *sen'thar* with the copper box, having concluded her duties, had unobtrusively retired. And now, a woman from the nomad ranks raised a reedy, high-pitched ululating cry into the hush in the Hall, taken up by several more in the next instant; it was a signal of great joy and approval, and the nomad ranks were agleam with broad, white-toothed smiles.

The rest of the morning was anticlimactic—ai'Farra descended from the galleries to reclaim her seat in the council semicircle as a handful of cases were brought to the lord and his council for judgment by the city folk. Most of them revolved in one way or another around issues concerning real or imagined transgressions of clan or family honor. Many of the *sen'en'thari* left before the end, as did the nomads, who settled their own disputes the hard way and had no patience with this kind of protocol. Touching Anghara's elbow lightly, ai'Jihaar motioned for them to slip out also, although it was asking too much for them to do so unobserved.

"Nothing you do from this time on will ever be done unobserved," said ai'Jihaar, sounding amused, answering Anghara's never-quite-uttered thoughts as usual. "If you plan on doing any plotting, Anghara ma'Hariff, you may as well do it sitting out in the square in broad daylight and calling all your secret orders out loud."

An image of ai'Farra's hooded golden eyes rose in Anghara's memory. "That does not stop others from plotting against me," she said, giving ai'Jihaar the image as well as the words.

"She can do little, now," said ai'Jihaar, dismissing ai'-Farra with a wave of her hand. "She could have been trouble in the Confirmation, even after the temple—but between us, al'Jezraal and I handled that. But now you have been accepted into the *sen'en'thari* and into the Hariff—*hai,* I still do not know what made you do that, but it was well done! In either there will be those who would take it amiss if anything ill should befall you, and who would know from whom the ill had come. The Sayyed are a rich clan, and powerful— they breed the best dun'en, and get good prices for them— but they could not stand alone against a clan alliance if they tried to cross the Hariff here in our own country. Speaking of the Sayyed—ai'Farra still does not know about the other oracle. Let us go to the *Sa'id* tower and wait for the meeting, al'Jezraal will be there as soon as he can escape."

When ai'Farra arrived before al'Jezraal it was al'Tamar, golden eyes studiously blank, who showed her in, and then withdrew with alacrity. If there were to be fireworks between the *an'sen'en'thari,* he did not want to be close enough to feel the heat.

She stood for a moment, staring at Anghara with smoldering eyes. "It could be said," she said softly at last, ominously rephrasing her earlier words, "that things weren't done according to tradition today, and you were never confirmed. The dissenting voices have been allowed into the Hall Ceremony with good reason. It could be said you wear the gold robe by the word of an *an'sen'thar* alone—and that has never been enough."

"After what you tried to do at the temple," ai'Jihaar said cuttingly, "had you tried to raise a dissenting voice your own tower would have shouted you down."

"We had not met before today," said Anghara calmly. The golden glow of her soul fire kindled and wreathed her form like a cloak, striking sparks from the burnished hair confined by the silver circlet. She rose, offering the most graceful desert salute she could muster, the golden flame of her power rippling from her fingers and leaving starbursts where she touched the aura over her heart, her lips, her brow. Her voice was still serene, as though she was completely unaware of what she was doing, and tinged with subtle irony. "I am happy to make your acquaintance at last, Keeper of the Records. I have heard much about you."

Taken by surprise as she turned to answer ai'Jihaar, to her great credit, ai'Farra recovered quickly. Her own aura, the crimson of newly spilled blood to ai'Jihaar's white and Anghara's own gold, blossomed to meet theirs even before Anghara had a chance to straighten from her bow.

"Very well," ai'Farra said tightly, "you have the power. I hardly doubted that, not after . . . Still, you are *fram'man* before anything else. They should never have even considered . . ." Her voice dropped for a moment, sounding silky and dangerous. "Do you know what happens to strangers who stray into Kheldrin unasked?" she said, her long fingers stroking the haft of a dagger in her belt, twin to the ones ai'Jihaar and now Anghara herself wore.

"Who strays into Kheldrin?" asked Anghara. "This is hardly a country for stumbling into unawares."

"Oh, but they come," said ai'Farra. "There are, after all, riches here of a kind, enough to tempt a few beyond prudence. They come from Shaymir—there are paths through the mountains, if one cares to look for them; or they brave the Se'thara by night. They come." She drew the dagger, and within her red aura the blade seemed immersed in blood. "They never return. And they had not even dreamed of crossing the Empty Quarter with their profane feet, nor bringing down a holy shrine with a sacrilegious touch."

"That is enough, ai'Farra. You speak of what you do not know," said ai'Jihaar sharply.

"It is done, ai'Farra ma'Sayyed." The new voice at the door heralded the arrival of al'Jezraal and, in ai'Farra's case only very reluctantly, the three women allowed the flame of their auras to flicker out and die. Slipping the scarlet cloak from his shoulders, al'Jezraal strode in and tossed it aside. "We need your knowledge, and your help," he said levelly, staring directly at ai'Farra, "and I will have your word, *an'sen'thar,* that you will work with us on this. What we seek will be a gift to all of Kheldrin's people."

"All of *Kheldrin's* people, *Sa'id?*" ai'Farra said softly, her eyes flicking once again in Anghara's direction; al'Jezraal could not fail to notice this. His mouth tightened.

"Here, she is Hariff. In Sheriha'drin, she is Kir Hama, and royal. In the temple, she is confirmed amongst the highest of the God-spoken. I will have an end to this, ai'Farra."

Finally ai'Farra dropped her eyes. She was still far from happy, but her support base in Al'haria, at least on this issue, was not big enough for her to pursue the matter at this time—there were never many Sayyed here, and her own tower was divided, with too many on ai'Jihaar's side, and Anghara's.

"Very well," she said coldly.

That would hold for only as long as there were three powerful Hariff ranged here against her, and enough *sen'en'thari* held out against her prejudices—unless something extraordinary happened to change her mind.

And al'Jezraal held something extraordinary to offer her.

He nodded, now, as though her words sufficed, and then, while she was still braced against this grudging acceptance which had been forced from her, he flanked her and changed the subject, exploiting the vulnerability.

"Keeper of the Records," he said formally, but his voice was intense, "we seek a place called . . . Gul Khaima."

Whatever her faults, ai'Farra had the gift of power in no mean magnitude. There was no way in which she could have learned of this name, or of its meaning, but she stiffened in sudden reaction.

"I do not know of such a place," she said after a pause. "And yet . . . why do I feel as though I should? What is Gul Khaima, *Sa'id* al'Jezraal?"

"Anghara," said al'Jezraal, inviting her to take over by voice and gesture.

Anghara told once again of her encounter with Gul Qara in the Empty Quarter, the full story of which ai'Farra had never heard from the source; ai'Farra's hands clenched tightly in the folds of her robe, but she heard the story in silence. And then Anghara told of the dreams, of the talisman-given vision, and of the interpretation.

"A second oracle," she said. "A new oracle. It exists, or will exist, in a place called Gul Khaima, somewhere close to the sea. Is it possible there might be a trace of this somewhere . . . would the Records speak of it? Did Gul Qara never mention this place before?"

"The last recorded prophecy of Gul Qara," said ai'Farra with some bitterness, "took place almost three hundred years ago. I knew this name when you said it . . . but I do not think I learned of it in the Records."

"May I . . . see what the Records say about Gul Qara?" Anghara's question was a request, although as full *an'sen'thar* she had the right to demand access to Records and ai'Farra could not refuse. But she had chosen to bow to ai'Farra's standing as the Keeper; in some ways ai'Farra had the right of it. There might be things in the catacombs not meant to be seen by *fram'man* eyes. The Kheldrini woman straightened, lifting her chin, her eyes meeting Anghara's with defiance, resentment, a grudging respect.

"We can go now," she said. The words were heavy, like stones, but her interest had been kindled, and the very speed of her assent, despite the tone in which it had been uttered, was proof of piqued curiosity.

"Thank you." Again, the courtesy, from supplicant to Keeper; ai'Farra could not but respond to it. It was far from acceptance—but perhaps it was a beginning.

They all went in the end—ai'Farra in front, with a massive key black with age, unlocking a great door whose carvings had all but vanished into blank oblivion over the passage of uncounted years; al'Jezraal only a step behind her, a smoking torch in his hand; ai'Jihaar, holding onto Anghara's arm. They passed along a corridor hewn into the mesa at the city's back and down endless spiraling stairs into the bowels of the catacombs. These opened up with almost no warning, a vast darkness swallowing the guttering torchlight at the foot of the stairs, but there were cressets here, and unlit torches prepared against a Keeper's need. When al'Jezraal lit three or four, suddenly there was light enough. Stone archways revealed themselves, leading off in various directions, darkness beyond them; two or three were barred with great doors, similar to the ones at the top of the stairwell, bearing seals of various clans—Anghara recognized only Hariff, from a hanging in al'Jezraal's chambers which al'Tamar had pointed out to her earlier. A great stone table stood in the middle of the small amphitheater, which opened out from the stairwell.

"Stay here," said ai'Farra, her words a warning but her tone almost a regret that she was issuing it at all. "This place is a labyrinth; my predecessor took years to teach me how to find my way around. I will fetch what is needful."

She took one of the torches, and moved into the darkness of one of the side corridors. For a brief while they could see the flickering light, and then it abruptly vanished, perhaps as ai'Farra turned a corner. Or simply disappeared.

His eyes darting amongst the shadows as though he expected every one to spawn a demon, al'Jezraal stood tense and ready to fight. He started as ai'Jihaar reached out to lay a delicate hand on his arm, then had the grace to smile sheepishly at the sound of her silvery laughter.

"I have never liked this black dungeon," he admitted. "I was born to the light."

*Dungeon . . .*

The word leapt out of the dark, and the vision was upon Anghara before she could draw another breath.

Roisinan's princess-heir had had little to do with dungeons—there would be time enough to consign miscreants and traitors to them when she was grown and crowned. And yet . . . the dank gray walls that abruptly reared about her were as familiar to Anghara as the banks of Cascin's wells—these were the dungeons of Miranei, which she had never seen with living eyes. Somewhere, a long, long way away, she could hear the ominous clang of a closing door—and she was on the wrong side. The darkness rushed in upon her, and she heard a long, drawn-out cry, dimly aware it was her own. When she opened her eyes, blinking furiously at a welling of tears, she found herself lying on the cold stone floor of Al'haria's Catacombs of the Records, with ai'Jihaar kneeling beside her and al'Jezraal's worried face, shadowed from the flickering torch, bending over.

"What was it that he said?" demanded ai'Jihaar, who had spent enough time with her young charge to recognize these occasional visions for what they were.

But the memory was scrubbed from her mind, shredded into trails of dark mist. "I don't know," Anghara said. "I can't remember. And . . . it was . . . important . . ."

"Can you stand?" asked al'Jezraal.

"Yes," Anghara said, scrambling to her feet. Her face was set. Perhaps Sif had the right of it, after all—a fine queen she would make, with an unexpected word or an unguarded glance into the fire enough to pitch her into these uncontrollable fits of vision. But she knew better than to start philosophizing about that here, and it was only just given to her to return to some kind of order before a flickering of torchlight announced ai'Farra's imminent return.

The Keeper, who appeared to have been out of earshot during the drama of Anghara's brief vision, came staggering back with a mammoth pile of book rolls under her arm, piling them with care and a sigh of relief on top of the stone table in the hallway.

"That is most of it," she said. "There are more, but a lot of them are in a language or an alphabet too archaic even for me to understand."

"Then we will start with these," said al'Jezraal. "I think we should begin with the oldest."

"This one," said ai'Farra, extracting a scroll delicately from underneath the others. "This is the oldest comprehensible one."

As she ran gentle fingers across the parchment, ai'Jihaar said, "It is beginning to crumble." There was deep regret in her voice.

"It is almost eight hundred years old," ai'Farra said cryptically. Her eyes gleamed oddly in the torchlight and it was hard to gauge whether she meant it as a boast or a gentle rebuke. "Here, let me see. I am probably the only one who can still understand the half of this tongue."

They relinquished the parchment and al'Jezraal held the torch high as she began to read.

They lost all track of time in the darkness, tracing the life of a vanished oracle over the centuries. When ai'Farra closed the last book roll she had brought, they were all conscious of a deep weariness, and a pang or two of hunger. While al'Jezraal had taken time for breakfast that morning, none of the *sen'en'thari* had eaten anything since dawn, and it felt as though it was time for the sun to rise again.

They had found nothing.

For some reason not one of them, not even ai'Farra, took that as proof the vision from Anghara's dream was at fault—if anything, the contrary. This was the last vision of Gul Qara, almost a kind of farewell; it was hardly to be expected they would find prior references to it scattered freely through the Records. But the absence of any clue left them adrift; they would have to try finding Gul Khaima the hard way.

"Put them away, ai'Farra," said al'Jezraal, gathering the rolls together. "The answer lies elsewhere. We will not find the place in here, not today."

"It would not have been that easy," murmured ai'Farra, hoisting her load back under her arm.

They waited in silence while she vanished again into the mysterious dark with her books, and presently reappeared again empty-handed to lead them back up the stairs and through the ancient door, locking it behind. A glance through a nearby window showed the reddish light of imminent sunset.

"I will have a repast brought to my chambers," said al'-Jezraal. "Please join me . . ."

For a moment the thought of food excised Gul Khaima from their minds. They climbed the stairs to al'Jezraal's rooms, his guards bowing deeply enough now to the approaching company. Once again it was al'Tamar who handed them into the inner chamber, and he who brought them the trays of food al'Jezraal ordered.

". . . anything to go on?" al'Tamar heard as he entered the room, trailed by another, junior servant carrying the trays he did not have enough hands to bear himself. "You saw a stone, and there is not much stone on Kheldrin's shores, but what there is lies scattered facing three different seas. It would take months to explore everything, especially if you were to go to every place yourself."

"Gul Khaima," muttered ai'Farra, tapping her nose with one long finger, once again deeply into the mystery, oblivious to al'Tamar's presence. "Why do I know that name?"

Even before al'Tamar's silvery-blue aura flickered in surprise at the overheard words Anghara had felt his reaction, and was on her feet.

"Where?" she said, very low, gazing at him steadily.

They had all risen now, and al'Tamar took an involuntary step backward under the concentrated gaze of so many eyes filled with power. Then al'Jezraal's face softened. "*Hai,* lad, the look on your face! No, we will not breathe fire upon you. But if you do know anything of a place called Gul Khaima, you must tell us."

"Not quite . . . that," said al'Tamar. "Ul'khari'ma. But you spoke of stone, and sea, and it fits. It bears a different name on the maps, but its folk name it thus. Ul'khari'ma is in the north, I fostered there briefly with al'Talip ma'Shadir, my mother's kinsfolk. It is a small place, a handful of people— a place where they fish for had'dan and for amber, beneath a great cliff."

As al'Jezraal looked around, he met first Anghara's eyes, then ai'Farra's.

"It is the best we have," he said. "At least it is a start. You will take us to Ul'khari'ma, al'Tamar, as soon as it might be arranged."

## 22

There was a word for this too—it was simply another kind of sand, in a land made of it. But this sand sloped gently toward a whispering ocean, indigo in the starlit darkness. Anghara sat with her burnoose laid on the ground beside her and her knees hugged in the circle of her arms, watching the silver glimmer of breaking surf and listening to the murmur of the water on the shore.

It was Sight more than any other sense that warned her of a presence approaching at her back, but it was a physical and rather disagreeable noise, at once a snap and a wet squelching sound, that made her turn. She saw al'Tamar bending to examine something he had just ground with his heel.

"Red crab," he said by way of explanation, without looking up. The silvery-blue soul fire Anghara had first sensed in Al'haria played about al'Tamar's bright hair like a faint halo. "If not quite poisonous, then relatively unpleasant. They bite anything that moves, and the consequences are . . . uncomfortable, to say the least."

Anghara accepted his presence, his action, without question. *Hama dan ar'i'id,* the saying went, You are never alone in the desert. Anghara had learned what that meant, out here in the caravan. It was a simple truth that not a single Kheldrini in the desert watched his own back—but always that of his companion. If there were no companion, there were always the Gods, who were understood to take on the role of watcher as well—given the right rituals had been followed beforehand. Something like this, in effect an enforced altruism, might have been thought unusual in a society where feuds could start with such ease—but defending against a feud was always better done when someone else stood between the man and the deed. In Kheldrin, whenever one man wished ill to another, there was always a watchful third to warn of its coming, eyes in a man's back. And in this caravan, al'Tamar had chosen to become Anghara's particular shadow.

It had not been a large caravan that set out from Al'haria in search of Gul Khaima, and al'Jezraal was happy to have it so. To accompany her, ai'Farra brought along only one other *sen'thar,* a gray sister being groomed for gold, whom she trusted implicitly. Her presence was a hedge against Hariff supremacy—if she wasn't Sayyed, which was what ai'Farra would probably have preferred, at least she was Sabrah, a clan whose fortunes were closely allied to those of ai'Farra's own. Clearly ai'Farra had accepted this quest and was throwing her full weight behind it, but she was not going to allow this covenant of a new oracle to become something the Hariff could claim for their own—and just in case they tried, ai'Farra had brought along a witness.

The secular part of the company was made up of al'-Jezraal and al'Tamar. A handful of trusted Hariff servants to care for the needs and comforts of this illustrious party completed the cast, and if one or two looked more at home with a bright martial blade than a simple kitchen knife, they managed to remain relatively inconspicuous. They were only there as insurance, in any case al'Jezraal hardly expected to have to put his guards to use on this trip.

For the most part, the route they followed was well established—the trade passage from the coast, along which sea-amber flowed into Al'haria for her craftsmen and dried fish for her people, with livestock and commodities manufactured in the cities and the nomad hai'r'en making the return journey. The trail was well known and routine for most of al'Jezraal's small caravan—everyone except Anghara had made this particular trip up the coast at least once. Inured to Kadun Khajir'i'id's sights, they appeared content to ride blind and wrapped in their own thoughts and largely ignore the vistas which broke into new wonders every time Anghara looked in a different direction. The red desert had not failed to astound her, yet again, with its infinite variety.

It was not something she could easily share with ai'Jihaar—she could hardly exclaim "Look!" to the blind *an'sen'thar* when she saw yet another thing which left her breathless with its beauty, and expect ai'Jihaar, however augmented her senses were, to respond. She hardly knew the gray *sen'thar* and ai'Farra was only just reconciled to tolerating her. By the same token, she could hardly ride at al'-Jezraal's knee like an exuberant child. While he would have been happy to explain, or teach, he always treated her with the grave courtesy due both to her royal rank and the *an'sen'thar* gold, and somehow she felt foolish at the thought of giving way to her enthusiasm beside him.

Which left al'Tamar.

Anghara had not been able to figure him out yet—he was still an anomaly, al'Jezraal's right hand when he should have been ensconced in the *sen'thar* tower years ago. But ai'Farra seemed blissfully unaware of his gifts, as was her companion; Anghara had tried asking ai'Jihaar about male *sen'en'thari* without being specific, but they had been sidetracked by other things and the subject had been lost in the chaos of the preparations and then the journey itself. But once on the trail, al'Tamar seemed to sense her curiosity and awe of Kadun Khajir'i'id, and it was soon customary for the pair to ride out together in the van. He became an enthusiastic guide and teacher, and, before long, a friend.

"See that?" al'Tamar pointed at an insignificant-looking pile of what seemed to be shrivelled brown leaves on the red sand. "That is sarghat. The desert is full of it, for those who know where to look."

"What's sarghat?"

"Below that mop of leaves is a root as long as your arm and as thick as your thigh," al'Tamar said, with a fine disregard for proprieties. "When you are lost in the desert that root can let you live long enough to get to help. Nomad tribes will sometimes offer you sarghat when you arrive into their camp, usually immediately followed by something much more palatable."

"Something like pa'ha?" Anghara grinned, remembering ai'Jihaar's fastidious shrinking from the pungent liquor in the Kadun's Shod Hai'r on the night Anghara had first met al'Jezraal.

"Something like sweetmeats," al'Tamar said, but he was not quite able to hide a quick grin of his own. He was all too aware of his aunt's tastes. "It is very symbolic, and their way of saying that their tents are offered as sanctuary against the desert—sarghat root, which is hardship and privation, followed by nomad hospitality in terms of something that is their own specialty."

Another time it had been the edge of a desert hai'r, and Anghara had succumbed to the desert heat to the extent of giving in to a massive headache, pain buzzed inside her skull like a hive of disturbed bees. Once again, al'Tamar had come to the rescue with his herb lore. "Khi'tai," he'd said, pushing a pair of thick, waxy leaves into her hand. "Drink it as an infusion, or just chew it raw, and the headache will go away."

It was fleshier, but the shape of the leaves looked familiar. "It looks a bit like wirrow," Anghara said, peering at the glossy leaves. "We use it in Sheriha'drin too. Headaches, and fevers . . . once, in Cascin . . ."

When she fell silent, al'Tamar allowed himself a small sigh. "Perhaps there will come a time," he said, "when I too will be allowed make the pilgrimage."

"Allowed?" asked Anghara, folding the khi'tai leaves into her palm. "Who is to give you permission?"

"It is usually only *sen'en'thari* who go," said al'Tamar briefly.

It had been a perfect opportunity, but Anghara had been rattled and dazed by the headache and missed it completely—and al'Tamar had turned away, offering nothing further. The next day neither made any reference to what had been almost a confidence; it remained unspoken between them. Toward sunset al'Tamar pointed out a silkseeker descending in slow spirals, which could only mean a jin'aaz spider lair nearby. When they peeled off to look for it, al'-Jezraal came with them. They found it in time to see the silkseeker tease out several fat silk-wrapped cocoons with its long sharp beak and begin feeding. It was a neat and utterly pitiless spectacle, the beautiful gold and white bird dispensing impartial death; they were too late to save any of the cocoons for their silk, but Anghara watched the episode with a feeling that was half fascination and half revulsion.

"Survival," said al'Jezraal on their way back to the others. "Out here, you are the eater or the eaten. The desert harbors nothing soft."

"What eats the silkseekers?"

"The vultures," said al'Jezraal. "And sometimes the jin'aaz."

"The *spiders?*" asked Anghara, her eyes wide. "But I just saw . . ."

"It fed on the cocoons," said al'Tamar. "The young. The adult spider was not at home. Sometimes even silkseekers get unlucky."

"How big are these spiders?" gasped Anghara, trying to envisage something that could consume the silkseeker. The bird was not large, but it was certainly bigger than any spider she had ever seen.

With a wide grin al'Tamar dropped his reins, showing a size as wide as an Al'hariani serving platter between his open palms. "But do not fear," he added, seeing her eyes go even wider. "They are largely nocturnal and very shy. They would not come near a man."

"And when you go to get the silk?"

"The spider is lured from the den first, with bait of food," said al'Jezraal.

"I suppose they're poisonous, like everything else," said Anghara.

"Is that what you think? We have been remiss, then, in showing you the things that bring life in the desert," said al'-Jezraal with a smile.

"No," said al'Tamar, his own answer far more specific.

"Not exactly poisonous. But a spider bite is liable to lead to swelling and, if it is about the face, sometimes to temporary blindness. Not life-threatening, but largely unpleasant."

The words were almost the same as those he'd used to describe the red crab he had just pulverized on the Kadun Khajir'i'id shore. It had been another lesson. *Hama dan ar'i'id.*

"Sit with me," Anghara invited, patting the sand. "You said that you fostered at this place which we seek?"

"For a while," said al'Tamar, sitting beside her. "They are cousins, my mother's kin. Her mother was sister to al'Talip ma'Shadir, the village headman. He is old now, but he still leads the fishing fleet at Ul'khari'ma."

"Why did they send you there?" asked Anghara, staring out to sea.

It had been an innocent question, but the silver-blue aura flared briefly into an incandescent glow before being furiously damped down. Anghara turned sharply.

"You know," he said flatly, glancing up in resignation at this reaction. "Of course you know, *an'sen'thar.* And one other does—my aunt, ai'Jihaar, because she was the one who hid me from the rest."

"Hid you? But why?"

"I could not join a tower," he said, rather bleakly, kneading the sand with restless fingers. "I am my father's only son, his heir, the heir to a Hariff silver mine. If I went, it would lapse—to another clan, perhaps. So they sent me first to the furthest place they knew where I had kin, and where *sen'en'thari* were few. And when a *sen'thar* came to Ul'khari'ma, I left, and came to my uncle at Al'haria."

"But there are more *sen'en'thari* there than just about anywhere else in this entire land," said Anghara, frowning.

"Yes, and my uncle is the one man who can keep me from ever being near one for long enough for them to suspect," said al'Tamar. "And my aunt has placed some kind of a block on me, something that prevents them from seeing what I am. I do not understand it, but then, I was never trained. I never will be."

"Would you have liked to be?" asked Anghara.

"A man has never yet worn the gold," said al'Tamar, and his voice was very soft. "I think I would have liked to try."

"Perhaps you still may," said Anghara, very gently.

He tossed his head, sending the long loose copper hair swinging. "It is too late."

"It's never too late," she said. "Look at me."

He did, and offered one of his quick grins, tinged, however, with sharpness. "I said I thought I could wear gold, *an'sen'thar.* Not hear dead oracles and raise the dead."

"But . . ."

"I was there, Anghara. I saw you heal."

"Others can heal also," she said stubbornly.

"Not," he said, "without knowing how, without knowing what they were doing—and that is what you did that night in Shod Hai'r. I made you do it—I saw it—I have never forgotten it. And I have seen Gul Qara; I have seen it before you came there, and I have seen it afterward. There has always been an odd power there—now no more, and I can often sense that power in you. You carry Gul Qara in you. As I said, I thought I could wear gold. But take an oracle and carry it in my blood . . ." He shook his head again. "No. It could never be too late for you. But for me . . . I do not know. Even if a tower would have me, I do not know if I could ever regain all the lost time that lies between me and what might have been."

"But you cannot . . ."

He lifted his hand, and she closed her lips over the words she had been about to say. "If, one day, they let me go to Sheriha'drin, I shall be content," he said. "But otherwise I have to do my duty, to my family, to my clan."

Duty. Anghara knew the word well, and its weight. Though al'Tamar's were young shoulders to carry that weight, he would not bow under it. What she felt was beyond words—an odd sense of companionship with this lonely young man, a strange, bittersweet sadness no less potent for that it was tinged with so much understanding. So he wasn't trained, but there were some things Sight didn't need training for—emotions and feelings did not need interpretations and special skills, they simply were. The gold kindled, very soft, no brighter than, perhaps, candlelight; the soul fire reached, touched, gentle as a whisper.

At its touch al'Tamar's own aura brightened into a cloak of silvery blue; the two fires brushed, merged, trembled for a moment ravelled and twined into one another, and then Anghara pulled away, and al'Tamar allowed his own soul fire to die down to a banked glow. His eyes were huge in the luminescent ocean night.

When he finally spoke, after a long pause, his words were unexpected. "It is a hard gift," he said, and there was surprising compassion in his voice. Evidently he had received so much more than Anghara had originally meant to convey. Some of her own loneliness had gone into her touch, and where she had thought to communicate only her comprehension of his sense of duty, it seemed obvious, in retrospect, that this would have been colored by a vision of her own, and the way her Sight affected it.

"You could wear gold," she said. He was strong. Stronger than many in ai'Farra's tower. Stronger, perhaps, than most.

His eyes glittered. "One day, perhaps," he murmured. "When I have produced a son of my own, and the line of succession is secure. If they accept a grown man into the novice school."

"The Gods will take you," Anghara said with conviction. "Even if those in the temple balk, the Gods will take you. You are close to them."

"*Sen'en dayr,*" he said with a smile, "but do not put it quite like that. In Kheldrin, when people speak of the Gods taking someone, it usually means death."

She reached out impulsively to squeeze his shoulder. "You won't die," she said. "There are too many important things left for you to do."

She did not hear the echo of prophecy in her voice, but al'Tamar did, and shivered. He had told her she carried Gul Qara within her, and she had just allowed a glimpse of the oracle's light to escape. There was a vision in her words—a vision of a life that was much more than taking over a silver mine from his father and holding it for his clan. There were many things to which al'Tamar had felt he had no claim; this slim hope of unspoken promise he hugged to himself like a talisman, carrying it like a charm of brightness against the dark of everything that had been impossible for so long.

They left the ocean then, and returned to the caravan camp. Everything that could have been said had been said, and it was back onto the desert trail in the morning.

But they were no longer far from their destination. They now rode a narrow band between the sea on the one side and rising ramparts of Kadun's red stone on the other; sometimes seabirds swooped down on them from their nests on the cliff face with shrill cries. The occasional red rock rose from the sea, carved by the waves into fantastic shapes; one, sculpted into a massive arch, caught al'Tamar's eye.

"The First Gate," he said, pointing it out to Anghara with whom he was riding, as usual, at the front of the caravan. "The Second lies closer to the shore; the Last is part of the mainland, and it is there that Ul'khari'ma is."

"It's beautiful," Anghara said.

"And treacherous," said al'Tamar. "The currents are strong here. They carved rocks, after all. It is very easy for an unwary fisher to become caught and be dashed against the Gates. Three young men died that way while I was here."

He was pragmatic about it—the desert folk were all pragmatic about death, especially when it came by accident, unlooked for, out of the dark. They would simply shrug it off—*al'Khur knows his hour,* they would mutter, and carry on with their own lives. But Anghara stared at the sculpted red stone gate as they rode past, thinking of the lives it might have taken. In some things she was still of Roisinan, and there every life cut short prematurely was a tragedy. There were times she despaired of ever being whole again, fitting seamlessly into one country or the other—every time she thought she understood, something else would leap up to tear at the fragile equilibrium. Here, now, so taken up was she with thoughts of Roisinan she could almost smell the damp green grass and the wet, salty spray as the sea broke on the rocks around the bay of Calabra . . .

She blinked, stiffening. She'd thought herself in Calabra, but the memory of the scent of sea spray was of much more recent vintage. Even as she cast out for it, it vanished again, leaving behind only the murmur of lapping ocean.

"What is it?" asked al'Tamar quietly. He had noticed something was going on, but he had waited until her eyes had regained their focus before he ventured to break the silence.

"The scent," she said. "The scent Gul Qara gave me. It is only now that I have smelled it again. We're close. You were right; this is the place. Ul'khari'ma . . . you said the place was so named by those who live there. Why? What does it mean?"

"It is corrupted now, but I think the original meaning was the Place of the Stone," said al'Tamar.

Anghara's hands tightened on her reins, and then she laughed, tilting her head as though in acknowledgment of some kind of failure. "I should have known," she said. "How far still, al'Tamar?"

"We should be there before noon tomorrow," he said.

They could smell it before they saw it. A pervasive aroma of fish met them some way from the village, and it was soon obvious why—they passed the great flat stones where the fishers laid out their catch to dry in the sun some hours before the caravan actually laid eyes on the village itself. The spot had been chosen, al'Tamar told them, because the winds usually carried the smell away from the village when the catch was brought here—else it would have been impossible to inhabit the village unless it was with cauterized noses. While ai'Farra was seen to wrinkle her own aristocratic nose once or twice, she made no complaints—and once they were past the drying grounds it really did get better.

Ul'khari'ma was an untidy cluster of huts nestled in a protective horseshoe of rock. The cliffs at the village's back did a ponderous turn and waded out into the ocean, petering out into a tangle of rocky teeth around which the water seethed and foamed, breaking up into spectacular fans of white spume. Here at last was the source of the spray scent Gul Qara had given Anghara as her guide. But before the cliffs broke up into the rocks of the reef they reared into the most spectacular of all, the Last Gate of al'Tamar's description. It was actually a double gate. One had simply been driven through the cliff, a great reddish stone arch, broad at the bottom, narrowing at the top into an elegant pointed lintel which would not have looked out of place as a gateway in one of the exotic palaces of Algira, paintings of which Anghara had seen in Miranei. The other, more squat and dumpy, led into a cavern within the cliff itself, the darkness within broken up into a luminescent sparkle where sunlight touched the still waters just inside the gateway, sheltered from the open ocean as if in a womb.

"What is that place?" Anghara asked al'Tamar as they approached the village, unable to take her eyes from this second gate. It was as though the sparkle of light upon the hidden waters had hypnotized her.

"The grotto," said al'Tamar. "Boys are usually sent there on a dare; at least once is mandatory, before they are counted as men. The tale goes that a demon lives in there."

"Did you go?" asked Anghara.

If it had been given to Kheldrini to blush, Anghara was almost certain al'Tamar did. He hung his head.

"Almost," he admitted at last. "But I put it off, and put it off, and then I left, and never went at all."

"Do you believe in the demon?"

He shrugged. "Anything is possible," he said. "I do not think there is one in there, though. Those who did go spoke of it to me, but there is probably just the echo, and perhaps a strange light, and the water, they say, is very deep."

"So why didn't you go, then?"

"And what if I was wrong?" He was grinning now, teasing himself. "Still, I am back. Perhaps now is the time for me to enter the grotto."

"Perhaps," said Anghara slowly, her eyes still on the grotto gate. "Perhaps you might have to take me there."

"But it is only the young men . . ." he began, and then caught a glimpse of the gray eyes in the face bared of its burnoose. His own changed, a glimmer of understanding lighting the gold. "I see," he said. "I think it could be arranged. But perhaps it might be best to speak of it to no one of Ul'khari'ma for now. Leave it to me."

By this time they had been spotted, and a welcoming delegation waited for them in the midst of the village. It consisted, officially, of a handful of the more senior fishermen led by al'Talip, al'Tamar's great-uncle and the village headman, and an elderly and dignified gray-robed *sen'thar* woman whose skin the sun and the sea had baked into a brown, wrinkled mask. But the delegation was something of a technicality, with the entire village hanging curiously about, hovering in doorways, peering around the corners of houses, finding urgent business that necessitated the immediate crossing of the village square. When her glance crossed with that of a chubby, round-faced girl who stared at her with undisguised astonishment, Anghara had to smile. It was obvious they knew whom they were facing, and the presence of *Sa'id* Al'haria and no less than two other *an'sen'en'thari* faded into insignificance when they realized the *fram'man* from Sheriha'drin was also in their midst. Perhaps she should have had the presence of mind to keep her burnoose fastened until al'Jezraal was done with the formalities.

Such as they were, these did not take long. The new arrivals were greeted, their animals taken into care, and al'Jezraal and al'Tamar ushered into what looked like al'Talip's own house while the *sen'en'thari* were whisked away to the local *sen'thar's* quarters. Anghara did not know how the men fared, but as far as the *sen'en'thari* were concerned the place was adequate, if a little cramped—ai'Jihaar and Anghara were given one tiny room, ai'Farra and her gray went into another, and the gray *sen'thar* to whom the house belonged slept on a makeshift pallet in a nook by the hearth which usually harbored a servant. The servant herself was banished to her own family's house for the duration of

the visit, the little house being simply too small to contain
all six women.

The villagers' curiosity was extraordinary, even stifling;
al'Jezraal had said not to speak of the purpose of their visit
until he had had a chance to talk with al'Talip, but that did
not prevent the locals from speculating furiously. Even the
*sen'thar,* who was trained to respect her superiors' silence
for as long as they chose to keep it, could not stop her eyes
filling with conjecture and deliberation every time she
looked at this unprecedented number of *an'sen'en'thari*
under her humble roof. The atmosphere was charged, and
*sen'en'thari* were by nature more sensitive to it than anyone
else. Anghara felt it wrapping around her, heavy and close,
reminding her of the air in Khar'i'id. Her mind was still full
of the scent of the sea spray and the sight of the gate to the
grotto, but she could not seem to marshal her thoughts into
any sort of coherent order inside the house. Waiting until
everyone was otherwise occupied, she threw her djellaba
around her shoulders, drawing up the concealing hood, and
slipped out into the night. It was as much to escape the constant sideways glances of the local *sen'thar* as to grab a
chance to think, alone, about how to unravel the puzzle Gul
Qara had left her.

She had half-expected to find the entire village gathered
outside the *sen'thar*'s house, but for a wonder nobody was
there at all; it was as if the Gods themselves were keeping
her path clear. Anghara wandered down to the small harbor,
with the fishing coracles drawn up and upended over the
sand above the high tide mark. The entrance to the grotto
was a yawning hole full of darkness, and the breaking waters on the reef rose ghostly white into the air and then fell
back to vanish once again into the inky sea.

The stone . . . the sea . . . the smell of spray . . .

Almost without thinking she sent out a tendril of gold, imperceptible to most—even, perhaps, to *sen'en'thari* who
weren't really looking—seeking a specific soul fire, silver
upon blue, like the moon on the waters. *Come. Come to me.*

And he came, stumbling dazedly on the sand, rubbing at

his temples, the sea breeze tangling his long, loose copper hair. "You called me?" al'Tamar whispered, coming to a stop as he saw her standing by the boats. "You *called* me?"

"You heard me," she replied.

The silver-blue light rippled, settled, died into a low glow around his brow, like a circlet of royalty.

"What is it, Anghara?"

"The grotto," she said. "Will you take me?"

"Now?" he said, taken aback. "Tonight?"

"Tonight," she said. Her voice was quiet, even, low; she was speaking to a friend, but there was Kir Hama command embedded somewhere within, and he heard it.

He rubbed his temple again, and then straightened. "We will need a paddle," he said. "Wait here."

He wore a dark djellaba and would have vanished into the night as he turned away had it not been for the faint aura of light which clung to him. It was still a source of endless astonishment to Anghara that ai'Farra was unable to sense this. Before long he was back, carrying a broad flat paddle in one hand, undoing the clasp of his djellaba as he walked.

"Leave yours," he said. "They are only a hindrance in the boat. If I had it, I would don my fishing breechclout. It might not go so well with your robe."

"It will go well enough," Anghara said, laying her own djellaba in a pile on the sand, next to where al'Tamar had let his drop. "Which boat?"

"A small one. That one will do. Big ones do not seem to like the grotto very much, at least two of my acquaintance came back in splinters. Hold this."

He handed her the paddle and hoisted the light, small boat onto his shoulder, laying it into the surf as they reached the ocean. Handing her inside, he waded into the water, pushing the boat out, and scrambled up into it when it floated in deeper water. He took the paddle and steered the small craft away from the angry breakers of the reef, toward the grotto's low entrance.

He did not ask questions, and Anghara was grateful; she was in the grip of something similar to that which led her to seek the Tanassa Dance in Roisinan years ago, leading in turn to her first meeting with ai'Jihaar. Pressed for explanations, she could give none—she went where the Gods took her.

The darkness of the grotto yawned ever deeper and more solid as they drew closer. Anghara could see al'Tamar's lips folded tight, his expression at odds with itself, exhilaration and dread warring on his features. This was a sort of proving he had never done while he was here. But it was certain he had never imagined doing it like this, with Anghara in the prow of the small boat, a film of gold clinging to her hair and hands much as silver-blue still hovered at al'Tamar's own brow. If there was an unwritten code governing the grotto, it was more than certain they were breaking it.

They passed under the archway suddenly, as though it had reached out to swallow them—which it had, in a sense, as they discovered they were in a low, gullet-like tunnel. Black as pitch, the tunnel seemed to curve slightly to the left; al'-Tamar steered by touch.

"We should have brought a lamp," he murmured, fending off the tunnel wall with the paddle yet again.

Then, with equal suddenness, they were out of it, and al'-Tamar's comment became obsolete. They found themselves in a high-domed cavern filled with a strange half-light, a pearly, faintly luminescent glow which seemed to be emanating from nowhere in particular and yet surrounded them. For a moment al'Tamar froze, with the paddle just touching the still water; but a stray eddy tugged at the boat, and that was enough for him to come to his senses. He dug the paddle into the luminous water with a gesture that was almost savage. The boat righted itself and glided further into the cave.

Anghara had seen such light before. The black hills of Khari'i'd had glowed with it on the night she heard the voice of Gul Qara in the hidden valley in the Empty Quarter. There it might have seemed to be no more than moonlight, but now, here, she recognized it once more, and there was no moon in this cavern. She sat quiet, very still, a slow exhilaration beginning to build within her; her fingertips tingled with the memory of the touch of Gul Qara's smooth gray stone.

"What now, *an'sen'thar?*" asked al'Tamar in a low voice. The boat hovered in the midst of the pearly waters, almost the precise color of al'Tamar's soul fire. His words raised a small echo, and his hands tightened involuntarily on the paddle. Anghara laughed, softly, and the echo threw that back as well.

"You said you didn't believe in demons," she said.

"I said nothing of the kind," he said, collecting himself. "I merely said I did not believe there was one here. But this . . . this is beyond my understanding."

"And mine," she said. "I do not understand it, but I know it. Can you get me up near that ledge?"

When al'Tamar guided the boat toward the flat stone shelf she indicated, she scrambled up onto it as he steadied the small craft against the rock.

"Where are you going?" he asked.

"Up," she said, and only now did he notice there was a cleft in the rock beyond the sill, and something hewn by no human hand but nevertheless a rough kind of a staircase spiraling upward out of sight. For a long moment he could only sit and stare.

"Well?" Anghara said, poised almost on the first step. "Are you coming?"

His head jerked up. "I? Is this for me?"

"For this night's work," she said, and again al'Tamar heard cadences of prophecy scintillate in her words like light on a knife's edge, "you may yet find yourself wearing the gold."

She was *an'sen'thar,* it lay within her hand to give that gift. And there was deep truth in her voice. Quickly al'Tamar dropped his eyes, made the boat fast, and followed her without another word.

The staircase was wickedly uneven, with one step nearly on a level with its predecessor and the very next necessitating almost a scramble; but at least the light was with them still. The staircase seemed to go on for so long that al'Tamar almost gave up hope of ever seeing again the freedom of the open skies. But then, quite suddenly, the walls simply fell away beside him. He stepped out onto a broad, flat plateau whose edges plunged sheer toward the sea on three sides, with a low escarpment falling away into the reddish expanses of Kadun Khajir'i'id on the fourth. It was empty except for a large stone lying on its side almost across the middle of the plateau. With silver-blue Sight al'Tamar could see the edges of the great stone shimmer in the night.

"Is this it?" he asked, awed.

"This will be Gul Khaima," Anghara said, breathing deeply of the salty tang of spray-spiced air. "All we need to do is raise the stone."

His initial exhilaration turned almost to dismay as he surveyed the massive stone lying before them.

"How?" he said. "Can you do it, with . . . Sight? With the gift?"

"I must not," she said, turning to him, and her eyes were luminous. "This is a place of the Gods, but this oracle is mortal-born. Look, there is the base which will hold it—but it must be set to stand there by mortal hands, with ropes, with willpower."

"We cannot do it," al'Tamar said, bending to gaze at the depression Anghara had named as the stones base. "It will never hold."

"It will," said Anghara. *"I have seen it."*

## 23

It had seemed such a small place in the night, but morning saw many people on the plateau at the top of the cliff— al'Jezraal, al'Tamar, a handful of the villagers led by wiry old al'Talip ma'Shadir, and all the *sen'en'thari*. Yet somehow it was big enough to hold them all with space to spare. It felt as though the plateau had grown to accommodate the number who climbed upon it.

Anghara had insisted the oracle stone be raised the hard way, and they had brought ropes, with the villagers providing the muscle and al'Jezraal himself pitching in with a will. This was yet another face to the man—his council at Al'haria would not have recognized him. Stripped to the waist, chest and shoulders gleaming with sweat, heaving with the rest of them to Anghara's directions, he found one of his sweet, grave, fleeting smiles for her whenever he looked up from beneath his burden and their eyes happened to meet.

He would have been far more recognizable to his council in the early hours of that morning, two or three hours after midnight, when al'Tamar, whom Anghara had sent back alone to the village, roused him at al'Talip's house. Then al'-Jezraal had been haughty and angry. Stoically al'Tamar had borne the brunt of his anger since Anghara was conveniently out of reach. And yet—alone up there with the stone that was about to be reborn as the oracle of Gul Khaima, Anghara had been as present at that meeting as if she had physically stood beside him.

"Uncle," al'Tamar had said, desperation driving him to try and squirm out from under the lash of al'Jezraal's ire by playing the kinship card, "it was hardly my idea! But it is not as though hundreds of village boys have not been doing it for years. And she seemed so insistent . . . so sure . . . you know how she can be . . ."

*The young wretch,* Anghara thought, up on her perch, grinning despite herself. *All injured innocence.*

But it seemed to work.

"It was dangerous and foolhardy," al'Jezraal snapped in reply to al'Tamar's admittedly lame excuse. But then al'-Jezraal's anger seemed to leave him all at once to be replaced by an eager enthusiasm. Although he realized that going to Anghara was absolutely useless until morning—there was nothing he or anyone could do before it was light—al'Tamar had been forced to do an abrupt about-turn in mid-argument and try and restrain his uncle from leaving for the grotto there and then.

By this time half the village had roused, and both ai'Farra and ai'Jihaar, who had inevitably missed Anghara's presence given the cramped living quarters, had naturally arrived at al'Talip's house almost before al'Tamar had finished the first telling of his tale. They had difficulty restraining the entire village from coming to the grotto at the crack of dawn. Eventually most of those not invited to climb up on the spire were bobbing about in their boats out in the bay, peering upward into the sun and trying to figure out what was going on from a distance.

Those who came brought rope, and ten men now labored to hoist the great stone into the depression Anghara had pointed out. It was not easy. A sharp edge frayed a rope to such an extent that it gave way, and the stone almost went over the edge into the ocean. Another time they thought they had it poised, but the base of the stone slithered on the smooth rock of the plateau and it crashed back down into its horizontal position with such force al'Tamar could not believe it had not cracked in half. The morning was half gone and still they struggled; and perhaps they would have given up already if it hadn't been for Anghara's words, relayed to the rapt village by al'-Tamar the night before: *It will stand. I have seen it.*

It was ai'Jihaar, the blind one, who "saw" it first—she cried out as the apex of the stone, guided carefully by panting men, finally slid into the cavity for which, ages before, it had been made. The stone trembled for a moment and then stood upright, poised, the ropes still wrapped around it like some bizarre decoration. Everyone felt it—the moment resonated like a bell, and hackles rose on even the most insensitive of the villagers—but the *sen'en'thari* could see cold fires bubble from underneath and spiral around the great stone. Only now, seeing it standing for the first time, did Anghara realize why it had looked so familiar. It was much bigger, of course, and the color was all wrong, but the shape of the Gul Khaima Stone bore an uncanny resemblance to the small sharp pebble she had planted with her own hand into soft moss on the bank of the well at Cascin. For a moment she wondered which talisman had done the choosing in Bresse. Seeing the power of the one they had just raised, it was hard to believe the little Cascin Stone had ever borne any power that had been its own and not drawn from this primal rock, toward which her steps now seemed to have led all along. Already, watching the stone, it was difficult to recall what the plateau had looked like before—the stone looked as if it had always stood thus, with no visible seam between it and the flat rock on which it stood.

First to break the stasis was ai'Farra, who stepped forward to touch the stone. "It is cool," she said wonderingly. "As though it had not lain in the hot sun all morning."

"What do you think we should do now, *an'sen'thar?*" asked al'Jezraal, himself completely unaware his hands had folded automatically into a gesture of prayer.

"It has been sealed into place," said Anghara. "Thus far I have seen; where the stone takes us from here, I do not yet know."

"Will it speak, *an'sen'thar*, as Gul Qara did?" Beneath the edge of wonder which would not leave it, ai'Farra's voice was as coolly analytical as ever.

But when Anghara turned to face her, the Al'hariani *an'sen'thar*'s eyes were blazing with something that had never been there before—ai'Farra had gone in the space of a few hours from tolerance past acceptance into something that was almost adoration. Anghara had spoken of her vision, and the vision had come to pass. Kheldrin had a new oracle where the old one was dust and ashes, and had been dead and silent for a long time before it met its fate. That, finally, was enough—ai'Farra claimed Anghara as *an'sen'thar* here, now, daring anyone to counterclaim—Anghara was of the Al'haria tower, ai'Farra's tower, and it was Anghara who had raised the oracle.

"I don't know," said Anghara in answer to her question, deliberately introducing a note of uncertainty to dampen the other's naked, possessive pride. "But this is an oracle raised by mortal sweat, by mortal hands, which I am not so sure Gul Qara ever was. It might happen that this oracle will need to speak with mortal tongue."

As though to corroborate this, the gray *sen'thar* ai'Farra had brought with her from Al'haria suddenly moaned. Her eyes rolled back into their sockets, the whites impossibly pale against her bronze skin, as some kind of trance took hold of her, shaking her slender body. A young fisherman who stood beside her scrambled away so fast he almost went over into the chasm and had to be retrieved bodily by a quick-thinking friend. The village *sen'thar,* the old gray who was sharing her house with the visiting *sen'en'thari,* stepped forward to try and help but Anghara stayed her. "No. Wait. I think . . ."

The young gray, whose name was ai'Raisa, shuddered violently once or twice, inarticulate sounds coming from her throat. It looked as though she were going to fall to her knees, but, as the others watched in rapt silence, she staggered forward until she touched the stone with her outstretched hands.

The touch seemed to galvanize her, and for a long moment she stood rigid, her throat arched and her head thrown back, the palms of her hands pressed flat against the stone. Then, very suddenly, she seemed to come back to herself. Her eyes rolled back, wide and gold, and there was almost a smile on her face. Only the *sen'en'thari* could sense her soul

fire had changed, deepened, to resonate with the flames
wreathing the stone, and only they could see the cobweb of
thin strands which now bound oracle and seer together. For
seer was what ai'Raisa had become. Even her voice was different when she spoke, darker, richer, more resonant, ringing like a bell with the truth of oracle-wrapped prophecy.
And when she did speak, it was looking directly at Anghara,
one hand still touching the stone, one stretched out toward
the Roisinani princess.

> *"Reaching from the dark, the bleeding land waits.*
> *A friend and a foe await at return;*
> *love shall be given to him who hates.*
>
> *In fires lit long ago the blameless burn;*
> *a broken spirit shall opened lie,*
> *a bitter secret to learn.*
>
> *Beneath an ancient crown the unborn die;*
> *the hunter is snared by the prey he baits;*
> *sight shall be returned to the blind eye."*

"With mortal tongue," said Anghara, who, for the moment, had been carried away from the message so obviously
meant for her by the self-fulfillment of her own small
prophecy.

"In threes," murmured ai'Jihaar, listening to the cadences.
"Gul Qara often worked in threes. Now this . . ."

"There's three gold *sen'en'thari here*, and a mere
gray . . ." muttered one of the Al'haria servants who had
come with the caravan and who, bred in the shadow of a
*sen'thar* tower, knew the hierarchy was wrong here. But ai'-
Farra heard, and her chin came up firmly.

"Not a gray," said ai'Farra. "For this, ai'Raisa, I raise you
to the gold . . ."

"I have no color any more," said ai'Raisa, perfectly
calmly, "unless I take the red of these cliffs to which I am
now so irrevocably bound. I think . . . I think I am no longer

truly *sen'thar,* ai'Farra ma'Sayyed. I am not sure if I am even ai'Raisa any more. I am the Voice of Gul Khaima . . . I *am* Gul Khaima."

This announcement was received by a moment of sepulchral silence; then ai'Farra, stubborn and unquenchable, set her jaw. "But when you come back to Al'haria . . ." she began.

"I will not return," said ai'Raisa, very softly. "I think I will never return. This place holds my life; I think that, if I left it, the stone would crumble . . . and I would die."

"A mortal oracle," said the gray *sen'thar* from the village, echoing Anghara's earlier words.

"This place is vulnerable as Gul Qara never was," said al'-Jezraal thoughtfully, seeing the whole thing from quite a different perspective.

"We will protect it," old al'Talip spoke up unexpectedly, standing very straight. "My people will be the threshold to the oracle of Gul Khaima; none will come here who mean harm."

At his words, al'Jezraal favored him with a long, measured golden glance. "That is well," he said finally, nodding gravely. "I think you will be needed."

"*Salih'al'dayan* must be done," said ai'Farra, accepting the situation abruptly and then suddenly changing tack in her own inimitable way. Her eyes blazed once again with pride and joy as she glanced up at the stone, and its seer— also one of her own, of the Al'haria tower. "We must thank the Gods. Something suitable . . . al'Talip, do your folk have a ki'thar lamb to . . ."

"No," said Anghara, and although her voice was very low it froze every person on the plateau into stillness, as all eyes swivelled to rest on her. "No blood. Not here. Not ever."

At this ai'Farra drew herself up to her full height. "The Kheldrini Gods have always . . ."

"No blood," said Anghara, meeting the rebellious golden eyes with a gaze that was gray steel. "Not here. This oracle will not accept death as payment for its truth."

*Not for death.* The words spun in ai'Jihaar's mind as she

remembered Gul Qara's fall; and now, here, at another oracle, death raised its head once again and once more Anghara stood in its path.

"She is right," said ai'Raisa suddenly, breaking a brittle silence which hung between ai'Farra and Anghara like ice.

The color in her cheeks high, ai'Farra swung to face her. "What do you mean?"

But ai'Raisa had turned to face Anghara. "This place . . . is not of the old Gods, is it, *an'sen'thar?*" she said hesitantly; her eyes were clouded, but if there was a trace of incomprehension there, there was none at all of doubt.

*It is yours,* said ai'Jihaar, into Anghara's mind. *It is yours, isn't it? You were led to find this stone, you were told how to raise it, and it is your rules it stands by.*

"No blood," Anghara said again, and her words were in answer to all the questions channelled her way. "Make your sacrifice down in the village, ai'Farra, if *salih'al'-dayan* must have blood flowing to make your thanks acceptable to the Gods." She turned, held al'Talip's eye. "Your folk must be the threshold to Gul Khaima in more ways than just standing between her and harm," she said to the old man. "The blood stops at the edge of the water. It must not touch the rock from which the stone draws its truth. Do you understand?"

"We will make it so," said al'Talip.

"Leave me now," said ai'Raisa after a beat of silence, and her voice rang with the power of the oracle.

As he took his leave al'Talip bowed to the young *sen'thar* deeply, in desert-fashion. "My people will see you have all you need," he said, his voice full of reverence. "You have but to ask, and it shall be given to you."

One hand still curled tenderly around the stone, as though she were cradling a lover or a child, ai'Raisa gave al'Talip the other, together with a smile which had something immortal in it. "I am content," she said, and she who had been a simple nomad girl before she had come into Al'haria's tower spoke now as a queen. Her simple sentence was blessing, acceptance and dismissal all in one. As al'Talip walked away his face was transfigured, as though he had just seen a vision.

In stubborn silence ai'Farra went about preparing for the rites of *salih'al'dayan* once they had all regained the village shore. She sent the local *sen'thar* to procure the necessary sacrifice; no ki'thar'en could be spared from the village, and ai'Farra had to be content with a single scrawny chicken from al''Talip's own yard. As with many *sen'thar* ceremonies, this one had always been done in secret, away from *non-sen'thar* eyes, and the village gray had a private place for such occasions. Anghara withdrew into an odd solitude on the journey back from the stone, and the three remaining *sen'en'thari* had all gone there, with their doomed chicken, by the time she came to follow them. But to her vision no place was secret, and the three gathered there showed no surprise when she suddenly materialized amongst them just as ai'Farra was beginning the rite.

The Al'hariani *an'sen'thar,* her slim sacrificial dagger already laid ready, looked up as Anghara stepped into the stone semicircle beneath the cliffs where the ceremony was taking place. A fierce pride still burned in her face, but there was a coldness there, too.

"In some ways I was right, Anghara, whom some name ma'Hariff," ai'Farra said, and her voice was unexpectedly soft, as though she spoke to a child, at odds with her expression. "A tide and a name you took from the desert do not make you of it. *Salih'al'dayan* is our Gods' due; and if you raised an oracle where such dues are forbidden . . ."

"I know, ai'Farra," Anghara said. "But we are not at the oracle now. Let me perform the sacrifice."

In a moment of unguarded astonishment, ai'Farra's eyebrows actually rose, and even ai'Jihaar looked blank for a moment.

"I took nothing the desert did not give me," said Anghara into the silence. "I am *an'sen'thar,* ai'Farra, just as much as you, by your own word. Let me make the sacrifice."

Without taking her eyes from Anghara's face, ai'Farra stepped aside mutely and motioned Anghara to take her place, pausing only to sheath her dagger. The chicken sat quiescent on the slab of red rock that served as their altar. Anghara laid her own dagger, the one that had once been ai'Jihaar's, beside it and raised her voice into the *salih'al'-dayan* invocation she had first heard one night at the edge of the Stone Desert, where an oracle had just died. And now, here, they were giving thanks for another, newly born.

There was no blood on Anghara's sleeves as she laid the chicken's lifeless body down on the altar, the sacrifice done. But, seeing through a shimmering haze of power and a god-presence almost thick enough for the Gods' faces to manifest in the air between them, ai'Farra stared in silence at the tear tracks sparkling on Anghara's cheeks. Once before, on the roof of the temple in Al'haria, Anghara had wept at the moment of sacrifice . . .

As though sensing these thoughts, Anghara looked around to meet her eyes.

*This is the way it has always been done,* ai'Farra said, more to reiterate this to herself than to tell anyone else, but Anghara picked up the stray thought from the surface of the other's mind and replied in kind. It was the first time the two had come into this close a contact.

*I would not take the gold for death,* she said, and the tears still sparkling in the gray eyes held ai'Farra almost hypnotized, *and yet death is all that it means . . . or does it? I weep for every life spilled for the Gods to feed on. There are other ways, ai'Farra. There are other ways of reaching for them.*

*Are there, Anghara? For our Gods?*

*I do not yet understand completely, but I will. And once already I have made one of your Gods a different kind of sacrifice.*

*Twice before. First there was al'Jezraal's sister, whom you snatched from al'Khur . . . I still do not know how. You gave something instead for her, and we still do not know what bargain you made there. And then there was the silk-seeker I tried to have you slay in the Confirmation Service. Twice; and both times the Gods came for you. But for us, Anghara . . . for us, there may be no other way of touching the Gods whom we revere. Blood has been the bridge between us for too many ages.*

Anghara's eyes were silver, luminous. *One day, there will be other bridges,* she said, gazing up at the cliffs towering above their heads. Lost amongst those crags somewhere was the Stone of Gul Khaima. *They are already being made. The first prophecy of Gul Khaima was made without a blood price.*

"But there *was* a blood price," said ai'Farra, very softly, out loud; her eyes came to rest on the bloody altar stone.

"But only because you chose to pay it," said Anghara. "It was not demanded. The first prophecy of the oracle we have raised was given freely."

"Yes," said ai'Farra, smiling cryptically, looking at her again. "Freely. To you. The only one amongst us who does not offer blood as a price for knowledge, and for power."

Things had moved so fast Anghara really had little chance to think through the enigmatic phrases ai'Raisa had uttered earlier. Not being able to refute this statement—the words had indeed been offered to her directly—Anghara turned away. The village gray had already removed herself and the remains of the sacrificed chicken from the scene of the rite; ai'Jihaar stood waiting a little distance away. Anghara's eyes softened as she looked at her teacher and friend; all of a sudden ai'Jihaar looked almost impossibly frail.

"Take her back," Anghara said to ai'Farra. "She needs to rest."

"And you?" said ai'Farra, something sharp and almost motherly in her own voice. "Of all of us, you . . ."

"Probably did the least," smiled Anghara, "aside from talking al'Tamar into the midnight excursion and finding the stone . . . and then standing around and telling everyone else what to do. I'll be all right, ai'Farra. I just . . . need to be by myself for a while."

For another long moment ai'Farra looked at her and then, unexpectedly, bowed deeply before she turned away. Anghara saw her lay a light hand on ai'Jihaar's elbow and heard the murmur of soft conversation, too far away to make out.

Then the two women, gold robes glimmering amongst the reddish rock, walked away.

Anghara waited until they were well out of sight and then left the place of sacrifice, wandering aimlessly toward the ocean. The shore, with its upturned fishing boats, was once again deserted when Anghara came to the water—except for a few children scrambling in the surf who, once they had seen her, seemed to vanish almost before her eyes. If she had been asked, she would have said they had quietly dissolved into the foam which had up until a moment ago been washing their feet. But they went, and Anghara found herself alone. She walked slowly along the shore, turning her back on the Gate and the village, and the spire of rock her hand had hallowed. Her thoughts were strangely vague; her senses, as though to compensate, almost preternaturally sharp. She watched the way the bubbles of white foam caressed her ankles as she stood shin-deep in the water, aware of every individual lacy sphere. Twice she bent over the ruined beauty of a shattered shell, whose broken carapace seemed to have been wrecked simply so that she could see the intricate convolutions which had lain hidden within. And then she saw the jellyfish.

It was almost dead, tossed by the ocean to the edge of the water line where the sand had just enough traction to hold on to it against the water's occasional attempt to reclaim it. Beached, dying, out of its element, it still retained an iridescent beauty—the sun caressed the slowly deflating bubble that was its body and coaxed coruscating rainbows which shimmered like jewels. Ordinarily it would have been just another casualty of the indifferent cruelty of the ocean—but Anghara's senses were not her own. The rainbows glittered and sparkled before her eyes, filling them with radiance, making her dizzy to the extent that she had to sit down suddenly before she collapsed. And still she could not take her eyes off the jellyfish. The colors ran together and spiraled into endlessly changing patterns—then everything flashed up into a brilliant white light, and beyond that there were shadows . . . shadows playing on a stone wall . . . firelight . . . cool mountain air . . .

It took a moment before Anghara recognized her, but the last time she had seen this girl she'd been a veiled bride, and then, later, there had been the vision of Sif's hands over the child-queen's in the bedchamber. It was only now that Anghara saw the face of Sif's queen.

Senena sat on the wide hearth, hunched by the fireside, prodding the flames desultorily with an iron poker. Everything about her was still childish—her body was hardly formed, her breasts still small and high, her waist a handspan. At that moment, drooping by the fire, wearing nothing but a loose shift and with her wheaten hair unbound over her shoulders, she looked as if she still belonged in the nursery. But a marriage ring glinted on her finger as if in mockery, and her eyes were older, much older, than any nursery child's.

She was not alone; another girl sat with her, older, more decorously garbed. But even though the latter's hair was gathered and held back by a pearl-studded net it was unquestionably the same golden shade as Senena's and there was something about their faces that instantly proclaimed them sisters. Lliant was Senena's elder by less than two years, wed just before Sif had come to carry Senena off; neither ever forgot for long that he might well have taken Lliant, if she had been free. For a while Lliant had been jealous of her sister's fortune—she, Lliant, the elder, was a mere knight's wife, where her sister was a crowned queen—but it had not taken long for envy to disappear. The reason was simple—Lliant had found contentment in her marriage. It was patently obvious Senena had not. Lliant's initial envy soon metamorphosed into sympathy, and then pity, for Sif was not easy on his queen. He had picked her because of her pedigree, and her youth—she could be expected to provide a sturdy heir, of good lineage, and she had been young enough to have been no man's before him. Love had nothing to do with his choice. He was fond of her, but in an impersonal sort of way; he tended to treat her a little like a favorite niece most of the time. But there was always the night—night, when she ceased to be anything but a vessel for his seed. He wanted a son; the impatience burned in him, and reached out through him to burn her—the king did not see the terrified child's eyes on the body which lay waiting for him in his bed every night. Passion was Sif's nature, and he brought it to everything he did, but he could not take the time to teach it to this naive young girl. As a result, it was inevitable that Senena came to look on passion as violence. And the idea of a child born of this violence sickened her to the core—it was as though Sif was tearing her very insides from her. Nothing was her own any more.

And there would be a child. She had known for almost a fortnight, and had not had the courage to tell Sif. Nobody knew, except a wise woman of her chamber. And now, because it was tearing her apart to know and not tell anyone else, she had summoned her sister to her chambers one night when she knew Sif would not be there.

Lliant sat clutching the arms of the chair in which she sat, staring at her sister's white, pinched face.

"He does not know? You are with child and you have not told your husband?"

"What will he do, Lliant?" Senena asked, and her voice was very small. "What will he do when I do tell him?"

She was asking for reassurance, but there was none to offer here.

"He has a right to know, Senena," said Lliant, gently but firmly. "Avanna! You carry the heir to Roisinan!"

"He will take it away from me as soon as it is born," said Senena dully, poking the fire. "I am not the kind he would allow to rear his son. The minute he is born he will be taken from me. Even that I will not have."

Lliant slid from her chair and knelt on the floor beside Senena, taking a cold little hand into both her own. "Senena, Senena, you cannot know that. And perhaps . . . perhaps it will be a daughter . . ."

"Yes . . . maybe I will have a daughter," Senena allowed dubiously. Her eyes sparkled with tears. "But then . . . it would all start again . . ." Her eyes were unfocused, staring somewhere past the flames in the hearth. "He is kind . . . sometimes," she whispered. "But most times I do not exist for him, I am a gnat who annoys him and gets in his way; he comes to me at night, he takes his pleasure, and if he bids me a gentle goodnight then that is truly a good night. I do not think he has talked to me—truly talked to me—since the first night he bedded me, and even that was only to explain to me he needed a son. After that, all that was important was the begetting of him." Her breath broke into a sob, and she snatched her hand from Lliant's and buried her face in her palms. "Oh, Lliant! You do not know how lucky you are! Nobody has loved me . . . since I left Father's house . . . and my husband has me smile while I am sitting on my throne beside him, so nobody will see I am unhappy. And he will never understand—what do I have to be unhappy about? I am queen, I wear jewels and silks like no other woman in the land, and all I need to do for all this is give him a dynasty."

"He is a king, Senena," said Lliant, and it was hard to know if she meant it as a rebuke or a lofty explanation of Sif's behavior to a child incapable of understanding otherwise. Or perhaps neither—simply a bleak statement of fact. Senena shuddered, lifting her head and wrapping her arms around her still flat belly. Lliant recoiled at the pale, implacable flame in her younger sister's eyes.

"He is a man, and then he is king," Senena said. "I carry his seed—son and prince, perhaps, if the Gods have willed it; Sif has commanded it, and so it came to pass. But if he can lay claim to this babe's body and blood, I swear to you, Lliant, I shall never let Sif have his heart, or his soul. That much of my son I will keep. Enough of him I will keep to be able one day to tell the king he is my son, not his—and it will be true. It will be my dynasty that rules Roisinan; Sif's blood, but my heart. And I will not let Sif die before he knows this—knows that he has failed."

She moved her hand, and the wedding ring sent a lance of firelight into Anghara's eyes. Anghara blinked, and was instantly back on the shore of a strange ocean, sitting beside the dying jellyfish. The thing was dull now, fading fast; the vision died with it.

A line of ai'Raisa's verse came back to her: *Beneath an*

*ancient crown the unborn die.* The unborn. The unborn in Senena's womb? Die? How?

And how did the rest go? Something about a bleeding land . . . *Reaching from the dark, the bleeding land waits . . .* and then, a line or two later, *In fires lit long ago the blameless burn . . .* That was Roisinan, surely. A Roisinan which called to her. A friend and a foe—indeed, more than one—might well be waiting for her on her return, as another line went, but the rest of it was hopelessly cryptic. Whose was the broken spirit spoken of, and what was the secret? And what was the prey that would snare the hunter? One hopeful interpretation, fueled, perhaps by the very last line, would be that Roisinan's Sighted would regain what they had lost and, somehow, take their revenge against Sif. But then, there was the line about giving love to him who hated . . .

A soft step sounded behind her, and Anghara spoke without turning her head. "I think it is time I went home," she said quietly but steadily.

The old *an'sen'thar*'s voice bore a world of sorrows, but also pride, knowledge and understanding. "Yes," she said. "I know."

24

$P$erhaps the Kheldrini were all endowed with more gifts than they knew, or maybe it was just a combination of sharp intelligence with the proverbial ability of the desert nomads to glean news from the whispering of the sand at twilight, but Anghara's decision to leave was no sooner made there on the shore than almost the entire village seemed to be aware of it. Although al'Tamar was not there when Anghara and ai'Jihaar returned, al'Jezraal met them on the beach with an offer of sturdy ki'thar'en and supplies, as well as an escort as large as Anghara wanted and the promise of a safe sea passage once in Sa'alah. With both her customary stubbornness and a blunt affection she had no other way of expressing, ai'Farra said she would attend to the necessary ceremonies to ask the Gods to look kindly on Anghara's journey. And when her eye locked with Anghara's, it held a wry amusement of which Anghara would hardly have believed her capable.

When al'Tamar returned, toward sunset, he sought out Anghara where she sat outside the village *sen'thar's* house with ai'Jihaar; it seemed that he alone had not had the news, or, at the very least, he made no reference to Anghara's leaving.

"I have a present for you," he said instead, cradling a package. The outer wrapping looked suspiciously like his own burnoose. "Have you ever seen raw sea amber?"

Anghara shook her head, and al'Tamar emptied the burnoose onto her lap. Six or seven large, creamy yellow globes tumbled out, gleaming dully and ai'Jihaar reached out to draw the tip of a sensitive finger along one.

"These are deep sea," she said, and her voice had the edge of accusation on it. "What have you been doing, al'Tamar?"

"Deep sea?" asked Anghara, staring down into her lap with fascination. She lifted one globe; it was oval, smooth, and very heavy. "Are there other kinds?"

"There is the kind that washes onto the shoreline," said ai'Jihaar, a little grimly, "but those are smaller, rougher, often irregularly shaped. These, they had to be dived for—and diving for sea amber is not the kind of prank untutored boys who have not seen the sea for years should be attempting."

Anghara looked up. The silvery-blue soul fire was kindled, the aura bristling defensively; al'Tamar was guilty as charged. More; he knew of her leaving. He must have known even before she did. When he heard ai'Raisa speak the oracle's words, he had known at once. And the knowledge was there in his eyes.

"Thank you," she said simply.

"If you bring them back to Al'haria," he said, "I can make them into a *say'yin* for you."

"*You?*" asked Anghara in surprise. "You know how?"

"My uncle is generous with free time, and my duties are often light," al'Tamar said. "I learn that which is offered. Yes, I know how."

Anghara gathered the amber into a fold of her robe. "I would treasure such a *say'yin*," she said.

"Making a *say'yin* takes time," said ai'Jihaar laconically. "How long did you mean to stay at Al'haria, then?"

Anghara bit her lip, closing her hand over the amber. Now that the decision to go had been made, it burned in her like a slow fire. "I meant to pass through, because it lies in my way," she said. "I had no wish to linger . . ."

But ai'Jihaar suddenly seemed to regret her sharpness. She reached out to cover Anghara's hand with her own. "There is time still, child. You are not yet seventeen . . ."

"Sif was only three years older when he took Miranei," said Anghara after a pause, with an edge of defiance.

"And he was a trained warrior," said ai'Jihaar, "a knight in all but name."

Anghara laughed, lifting her arms to show off the gold robe she wore. "And so am I," she said, her voice silky. "Perhaps not quite a knight, but thanks to you, I am also trained. I am not one of those poor Sighted wretches in the villages who have nothing to raise against him. I am Sighted, I am *an'sen'thar,* I am queen by right of blood."

"Using your gifts as a weapon . . ."

"I would not, and you know it. But it is time I returned, ai'Jihaar. It is past time," Anghara said, more gently. "And time . . . I do not have." She glanced up at al'Tamar, and then stood and pressed the handful of amber back into his hand. "Guard them for me; make the *say'yin.* One day, *sen'en dayr,* I will be back to claim it."

He accepted them almost mechanically. "Wait," he said. "You need speed?"

"Yes," Anghara said. "As much as I can muster."

"And you really mean to go all the way back to Sa'alah to return to Sheriha'drin?"

Anghara blinked at him, startled. "There is a choice?"

He scuffed the sand with the toe of his sandal, looking down. "The mountains," he said, almost inaudibly. "Shaymir."

Even as Anghara opened her mouth to speak, ai'Jihaar was on her feet but Anghara's hand on her shoulder silenced her. The old *an'sen'thar* waited, tense, as Anghara gazed thoughtfully at the young man before her.

"You know the way?"

"Paths can be found," he said.

"There is death in those mountains," said ai'Jihaar at last, unable to hold back. "That is the only thing that can be found there. And if you stray onto the Se'thara while the sun is still in the sky, you will find it swiftly; if you blunder in the mountains until you fall off a cliff or run out of supplies in some dead end, you will find it slowly, and agonizingly."

"There have been those who have lived to tell the tale, ai'Jihaar."

"He is right," said Anghara. "I remember, the day of the Confirmation, ai'Farra telling me what became of those who crossed from Shaymir into Kheldrin."

"And there have been those who went the other way," said al'Tamar, "and returned."

Anghara suddenly connected the *Sa'id*'s Shaymir-accented Roisinani with the road through the mountains; "al'Jezraal," she said.

"He has been," ai'Jihaar admitted. "Often. He trades with some of the far-flung outposts. Some of those who dwell in your desert . . . they are not so very different from us."

"And I went with him, once," said al'Tamar. "Nobody will be expecting you to return that way, the mountains will not be watched. And we are so much closer to Se'thara than to Sa'alah here."

"Nobody is likely to be keeping an eye out for me anyway," said Anghara with a laugh, forgetting for a moment the warning in the oracle's words. "For most in Roisinan, I have been buried in the family vaults these many years. But the time I would save . . ."

"Do not tell ai'Farra I know the way," said al'Tamar hastily. "She would flay me, and my uncle too would know the lash of her wrath, *Sa'id* or no *Sa'id*. She seems to have put aside her obsession with keeping Kheldrin from prying eyes where you are concerned, but that does not change her edicts—not every *fram'man* comes with the power to raise oracles for the Kheldrini, and everyone except you is still an intruder. She has never liked the idea of the mountain passes; the Sayyed patrol them, and they are not kind to anyone who falls into their clutches."

"Then it is a dangerous gamble . . ."

"Of course it is a dangerous gamble," said ai'Jihaar, latching on to the words gratefully. "Between the Sayyed and the mountains . . ."

But al'Tamar was smiling, and there was an echo of that smile in Anghara's own eyes as she looked at him.

"We can leave before tomorrow morning," al'Tamar said quietly.

"Anghara!"

Anghara closed both her hands over ai'Jihaar's, lifting the other's close against her breast and leaning over to plant a kiss on her brow. "I will be all right, ai'Jihaar. Remember, I will be home in the time it would take me just to reach Sa'alah . . . I will be home . . ." She drew a ragged breath. "Don't tell them," she said, pleading now. "I'm truly grateful for all al'Jezraal's offers of help, but you know that while he would think it perfectly all right for himself to brave the mountain passes, I would be quite a different matter. And ai'Farra . . . well, she seems to be a law unto herself."

"But to go alone like this into danger . . ."

*"Hama dan ar'i'id,"* Anghara reminded her. "You are never alone in the desert, or so everyone has been telling me ever since I got here. And I won't be alone. There's al'Tamar."

"The whelp," ai'Jihaar laughed sharply. "He'd better take care of you, else he will have me to answer to."

Anghara's smile widened. "So you'll let us get away?"

"If you say you need to get home quickly . . ." said ai'Jihaar. "Still, I would have preferred you went properly escorted . . ."

"I have to go alone into Roisinan anyway," said Anghara gently. "I can hardly march in at the head of a Kheldrini caravan."

"I will miss you," said ai'Jihaar. "But I always said I would know when it was your time, and I think it is now. Go, child, with my blessing; and one day . . . one day, come back to us." Anghara dropped onto one knee before her, suddenly overcome with emotion, and ai'Jihaar reached out with a gesture of blessing which quickly turned into a gentle caress of her bright hair. And then the old, practical ai'Jihaar emerged once again. "Do not come back to the house," she said. "I will pack for you. When everything is ready I will leave your gear beneath one of the fishing boats." She paused, and then, even as she was turning to go, held on to one of Anghara's hands. "I will perform the ceremonies for you myself," she said. "May the Gods watch over you both."

With no further farewell, she was gone. Anghara stood up, gazing after her for a long moment, and then turned to al'-Tamar. "When do you think we should start?"

"She will have things ready by the time it is dark," he said. "I will prepare a few supplies, and bring out the ki'thar'en. We can leave as soon as we have everything."

They rode out into the gathering twilight on two ki'thar'en and with a third pack-animal on lead rein—all three with burnooses tied around their muzzles to ensure silence at least until they were out of earshot of the village. There was no way of climbing the cliffs behind the village to reach the dunes of Kadun, and they had to retrace much of their original path, riding at a steady pace back along the same caravan trail beside the ocean. But al'Tamar cut into the red desert a lot sooner than al'Jezraal's caravan had dropped down to the ocean, through a barely visible gap in the cliffs, and they were quickly plunged into one of Kadun Khajir'i'id's more improbable landscapes, coral dunes streaked with yellow, gold, and occasional black stripes. Tall buttes of red rock reared around them every so often, and they had to pick a meandering path around their roots; al'-Tamar bowed to the necessity of this, but kept them moving steadily east and south. They rode fast—there was no time on this trip to linger and follow silkseekers to jin'aaz lairs, or to pause to admire the scenery. This time they rode a race, yet al'Tamar managed to pass a nugget of information every now and again.

"This is silver country," he said. "We will be passing quite close to my family's mine. They will have good silver for your *say'yin*."

"They would no doubt be astonished to see you," said Anghara, unable to repress a quick grin.

"They would chew me out as an ignorant pup who cannot be trusted out of his elders' sight, and probably send me straight back to Al'haria under guard," he admitted without a trace of remorse at this unsanctioned adventure. "Perhaps it is best if I went back for the silver after you are safely through the passes."

The weather held for them for almost a week, and then, without warning, everything changed. Anghara, shaken awake out of a dream where she was slowly suffocating, with two faceless men holding her down and another pouring sand down her throat with sadistic slowness as though it were wine, found that aside from the fancy of the three torturers, it had been no dream. Sitting up with a paroxysm of coughing, she reached instinctively for the burnoose which was always laid within arm's reach by her bed. There was still grit between her teeth even after she fastened it, and she stared at al'Tamar, whose own desert veil was up, across the rim of her own with eyes which stung with the granular atmosphere. It was dark, but it was an oddly amorphous darkness—Anghara couldn't tell if it was midnight, or simply mid-afternoon smothered in gales of flying sand.

"What in the name of all the Gods . . ." she managed to croak.

"Sandstorm," he said. "Bad one. But it is too fierce to last long; I think it is best we wait it out."

There was little time to talk. Anghara merely nodded. "The animals?" she asked.

"I took care of them."

It was not a boast, simply a flat statement of fact, but he had accomplished a task which would have taxed two grown men. The walls of their tent flapped violently in the gusts of wind, and the scouring sand was merciless, even inside.

"Lie down," he said, "it is best to move as little as possible."

She nodded; he quickly followed his own advice, padding over to his own camp bed and dropping down full-length onto his stomach, drawing a fold of his blanket across his face for additional protection against the elements.

They survived, although the storm held them pinned to the camp for almost two days. They managed to gain a hai'r, and recuperated there for a whole precious day before they could go on again.

"Odd thing, this storm," the nomad chieftain whose base the hai'r was remarked to them, as he gravely accepted the water-price from al'Tamar and then stood watching while they watered the animals and filled their water-skins. "They are not common this time of year. This one, it came out of nowhere. Like you two. Where are you bound?"

It was discourteous to lie to those whose water one drank in the desert, but then, this was hardly a pleasure trip. "Home," said al'Tamar after mulling over the possibilities for a moment. That wasn't quite a lie. Anghara was indeed going home, and there was every possibility he would visit his own on his way back to Al'haria.

But it was useless—these were nomads, and already they knew everything before it happened, as usual. The chieftain chuckled.

"Your prudence does you credit, youngling," he said. "This can only be she who raised the oracle at Gul Khaima; my people mean to make a pilgrimage there soon. And 'home,' then, means a great deal more than you would have cared to admit. But I will not pry," he added, drawing his djellaba over his substantial stomach with a dignified gesture. "You are welcome to stay as long as you wish; and all our good wishes upon you when you choose to depart. Will you give us a blessing before you leave, *an'sen'thar?*"

Anghara pronounced the blessing, calling it down both on the nomad clan and on herself and al'Tamar. She had no way of knowing if the nomads reaped any benefits from it, but as far as the two of them were concerned it seemed as though the Gods had not been listening. On the second morning, al'Tamar led them out from the hai'r and they were only two days out when another storm hit, again from out of nowhere. It was as furious as the first, costing them another precious day and a half while it raged and an afternoon, afterward, to pull themselves together again.

"I should be able to see these coming," muttered al'Tamar unhappily. "This is unnatural."

"This stuff clings," said Anghara, trying to shake off the soft sand, which seemed to have worked its way into every fold of her clothing.

The words seemed to surprise al'Tamar. He came over to peer at the residue on her robe, and chewed his lip thoughtfully. "That is *omankhajir,*" he said. "Soft sand. There is none around here for miles. Look." He bent to rake a handful of the coarse, crystalline reddish sand at his feet into his palm and allowed it to trickle through his fingers. *"Kharkhajir,"* he said. "Rock sand. We are amongst the mesas that give birth to it. *Omankhajir* belongs much further south . . . and much further north, out beside the Se'thara. But not here."

"So where," asked Anghara, shaking still more clinging *omankhajir* from underneath a fold of her sleeve with some impatience, "did all this come from?"

"I do not know," he said, and he sounded worried. Anghara looked up, startled. His golden eyes were dark with apprehension. "Sandstorms which carry soft sand can kill. Whole caravans unlucky enough to be caught in one have been found buried years after their journey; every man and beast perished."

"But you said there is no soft sand here," Anghara said, frowning.

"There ought to be none. But . . ." He stared at the powdery stuff she was still dusting off her person. His lips tightened. "We go on," he said at last, after a pause. "Perhaps it was only chance, a few grains caught in the wind . . ."

But less than a day after this, storm number three blew up out of a clear sky. It was different from the others—duller, somehow, with less sound and fury but with a disturbing air of permanence—al'Tamar needed less than an hour to admit defeat.

"This is the kind that buries," he said grimly. "We have no chance. Back, before we die in it; we had better hope we can outrun it."

He turned his ki'thar, and the beast they had brought to carry supplies, tied to his own animal's saddle, wheeled with him and followed him in retreat. But Anghara hesitated, staring into the teeth of the storm through narrowed eyes—and it seemed to her that somewhere in its midst stood a woman's shape, motionless in the tumult of wind-tossed sand, so still that not a hair on her head moved. And through the whirling, blinding sand Anghara thought she could clearly see amber eyes that watched her with a sort of compassion. *Your paths are still those of the Gods, and the paths that lead you this way lead nowhere but to futile endings.*

The thought was so pure and sharp, so alien, that Anghara knew she could not have imagined it; but it was distant and faint, and seemed to reach her across a gulf of unimaginable dimensions. *Forgive the suffering, but it is the only way I have to tell you that you must turn back.*

It was ai'Dhya, ai'Dhya of the Winds . . .

"Anghara! Hurry!" al'Tamar's voice broke the spell, and when Anghara looked again there was nothing where the Goddess had stood except a tornado of twisting sand. She bowed, nonetheless, to where the presence had been, and turned her back onto the storm, to where al'Tamar stood waiting for her, eyes screwed into slits against the grit. He lifted his head as she approached, as though he were sniffing the air.

"It seems to be abating," he said. "Perhaps, if we did wait it out . . ."

"No, al'Tamar. It was a gallant idea, but it is not to be," Anghara said, her voice firm but gentle. "I should really ride back to Al'haria and ask al'Jezraal for all the help he promised," she mused, "but I cannot face ai'Farra, not after sneaking out on her like that. If I do, I won't be able to leave the city until she's told me exactly what she thinks of me and of what I have done, and I don't have the time to listen to it all, not now. And already I have lost over two weeks . . . Will you come with me to Sa'alah?"

"Willingly," he said instantly, without a trace of hesitation. He glanced once again at where the storm seemed to be settling down into nothing more than a slightly high wind behind their backs. "What was it you met back there, *an'sen'thar?*"

"Only a God," said Anghara, smiling. She dug her heel into the ki'thar's flank. "Come, we must make up for lost time. *Akka! Akka! Akka!*"

The ki'thar broke into a shambling, loping run; after a moment of shaken silence, al'Tamar followed, dragging the volubly protesting pack ki'thar behind him.

The moment they decided to forego the mountain road, everything settled down, and it seemed as if the blessing

Anghara had called down on the nomads finally brought
good fortune. They skirted carefully around al'Tamar's
home, passing so close he was able to point out the mesa it
lay within. Other than the occasional hai'r, they tried to
avoid most places which might be inhabited, and moved
swiftly and freely across the face of Kadun Khajir'i'id. This
time there would be no ordeal of the Khari'i'd between Anghara and the coast—they were too far east for the Empty
Quarter, and, anyway, there was nothing there for her to seek
any more. This time Anghara would take the High Road
ai'Jihaar had wanted to take before her own Gods had told
her otherwise—she would cut across Sayyed land, the
plateau of Kharg'in'dun'an, the place of horses. There was
only a narrow belt of the Stone Desert, less than a few hours'
worth, between the red desert of the north and the winding
road which led to the high country.

The horse clans could hardly have been expecting them,
but Anghara was not surprised to find a welcoming committee waiting for them on the edge of the plateau, forewarned by
their scouts and the inevitable desert grapevine. Anghara and
al'Tamar had ridden hard, and it showed both on themselves
and on their ki'thar'en; Anghara was bone-tired, too tired to
favor the dun'en on which the clansmen were mounted, which
she would have gasped to see under ordinary circumstances,
with more than a cursory glance. Khari'i'd had done it to her,
again; she could have endured a week in the Kadun easier
than she coped with an hour in the Stone Desert.

They could not help but know who Anghara was—by this
time there were few in Kheldrin who had not heard of her.
These were ai'Farra's kinsmen, and most of them shared her
aversion to strangers—but they were also imbued with the
pragmatism of the desert folk. They might not have wanted
Anghara in the first place, but she was here, and, after all,
she had earned the right. So they did their best to ignore the
alien gray eyes and the foreign lines of the face revealed
when Anghara dropped her burnoose, and tried to see only
the gold robe of a Kheldrini *an'sen'thar,* a holy woman filled
with power who was said to have the ear of the Gods.

"Our home is yours," said one of the delegation, bowing deeply from the saddle, without smiling.

"We are honored," Anghara said, returning the courtesy as best she could.

"The honor is ours," said another, a younger man with the yellow eyes of a Roisinani wildcat. He did smile; alone of the committee, he looked as though he might truly welcome Anghara's presence. She thought she could vaguely sense a flicker of an aura around him, but she was so tired . . .

"We will not impose on your hospitality for long," she said, "I have need of speed, and would be on my way as soon as we have sufficiently rested."

*"An'sen'thar,"* said a Sayyed elder, his hair almost white with age, with grave and unexpected sympathy, "you are welcome to stay as long as you need. A day's rest now will speed your journey all the more. Stay and gather your strength, and we will give you fast dun'en for the last lap to Sa'alah. You will reach your destination as though you had never tarried. But leave now, and the weariness will cling to you, and slow you down. My daughter said you might pass this way, and bade us give you our assistance should you do so; it is no more than we can do to offer you a place of comfort and safety to rest in."

So they had been expected, in a way.

"Your daughter . . ." asked Anghara fuzzily.

"That is ai'Farra ma'Sayyed's father; he is *Sa'id* Say'ar'-dun," said al'Tamar in a low voice close to her ear.

Say'ar'dun turned out to be a small city, less striking than spired Al'haria but far more focused in its existence. The reason for its being was dun'en, and everything in Say'ar'-dun revolved around the beasts. Anghara, whose idea of the animals was shaped by their rarity and preciousness in her own land, could not get over seeing herds of them in one place. There were dun'en being groomed, or exercised, or doctored, or if the physical beasts were absent, then the residents of Say'ar'dun surrounded themselves with records of their breeding, with distinguished pedigrees stretching back generations. When Anghara, whose weariness seemed to have abated after a good meal and a short nap, requested to be shown the city, it was the yellow-eyed Sayyed youth who acceded.

Dogging Anghara's footsteps as always, al'Tamar commented whimsically in the Records House, "Some of these dun'en know more about their ancestry than I do."

"The records go back hundreds of years, in some cases," their guide said, unrolling one long scroll. "Here, for example, is one where twenty-five generations have been tallied."

Anghara peered at it. "But how long does a dun live?"

"Twenty years, sometimes thirty," said the guide. "A lifetime companion for a man."

"Twenty years?" she repeated. "But that means this scroll is . . . over five hundred years old!"

The young man bowed lightly, allowing the scroll to roll up again under his fingers. "A copy," he said diffidently. "But yes, that is correct."

"I have not seen many dun'en in my land," Anghara said thoughtfully, "but I do remember my father had at least two separate sets from Kheldrin in my own lifetime. I do not recall ever hearing of any surviving for longer than ten years."

"Taken away from their country," said the Sayyed guide gravely, "it is possible they do not live as long. Perhaps there is something we do not understand—a tie which, severed, means they cannot exist beyond a certain number of years. I know of this; my own dun'en, and my family's, are like children to me, and I grieve for their lost years as I would sorrow for those lost to any child of mine."

"And yet they are still taken," murmured Anghara softly.

"Those that go," said the youth, "help those that stay behind, both dun'en and their masters, to survive the dry seasons. The wealth they bring in provides food for those who might otherwise go hungry. And it is never the best who go." The smile that crept onto his face as he tapped the ancient pedigree in his hand with one long tapered forefinger was almost sly. "None of his line will ever be sold beyond these shores . . . and these are the real dun'en, the jewels of the desert. They are companions, not servants—they are ridden for the joy of it, not for need or necessity. They are kings here, and what is a king when you send him away from his country? He is diminished when torn from the place he was born to rule."

"Perhaps there are other callings," said Anghara.

The youth bowed in a graceful apology. "Forgive me. I forget myself sometimes when I speak of these animals; I do not often speak of these kings to one who is queen in her own right, and in whose presence it might be more prudent to hold my tongue. But you will see; we will give you one for your journey. And afterward, nothing you ever ride will be the same again."

He was right, of course—in everything. It would have been all too easy to stay there, resting in the high cold breezes that swept the plateau, watching the proud herds of dun'en graze on the banks of the small lake which made their life in that place possible. But it was this young man's words, inadvertent or not, that made Anghara look with fresh passion on her journey. Yes, there were other callings, as she had told him—and she would never regret her Kheldrin years and the gifts the Twilight Country had chosen to bestow upon her. But she was a queen, and yes, she was diminished by her distance from the land that was her own. Her home. It was time to go back.

The Sayyed were true to the young man's promise when Anghara prepared to depart; Anghara's mount, a rare gray in a breed that was usually sleek and dark, was truly a prince amongst dun'en. The yellow-eyed youth himself held her reins as she came to mount up, and his eyes gleamed.

"This is one of my own," he said, with not a little pride. "One whose ancestry lies revealed on the scroll I showed you. A king, who has never been away from his kingdom."

"You do me great honor," said Anghara.

He tilted his head in respect, accepting her thanks with his usual grace. "What greater honor," he said, "than for him to bear an *an'sen'thar* on a journey . . . and a queen back to her realm?"

Here, she was *an'sen'thar* first, queen second. It was a dif-

ferent world; but hers, also, just like Miranei. She reached to
pat the horse's arched neck. "I will see he is well cared for,
and returned to you to reign in his kingdom again," she said.

*"Sen'en Dayr,"* he said, stepping back. "God speed,
*an'sen'thar."*

The gray dun's paces were silken, but it could fly like the
winds of ai'Dhya herself, and Anghara sped across most of
Kharg'in'dun'an at a flat-out gallop, for once not because
she wished to hurry but for the sheer joy of it. But that meant
they were upon the southern desert almost before they knew
it, and the first glimpse of Arad Khajir'i'id from the edge of
the high country, her first after many months in red Kadun,
smote Anghara with an almost physical pain. She seemed
transfixed by it, so much so that al'Tamar, himself mounted
on a princely chocolate-colored dun, had to all but lead her
down into the yellow sand together with the pack beast he
still dragged behind him.

They crossed the Arad without meeting another living
being, and all too soon the mountains that were the desert's
barrier swelled from a distant shimmer into the great but-
tresses of naked rock she recalled, as if from a dream. And
then the mountains shrank down to a point—Ar'i'id Sam'-
mara, the Desert Gate, the place where an exiled Roisinani
princess had first set foot into a hidden, forbidden land. Anghara stood for a long time, looking back into the yellow
desert—treasuring this parting glimpse as much as she treas-
ured the memory of her first. And when she finally turned to
follow al'Tamar into the maw of the Gate, she felt a ghostly
self fall away from her, to stand guard at the gate and watch
for her return. Much as she had once done on a ship's deck,
watching the shape of the land of her birth fold away under
the horizon, now she made the same vow to the land she was
leaving behind: *I will return.* And then, with tears stinging her
eyes, she wished bitterly that somewhere in all the knowledge
she had gained over the years she could find, in this moment,
a single iota to tell her how to cope with her divided heart.

It was close to dusk when they reached Sa'alah. Anghara
left al'Tamar in the serai where they had bespoken rooms,

the same one from which she had once started out on this adventure, and went alone to the quays to bargain for a passage to Roisinan. It was full dark when she returned; al'Tamar had not been idle, she found supper waiting, and lais tea steaming in delicate porcelain cups.

*To you, ai'Jihaar,* thought Anghara, sipping the hot tea with a smile.

"Sit down," she said to al'Tamar, who showed every sign of hovering at her elbow as she ate, ready to wait upon her as he did with al'Jezraal. "We are not in Al'haria, and I am not your *Sa'id.* It is your supper, too."

He did as he was told, breaking a handful of flat panbread to sop the juices in the bowl of stew. "Have you found your passage?"

"A ship leaves in two days; there is nothing before," she said. "I took it . . . al'Tamar . . ."

"I know what you want," he said, staring down into his lap. "And I will not, Anghara. I will not go back until you leave. You might not want to have someone wave goodbye to you from the shore, but I came with you to Sa'alah, and I will stay until you leave." He glanced up, briefly, and Anghara could read his soul in his eyes, the soul he tried to keep so carefully hidden, the pain of what he knew could never be.

*He loves me,* she thought, without surprise. "Even if I gave you a task to do for me?"

"I would do it," he said, after a small hesitation. "But what could you need to have done with such urgency that you would send me away at once?"

"There are the dun'en to return to Kharg'in'dun'an," she said, "but that you can do at any time on your way back. But there is something else. Have you forgotten the *say'yin* you promised me?"

"But you will . . ." *You will be gone by the time I am done. Gone. And will you ever come back?*

"It will be a special *say'yin,* al'Tamar, and not only because it will be a friend's gift and a friend's hand will have made it," Anghara said. "You already have the amber, and the promise of the silver. But there is something else I want you to put in it."

He looked up, hooked despite himself. "What is it?"

Anghara ducked her head, drawing off a fine chain and withdrawing something she had kept hidden beneath her robe for all these years, something that had kept her faith burning through all the dark times, that her mother had given her with her own hand. Anghara's own trembled a little as she held out Red Dynan's Great Seal for which Sif had searched so fruitlessly, and met al'Tamar's wide golden eyes with a calm gray gaze, full of a serenity she was far from feeling. "The Royal Seal of Roisinan," she said quietly.

He reached out, and then his hand jerked back. "I cannot—I cannot take that . . . How will you go into your country without it? How will you prove what you are?"

"When I have need of it," Anghara said, "I shall send for it . . . or return for it. For now . . . there are other ways; or I will simply have to be enough in myself." In truth, Anghara had no arguments, for her gesture had been pure instinct, a decision made in that instant. She did not know how she knew the seal would be safer here with al'Tamar than with her, but she did—and she gave it into safekeeping, without a pause.

Reaching out again, this time more slowly, al'Tamar took the seal from her open palm as though he was handling something that would burn him, or else disintegrate in his hand. It did neither, and he sat holding it for a moment, frozen, as Anghara's own hands fell into her lap; he did not see her fingers twist into her skirt there, against an almost uncontrollable urge to snatch it back. The seal lay in the palm of his hand, still warm from the heat of her body.

His hand closed over it abruptly but very gently, and he nodded stiffly.

"I will make your *say'yin* for you and hold it safe; none will know of this until you claim it." He had gone cool, detached, his soul fire more a barrier than a reaching out; his mind had accepted the role of a companion, a friend, but his heart railed against the circumstances that made this girl a *fram'man,* an *an'sen'thar,* a queen—three times removed from him. Friendship, and the trust she had bestowed upon him, would have to be enough.

He rose to take his leave, and bowed to her, deeply; her eyes glittered suspiciously in the lamplight as she shook her head and embraced him once, as she would a brother.

"Good-bye, al'Tamar, the blessing of al'Zaan be upon you," she said.

"And with you," he said.

"I will come back," she whispered, not even sure if he heard as he ducked under the curtain and stepped out of the room, carrying the Great Seal in one tightly clenched fist. "Or I will make you *an'sen'thar,* and you will come to Sheriha'drin—and if I ever regain Miranei you will sit at my right hand and I shall call you my brother, and my friend . . ."

Her brother. Her friend. But the love that burned in al'Tamar's soul fire was of a different kind. They had shared deeply on the shores of the Kadun ocean, learned perhaps more of one another than was altogether prudent. Under ordinary circumstances, this would have been a binding experience, something that should have twinned their spirits, melded their lives. Instead . . . all al'Tamar had was a deeper understanding of the barriers which conspired to keep them apart. He understood, in his mind. It would take time, however, for his heart to accept that understanding.

He was gone from the serai in the morning, and so were the dun'en. Anghara, who had claimed her quarters on the ship upon which she would sail, stood at the prow and lifted her eyes up to the mountains, imagining him galloping across the flat yellow sands of the Arad, the two other dun'en thundering in his wake. And then he was climbing the High Road, taking back his ki'thar'en, descending down into the red desert to finally gain the spires of Al'haria, his entire journey telescoped into the space of a few minutes, into the image of Kheldrin she carried in her heart.

But al'Tamar was not on Kharg'in'dun'an, nor even yet in the Arad. He had been hiding from *sen'en'thari* for years, and had it down to a fine art. For all her gifts Anghara was utterly oblivious to the fact that one of the myriad pairs of golden eyes which watched her ship cast off from the dock were his. He stayed on the quay, alone, staring out to sea for a long time after her ship had vanished from sight and the rest of the quayside crowd had departed. Then he turned and retraced his steps to the new serai in which he had spent the previous night. As much as he had felt the need to stay in Sa'alah while she was still in the city, now he felt the pressing urge to leave—and he was on his way within an hour of returning from the quay.

They crept into each other's dreams that night, the first on both their journeys—she returning home at last, he travelling toward his own. He dreamed of the *say'yin* he would make of sea amber from the foot of Gul Khaima, Kadun silver, and the Royal Seal of the land of Sheriha'drin. He dreamed of her to whom he would give it, the glow in her gray eyes as he reached out to place the *say'yin* around her neck—dreamed of what might be, or of what he wished could come to pass. Anghara, *an'sen'thar,* dreamed of what was. She saw him sitting outside his tent in the starlight, just before he retired inside to sleep, turning the seal over in his hands so the pale light cascaded from it like water. She wept in her sleep at the things she had given him, and those she had taken away. He would never again be the carefree young man who had set out from Al'haria to look for an oracle— and found the answers to questions he had never thought of asking, before he had first laid eyes on the stranger from the land called Sheriha'drin.

# Glossary

Some names and concepts originating from different parts of the world have been annotated for ease of placement, i.e., Kheldrin (K); Roisinan (R); Shaymir (S); Tath (T).

Adamo Taurin: twin to Charo Taurin (q.v.), Chella's younger sons, later important to Anghara's cause

-ah (K): feminine suffix added to words to indicate feminine gender; sometimes occurs within a word (as in havallah), implying an inherent grace, beauty, or feminine quality in the concept the word describes

ai'Dhya (K): Kheldrini Goddess, Lady of the Winds

ai'Farra ma'Sayyed: Keeper of Records in Al'haria, chief an'sen'thar of the Al'haria Tower

ai'Jihaar ma'Hariff: blind Kheldrini priestess (see an'sen'thar); Anghara's friend and teacher

ai'Lan (K): the Sun Goddess; similar to Roisinan's Avanna except that her worship is more bloodthirsty—can offer great power and protection in return for the right sacrifice

ai'Raisa: young gray-robed sen'thar who remains as the voice of the oracle of Gul Khaima (q.v.)

ai'Shahn, often known as ai'Shahn al'Sheriha (K): messenger of the Gods, Water Spirit; a holy entity

Akka! (K): ki'thar command: Go!

Algira (T): a beautiful canal city in Tath, once pride of Roisinan; a training center for the Sighted, similar to Castle Bresse, lies nearby

Al'haria: red city of Kheldrin, place where the Records are kept, city of scholars, priestesses and craftsmen al'Jezraal ma'Hariff: Lord of Al'haria, brother of ai'Jihaar

al'Khur (K): Lord of Death and also of dreams that come in the Little Death that is sleep, half-man, half-desert vulture

al'Shehyr ma'Hariff: son of al'Jezraal

al'Tamar ma'Hariff: nephew of al'Jezraal, son of his brother; sen'thar-gifted, but untrained because he is heir to an important Hariff silver mine

al'Zaan, Sa'id-ma'sihai (K): al'Zaan the One-Eyed, Lord of the Empty Places, Kheldrin's chief God, cannot be worshipped in any confined place, only in the open

Anghara Kir Hama (ma'Hariff): Princess of Roisinan and an'sen'thar of Kheldrin, heiress of Red Dynan whose crown was usurped by her half-brother Sif when their father died in the battle at Ronval River, powerfully Sighted, events turn around her

Ansen Taurin: Anghara's oldest foster brother and cousin, son of her aunt, Chella

an'sen'thar (pl. an'sen'en'thari)(K): wearer of the gold robe in the sen'thar priestly caste of Kheldrin; high priestess, used both as noun and form of address

arad (K): south

Arad Khajir'i'id: the Southern Desert, sometimes also known as Mal'ghaim Khajir'i'id (q.v.)

ari'i'd (K): desert

Ar'i'id Sam'mara: Desert Gate, name given to the canyon which forms the passage between Kheldrin's coastal plain and Arad Khajir'i'd

Avanna of the Towers (R): Lady of the Lights, Roisinan's harvest goddess, patron of all that is bright, glowing and growing; she created the sun, the moon, and the stars, and blesses everything grown under them; Roisinani infants are presented to the Gods within her towers

Aymer: capital of Shaymir, semi-desert independent principality to the north of Roisinan, origin of the Aymer Harp (q.v.)

Aymer harp: a difficult Shaymiri musical instrument.

Beit el'Sihaya (K): the Empty Quarter, from beit (geographic quarter) + sihaya (empty)

Beku: city of Kheldrin

Bodmer Forest: large forest in the heart of Roisinan

Brandar Pass: mountain passage from Roisinan into Shaymir through the range behind Miranei

Bresse: see Castle Bresse

Brynna Kelen: Anghara Kir Hama's alter ego, the name by which she was known at Cascin

burnoose (K): a head covering and desert veil against sand and heat

Calabra: main port city of Roisinan, at the mouth of the River Tanassa

Cascin (Cascin of the Wells): the ancestral manor of Anghara's mother Rima, Anghara's sanctuary in the first years of her exile, held by Lord Lyme, married to Rima's sister, Chella

Castle Bresse (R): training school for the Sighted, where Anghara first learns a measure of control over her gifts, levelled by Sif in the first stroke of his anti-Sight campaign

Cerdiad (R): Midsummer Harvest Feast with connotations of ancient fertility rites when harvested fields and the harvest are blessed on midsummer's eve by a priestess of Avanna of the Towers, patron goddess of the feast and the rest of the night given over to celebrations; romantic superstitions practiced by girls wanting to know who they will marry are commonly associated with this night

Charo Taurin: twin to Adamo Taurin, Chella's younger sons, Anghara's foster-brother

cheta (R): a military company in the Roisinani army

Colwen: Sif's first queen, put aside because she could not give him an heir

dan (fem: dan'ah) (K): alone

Dances (R): circles of huge hewn stones with an ancient and often feared power; there are four in Roisinan: in the hills by the river Tanassa, in the middle of the central plain in Shaymir, on the edge of the Vallen Fen in Tath, and in the

Mabin Islands (now largely ruined); the three mainland Dances are more or less intact, their original purpose or ancient builders unknown; there may once have been more, as there are solitary stones in other places, which exude something of the power of the Dances, known as Standing Stones (q.v.); both Dances and Standing Stones are avoided at night, and especially during the high festivals as they are believed to be the haunt of spirits

desert sage (S): a herb with a sharp, bittersweet scent which grows in the Shaymir desert

diamondskin (K): lethally poisonous lizard found in the Khari'i'd; no antidote to its poison, which is almost instantly fatal; gray with black diamond-shaped markings on the skin

djellaba (K): desert cloak

Duerin Rashin: King of Tath; scion of the Rashin Clan who once wrested the Throne under the Mountain (q.v.) from the legitimate Kir Hama incumbent—Duerin's ancestor failed, but Duerin still wants Roisinan, and went to war over it

dun (pl. dun'en) (K): desert horses, exported to Roisinan, Tath and Shaymir from Kheldrin but affordable only to the very rich; beautiful, graceful animals, faster than the wind, dun breeding is largely the province of the Sayyed clan

Dynan ('Red Dynan') Kir Hama: Anghara's father, King of Roisinan, killed in battle against Duerin Rashin of Tath

Empty Quarter, the: see Beit el'Sihaya

Favrin Rashin: Prince of Algira, son of Duerin Rashin of Tath

Feor: ex-priest of both Kerun and Nual, Sighted tutor in the household of Cascin who grooms Anghara Kir Hama for queenship

Fihra Hai'r (K): literally, The First Oasis; the first water-bearing oasis a traveller encounters upon emerging from the Khar'i'id—depending on which direction the voyager is travelling in, the same oasis can also be known as Shod Hai'r (q.v.)

Fodrun: Dynan's Second General, on whom leadership devolves during the Battle of Ronval when Dynan is killed and Kalas, the First General so badly wounded as to be permanently disabled; seeing the conflict ahead, he chooses to support Sif Kir Hama, Dynan's grown son, in preference to his legitimate heiress, the nine-year-old Anghara, but not without some misgiving; also known as Fodrun kingmaker

fram'man (pl. fram'man'en) (K): stranger

Glas Coil (R): Gray Wood, something along the lines of the Celtic Tir'na'n'Og, land of youth—Roisinani believe in it as an afterlife

Gul Khaima (K): Oracle Anghara raises in Kheldrin, on a stone pillar by the sea; human oracle

Gul Qara (K): the ancient oracle in the Empty Quarter, which gives Anghara the name of its successor

had'das (K): species of fish caught off the coast of Kheldrin

Hai! Hai haddari! (K): an expression of amazement or admiration

hai'r (pl. hai'r'en) (K): oasis

Hama dan ar'i'id (K): Kheldrini adage: "You're never alone in the desert"

han (R): inn, as in Halas Han (inn on the river Hal)

hari: red (Kadun Khajir'i'id is sometimes known as Harim Khajir'i'id)

Hariff: Powerful Kheldrini clan or family involved with silver mining; root hari, red, may indicate they originated in the Red Desert

Harim Khajir'i'id: the Red Desert (see Kadun Khajir'i'id)

iri'sah (K): hot desert wind

jin'aaz spiders (K): large desert spiders who cocoon their larvae in a chrysalis of silk; Kheldrini use silkseekers (q.v.) to find jin'aaz spider lairs and extract this silk; much prized and very expensive—one of the main Kheldrini exports

kadun (K): north

Kadun Khajir'i'id: the Northern Desert; sometimes also known as Harim Khajir'i'id (q.v.)

Kalas: Dynan's First General, badly wounded at the Battle of Ronval Keda Cullen: sister to Kieran Cullen, gifted musician from Shaymir

Kerun (R): Roisinan god, also known as The Horned One; he is the Guardian of the Gates to Glas Coil (q.v.). He is the avatar responsible for death and life through death. He is the God of War, of Destruction, of Catastrophe; he must be propitiated at the beginning of every new venture, lest he claim it for his own; his sacrifices often involve gold, and he has his own incense, manufactured specially by the priesthood

khai'san (K): hot storm wind of the desert

khajir (K): sand

khar (K): stone

Khar'i'id: black stone desert of Kheldrin; deadly, hot and poisonous, but also strange and generous with occasional obscure and hermetic gifts; sometimes known as Rah'honim Ar'i'id, the Black Desert

kharkhajir (K): coarse sand, rock-sand

Kheldrin: Land of Twilight, from khel (dark, twilight) + drin (land, country); desert country to the west of Roisinan, for many ages closed to outsiders, except for a tiny cultivated strip in the lee of the coastal mountains, where Roisinani visit the trade port of Sa'alah to bargain for silk, esoteric drugs or dun'en

khi'tai (K): medicinal plant; reduces fevers, acts as a painkiller for minor aches; can be used as an anesthetic in conjunction with lais (q.v.)

Kieran Cullen: a Shaymiri boy, Anghara's foster-brother, already fostering at Cascin manor when she is sent there; later knighted in battle

ki'thar (pl. ki'thar'en) (K): camels, desert animal of Kheldrin

lais (K): squat, ill-favored small bush found largely in Kadun Khajir'i'id; lais tea, soporific, slightly opiate and possibly addictive, can be made either from the whole leaf or from dried leaf powder; sometimes exported from Kheldrin into Roisinan and Tath; well known in Shaymir, where the plant is named selba

mal'gha (K): yellow (Arad Khajir'i'id is sometimes known as Mal'ghaim Khajir'i'id)

Miranei: Roisinan's capital and the King's Keep, a powerful fortress never taken by force—and only a few times by treachery

Morgan of Bresse: the head of the Sisterhood of Bresse, she chose death by martyrdom at Sif's hand in the knowledge that this would hasten the return of Sight to Roisinan's persecuted people

Nual (R): Roisinani God of the Waters; not as powerful as Kerun and Avanna, but noteworthy because his temples are sanctuaries which cannot be breached; as some stay a lifetime Nual is sometimes also known as the God of Exile; his temples are always found near water, and anything found on or near the water has always been his; every shipwreck is salvaged by his priests; usually content with light offerings; a garland of flowers thrown into a river is pleasing to him; his priests are as simple as Kerun's are devious and plot-ridden, and dress in blue in honor of his element

omankhajir (K): soft sand

pa'ha (K): fermented juice of the pahria fruit

pahria palms (K): desert palm bearing large, hard-shelled fruit, soft inside, juicy but tart—an acquired taste; sometimes cultivated, but usually grows wild in desert hai'r'en (q.v.)

rah'hon (K): black

Rah'honim Ar'i'id (K): see Khar'i'id

Rashin: Tath clan of pretenders to the Roisinan throne

Rima of the Wells: Red Dynan's queen, Anghara's mother; dies during Sif's takeover, but is instrumental in saving Anghara from his avenging arm

Roisinan: Ancient land, lush with wood and field ruled by the Kir Hama dynasty until the Rashin clan from south Roisinan rose in revolt and took the throne in blood and rebellion, when the Kir Hama king, Connach Kir Hama, was killed in battle. His son Garen went first into a Nual Sanctuary and then took himself into the mountains, living as an outlaw while he gathered together his father's shattered army. He took his kingdom back two and half years later, in a successful summer campaign. The Rashin usurper was killed, but his son fled south into what had once been a province of Roisinan and declared it to be the independent kingdom of Tath with its capital at Algira, one of the jewels of Roisinan. Shaymir in the north, once also a part of Roisinan, chose to break away as well, but remained a vassal principality, with Garen Kir Hama as High King in Miranei. Tath was not rooted out, but subdued, and forced to pay tribute. The border, marked by the River Ronval, lies ever uneasy. Garen was succeeded by his son Connach II, and he by his son Dynan, known as the Red for his fiery hair, who in his turn would meet his death at Tath hands like his great-grandsire

Saa! (K): ki'thar command: Stop!

Sa'alah: main Kheldrini port and trade city on the coastal plain

Sabrah: Kheldrini clan or family

sa'hari (K): Are you there? (Equivalent to knocking on a door requesting permission to enter)

Sa'id (K): Lord

Sa'ila: stream close to Sa'alah, only running water in Kheldrin

saliha (K): thank you

salih'al'dayan (K): ritual of giving thanks to the gods, thanksgiving

sarghat (K): a desert root, distinguished on the surface only by a pair of insignificant-looking leaves, easily overlooked by an inexpert traveller, it can sustain life for a long time

Say'ar'dun: Kheldrini city, stronghold of the Sayyed clan, capital of dun'en breeding country

Sayyed: Kheldrini clan or family

say'yin (pl. say'in'en) (K): necklace of rank, usually of sea amber and silver

sea amber: soft yellow globes found in the sea off Kheldrin—deep sea amber is much prized, but smaller and less regular pieces are often found washed up on the shoreline. Exported to Roisinani and Shaymir

se'i'din (K): Khar'i'id plant. A swift-acting poison, no known antidote (Roisinani name: rosebane)

Sen'en Dayr (K): gods willing

Senena Shailan: Sif's second queen

sen'thar (pl. sen'en'thari) (K): Kheldrini priestly caste, usually female, but sometimes also has male acolytes, none are devoted to a single god—all belong to all gods, and must know all their rituals; there are four levels: novice, white robe (first circle), gray robe (second circle) and gold robe (an'sen'en'thari, q.v.) (Linguistic roots: sen, or sen'en, meaning God or deity, and thar, thari—serve, server, service)

Shadir: Kheldrini clan or family

Sheriha'drin (K): Kheldrini name for Roisinan, Land of Running Water

Shod Hai'r (K): literally, the Last Oasis—the last place to find water before stepping into Khar'i'id; there are two, one in the Kadun and one in the Arad, depending from which direction the traveller is coming, both also known as Fihra Hai'r (q.v.)

Sif Kir Hama: Anghara's half brother, Red Dynan's son by a Clera; Sif seizes the throne when it is offered to him at the battle which saw the death of his father, he hates and fears Sight—seeing his own bastard birth due solely to the fact that Dynan chose to marry Rima (who was Sighted) instead of Clera (who was not), this plays a large role in his later violent campaign against Sight

Sight (R): a power with roots in Second Sight, or prescience, granted to those born with it—usually but not exclusively women; current usage covers a multitude of gifts, some rare; a Sighted person may exhibit an ability to "eaves-drop" on conversations many miles away, move objects without touching them, dream true, establish when truth is being spoken (and, more importantly, when not), and sometimes the ability to control their immediate environ-ment (invoke a rainstorm, for example); some of these gifts are taught to aspirant Sighted initiates at Castle Bresse and a similar establishment near Algira in Tath, run by a Sisterhood of Sighted women who have devoted their lives to teaching; largely accepted as a fact of life in individuals—many women are Sighted in Roisinan—but often feared in large numbers

silkseeker: golden-yellow and white bird often used in Kheldrin to seek out nests of jin'aaz spiders (q.v.), on whose larvae it feeds; the larger adult jin'aaz, in turn, has been known to devour unwary silkseekers; wild silkseek-ers are seen as Gods' birds, and are protected

soul fire: aura around Sighted people, visible to others with Sight; of a shade specific and unique to every individual (Anghara's is gold, ai'Jihaar's is white, ai'Farra's is crimson)

Standing Stones (R): huge, hewn, solitary stones, often but not always upright, scattered across Roisinan; thought to have been part of an ancient Dance; sometimes used as a focus for sacrifice by underground worshippers of the Old Gods and practitioners of black magic, but even without this connotation they possess power and are avoided at night, especially on major festivals like Cerdiad

Tath: ancient province of Roisinan, now an independent kingdom ruled by the Rashin Clan, pretenders to the Throne Under the Mountain

Throne under the Mountain: ancient name for the Roisinan Throne, in the mountain fortress of Miranei

Ul'khari'ma: village of al'Talip ma'Shadir where al'Tamar fostered; a corruption of "The Place of the Stone"—the place Anghara knows as Gul Khaima, and where she raises the second Kheldrini oracle

Vallen Fen (T): broad, malodorous swamp at the mouth of the River Ronval, largely on the Tath side

wirrow (R): a medicinal herb in Roisinan